Finch Books by Hannah Kay

Single Books
The Artist and Me
Project Emma

I0646172

PROJECT EMMA

HANNAH KAY

Project Emma
ISBN # 978-1-83943-855-4
©Copyright Hannah Kay 2020
Cover Art by Louisa Maggio ©Copyright February 2020
Interior text design by Claire Siemaszkiewicz
Finch Books

PROJECT EMMA

Dedication

I will write about the good times because they were as real as the bad ones.

Chapter One

Light bleached the worn book under my hand, and I shifted, listening to the wail of the chilly Mississippi winter wind. Humming, I cursed the ever-present sun and breathed in the earthy scent of freshly mown grass, somehow still thriving in the recently arrived colder temperatures. As I squinted to see the page in front of me, a fly landed on my arm and I swatted it away. *Three cheers for nature*, I thought.

The bell rang, so I slammed the crumpled envelope between the pages. A month ago, that very envelope had housed an acceptance letter. Now, it was a reminder that I was just biding my time.

I hurried into the school and stopped at my locker. I was a senior. I would graduate in a little over six months, then I was leaving Nomansville in the dust.

At the locker, I thrust my lunchtime light reading into its confines and slammed it closed. Just a few paces down the hall, I arrived at my last class of the day, English composition. It was funny how Nomansville rotated the same teachers. Mr. Zelner, the bright spot in all of this high school madness, had taught my freshman English class too. Before I'd stepped into his room... Well, I'd hated reading. The concept of it had baffled me. He'd opened my eyes to an entire world — a world of books and literature — and, for that, I could not be more grateful.

Inside his classroom, Mr. Zelner sat with his back to the students, examining something on his bookshelf. A tuft of dark brown hair stuck out in the wrong direction and the collar of his red button-down shirt sat uneasy, but a mug of warm coffee steamed on his messy desk. They say that the wisest people live in a state of chaos. For Mr. Zelner, that much was true.

He spun in his chair, shocking a couple of blondes on the front row. They stuffed their cell phones into their handbags in awkward unison, and Mr. Zelner nudged his glasses up the bridge of his nose. He was crookedly handsome, with little attention to it. He smiled at me. "Miss Cage," he said, just as I slid into my desk. I startled at the attention. Catching my reaction, he grinned. "See me after class, all right?"

Great, I thought. Had I missed an assignment? Drifted off in class again? I hadn't been sleeping that well recently. I had been too worried about college applications and surviving these last months of high school. But the handwriting was on the wall and the end was spiraling toward me. I could feel it. I could already hear the screaming and feel the whir of caps in the air. *It's so close*, I thought—and that made me happy.

Zelner stood, smoothing his khakis and grabbing the mug from his desk. "Nothing is wrong," he added then turned to address the class thoughtfully. He scrunched two bushy eyebrows together, calculating as the last few stragglers rushed into class, and he lifted a paperback from his desk, gingerly flipping it in his hands. That was Zelner's thing. A nervous habit from college, I guessed. The little I knew about Mr. Zelner's past dated him to a late twenty-seven. University pending, he had been an anxious scriptwriter but apparently that hadn't gone far enough to feed his wife, so he'd become a high school teacher. *Some trade out*, I thought, as he walked to the chalkboard.

He wrote only three words, and the entire class released simultaneously awkward chuckles. *May twenty-fifth*, he'd scribed. Twenty-three some-odd seniors danced in their seats for the date of sweet, liberating graduation. I guess, in a way, that was something we all had in common. We were ready to escape.

He slapped the chalk onto the tray, and I straightened to attention. Mr. Zelner leaned against the wall, surveying us. Sometimes it seemed that he forgot his stature at the head of the classroom and became that twenty-two-year-old, straight out of college again. He looked confused—concerned, a little bit like he was the blind leading the blind. Then he forced a smile and recovered.

"Your final for this class will be a creative project," he said. Now he walked an uneasy line away from us, shrugging his lanky shoulders. "I have assigned you a partner, and together, you and your partner will choose the medium—a song, a short story, a play…" He ran a hand through his hair. "I don't care which, just be creative. Think," he probed, and we all sniggered, cogs in his machine. "The idea is to be original and immerse yourself into something real."

Everyone looked around, confusion rippling throughout the room, and he held up a hand to questions.

"The purpose of this exercise is to remember that art is just that. We can interpret, we can guess, but can we really know the inner mind of an artist? No," he said, shaking his head. The screenwriter's head had suddenly popped into frame, seemingly cautious and idealistic, all at the same time.

"English as a discipline broadens the mind to other possibilities, and it requires you to think past the literal, but for this project, I want you to act as the artist." There was a wicked gleam in his dark eyes, and I reveled in it.

A hand shot up from the back of the room, but Mr. Zelner lifted a pale finger. "Don't knock it until you try it, Mr. Roberts," he said. Chuckling, he turned toward the window. "Now. How many days until graduation?"

My classmates' hands darted skyward, and Mr. Zelner smiled. "Exactly," he said. "It's a date you all know. Well, subtract five days from your countdowns, and that is the due date for this assignment." He rubbed his temples, a methodical gesture, and he shook his head. "I'm telling you this now so that you can forget about it until March." He chuckled. "No," he said. "Take Christmas to think about your project. Spend time with your partners. Become friends or cherish your luck that you are already friends. After all, you'll be spending a lot of time together over the next semester." He retreated behind his desk once more, shuffling papers. "Good luck."

Chalk to chalkboard, now he set our fates as he began to post the partnership assignments. I poised my pencil on my notebook, swallowing hard. I hated partner projects, but who didn't? Nibbling my bottom lip, I watched as he scribbled names along the board. As he wrote, there were a couple of snickers and a groan or two, but when I saw my fate, I merely stared at the blank sheet in front of me, stomach twisting with the cruel joke of it all.

Maverick English stood between me and my diploma.

Chapter Two

Maverick English, I thought, my heart pounding in my ears—anyone but Maverick English. Swallowing hard, I cast my gaze to peer at his vacant seat in the back. *Maverick, the mystery man*, I thought, exhaling. He wasn't exactly a raving intellectual, not to say that he was dumb. I wouldn't know. He didn't exactly like school enough to show up most of the time. He ran track and worked on the family farm, but that was the extent of my knowledge about Maverick.

"Now," Mr. Zelner said, segueing with a deep chuckle, "in an effort to facilitate the introduction process, let's take these last thirty minutes of class as something of a meet and greet."

The classroom escalated into chaos, voices raising in rapid fire without restraint, and he held up his hands. "It's such a nice day. Why don't we take it to the courtyard?" The introvert blossomed from our English teacher as he shooed my peers from the tiny classroom. They fell into step, two by two, and soon they were gone, leaving just Mr. Zelner and me in their wake.

I stared at my notebook, offended, my heart in my throat. Mr. Zelner had been my ally in this place.

Now he smiled, leaning against his desk and crossing his arms. "Hey now," he said. "You look like a wounded puppy."

I straightened the sticky note dividing my notebook, suddenly aware that I had been unconsciously pouting. "Maverick isn't even here."

"Yeah," he said. He crossed to the big window that faced the courtyard, scanning the class as it mingled. "Emma, about Maverick…" Mr. Zelner's voice trailed to silence as he tallied, accounting for everyone before his attention returned to me. I listened to the hive of seniors buzzing outside the window and wondered how it felt not to be trapped inside my own mind, inside a dream for something more.

"Emma? Are you with me?"

My cheeks warmed. "Yes, sir," I said. "Sorry."

He nodded, not dwelling on my lengthy loss of focus. Instead, he forged on with his speech. "Emma, don't take Maverick at face value."

I frowned, scanning his bookshelf to the spiderweb in the corner of the room, looking at anything but Mr. Zelner. "I know," I said. I sighed, stuffing my notebook into my backpack. "I know… Don't judge a book by its cover."

He laughed apologetically and twisted the wedding ring on his finger—a slim golden band he'd gotten when he'd made Ms. Martinez a Mrs. Zelner. "Exactly, Emma," he said. A grin spread across his face, and he exhaled softly. "There is always so much more underneath the appearance."

I stood, tossing my backpack over my shoulder. "I can't even contact him," I said.

He shrugged a shoulder and spun to grab the laptop he'd earlier tucked away under a pile of essays to be graded. He slid into his desk chair, opening the laptop. "I can give you his email address," he said, clicking through documents on the computer then scribbling the email address on a slip of paper. "But you know where the farm is. That might even be easier."

I swallowed, annoyed, and grasped the paper in my hand. "Yeah," I said, "okay."

He sighed and a genuine grin slipped onto his face. "You'll be fine, Emma," he said. "Just give him a chance. He might surprise you."

* * * *

I heaved my backpack into Alex's car and sighed. "Maverick English...," I said, tucking a strand of dull brown hair behind my ear in frustration.

Alex snorted, leaning against the driver's side of the car. Her copper highlights gleamed in the sun. "I mean, I got Caroline Pryor. She's not exactly top notch."

I groaned. "You're laughing at me," I said, hopping into the passenger seat with an exasperated sigh. "Caroline's smart too."

Alex nodded. "I'm sorry," she said, biting back a giggle. "Just calm down."

"This is graduation we're talking about," I said, buckling my seat belt.

Alex shrugged and pulled out of the parking lot. "I know," she said. "It's going to be okay, though. Seriously... I doubt they can make 'Miss Highest Honors' fail senior English 'cuz the town farm boy doesn't come to class."

I sneered. "That isn't the point," I said. "Now I have to find this guy."

"You don't have to," she said. "You can just wait until January. He'll have to show up one day. You can just plan then."

True, I thought. *If only...* "No," I said. If only that was how it worked. I rapped my fingers against the dashboard, listening to the roar of the engine. "It would drive me crazy to wait."

Alex slid to a stop at one of the three red lights in town and swept her hair into a messy bun. "You are strange," she said. Her hazel eyes twinkled as the light turned green, and she hit the gas. "But I love you."

I peered out of the window as the town fluttered by. She rolled the windows down, and I groaned into the wind. She laughed and, soon, I was too. That was the two of us. She leveled me and I steadied her. Somehow, together, we made a complete person. "I love you too," I said.

Alex smiled, broad, bright and without limits. "Oh," she said, "I know."

I leaned out of the window, humming, and she twisted the radio dial. Music filled the car and Alex lit up from the tip of her red toes to her freckled nose. The corners of my mouth twitched skyward. She loved this song, and so did I. Within seconds, we were singing at the top of our lungs.

Alex and I were like that. We'd hit our stride, driving with no plans to go anywhere but away from here. Sometimes, I thought it would be perfect if we could just stay on this highway until we hit the ocean or a big city. I wouldn't care, as long as we were together.

But no... We only had six months to go before life—and college—would separate us.

Blinking over at her with her fluorescent highlights and signature white bomber jacket, I grinned. I don't think there could be two people more out of sync with this place than Alex and me. I was just glad Alex was along for the ride.

I remembered middle school. Hell, I even remembered elementary school. I'd sat on the sidelines. I'd observed, and I'd never known what was missing, though I'd felt the distance.

Then, Alex had moved in next door. Mom had made a strawberry cheesecake and sent me over to give it to her mom, but Alex had opened the door. It had been freshman year. Alex's hair had been dyed black and cut in a sharp bob, and she'd had on the bomber jacket despite the eighty-seven-degree Mississippi-in-July weather. Recklessly smart and independent, she'd instantly become my best friend. She'd cocked the pair of dark sunglasses from her eyes, and a toothy grin had spread across her face. *'Cheesecake?'* she'd said, and I'd flashed her a toothy smile.

'Yes,' I'd said. *'Strawberry.'*

She'd grabbed the tray and invited me in for a slice. Her mom had poured us milk, and we'd eaten with satisfied sighs and a discussion about indie rock and our favorite books. Our sentences had tumbled over one another, each of us finishing the other's almost before they'd started, and we hadn't been able to stop giggling.

I swear that before Alex, I hadn't really *laughed* with anyone other than my mom, and I think she could feel it too. We'd been fourteen then, and sometimes it felt like so little had changed in the three some-odd years since that epic meeting. But other times it felt like a lifetime of clashing memories. We had grown, but we hadn't missed a beat.

"So," she said, glancing across the cluttered cup holder. She had turned around, and now we rolled to a stop in her driveway. Her expectant gaze bore into my skull, and I groaned.

"So?" I rummaged through my backpack for my keys, a distraction from the eye contact that would give me away.

Alex smirked over the console. "Are you gonna go see Maverick?"

For a moment, I'd nearly forgotten Mr. Zelner's assignment. "I don't know," I said.

She quirked a knowing eyebrow toward me. "Oh?"

I grappled through the bottom of my backpack, weaving past the gum wrappers and loose pencils, and jerked my lanyard from the contents. As the keys jingled to life, I realized I should probably clean the backpack out.

"Maybe tomorrow," I said, shoving the car door open and tossing my legs over the edge.

She giggled. "Maybe tomorrow?"

I popped my head into the car again. "Yeah," I said, "maybe tomorrow."

With that, I threw her a last wave and rushed inside.

Chapter Three

I shucked my coat from my shoulders and tossed it over the back of the couch. Idly, I warmed my hands over the radiator by the bookshelf in the corner.

"Mom, I'm home," I called.

"Hiya," she answered, likely moving through the motions of getting ready for work. Mom had a late shift at the hospital, so I had a date with a book, a steaming cup of hot chocolate and a microwave dinner.

Kicking my shoes off by the couch, I padded to the back of the house to lean against her doorway. "Hey," I said.

She was sitting on the edge of the bed and tying her shoelaces. "How was school?"

I shrugged, sliding down into the chair beside her dresser. "It was fine. Mr. Zelner assigned us our final project."

She glanced at her watch. "Did I sleep through half a semester?"

"No," I said. "It's a partner project. He wanted to give us the break to bond or something."

"Oh," she said, standing from the edge of the bed and straightening her scrubs. "Who's your partner?"

I paused, biting my thumbnail. "Maverick English," I told her.

"Maverick English? You mean...?"

I tugged on my ponytail, exhaling sharply. "The very one," I said. Yeah, there was history—always history.

"That will be interesting," she said.

"Yeah," I said, "I'll say."

She gathered her things, shoving her bag onto her shoulder. "What's this project, then?"

"It's creative," I said. "A short story or play or something."

She smiled, leaning against the doorway. "Well, you'll like that."

I pouted. "Yeah." I was certain that my body language and expression clearly showed the sarcasm in my response.

Mom squeezed my shoulder and shrugged. "I bet it'll be fun," she said. Then, she sighed. "I guess I have to go to work."

"See ya in the morning," I replied, kissing her cheek.

She tucked a loose strand of hair behind her ear. "All right," she said. "Oh, and I'm going to talk to Stephanie tonight and see if she still has that desk job for you during break."

"Great," I said. "Sounds good."

She grinned and waved, heading toward the door. Seconds later, I heard it close with a soft click and I was alone.

I meandered back into the living room. The sun outside the window cast sidelong rays of light along the baseboard and I sighed. I sank into the armchair in the corner, fingering the books on the bookshelf. Mom and

I hoarded books. They were old, second-hand and from garage sales and thrift stores, crossing several genres. There were plenty of choices, and I pulled one out, flipping it over, but I groaned, shoving it back onto the shelf. I was far too unsettled to read.

Instead, I padded into the kitchen and grabbed a frozen dinner. I popped the tray of macaroni into the microwave and, with the push of a button, the machine buzzed to life. Deadening silence echoed through the house, so I walked into the living room to flip on the TV. A rerun of one of those mindlessly wonderful sitcoms flooded the vacant living room.

Smiling idly, I walked back into my bedroom to feed Stella, my brown and white hamster. She poked her head from under her log, squeaking. "Hi, Stell," I mumbled. Our landlord didn't allow pets, but he didn't mind Stella. Apparently, *she couldn't do much*.

After feeding Stella, I plopped at my desk, opening my laptop. I logged onto Facebook, the collective of lives flashing across the screen. They were bright and excited and full of college announcements, side by side with the breakups of our time—power couples torn apart by petty vendettas and the color of their graduation caps.

Our lives, I thought, pasted in technicolor and saved for no one person. Moments, I realized, that were not personal, and they made no impact. Frowning, I brought a single finger to the keypad, rolling over the chat list. Alex's bright-eyed selfie settled atop it, and I noticed *him* lurking in the corner. Maverick English's name peeked from the bottom of the active list, green-lit like Gatsby.

"Talk to him," I mumbled to myself, nibbling on the fleshy skin of my lips. I hovered the mouse over his name, clicked the link and a fresh chat box opened. His face popped up as small as an icon, and I blushed. He was tan and grinning—and a problem…my problem.

In the space of the single moment of gawking, the green light disappeared. *Moment lost.* I rubbed the bridge of my nose and sighed. "Damn," I said. I tipped my head toward the popcorn ceiling and clicked on his name again, directing myself to his profile. The previously small picture now popped larger on the upper-left corner of the screen. He wore a red T-shirt and his smile stretched across his caramel-tan face. I studied his pale brown hair, which was tousled skyward, and his clear blue eyes. Handsome, reckless… He was everything I didn't have time for.

A quick look at his profile told me what I already knew. He was trouble—handsome, beautiful trouble.

The microwave dinged in the kitchen and I snapped the laptop shut. I hurried to my closet and changed quickly, pulling on an oversized T-shirt and a mismatched pair of socks.

With that, I followed the smell of dinner. I pulled my plate from the microwave and sat at the kitchen table, listening to the hum of the evening outside the window.

Darkness overtook sentiment and I settled into normalcy, craving to leave Nomansville. *Nothing*, I thought. *Nothing matters here. I just want to leave this town and get to college. I need to build a new normal—to build my new normal.*

My phone buzzed on the kitchen table beside me, and I poked at the noodles on my plate. They were now lukewarm and tasted of pepper and melted cheese. Instinctively, I grabbed the phone and opened it to silence its insistent vibration.

"Hello?" I took another bite of the macaroni.

"What are you doing?" Alex's voice overtook the speaker, and I sat up a little straighter.

I frowned. "Eating dinner," I said.

She sighed. "It's your first night of winter freedom," she said. "Please don't tell me you're eating macaroni and cheese alone."

I teased my fingers through my hair. "No," I lied, and I could practically hear the roll of her eyes.

"Let's do something," she said.

I took another bite. "Like what?"

A pause...then, "A movie?"

"There isn't anything on," I said.

"Oh," she said, "I forgot. You don't like to have fun."

"It isn't that," I half whined.

"Then what is it like, Emma?" she pressed, and I shrugged, even though she couldn't see me.

"I don't know," I finally answered.

"I'll be over in five minutes." She snapped her phone closed and I groaned inwardly. Introvert meets extrovert in another episode of *Emma and Alex*. See your local listings for more information.

I stashed my phone in my pocket and my macaroni in a to-go container. God only knew where we would end up, I realized, shuffling back into my room to pull on a pair of sweatpants. *These must be appropriate, right?*

A knock came from the front door, then it swung open. "Okay," she called, strutting into the room with a smirk. She wore a gray skirt and a white T-shirt. Her dirty-blonde hair was pinned up, and she surveyed me with a frown. "Come on, Emma," she said. "I love you, but you can't wear that."

I frowned. "What *can* I wear?"

She twisted the ring on her finger. "The gray dress," she said.

"Where are we going?"

22

"A place," she said.

I stared over her head. There was no arguing, so I went to my room, put on the gray dress and swallowed my awkwardness for the night.

Otherwise, I would never hear the end of it. *Bless my best friend*, I thought.

The gray dress flared to my knees and tightened at the waist — simple, easy — and now Alex was twisting my hair into a carefully tousled topknot.

She studied her creation and squeezed my shoulders. "You look great," she said. "Now, let's go have a little fun, why don't we?"

I watched her in the mirror, twirling her fingers around the bracelet on her arm, and she grinned. Her smile was infectious, so I grinned back. "Where are we going, Alex?"

"Let's go," she said. *My best friend*, I thought. *That girl is full of mystery.*

We headed outside and, minutes later, we pulled out of the driveway. I blinked, closing my eyes. The clock on the dash illuminated a somber darkness, and I heard the constant mental timer — *tick, tock, tick, tock…* The ever-present countdown to our departure from this place.

She drove down the silent streets, and I sat at her side with my feet kicked up on the dash. She turned up the radio, drowning out my doubt, and I rolled down the window. I grabbed my phone from where I had stashed it in the cup holder between us. Quickly, I opened a note, and I did what I do… I began to write.

We drove, and it was like we were flying. We floated through the stars, through the planets, and even though we didn't know where we were going, it was perfect. We were together, and that was enough.

"Whatcha doing over there?" Alex interjected, noticing my distance, but I shrugged it off. In the three-odd years I'd known her, I'd yet to tell her about my writing. My words were personal—a quiet simmering in my heart. They had to come out, but they didn't have to be shared, so I slid my phone closed, tucking it under my thigh.

"Nothing," I said. It wasn't a lie. The words would never reach anyone. It was just journaling. They were just thoughts.

"You're lying," she said, glancing over at me in the light of the dashboard. She grazed her fingers through her hair and smirked. "Are you talking to your *other* best friend?"

I rolled my eyes. *As if*, I thought. There had only ever been Alex. "That is crazy," I said. I leaned my head against the headrest in an earnest attempt to catch the moon with my gaze. "You're my *only* best friend." *Hell*, I thought, *Alex is my* only *friend*, but that didn't diminish the gravity of her friendship.

Alex beamed. "I know," she said.

I peered over at her. "Where are we driving to, anyway?"

"I don't know," she said. She stared out of the windshield. Her gaze screamed fearless, wild and reckless. "I'm just driving."

I suppressed a grin. "Driving," I said.

"Yeah," she said, "just a drive."

I rolled my eyes. "And why could I not wear sweatpants on this drive?"

Her gaze darted across the dash, and she shrugged a shoulder. "It's more fun this way," she said.

"Yeah," I said, relishing the brisk breeze from the open window, "it is."

Together, I thought, *our lives are just better*.

Chapter Four

Sunlight broke through the windows, seeping into my skin through the cool glass and jerking me from blissful sleep. Groggily, I rolled to the edge of the bed. Morning croaked to life with the squawk of a sparrow, and I rubbed my fingers along the bridge of my nose. "Morning," I mumbled to myself and the bird.

The first day of Christmas break, I thought, and the annoying birds remained as a not-so-gentle reminder of Mississippi weather—warm today, in spite of the previous cold snap, and maybe even until Christmas. The closest thing to a white winter we'd had was the random snow shower of March.

I stepped into the bathroom and peered at my reflection in the mirror—pale skin and dark hair. I discarded my faded T-shirt on the counter. My stomach was lined from year to year as my weight yo-yoed, but I shrugged it off. I was on a mission. "I've got to find Maverick," I said, convincing myself to take action. There was no point in dwelling on the imperfection that was my body today.

One shower later, I stepped into a cloud of humidity and pulled a towel around me. Music hummed from my clock radio, and I rolled my eyes. *Yes*, I thought. *I'm awake, thank you.* I towel-dried my hair, humming along with the staticky song. The towel hung from my not-so-thin shoulders, and I straightened thoughtfully.

I meandered back into my room, listening to the bird outside the window twitter along with the radio. After dropping the towel, I jerked on a pair of leggings and a T-shirt, avoiding my reflection in the mirror. I felt inadequate and not worth much, period—not to mention my strange fascination with Maverick. I wouldn't admit that to Alex, but it was true. Well, he was…handsome.

I frowned, my heart in my throat, and shoved the brush through my hair before spinning to face the pale girl on the other side of the mirror. "You've got this," I said.

I bopped down the hallway to my mom's door. It was open, waiting, and I leaned against it. "Hey," I said.

"Hi," she said, twisting her gaze from the speckled ceiling. "Where are you off to?"

"The Englishes' farm."

"Good luck," she said.

"How was work?"

She wrapped her arms around her pillow. "Fine," she said. "Lots of ice chips, ya know?"

"True," I said. "Get some rest."

She laughed. "I'll try my best."

I backed away from the door. "See ya in a little while," I promised.

She nodded against the pillow. "Oh," she said, "and you have a job for the break."

"Awesome," I replied.

"Yeah," she said. "See ya in a little bit."

I waved and rushed into the living room to grab my keys. I retrieved my shoes from beside the couch, shoving them onto my feet, and hurried out of the door. A mid-December breeze whipped past me, and I unlocked my car door, ducking inside.

I flipped on the radio and drove through the nearly vacant streets, wondering where the productive citizens of our little hamlet were. Humming along to the near-silent radio, I turned down the wide road that led out of town.

As I drove, houses got farther apart and larger. The countryside was riddled with cows and hay, and there was something nostalgic about all of it. I barreled toward Maverick's family's farm. It wasn't terribly far, but the road felt like it went on forever.

Then, suddenly, I was there. The farm bloomed thousands of flowers a year, but now the fields were mostly bare. The long drive led up to a tiny red brick house and what appeared to be a dark barn.

The barn door slid open, and I slowed the car on the gravel. I swallowed. Maverick led a horse from the barn, steering it toward the field opposite the house. His black T-shirt and jeans stood out and I bit my bottom lip. *Well*, I thought, *here we go*.

I slowed to a crawl, listening to the increasing hum of static from the radio and gravel against the underside of my car. Blinking, I watched Maverick move. He was all shoulders, swagger and sweet temptation.

He slowed to a stop at the sound of my approach, and I imagined the smirk on his thin face. In the morning light, his hair seemed darker, his skin paler with winter, and I rolled to a stop in front of his house then opened the car door.

"Back so soon, Katie?" he called from where he stood, just feet away. He rubbed the horse's head. It was a strong, beautiful speckled gray, and it leaned into Maverick's touch.

Inwardly, I smiled at the gesture. There must be a hint of compassion in him. I stepped out of the car and slammed the door. "Not Katie," I called back. Katie, his younger sister by a year and a half, played things different than Maverick. She kept to herself in school, and he kept to myself out of it.

My voice had gotten his attention. Finally, he turned around. With a lift of his eyebrow, he led the horse my way, and I frowned. *Great*, I thought. *I didn't come here to interact with the wildlife…just check in about this crazy project and get out. I didn't come to bond with anything – or anyone, for that matter.* Although I had to admit that bonding with Maverick had always been a childhood dream.

"Emma Cage? What're you doing here?" He continued walking until he stood in front of me. The horse huffed a breath, and I begrudgingly wondered what I was interrupting.

I leaned against my car door. "Nothing," I said, stupidly, and he laughed, so I forced a timid giggle right back. "No, I mean, I'm here because you're my partner for this big English project. You weren't at school yesterday when Mr. Zelner assigned groups, so…here I am."

The look on his face darkened, and he chuckled. "That was fast," he said. He stuffed his hand into his pocket and pulled out a peppermint. "Want to give Pacman a treat?"

I frowned, just staring at Maverick with my mouth slightly ajar. *No,* I thought. "Maverick, no."

"Why not? Pacman doesn't bite. He loves the ladies," he assured me.

"I'm sure he does," I said.

He unwrapped the peppermint and held it out to the horse. "Did I do something to offend you?" Shoulders lax, he didn't seem to mind either way.

I groaned inwardly and shook my head. "No," I said. *That* wasn't exactly the gnawing feeling in my gut. I blinked, watching the horse eat Maverick's peppermint. I had never seen anything like it, but, to be fair, I hadn't been around many horses to know the odd things they might eat.

He patted the horse's back then he looked at me. "Well," he asked, "what is this big project you're so worried about?"

I'd never said I was worried, but I didn't take the time to correct him. "It's for English," I said. "A creative project. A story, a skit…something like that."

He peered at me thoughtfully. "A skit?"

I looked at him with a hand in his hair, his eyes smiling, and I flushed. "Or a short story… Just something creative."

He turned toward Pacman and smirked, tossing his leg over the side of the horse. "We'll get right on that."

I frowned, forehead wrinkling. He loomed over me, and I was dwarfed under his gaze. "Well," I hedged, rubbing my forearm slowly, "can I get your number?" I heard myself talking and realized that I sounded bizarre, but it was too easy to ignore a Facebook message or even an email, for that matter.

He petted Pacman's side. "I'll be at school," he said. "We'll talk then."

I sneered. *Sure*, I thought, *you'll be in school*. I twisted a piece of hair around my finger in thinly veiled frustration. "We shouldn't just throw it together."

He twisted back to face the barn, shaking his head. "Don't worry," he said. "We won't throw it together."

With that, Maverick leaned forward and Pacman took off, leaving me in the dust.

"Okay," I said to myself. "Okay."

I stared after him, dumbfounded, and spun back toward the car. *Well*, I thought, *that went well*. I slumped into the front seat and grabbed my phone from the passenger side. Instinctively I hit Alex's name and put the phone on speaker, shoving it under the mirror so I could drive away.

The phone rang and the gravel rolled, but no one picked up.

I frowned, staring out of the windshield.

Well... I thought.

Her voicemail ticked on, and I said a little bit of nothing. What was there to say to a voicemail?

Chapter Five

My phone vibrated, clattering against my desk. I'd been writing or reading or both, but Alex's face lit up the screen.

"Hey," I said after sliding the bar to answer.

"What's up? Sorry I missed you."

"It's fine," I said. "Are we still on for tonight?"

"Is that even a question? I'm outside."

Seconds later, we were in my car and I was driving.

"He just rode off?" Alex was sitting in the passenger seat. I drove toward Hal's Burgers, ready for the Friday night special — a double-sized everything. "On a horse? Really? I mean, that is so cliché," she said.

I groaned. "Don't make fun," I replied. I leaned out of the window, shouting my order into the speaker.

"I'm not making fun," she said, but we both knew she was.

I pulled around the front of the building and paid for our dinner from our collective Hal's budget, and we pulled out a few seconds later. "Sure, you're not," I said, shaking my head and taking a sip of my drink.

I drove out of town toward one of our favorite spots in the city—a vacant parking lot of the old drive-in movie theater, where we would prop up her phone as a makeshift movie screen.

It had become a sort of Friday night tradition—drive out to the pavement paradise that had once been the theater, bring a bunch of junk food and watch a really bad movie on a really tiny screen. Half the time, though, we didn't actually watch the movie. We talked and ragged on each other and everyone else. It was a good tradition. Steady.

She set her phone up for our newest showing. Soon, a leggy blonde made a bad joke and her suitor sniggered, because he wanted to get laid. Patterns, I realized, were essential in Friday night movie land.

Alex ran a finger through her hair, and she grinned a little. "So," she said, "*the* Maverick is a hard case to crack. You'll make it through. Seriously, Zelner wouldn't pair you with an anchor."

I shrugged, not so sure Zelner was Team Emma anymore. "Yeah," I said. I peered over at the tiny screen. "Maybe."

"No 'maybe' about it," she said. "Zelner's a good guy, and you're one of his favorites. He isn't going to let this guy drag you down. Just give the dude a chance." She popped a fry into her mouth. "He probably needs an Emma, ya know? Someone to set him straight," she clarified.

I rolled my eyes, because, really, who wants to set the Maverick Englishes of the world straight? I didn't have time for that and Zelner knew it. Alex and I were on our way out. This semester would be the upward swing, and we would not be trampled by that track-and-field, flower-child cowboy, no matter how delicious he looked and how long I'd crushed on him. I crossed my arms, staring at Alex's smartphone. "Yeah," I said, "well, it isn't right."

"Hey, you might come out of it for the better." A sly smirk slid across her face, and I regretted the conversation at once. "I mean, English is pretty cute...if you like that mysterious loner kind of chic," she said. She twisted in her seat to grab another drink from the tray and flashed me a winning smile. "Think about it," she said. "Will working with *that* face be so bad?"

I groaned. Of course, she was right. Alex knew every thought, every nerve, every facet of my personality. I guessed she'd picked up on the crush I'd developed on Maverick during freshman year, regardless of how much I'd tried to hide it. "No," I said.

"Thought so," she replied, and her grin broadened even more. "Ya know what?"

I peered over at her, silhouetted in the setting sun. "What, Alex?"

She reached over and squeezed my hand. "It might even be good," she said.

"Yeah," I replied, "it might even be good."

But I didn't believe it for a second.

Chapter Six

Ever since Dad had left, Mom and I had been second-row Methodists. Every Sunday, without fail, we woke up at seven, put on our Sunday best, had a nice meal and drove to the church three minutes from our house. First Methodist was a brick building with a steeple and Southern charm. The stained-glass windows painted pictures on the floor at sunset, and I loved to sit in the empty sanctuary and sing. My voice would bounce from the walls, amplifying itself ten times over.

The Monday after the school holiday had begun, I started my desk job at the hospital. I made appointments and took calls. Mostly I daydreamed about leaving this godforsaken town and doodled on hospital stationery. They didn't seem to mind.

Tuesday, as I sat with my back to the TV that blared the news, I heard a rustle. Our corner of the hospital wasn't far from the emergency room, so noise wasn't uncommon. Curious, I glanced up just in time to see

Maverick English arguing with the automatic coffee machine in front of our station. He kicked it, arm against the wall, back arched over a black shirt and jeans, and my cheeks flared with color.

He turned around, having given up on the coffee, and looked at me. *Definitely not Maverick*, I thought, but the thirty-something man *was* concerned that the receptionist in the ice-cream-cone scrubs was staring at him. "Do *you* know where a person can get a decent cup of coffee around here?"

I reached for the pot just inside our window. Stephanie, the nurse I worked with, needed coffee to survive and had requested a coffee pot when she'd been reassigned from the upper floor. "I don't know about decent," I said, but I poured him a cup of coffee and, honestly, he looked grateful.

"Thanks," he said and shuffled off.

I huffed a sigh and ran my fingers through my hair. "Well," I said to myself, "that was strange." *Yeah.* It was strange — but not so strange that I was surprised. Alex had been right. I'd once had a crush on Maverick. One of those borderline obsessive ones at that, but it had been years ago. Now Maverick was just a means to an end. *Right?*

Frankly, he was an ass. There was no reason to like him, much less to *like*-like him. I mean, other than his ass. I shook my head.

Eighteen years and an Ivy League acceptance, and this track-and-field farmer occupies my mind like a disease.

I poured myself a cup of coffee and took a sip but nearly spit it out. *No*, I thought, *I just don't like coffee.* I inhaled the smell of it, rich and warm, and decided to leave it on my desk, nonetheless. What could it hurt?

My phone, face down beside the keyboard, vibrated and I flipped it over. It was a text from Alex —

Hey. Plans tonight?

I frowned before responding.

Thought I would order Chinese and watch reruns of reality TV.

Seconds later a single word.

Wrong.

Sorry. Let me check my calendar... Yeah, Chinese and reruns.

The bit could go on forever, but we both know who would win. Finally, Alex made a suggestion.

There's a party tonight at the lake.

I sighed. There was the punch line. And she soon followed it.

You want to go?

And while I considered her suggestion, she didn't give up.

Yes! Let's go. It could be fun.

I glanced around, listening to the squeak of tennis shoes on linoleum.

I don't know, Alex.

Come on, Emma. Live a little.

I sighed, rubbing my forehead. I doubted there would be any convincing her to *not* go, and I didn't like it when she went to parties alone, since there is safety in numbers and all that jazz.

All right, all right. Let's go.

Yay! Wear your purple dress?

I laughed. *My fashionista best friend*, I thought.

Sure.

I'll pick you up at 7:30.

I shook my head and flipped my phone back over. *Well*, I thought, *I guess I have plans now.* I turned back to the notepad and the doodles morphed to words. I guessed that was just what became of my mind. *It structures itself into words, fragments and phrases.* By the end of the day, my doodle paper would be another explosion of writer brain.

* * * *

I flipped off the lights in the office, hung the sign in the window and punched my card in the back. My stomach lurched as I passed a man on a gurney who was in dire need of stitches. Inwardly, I reaffirmed that the medical field was not for me, because I couldn't handle the sight of blood. I smiled politely and pulled my jacket on for precautionary measures, even though I doubted that the temperature would be below forty-five degrees, even now.

I stepped into the parking lot and pulled my keys from my purse. The drive was short, just long enough for me to sing along to my favorite song on the radio. Inside the house, Mom was performing her own concert in the kitchen, so I hung my coat on the rack and sang along.

"Way to make an entrance, Emma," she called between verses, and she stuck her head around the corner. She wore a white apron over her scrubs. "Hey," she said. "How was work?"

I shrugged. "Steph was out today," I said. No need to mention not-Maverick showing up. "So, more boring than usual."

"Sounds about right," she said. She was plating dinner, so I took to filling glasses of water. Mom tended to run off coffee and dehydrate herself. "Any plans for tonight?"

I glanced down at my watch. Five-fifteen. *Two hours,* I thought. Two hours until Alex appeared, probably wearing something sparkly. "Well," I said, "there's a party at the lake."

"And Alex wants to go?" Mom asked, easily filling in the blanks.

I leaned against the counter. "Yeah," I replied.

"I knew Alex would be good for you," she said.

I rolled my eyes. "By taking me to a party?"

"Yes, by taking you to a party," she replied. "What are you going to wear?"

"Alex mandated that I wear the purple dress," I told her.

"Alex does have a sense of style. You should curl your hair," she said.

I groaned and took a sip of water. "Yeah."

Mom slid a plate to me and smiled. "A party will do you good. You'll be careful?"

"Of course," I replied.

She nodded, took a sip of water then said, "Good."

Chapter Seven

At seven-twenty, I stood in front of my mirror, tugging the purple dress into place. I ogled at my reflection—hair curled and pinned out of the way and awkwardly straight posture. I sighed, jerking a white wrap from my dresser. My pale arms and the sleeveless dress didn't exactly add up, and I'd added a pair of black tights for modesty and potential wind chill alike.

I slid down onto the edge of my bed to zip up my boots, just as my phone buzzed on the nightstand. Groaning, I thrust myself across the bed to grab it. "Hello," I said, my voice clipped from the laughable position.

"I'm outside," Alex practically sang. "Are you ready?"

I rolled off the side of the bed, zipping my boots the rest of the way and righting myself. "Will I ever be?" I teased and hurried out of my bedroom and through the house. I waved at Mom, who sat at the kitchen table doing a crossword puzzle and waiting for time to leave before her shift started. "Have a good night at work, Mama," I told her.

She looked up. "You two be careful," she said.

"We will be," I replied.

"No," Alex said through the speaker, "we're going to get plastered and have some *real* fun."

I rolled my eyes at the phone. I was inwardly glad that I was off tomorrow. Lord knew how long tonight would be. I smiled at my mom and walked outside. Alex's car was idling by the curb, and she rolled down the window.

"Come on. Come on," she said. She waved, and I hopped into the car. Alex's dress was green and flared, just like mine. *Surprise, surprise...* We'd bought them from the same store at the same time.

"We're matching," I noted, and she giggled.

"Yes," she said. "They're *our* colors."

I replied, "Go ahead. Drive."

She pulled into the road and nudged my shoulder. "Come on," she said. "I know how we normally feel about these people, but they aren't all bad."

I frowned, surprised by the revelation. "Where did *that* come from?"

She dialed idly through the radio stations. "I don't know," she said. "I've just been thinking. They aren't all bad."

I picked a loose straw wrapper from the cup holder, folding it, accordion style. Suddenly, I felt like the conversation wasn't hypothetical, but I didn't want to get into the semantics of her sudden change of heart quite yet. "Okay," I said, "they aren't all bad."

Silence lay between us. I peered out of the window. As we drove, the houses got farther apart and the stars got brighter.

"And...I mean," she hedged, quieter now. "I just think we could make some memories, ya know? Here and now." She paused, swallowing. "I mean, next year...things will be different."

I frowned. *Yeah*, I thought, *things will be different.* "Yeah," I said. "You're right there."

"It'll be all textbooks and future and focus," she said, leaving out the most important part—that we wouldn't be together—and stepping into the pragmatics. She cut a glassy-eyed grin toward me. "We won't have time to be wild."

"Who said anything about being wild? I'm not even convinced I know how to be wild," I said.

"Good point. You're a little uptight," she teased.

I rolled my eyes, playing along. "Hey!"

Alex shrugged. Her green-clad shoulders bounced and she smiled. "Let's live a little," she said, but I stared out of the window.

We flew up a hill, sky and grass becoming one, and at the crest, suddenly I could see fairy lights across the lake. Flashy figures dotted the grounds, and bag-covered lights led up to the house. It belonged to the family of one of the football players for the sole purpose of events such as this.

"Oh," I said, and she laughed halfheartedly, pulling around to where cars were lined up on the grass.

"Oh?" she asked.

"That's just a lot of people," I explained.

She reached across the car to squeeze my hand. "Don't worry," she replied. "This will be fun."

I watched our peers stumble across the grass, out of their cars, into the house and I swallowed hard. *Yeah*, I thought, and she shut off the engine. The sound of the party echoed off the water. "Fun," I replied.

Funny... All I could wonder was... *Will Maverick be here?*

Chapter Eight

I rounded the car and Alex squeezed my shoulders. "Stop worrying," she said.

"I'm not," I replied, not a one-hundred-percent lie. I wasn't worried, per se, but I was anxious. Crowds and Emma weren't the best pair.

The party teemed before us, and I scanned the crowd thoughtfully. These faces, I realized... I had walked by them my entire life, but I had never really seen any of them. Here, they wore dark colors and leather, and they stumbled as they walked. They spoke a little too loud. *Seems like a weird time to mingle*, I thought. But, here I was.

We walked until we met the edge of the party, and I paused. "So," I said, "how do we do this?"

She snorted, but not in a mean way, and released my hand that she had been idly holding. "We have fun," she said and crossed into the chaotic grounds.

I blinked. One of the football players was chasing a giggling girl in a red dress. Another girl, clad in silver, leaned against a tree with a beer in her hand. A guy walked up to her, grinning like the Cheshire Cat, and wrapped his arms around her waist. A symphony of chuckles and voices mingled in the air, and I bit my bottom lip.

"Well," I said, "okay."

Alex waved at a couple, they waved back and I blinked. Had Alex gotten popular and I'd missed it? She trained her gaze on me, smirking. "We've never spoken," she told me. "Don't make interaction harder than it has to be, Em."

Awkwardly, I nodded. That could be true. I followed her, approaching the house at a slow crawl. Alex let herself in. She glanced toward the dance floor, still waving, but her tight-lipped smile told a tale of something under the surface. She maneuvered through the mass of dancing figures and into the kitchen.

"The first step of having fun at a party," she said and scooped a beer from the ice chest on the counter, extending it to me, "is getting a little artificial courage."

"Where did they get that?" I asked, instinctively, and a chuckling guy in the corner walked up. He extended a hand.

"I'm Max," he said. His name was completely unfamiliar and the hand was one that I didn't really want to shake, but Alex automatically swooped in.

"Alex," she said. She offered an off-kilter grin and he winked.

"I'm Michael's older brother," he offered, and he looked me over. "I'm twenty-two."

Charming, I thought, but I smiled politely. "Nice," I replied, still not thrilled with the prospect of touching the guy's hand — or anything else.

"That is Emma," she said. "She doesn't talk much."

An easy lie, I thought, crossing my arms and leaning against the wall. I talked plenty, but I figured being the quiet one at the party could pan out in my favor. Maybe he would just go away and find some blonde bimbo that was more...well, *chatty*.

After a beat of utter silence, the guy, Max, nodded. There must have been something between his shoulders after all. "All right," he said. "Well, you ladies enjoy the party."

I blew out a breath, and Alex prompted me to take the beer, but I shook my head. "No thanks," I said, and she smirked.

"All right, then," she said. "That means *you're* driving home." She popped the can open and took a long drag.

In the space of a blink, her gaze darted away from mine. I frowned but didn't say a word. *I don't know...* Maybe I was imagining the whole thing, but she seemed agitated somehow. Maybe it wasn't even her. Maybe it was me.

"Stop thinking so much," she said and took another sip.

Music blared from the other room again, the mismatched sting of a guitar tuning. Then, suddenly, someone was playing—loud, electric—and a cymbal crashed. The party was really getting started, and the crowd revved up to join the noise of the music.

She reached into the tub and pulled out a root beer, outstretching it to me like a peace offering. *At least I won't be thirsty*, I thought. "Thanks," I said.

"Now," she said, "wanna go listen to the band?"

"Ugh," I replied, not so sure, but she rolled her eyes.

"Come on," she said, tweaking my nose then stepping back into the hallway. She maneuvered into the living room, and I followed. There was no furniture in there, save a couch pushed against the wall. A fire roared in the brick fireplace and the band staggered around the room at odd intervals—a drum set in the corner, the guitarist to one side, a singer dancing through the crowd... Meanwhile, my stomach lurched with the chaos of it.

I blinked, gravitating toward the wall, but I was soon lost in a sea of bodies. My throat contracted, dry as a bone, so I twisted off the top of the root beer. *Easy*, I thought, and I took a long drink. A lanky guy wearing hipster glasses bumped into me, and the bottle crashed from my hand, sloshing as it fell to the ground and shattered.

"Shit, sorry," he said, kicking the glass away.

I blinked. My hand was sticky, so I tried to step away to find a place to rinse it off, but I hit another body. *Full-on collision*, I thought, but the guy kept looking at me. I wondered how many beers he'd had already.

"Yeah," I said, hoping he would just leave, "it's fine."

He nodded, not-so-riveted, and shuffled away to a blonde not dressed for the weather. I spun to look for Alex, but she had already been eaten by the crowd.

I shuddered, backing farther into the wall. The band wailed, and my heart thumped in my eardrums. I was lost and unsure of myself and my surroundings. Blood rushed as I swayed in the stale evening air, and I ran into another body, warm and steady and strong. Color flooded my cheeks. *This is why I don't like crowds*, I thought, as hands came down on my shoulders.

"Emma," he breathed. *Maverick's voice.* I swallowed hard. "You've got to be more careful."

I tugged away from him, embarrassed. "Yeah," I said, "sorry."

He exhaled, sobering. "Are you okay?"

"Yeah," I said. "I'm fine." *Like he cares*, I thought.

"You sure?"

Music and people swarmed around us. "Yes, I'm fine," I replied. "I've got to get back to my friend."

I frowned, peering anxiously toward the swelling crowd, and he nudged my shoulder. "You were saying?"

I crossed my arms, biding my time and trying not to panic. "Well, I've got to find her."

"You'd better stick with me, kid," he said. "People get lost at these parties."

I stared blankly at the glass on the ground, blinking. His words, his warm hand on my arm... They overwhelmed me, and I could hear the roar of the party from what felt like miles away. *Tunnel vision*, I thought, and I trained my gaze on him. Up close, he wasn't so perfect. There was a dark line of stubble across his chin and his hair was pushed back, but there were deep circles under his eyes. He looked like a mystery, *my* mystery, and I cursed Mr. Zelner and the fates for shoving us together.

I shook my head. "I'll be fine," I said. I backed away, nearly tripping over the guitarist's amp chord, but Maverick gripped my arm harder.

Chuckling, he shook his head. "Come on, Emma," he said. "I'll help you look for Alex, and hey, if you play your cards right, we can even talk about this project of ours."

I sighed. Well, I couldn't exactly say no to that. "Okay," I agreed.

He shook his head. "You really do have a one-track mind," he said, and he pulled on my arm again. I almost resisted but I didn't. He was steady, and the party was making my head spin.

"So," I said, "where do we look?"

He shrugged and glanced over his shoulder. "Well," he said, "let's start outside."

In an awkward beat of silence, he skimmed his hand down my arm to grip mine. The flush that surely tinted my cheeks intensified and chill bumps rose on my arms. Swallowing hard, I followed him through the current of bodies, and he shoved the sliding glass doors open to stand on the back porch. Just outside the door, other seniors squatted on the stairs, drunkenly cackling, and there was a pool emptied for winter. The air was crisp, and Maverick held up a hand in half greeting to the others.

"Yeah," he said, half under his breath, "I don't think she's out here."

I had guessed as much. Unless she was in the pool, she was nowhere to be seen, but something in his gaze made me ask anyway. "Why?"

He smirked and gestured for me to look more closely. I frowned, glanced toward them then laughed halfheartedly. Still, I didn't get it.

"They're high," he said, and I blinked. I looked back at them and frowned. They were swaying, red-eyed, and they giggled, munching on chips from what I assumed was a communal bag.

I blushed and shook my head. "Yeah," I said, "maybe she's not here."

"See ya later, guys," he said, shaking his head. He shuffled back to the door, squeezing my hand once. "Maybe she went looking for the bathroom."

"Maybe," I said.

"Are you sure you're okay there, dolly?"

"My name's Emma," I said.

He spun to face me, his gaze somber and tempting. "I know that, Emma," he said. "I've known you since we were seven. I remember that yellow and black bumblebee costume you wore in that cheesy first grade play—the one with the dancing guitars or something?"

I blinked, my heart in my throat. Suddenly he was hardly an inch away from me, and I gasped his air. "They were mandolins," I corrected him stupidly.

He chuckled, a deep rattle in his throat. "I'm teasing you," he said.

"Oh," I replied, listening to the word drop like a boulder between us.

He nudged my chin. "Come on, dolly," he said. "Let's go find your friend."

He ducked down a hallway, weaving through the crowd. He stopped at an intensely long line, and I bit my lip. *No Alex*, I thought,

Maverick groaned. "No Alex," he mumbled, shoving a hand through his hair and stepping out of the hallway with a thoughtful frown.

The hall ended at a nearly deserted den, and he stopped, peering at something on the wall. I turned and he caught me, chuckling. Suddenly, we were close again. The air simmered, and I felt like his magnet. The skin of his forearm grazed mine. The party, the project, Alex… All of it melted away.

Then, he was kissing me. He cupped his strong hands on my face and my tension melted. I gasped against his lips. Heat flooded my cheeks instantly. It wasn't like I'd never been kissed, but I had never been kissed like this…at a party, with people so close, by an incredibly attractive boy with alcohol on his breath.

My pulse raced, and he cornered me against a door, smirking ever so slightly. He fumbled with the doorknob behind me and broke away long enough for two words. "Should I?"

Obviously out of my mind, I nodded, and I grazed the stubble along his cheek with my lips. Alex's voice was in my head, reminding me to have fun, and years of crushing and crushing hard for this face, this boy, this man, kept me wanting.

The door swung open, and he lowered his lips to my shoulder. We both giggled, half at the situation, half at ourselves — or at least that was what I imagined as we tumbled to the ground, a pile of limbs.

There was a gasp, a groan, then the sound of my name.

I frowned and looked up. We were in a bedroom, sparsely furnished, and Alex lay in a disheveled mess beside… I frowned then said to Maverick. "Is that your sister?"

He straightened, shifting, amused, and I realized with a sinking feeling that he was drunk — or at least buzzed. His gaze darted toward the bed, but mine burned a hole in the floor. My mind raced, and I shifted, scrambling to my feet.

He frowned. "Katie?"

I blinked then ran around the corner, my heart in my throat and confusion bubbling to the forefront of my mind. Voices swelled, calling out to me, but I couldn't stop. I swallowed hard and pushed through the party. I saw red, the secret I'd happened upon swirling in every step, because Alex and I told each other *everything*, and what we didn't tell each other, we just *knew*. My heart shuddered a beat. *I should have known.*

Cheeks burning, I didn't stop until I'd reached the car. My stomach in knots, I leaned against the car door and a torrent of voices followed, laughter and the sound of the party. For a split second, I contemplated walking home, just to avoid the situation, just to clear my head, but Alex called my name, strangled between disjointed conversation.

"Maverick, calm down." An unfamiliar voice rose over the crowd, and I faced away, feeling small. The wealth of my best friend's secret bubbled in my chest, and I wished I were invisible.

"Calm down," he scoffed, voice high-pitched, *confused*. He hadn't known anything either, I realized, my head spinning.

"Maverick, you're drunk," she said, and I glanced back. My rose-colored glasses had clattered to the floor of the off-den bedroom, and I realized it now. His words, slightly slurred yet somehow still utterly charming, clearly showed his rash lack of inhibitions. *Sure*, I thought, *we'll talk about the project*. My eyes welled with angry tears. *God*, I thought, *why am I so stupid?*

"God," Kate mumbled. "Mom is going to be *so* mad."

"Emma!" Alex's voice broke the argument, and Maverick's and his sister's voices tapered off. I assumed they'd gone to their car, but I really didn't care. I closed my eyes, but Alex was warm beside me.

"Keys," I said, and she dropped them into my hand after only one drink.

Chapter Nine

I whipped out of the makeshift parking spot, unfoundedly angry and listening to the heavy sound of our breath as the party music faded. Thoughts clouded the front seat but penetrating silence prevailed. My hands were firmly cemented at ten and two.

The irrationality of it wasn't lost on me, and, frankly, that made it worse. I groaned, my foot on the gas and my heart on my seat, because I should have known — and she should have told me.

"Say something," she said, shattering the glass-topped silence.

My gaze twitched from the pitch-black road to look at her, and I swallowed. My fearless Alex grimaced toward her lap, her fingers worrying a loose thread on that emerald-green dress. Her carefree attitude was shoved somewhere deep inside her, and she suddenly seemed so small.

I blinked back angry tears, shaking my head. "I don't know what to say."

A bitter laugh twisted from her chest. "Oh, you know what to say."

I slammed on the brakes, swerving into an abandoned parking lot and glaring over at her. "You don't get to do that," I said. My limbs ached, and I sprang from the driver's seat to pace the pavement. "You don't get to do that."

The door slammed behind her, and suddenly we were fighting. I hated it when we fought. "Oh, come on," she said, voice rising.

I stared blankly at her. The moon haloed her dirty-blonde head, setting her ablaze with something I couldn't identify. "Why are *you* mad?" I asked.

She scoffed, rolling her eyes. "Your opinion is clear, Emma," she replied.

I frowned, now confused. "What?"

"Your opinion," she said. "You've made it clear how you feel."

Her words sank in, and I dropped my gaze to the overgrown pavement. I hadn't exactly caught her with the captain of the football team. No, she'd been in a compromising position with a compromising person, and the shock of that hadn't even hit me yet, but she clearly thought my reaction applied to the gender of her companion and not the situation.

I blinked. I felt strange. My heart hung low, to the pit of my stomach, and tears burned in the corners of my eyes—but not for the reason she thought. I closed my eyes, battling to push the unfounded tears away. "You didn't tell me," I said, my voice quiet as daybreak.

"What?" She stilled, the frustration draining from her face and leaving her pale as a ghost.

I groaned, spinning away from her, in knots. "You didn't tell me."

"Emma," she mumbled.

"It's fundamental, Alex," I said, my mind churning.

A few paces away, she lifted her voice. "What is?"

"This monumental thing about yourself," I said, a little louder now, to get my point across. "I mean… I didn't even know you were dating anyone, and…you're my best friend."

She shifted her weight, obviously surprised by that particular reaction. "I'm…" She rubbed the back of her neck. "I'm sorry?"

"We're supposed to tell each other everything," I said. "Even the hard stuff."

She made a deep sigh, a broken kind of sound. "I know," she said.

I doubled back to lean against the car, my arms over my chest, quasi-defensive. "So, are you and Kate an…item?"

She shrugged. "Not really," she replied. She swatted a mosquito from her exposed ankle and sighed. "I mean, sorta, but not exactly."

"Did you just bring me to the party to…erm, see her?" *That too*, I thought. That stung.

Automatically, she shook her head. "No," she said. "I didn't even know she was going to be there." She sighed again. "I brought you to the party because you've been so stressed lately. I mean, first it was applications then it was acceptances and that huge decision. Then it was the English project… I just figured you needed to blow off a little steam." She shoved my shoulder and the ease of it softened the blow.

My cheeks warm, I shook my head. The memory of Maverick's breath ghosted my shoulders, my neck, my lips and I blistered under its fire. Gosh, I'd been the worst kind of idiot. "Don't talk about the project," I said.

"I guess that means I can't talk about the steamy make-out session with Maverick... Right?"

I groaned. "Yes," I said.

She shook her head. "Well, it's happening."

"Fine," I said, opening the car door and sliding in. "But let's go home."

She sat beside me just as I revved the engine. She was silent, staring at me in the hollow silence as I wove back onto the street. "Emma?"

In timid, undetermined silence, I glanced over the console. "Yeah?"

She studied her hands. "I'm sorry I didn't tell you," she said.

I sighed deeply. "I understand," I replied—and that was true enough.

I drove slowly and put down the windows. The air stirred my hair and caressed my cheek, and I leaned into it. Despite myself, I loved the smell of pine and the sharp scent of a Mississippi winter—just cool enough to need a jacket, not cool enough to cause me to curse winter's existence.

Still, she began to prod. After a prickly silence, she sighed a high-pitched whine and crossed her arms. "Oh, come on. You have to give me something, Emma," she said. "Anything."

I looked over. She looked different by the dashboard light. Her skin shone, and she was interested...maybe a little buzzed. Frowning, I tucked a strand of hair behind my ear. "He kissed me," I said.

"Obviously," she said. "How did it happen?"

I shrugged a shoulder, my lip raw from me worrying it. "Well," I said. I turned into my driveway and cut the engine. Fidgeting with my seatbelt, I continued. "This guy ran into me and I dropped my bottle of root beer. There was this super-awkward interaction there, and I was just trying to disappear altogether, ya know, but then I ran into Maverick, and —"

"Whoa, whoa," she said, holding up her hands. "Slow down, please."

I inhaled. "Okay," I said. "Well, we were looking for you, I guess. I mean... I wanted to and he said we would. We looked outside first, but you weren't there. Then we ended up along in this hallway and he just looked at me...like, *looked* at me. Then he was kissing me, and..." I trailed off because, well, she knew the rest of the story.

"Whoa," she said. "I can't believe it."

"Yeah," I said and shoved open my car door. "I doubt he will."

She frowned. "What do you mean?"

I walked toward the front door. She followed, knowing silently that she would spend the night, let the alcohol leave her system and go home refreshed. "He was drunk," I explained.

She sighed, shaking her head. "He was probably more sober than you think," she countered.

"Sure," I replied and stepped into the house. Mom's car was gone, so we were alone, and I trudged into the kitchen. "Want some popcorn?"

Normalcy pooled through the cracks of the secret, and she swallowed hard. "Yes, please," she said, sliding past me to grab a couple of bowls. I shoved the popcorn into the microwave. *There's no point in waiting,* I thought, trying desperately to believe it.

"So, erm... Katie?" I questioned without looking at her.

"Yeah," she said. "Kate."

I cringed at the blood on my tongue. "How long have you, uh, been together?"

"Well…" she said. "I mean, we've just been hanging out. We aren't *together* exactly."

The microwave plate turned. I stared at the countertop, thinking of new questions — or trying to — and I rapped my fingers against the countertop. "Well, how long have you *known*?"

Alex exhaled and rubbed her shoulders methodically. "I don't really know," she said. "I mean, I sort of started thinking about it a year ago. Kate and I met, and I'd never thought about a girl like that before, but suddenly she seemed like this interesting *possibility*."

I opened the microwave to grab the bag once it had finished popping. "Oh," I said — and thought of Maverick. He was a train wreck waiting to happen. Trouble, I knew, but I wanted it. I craved the poison.

She handed me the bowls. "What're you thinking about so hard?"

I dumped the bag of popcorn into the bowls. "You know what," I said. Sometimes, I felt Alex's eyes were lasers of X-ray vision. We were practically sisters, bonded by knowledge and awkwardness. She knew me like the back of her hand.

"Don't worry about him," she said, shrugging thoughtfully. "Seriously. Just don't give him the power here." She pointed to my head and smirked. "He isn't worth it."

I popped a piece of popcorn into my mouth and hoped she was right.

Chapter Ten

I rolled over at the mind-numbing squeak of Stella's hamster wheel and tossed my arm over my eyes. Alex lay beside me in a pair of my pajamas. Her blonde hair was fanned out across her shoulders and my pillow — a position we had been in countless times since she had moved in next door. It was an innocent position, but now not so simple.

Nibbling my bottom lip, I twisted to survey the clock and sighed. Three-twenty-three blared in red, and I tossed my legs over the side of the bed. The wood was cold under my bare feet, so I shuffled to the dresser and unrolled a pair of socks, pulling them on. Alex shifted in bed but didn't stir, so I trudged to the kitchen.

I grabbed a bottle of water and slid into place on a bar stool. My messy bun sagged on my head, so I jerked it into a high ponytail. A dull vibration rattling the coffee table startled me.

"It's three o'clock in the morning," I mumbled to myself. "Who calls at three o'clock in the morning?"

I abandoned the bottle on the kitchen counter and trudged to grab my phone from the cluttered surface, shoving popcorn bowls and soda cans out of the way. *Geez*, I thought, *I need to clean up.*

Finally seizing my phone from under a pile of magazines, I slid the bar to answer without glancing at the caller ID. "Hello?"

There was a garbled noise on the other end of the line. "Emma?"

His voice shocked me, and I glanced toward my lock screen — an unknown number but a very familiar voice. I blinked, but he was talking. "I'm, uh, sorry…for tonight. Katie said I should say sorry, but I don't think I should. Why would I?"

I frowned, sitting on the edge of the couch. "Maverick, are you still drunk? And how did you get my number?"

He chuckled but paused. "Drunk? No," he said. "I just… Everything got weird there at the party, and Katie said I should apologize, but why would I apologize? And Zelner gave me your number."

I heard something on the porch — a bump and a moan, magnified through the phone. Instantly, I frowned. "Maverick, are you outside my house?"

"Uh," he hedged and I flushed. "I'm here. Let me in?"

I sighed, shaking my head, then unfolded my legs from the couch and walked over to open the door. There Maverick slumped, holding his foot. He was wearing the same clothes as he had been at the party, but they were mussed, as if his sister had attempted to put him to sleep. "Maverick," I said, "what are you doing?"

He straightened and looked at me. "I took a walk," he said.

I just looked at him. Even disheveled and inebriated, he was still handsome. I crossed my arms. "It's three o'clock in the morning, Maverick," I said.

He grinned despite himself, delectable as he was. He straightened. "I'm sorry," he said — but he didn't seem very sorry.

I frowned. "I'll take you home," I said, but he protested.

"Not yet," he countered. "I want to talk to you."

"We'll talk in the car, Maverick."

He grasped my hand and my gaze darted up to his. "Kiss me again?" he asked.

I closed my eyes, prying my hand away. "No, Maverick," I said. "You won't even remember being here in the morning."

He shook his head but sighed. "Okay," he said, "fine. Let's go home."

"All right," I replied and stepped inside. I looked back at him and smiled weakly. "Come on in." I walked through the living room and glanced over my shoulder as he stumbled over the threshold. "Wait there."

He followed and stopped by the coffee table. I watched him for a moment and bit my lip as he peered at the photographs and books. Out of place and drunk, he stared down at the framed 'artwork' I had drawn as a small child.

My cheeks warmed and I rushed into my bedroom. I nudged Alex's shoulder. "Hey," I said, and she swatted my hand away.

"That could not have been eight hours," she groaned halfheartedly. Luckily, Alex had always been a fairly light sleeper. "What's wrong?"

I blinked, rubbing her shoulder gently. "Don't get up," I said and frowned. "I just wanted to tell you that I'll be right back...and I'm borrowing your car."

She frowned, rubbing her eyes. "What?"

I sighed. "Maverick is here," I said.

"What?" This time louder and more confused.

I suddenly realized I should have just gone. Knowing Alex, she would have slept through my absence. "I don't know," I explained. "He's drunk and he walked here. I'm just going to take him home. Go back to sleep."

She shook her head. "I'm sorry," she said. "He *walked* here?" She sat up a little straighter and peered at the clock. "It's three-forty-five in the morning."

"Yeah," I replied. "I've got to get him out of my living room, so I'm going to drive him home."

She frowned, staring at me, bewildered with mussed hair. "Is everything okay? Do you want me to come with you?"

I sighed and shook my head. "No," I said. "I'm all right. I just wanted you to know where I was going... Go back to sleep, okay? We'll talk in the morning."

"Okay," she said, leaning against the headboard. "Don't judge him too harshly for tonight. This isn't him at his best."

"Yeah," I said. "But it is real, isn't it?"

"Yes," she said. "Real is real, but he *is* a man and men are men."

I stared at her and barked a laugh. "You're asleep," I said. "Go back to bed. I'll be back soon."

She leaned back against the covers. "Fine," she said and snuggled into the blanket.

I watched for half a minute then quickly stood up, shoving my feet into my shoes and stepping into the living room. Maverick stood, still staring at the photographs thoughtfully, and he peered over at me.

"You ready?" I asked.

"Yeah," he said, so I scooped the keys from the coffee table.

"Okay. Let's go."

* * * *

We drove in relative silence past the church and the school and down the long, winding road to the farm. He hummed along to the radio, an awkwardly high-pitched murmur that contrasted with the alto from the speakers. I reached over and snapped it off. "We were gonna talk?"

"Yeah," he said. Then added, "About what?"

I groaned. "Oh, I don't know. Maybe let's start with why you walked to my house at three in the morning?"

He chuckled. "I wanted to see you."

Heartwarming, I thought, but I swallowed it. He was drunk and silly with alcohol, but my shoulders flushed under the thin straps of my tank top. "Sure," I said.

He crossed his arms, staring out of the window. "The moon is following us," he said, sounding like a little kid.

I bit back a smile, and the farm sprang into view. All was dark, so I assumed no one had noticed his absence, but I guessed that wasn't surprising. It was—a quick glance to the clock on the dash—four o'clock in the middle of the night.

"Emma," he said, "what if I don't want to go home?"

I glanced over at him. His voice was small now, and I wondered how much he'd had to drink to make him act like that. *Shouldn't he be puking or laid out on the bathroom floor?* Okay, to be fair, I don't know much about alcohol, but roaming the neighborhood didn't seem *exactly* right. "It's four in the morning, Maverick. There isn't anywhere to go," I informed him.

He shrugged. "Waffle House," he said, and I rolled my eyes, despite the point. Waffle House would be the only place open after the streetlights flipped on, but we were going home.

"We aren't going to Waffle House," I said, and I cut the engine in front of his house.

He looked at me, his eyes filled with something I didn't understand. "What if I wanted to kiss you again?"

I gasped and shook my head. "Try it sober," I said and opened my car door. He followed and we walked to the porch. I supported him up the steps, holding his side. "Do you have keys?"

He reached down, patting his pockets. "Uh," he said, "no."

I frowned and twisted the knob, hopeful, and to my relief, the door opened. The last thing I wanted was to call Katie — or, worse, his mom — to let drunk Maverick in at four in the morning. That would be tough to explain.

Well, yes, we were at this party, and we started making out... Yes, then I caught your daughter Frenching my best friend... Things got weird, and we left, but he just showed up at my door, so I brought him home. Plausible? Probably not...but it was true.

He led me to his bedroom. It smelled of sweat and boy, and I sneered, helping him into bed. I jerked a pen from his desk and wrote my phone number on the palm of his hand. Maybe, when he was sober, we could get *something* done.

Or maybe he wouldn't remember anything.
That might be good.

Chapter Eleven

I didn't go back to bed. I drove back home and cleaned the living room, listening to the slow crawl of jazz from the kitchen radio. Then I sat on the couch and tried to read, but my mind was everywhere but on the book in my hands. I fidgeted and could hear Alex shifting in the other room. Inwardly, I wondered if we would ever be the same again.

My head lulled against the back of the couch and my eyes flitted closed. I frowned and nudged the side of the couch. I sighed, letting sleep take over my body, relaxing despite myself. I slipped into a trance and into the party again.

Maverick grinned, rubbing my shoulders, and I giggled. Had I had a drink? Maybe, I thought, and I wrapped my arms around his neck to kiss him.

The colorful partygoers twisted and danced around us, and the music swelled to a peak that I couldn't understand. I felt free, and Alex laughed. I turned my head and saw Alex kissing Kate, and I looked at Maverick. He followed my gaze, and he smirked. "Oh," he said, "about that."

I blushed and kissed him again, washing the sight from my memory with the taste of his skin. He chuckled, and I brushed my fingers through his hair. "What?"

He shrugged, pulling me to his chest. "Nothing," he said, "just kiss me."

I wrapped myself around him, and it was like those big moments in the movies. We were all hands and skin, and there were no questions. The air smelled like spilled beer and pizza, and he jerked me even closer. "Wanna find somewhere?" His voice sent shivers down my spine, and I blushed against him.

"Yeah," I said, "let's go."

We wove through the crowd, and he leaned over and pressed a kiss to my shoulder. "How do you feel?"

I leaned against the wall, knitted my fingers into his hair then touched his face. "I feel good," I said. "I feel very good."

He twisted the knob behind me. I giggled, tumbled backward and gasped. Laughter escaped me, and Alex and Kate giggled on the bed.

My eyes flew open. "Oh," I said and straightened.

"You okay?" It was Mom. She stood over me and frowned. She had on her scrubs and her hair was tied up. She leaned over to brush a hand over my head. "Why aren't you in your room?"

"Weird night," I said, glancing toward the clock. *Seven-fifteen,* I read and rubbed my temples.

"Did you at least have fun at the party?"

I shrugged, not sure how to answer. "The party was fine," I said. "Alex stayed over. I hope that's all right."

"Yeah, of course," she said. We were past asking at this point, I knew, and the statement was out of place. "What was so weird?"

Again, I wasn't sure how to answer. "Just people," I replied.

"Yeah," she agreed. "People are pretty weird."

"Yeah," I said, glad she would accept that answer.

"Do pancakes sound good?" she asked.

"That would be great," I said. "Thanks, Mama."

She nodded and walked down the hallway.

I sighed, pressing my face to my palms. The dream... Maverick... All of it was intense and strange. I thought of Alex, and my cheeks burned against my hands. It was funny how one thing could so easily change everything.

Cheeks hot, I grabbed my phone from the coffee table and scanned the notifications. Candy Crush requests, Instagram likes, an email from one of those blogs I'd followed ages ago but never bothered unfollowing... No calls, no texts.

It's still early, I reminded myself. He had been drunk last night. He wouldn't be up yet.

Standing up, I padded to my bedroom. I shoved the door open, and Alex rolled over with a sleepy smile. "Oh," I said, "you're already awake?"

She straightened and tugged her hair into place. "Yeah," she said. "I heard your mom's car." She stretched with an implicative shrug. "When did you get back?"

"A little after four," I said. "I cleared off the coffee table then fell asleep on the couch."

She was silent for a minute before continuing. "Did you get the hunkie drunk home?"

I laughed because, to be honest, her phrasing had been hilarious. "Yes," I told her, "I took Maverick home."

"And?" she asked, "did you talk?"

"I mean," I hedged, frowning, "we talked a little in the car, but he was still pretty out of it... Ya know? He wasn't making much sense."

"Ah," she said, sliding out of bed and stretching. "Well, you'll see him soon... If nowhere else, then at school."

"Yeah," I said. *No need to mention my phone number in red on the back of his hand.* That choice might have been slightly irrational.

She grabbed a pair of knit shorts and a T-shirt that she'd stashed in my drawer a while ago, shucking them over her with a pause. "You okay?"

"I'm good," I said, half serious, but I knew it would be fine. My stomach twisted. *Lies*, I thought. *All lies.*

"Let's get out of here," she said.

I giggled. "Go where?"

"I don't know," she said.

"Mom's making pancakes," I answered, "then I've gotta get ready."

"Ready for what?"

I shrugged and checked my watch again. *Almost eight.* "Anything."

"Oh," she said, "I gotcha." She took my hand and squeezed once. "You're going to try to see him again."

"No," I said, and she smirked.

"Come on," she said.

Guess that cat's out of the bag. "Well," I said, "maybe I wrote my number on his hand so he would call — but it's for the project."

She grinned mischievously, shaking her head.

I sighed. "Well, how about that. I smell pancakes."

"Change of subject much?"

I choked on a laugh. "Yeah," I said, "change of subject."

We helped Mama make the rest of the pancakes. I think she could tell something was up. Her gaze darted between us when she thought we weren't looking, and I genuinely didn't know what to say.

Well, Mom, my best friend of years decided she's gay or bi or something but happened to skip telling me.

Alex went home, so I took a shower and stared at the water as it crawled toward the drain. Conflicted over Alex and Maverick and Katie the accomplice, I massaged my scalp and scrubbed my shoulders. In the confines of my shower, I cried, because that was all I could do at the moment. Luckily it didn't come out a loud, angry cry that I might have expected. No, this was a slow seethe. Hands on the shower wall beside me, I shook and giggled and sobbed, because, well, suddenly the future seemed so different for Alex and me.

I tried desperately to push thoughts of Maverick aside. He was a means to an end. He was a project I had to finish before I could move on to greener pastures — so to speak. Frankly, if it came down to it, I could just do it — fill up my journal with a story, *the* story maybe, and I could find peace.

I padded in a towel from the shower to my bedroom and sat on the side of the bed. I twisted my watch from my wrist and tucked it into my bedside table drawer. *No time*, I thought, and I closed my eyes. *No need to think.*

I rolled onto my side and jerked the pillow under my head. I scrolled through Twitter, scanning politics and cat pictures. I frowned. I didn't understand Twitter, so I closed the app because I didn't want to...ya know, *think.*

I opened an e-book and read until my eyes got tired and my heavy lids closed, falling back, finally, into a dreamless sleep.

* * * *

My phone gyrated to life, and I groaned, swatting my face with my hands. I sighed, grabbed the phone and answered on instinct. "Hello?"

"Damn," he said, and I frowned. *Maverick*, I thought. His voice was ice on coals, and blood flooded to my cheeks. "Who is this? Did you just wake up?"

I laughed, halfheartedly. "Maverick," I said and frowned, "it's Emma."

There was a pause. "Emma?"

I nodded like he could see me and shifted in bed, staring at the cork board of pictures over my desk. "Yep," I said.

He paused. "Why is your number on the back of my hand?"

Oh, I thought. So, he *didn't* remember. "Well," I said, "do you remember *anything* from last night?"

A stretch of silence, and I worried my lip. "Were you at the party?"

"Yeah," I said, "I was at the party."

He sighed. "What did I do?"

I shook my head. "That isn't why I wrote my number on your hand," I said.

"Oh," he replied, quietly. "Then, why?"

"The project, Maverick," I said. "We have to work on our *project*."

He sighed through a chuckle. "Oh," he answered, "right. I'll be over in an hour."

Silence…then the line went dead.

Chapter Twelve

The phone slipped from my grasp, clattering to the not-so-soft rug on the wood floor. I flinched, but it had merely landed with a soft thud. I stared at it, shock overpowering my now-uneven heartbeat, and I gasped, pivoting into action.

Hopping from the bed, I slid on a pair of jeans and a white blouse then braided my overgrown bangs. I slammed into my desk chair, and I blinked, suddenly infinitely interested in cleaning. I moved through the house, shucking clutter into wastebaskets and tidying pillows through the haze of my crowded brainwaves.

This is crazy, I thought as I moved through the house on impulse. *He doesn't remember,* but now I felt like I was going to be sick. After last night, after he'd kissed me, I couldn't stop thinking about it…or him.

The doorbell rang, and I slipped, tumbling headfirst onto my rug. I groaned, a bundle of battling emotions, but quickly straightened myself. "Calm down," I mumbled to myself, shuffling off the ground and to the door.

I closed my eyes, hand on the doorknob, and breathed deeply. *No awkwardness*, I thought, internalizing my stress, because — and I repeated — *he does not know*. There was no reason to make him suspicious or give him any ideas. As far as he knew, he got drunk and I wrote my number on his hand for this project.

I released the breath and twisted the knob, jerking open the door, and a blast of December bit my bare feet. Color flooded my cheeks, and I forced a smile, peering up at him.

He looked at me, all sunglasses and ripped jeans, and a shiver darted down my spine. He wore this sly grin that made me weak in the knees, but otherwise, he was silent.

I swallowed hard. *Okay*, I thought, *I'll speak first.* "Hi," I said.

"Hi," he replied, mocking my somber greeting.

I stepped away from the doorway. "Come in."

He stepped into the living room, and glanced down at the coffee table and the pictures. Then he made a face — curious, thoughtful, familiar. "Nice place you've got here," he said, feigning politeness.

"Yes," I said. "My mom has good taste."

"What about *your* taste?"

A weird question, I thought.

"Still trying to figure it out," I said simply, and he flashed a dimpled smile my way.

"Oh, right," he said. He exhaled, wringing his hands. He eyed me, his gaze lingering across my shoulders.

My heart clenched and I frowned. "What?"

"Nothing," he said. "I had a strange night."

The blood drained from my face. "Oh?"

"Yeah," he said but shook it off. "Can I see your room?"

"Sure," I said. "Follow me."

I shuffled down the hallway and into my bedroom, worrying the inside of my cheek. I rounded the door, leaving it open and watching him step inside. "Happy?"

He shrugged, scanning the room thoughtfully. "Not much personality," he said, his voice gravel and ice.

I followed his gaze. *Bare walls, a black and white bedspread with purple pillows... Pictures on my desk... A bookshelf of books, movies and CDs...* Frowning, I twisted to look at him as he picked up the little brown teddy bear from the black armchair in the corner. "That's Rori," I said, and he laughed.

"There," he said, looking at the bear then me. "There's the personality. I knew you had it in you."

"Don't be an ass." I jerked the bear from his arms and tucked it under mine.

"I'm not. I like the little guy," he said.

"Rori," I said. "Obviously a girl."

"Rory is definitely a man's name," he said.

I groaned. "The bear's a girl bear," I said. "Now...the project?"

"Yep," he replied. "So, what is it?"

"We talked about this," I reminded him.

He plopped in the armchair, making a show of crossing his arms. "Well, tell me again."

"It's creative," I answered, sitting on the edge of my bed. "Anything we want. A story. A play. A song."

He just stared. "Anything, huh?"

I nodded.

"That couldn't be too hard," he said.

No, I thought, *it wouldn't be hard if I didn't have to work with you.* Stomachaches and butterflies didn't really help the creative process. "True," I agreed.

"Well," he said, slapping the thighs of his jeans and standing up. The butterflies swelled in the pit of my stomach. "What's your pleasure?"

His wording struck me. I stared at my hands, because, at the moment, I was at eye level with — well, *not* his eyes. "Huh?"

He sank onto the bed beside me. My heart rate accelerated even further as the mattress shifted under his weight. *Damn,* I thought. He had me wrapped around his finger. "I think it's obvious, Emma," he said.

I frowned, staring at my hands. "Maverick," I breathed, because he was toying with me and I knew it. Inhaling sharply, I stood to grab my laptop from my desk so I could sit on the folding chair and make myself look busy finding a piece of paper.

I wondered if he was always this smug. "A story would be easiest, right?"

I bit back the part of me that wanted to argue. At least it would be a decision. "Sure," I said. "Yeah."

He ran a hand through his hair. "What should it be about? A murder mystery?"

I think that's a joke.

"I'm not great at keeping secrets," I said and he laughed — a genuine expression of pure joy, loud and rough and uninhibited.

"Yeah," he said, "I know."

I put down the notebook and crossed my arms. "What does *that* mean?"

He peered at me, all cheekbones and blue eyes, and my face burned. "You're lying right now," he said.

I frowned. "What're you talking about, Maverick?"

He groaned, strutting to peer out of my window. I watched the hard line of his jaw and the slope of his back, and something inside me snapped. I stowed my computer on the desk and went to peer over his shoulder. He smelled of aftershave and melons, and I shuddered. *Such a bad idea, being so close to him...such a bad idea.*

A bird flew from branch to branch in the backyard. It paused on one of them, eyed him, then flew away.

He spun to face me. He chuckled and framed my shoulders with his warm hands. "Your body language, Emma," he said, rubbing my upper arms. "You're nervous."

I groaned, stepping out of his grasp. "No," I said, "I am *not* nervous. I just want you to take this seriously."

He sighed, wheeling around to look out of the window again. "I don't think so. Well," he mumbled, "I'm sure that *is* true, and I will take it seriously, but I know there's something you *aren't* saying."

I sighed, twisting my hair into a loose bun, and stood up. "Why do you say that?"

He skimmed his fingers along my jaw. "Flushed cheeks," he noted. "You're fidgeting, and if every little school project makes you this antsy, then Harvard or Yale or wherever you're going is going to be hell for you."

"What do you want me to say?" I fumed, because what gave him the right to talk like that? To even *think* like that? Everyone knew about the Ivy League bias, and they judged those of us planning to attend one of those schools for it, like we were freaks just biding our time so that we could get out of high school. *Well, that much is true.* Now this guy had just thrown it in my face.

He shifted, falling back onto the bed. "You'll tell me whatever it is when you're ready," he said and grabbed a pen from my bedside table, tossing it over his head and catching it. "So, this project?"

"A story," I repeated. "About what?"

He twisted over to look at me and beamed. "Zombies," he said, and I laughed.

I rolled my eyes. "Can you *ever* be serious?"

He forged ahead. "A romantic comedy about two star-crossed pirates?"

"I liked you better when you were drunk," I mumbled, shaking my head, and he shot out of bed.

"What happened?" he asked.

"Maverick, lay off."

He crossed the room and smirked down at me. "Gimme time," he said. "I'm going to get you to admit what happened."

I closed my eyes, but his gaze burned on my face. "Maverick," I tried again, and tension bubbled under my skin.

His warmth radiated toward me, and he grazed my cheek. "What, Emma?"

I opened my eyes and inhaled softly. There was just a breath between us, and I shuddered and darted into the bathroom without another word.

Chapter Thirteen

The bathroom door slammed behind me, and I leaned over the sink. Mouth dry, I twisted the knob and splashed cold water onto my face then took a drink. The bathroom smelled of sweet berries from the wall plug-in, and my heart clenched in my chest.

I collapsed on the closed toilet seat, rubbing my forehead. My eyes burned with contemplation, and I swallowed, realizing I couldn't hide in the bathroom forever because I could hear Maverick shifting around in my room.

I frowned, unsure of myself. He had almost kissed me...again...and I had almost kissed him back. Suddenly, I wondered if maybe he did remember, after all, and was messing with me.

My skin prickled, and I closed my eyes. *Damn,* I thought, *calm down.* I peered at myself in the mirror then stared blankly at the peeling paint above it. I shook my head. "You're being crazy," I mumbled to myself. "Just go back out there."

I stood up and straightened my top. I took a deep breath then opened the door, and my frown deepened. He was standing with his back to me, mumbling quietly.

"What?" I asked.

He was reading aloud, slowly, evenly, and I leaned against the doorway, still frowning but now listening intently.

"I am beginning to speculate on the nature of the human condition of despair. I watch others and I feel it myself. Underneath all the high-pitched laughter and the tight grins, I see one common denominator. There is so much pain. But every once in a while there's a glimmer of something else, something whole and beautiful and bright as we're driving down the road to nowhere with the windows down, singing like no one in the world will ever hear.

"What I write are just words...pretty words...just to try to string those beautiful moments together, because how else do you capture the wind in your face? The brilliance of a sunset? The music of your best friend's giggle? You can't. A photo? A recording? All capture only one element, but the moment itself is lost to eternity. So, I write and hope that somehow that will be enough to calm the waters of my soul."

"What're you doing?" I asked him when I realized where the words were coming from, blood flooding my cheeks. No one read my writing. *No one...especially not him.*

He looked up, all eyes and a chuckle, and he peered at me. "Apparently, I'm reading," he said. "This is some heavy, sad shit."

I grimaced and jerked the notebook from his hands. "Don't look at it," I said. "Don't look at this ever again."

He sighed, walking over to me. "Hey," he said. He nudged my shoulder. "I'm sorry."

I tilted my head toward the mirror and peered at our reflection. He stood over me, grazing my waist with one hand, and the stubble on his chin caught on my hair. I closed my eyes with a sharp intake of breath. "It's fine," I said.

"Emma," he said. His voice was soft, quiet, "turn around and look at me."

The heartbeat sang in my ears, and I opened my eyes again to peer at him in the reflection. He was handsome and rugged and looking at me like I was his everything — or at least his something. A knot twisted in the pit of my stomach.

I breathed, low and steady, and turned around to face him. He drifted one big hand up my side, and I let out a breath I didn't know I'd been holding. "Maverick…" I breathed the word, and he dragged his fingers up to my chin.

"Emma," he said and pressed his lips to the apple of my cheek. He pulled back and grinned. "I'm not gonna kiss you now." Doubt crowded my vision, and blood flooded my cheeks. He slipped a hand around my wrist. "I *will* kiss you," he said, "just not now."

I stared at him and blood boiled under my skin. My cheek burned, a thousand pin pricks to the skin. *God, that guy*, I thought. My heartbeat thumped like a bass drum, and I pulled away from his grasp. "Oh," I said. My stomach twisted with his torture.

He took my hand again, intertwining our fingers like nothing I've ever known. A spark ran up my spine, and instinctively I leaned away from him. His even breathing unnerved me. He was far too good at this, too experienced, and I felt like a child in his grasp — like his toy. He smiled, one of those grins full of promise. "Unless..." He breathed, closing another inch between us, and the gravity of our nearness sizzled. I blushed and he laughed. "Unless you want me to."

"I — I — " I began, frowning to myself. *Yes*, I thought-screamed.

"Just say it," he mumbled, just a breath away, and I leaned into the scent of his skin. "Emma," he breathed my name, and I gasped.

"Maverick," I countered, air caught between us, and my face flamed.

He dragged his lips along my jaw, teasing the skin there. "Don't hide from me," he muttered and wrapped his hands around my face. "Do you want this?"

Yeah, I thought, *I do*, and I tilted my head to the side and realized that this moment defined my future — to kiss and be kissed, to feel something real instead of living in the fiction of my preference. So, I kissed him. I closed my eyes and closed the distance without any questions or replies — and no pretenses.

I kissed him. I could feel it in my toes and my heart as I leaned against him — his warm hands, the smirk on his lips, his heartbeat through his T-shirt... It was a crystalline moment overshadowed by the earthy sweat of his skin that shouldn't have been as sexy as it was and the scratch of Stella's tiny paws against her cage.

His gruff chuckle interjected, and he pulled back to peer at me. "What is that noise?"

I giggled awkwardly, brushing my bottom lip with my thumb. "That would be Stella," I answered, gesturing to the cage in the corner.

"Is that a hamster?"

My cheeks warmed. "Yes," I said. "What's wrong with a hamster?"

He shoved my shoulder. "Nothing... You named it Stella?"

"What's wrong with the name Stella?" I opened the cage door and pulled the hamster to my chest, grinning a little. "Stella's a good girl," I said. "Want to hold her?"

He laughed, watching as I sat on the edge of my bed. "I don't know," he replied.

"She doesn't bite," I told him.

He joined me on the edge of the bed with a shake of his head. "I specialize in...larger animals," he said.

"Don't be a baby, Mav," I told him, and I carefully placed the hamster in his hands. He looked at it, small and alive, and a smile sprang across his tamed face. "Who doesn't specialize in small animals now?"

He leaned down to talk to Stella. She was so small, I realized, as I watched them thoughtfully. He handed me the hamster. "She's cute," he said.

I grinned softly. "I know," I said. "I love her." I placed Stella into her cage and spun to face him.

"That was," he began, "just like my dream."

I frowned. "Your dream?"

"Yeah but *you* kissed *me* this time," he noted.

"Oh," I replied.

He smirked. "Well, I'm glad," he said, standing and wrapping his fingers around my wrist. "You looked like you were about to break."

I shrugged a shoulder and peered at him thoughtfully. "But I didn't," I said and nodded, leaning over to press an awkward kiss to his shoulder. "I might kiss you again."

"I wouldn't be opposed," he said, and a fresh smile peeled across my cheeks.

Okay, I thought, so I kissed him again. This was the kind of kiss that started at the head and went to the toes, and I blushed, knitting my fingers into his hair. The blood ran to my face, and I pulled back and pressed my face into the crook of his neck.

He wrapped an arm around my shoulders. "See?" he said. "You're getting good."

Another joke, I thought.

"Come on," I said. "We need to work on this project."

"Oh," he said. "Yeah, that."

I grinned. "Yes," I replied, "*that.*"

He hopped off the bed with a smirk. "Okay," he said, grabbed the notebook from where I'd discarded it and extended it to me. "But we've got to work this in somehow. We have to tell this story."

He was referring to my writing that he'd read.

I grasped the notebook between my fingers. "It isn't really a story," I explained.

"It's a feeling," he replied.

"But that isn't a story," I repeated.

"That isn't the point," he pushed.

"What is the point, then?"

He shrugged. "I don't remember."

And just like that, we laughed.

Chapter Fourteen

He left.

The door closed behind him and I collapsed against it. The blood rushed from my face, and I swallowed hard. Lips throbbing, I fumbled for my phone in my pocket to dial an SOS to Alex.

Even now, I felt him — the wonder and possibility and everything that was wrong with the situation. The last hour echoed in my memory, vivid and sinking into my chest, the anchor Alex had insisted Mr. Zelner wouldn't saddle me with.

Seconds later, my phone rang.

Alex's voice was tight, interested. "Is everything okay?"

"He might remember," I confessed.

There was a beat of uncomfortable silence, and she sighed. "All right," she said. "Is everything okay?"

I frowned, shoving my hand through my hair. "I mean... I guess." I laughed.

"Emma," she replied.

I picked at a loose thread on my T-shirt, and I asked, "Wanna drive?"

"Yeah," she said, "I'll be there in five minutes."

I sighed, leaning my head against the door behind me.

We'd sat on the bed, side by side, and batted ideas around. Most of them hadn't been serious. Then, he'd kissed me again, and I hadn't protested. I was wrapped up in the smell of him and the blood pulsing in my ears. He'd had to go—track practice—but he'd claimed he would call to set up a time for us to work on the project again. I didn't know that I believed it, but my heart thudded in my chest, nonetheless.

A sharp knock reverberated against the wooden door, signaling Alex's arrival, but she didn't wait for my response. Instead, she jerked the door open smack into me and I collapsed onto the ground. My hair fell out of place, and I skimmed my face along the rough carpet. *Well,* I thought, *that's a great way to start.*

"Earth to Emma," she said and knelt beside me. Tension melted between us as her lilting chuckle landed beside me. She grazed my shoulder, my best friend, and her lies shrunk with inadequacy. Some bonds couldn't be broken.

She smoothed my hair.

"Hey," I said.

She smiled weakly. "Are you all right?"

"Yeah," I answered.

"Why are you on the floor?"

I shrugged. "I don't know."

"Well," she said. She dangled her keys in front of my face, playfully. "Where are we going?"

I snatched the keys away. "Tyler's Tacos," I said.

She laughed. "Okay," she agreed and backed toward the door with a smirk. "And when are you going to tell me why we're driving thirty miles out of town for week-old, greasy tacos?"

To be fair, she was right, but I didn't care. "Into the car," I ordered her.

"Let's get going, then," she said, hedging me toward the door.

I tossed her the keys and grabbed my jacket from the table, listening to the battle between the wail of winter wind and our neighbor's angsty chihuahua. Shoving the jacket on my shoulders, I stepped into the elements, unsurprised by the not-so-timid breeze.

I glanced up, noting Alex's face and groaned. "Wipe that grin off your face," I warned, locking the door and hopping into the passenger seat of her car.

She shook her head. "Sorry," she said. Sobering, she hopped in the driver seat, and we pulled away from the curb.

Silence bubbled between us, and I switched on the radio. A slow melody wafted from the speakers, and I leaned back, watching the trees twist and whirl by. I followed them with my eyes, fingering a loose thread on my top and piecing my words together. "Maverick kissed me," I said, "again."

She blinked. "Please," she begged, her voice pleading, reminded me of what I was and what we were. I knew we would be okay together. "Tell me you're ready to talk about this. I need details. What happened last night? Start there."

I sighed. "Okay," I said.

She drummed the steering wheel excitedly and turned down the radio, adjusting the volume to background level and focusing on my words. "Go," she probed, expectant.

"Well, like I already told you," I said, not really sure how to explain what had happened, "when you disappeared, I ran into him, and he said he would help me look for you."

She glanced over with a wicked smile. She said, "I guess it was good I disappeared, then."

I glared over at her, the playful kind of glare you can only give your best friend, and she giggled. "Okay," she said, "not funny."

"That's right," I said. "Yeah, well, we went looking, and we couldn't find you — then suddenly we were just right there. He was drunk, and he started kissing me."

She nodded. "How drunk was he?"

"I don't know," I said. "I didn't even realize he was at the time." I continued to watch the trees, embarrassed. "But he seemed to be buzzed enough that today he acted like he didn't *really* remember what had happened. He just kept asking… I think he believes the whole thing was one weird dream."

"Did you tell him?"

"No," I said, leveling my gaze with hers. "Would you really want that?"

"Fair enough," she said. "All right, so how did you find us?"

"It was an accident, like I told you last night," I said. "I mean, we were just…ya know, kissing, and he had me against that door. He opened it and we fell — and yeah…"

"Okay, wow," she said, blinking over at me. "Have you thought about what coulda happened?"

"Yeah," I said, "but it didn't. It wouldn't have."

"Yeah, probably," she repeated but kept her eyes on the road. "Then he showed up in the middle of the night?"

I groaned, shaking my head. "He sure did," I said, artfully tucking my hair into a messy bun. "I couldn't sleep... I was just dreaming about the party, and it wasn't really, ya know, peaceful, so I got up and went into the kitchen. My phone started ringing, and it was Maverick."

She laughed. "Whoa," she said. "I didn't even know he had your number."

"Yeah," I replied, "I didn't either. He said that Mr. Zelner gave it to him."

"Well," she said, "what did he say?"

"Apparently Katie had talked to him," I explained. "She told him that he needed to apologize to me. He was all flirty and like *'but I don't know why I would apologize'* and I was just like... Well, you know me."

"Yes," she said, "I do know you. Then?"

"Then he announced that he was outside the door," I said. "I mean, I could hear him, bumping into the house." I shook my head. "At this point, I'm pretty sure he'd had even more to drink, because he was stumbling over himself and talking crazy."

"God," she said. "Why didn't you wake me up? That would have been hilarious."

I shrugged a shoulder. "Well," I explained, "I guess. But anyway... I drove him home, because he was a mess. I wasn't even sure if he could get himself inside, so I had to break into his house." I crossed my arms, excusing my hyperbole.

"You're funny when you're embarrassed," she said. "So, you broke into his house?"

"Yeah, well, the door was unlocked. Anyway, I took him to his room then I wrote my number on his hand."

She smiled, sly as a fox. "I knew you weren't just generally 'getting ready' for your project." She lifted one of her hands from the wheel to make air quotes. "So, this morning he called?"

"Yep," I said. "He called and was like '*why is your number on the back of my hand?*' So, I knew he didn't remember the night, which was pretty good, Alex, because the whole thing is *so* embarrassing."

She patted the steering wheel. "Yes," she said, "a boy kissing you is traumatic."

I sneered back. "You're funny," I said, leaning my head against the window. "He was drunk... It didn't mean anything."

She sighed. "All right, fast forward to the sober kissing that *did* mean something."

I watched the road, mesmerized, and I sighed. "Oh, I don't know, Alex." The taco shop became visible in the distance. "I kissed him."

Her eyes widened and she pressed the gas. A minute later, we jerked into Tyler's Taco's driveway, and she put the car in Park, swinging around to scrutinize me. "*You* kissed *him*?"

I nodded.

"What did he do?"

I stared at her stupidly. "Kissed me back," I said.

She gave me a blank look. "Then why are we at the taco shack?"

"I don't know what I'm doing," I said.

She laughed, shaking her head. "You're kissing a boy," she said. "You need to kiss somebody. You're wound too tight, Emma."

I sighed. "Come on," I said. "I need a taco."

We sat at a table in the back of the restaurant, eating chips and salsa, and Alex told me about Kate. "Do you remember when I was dating River?" River was a guy on the swim team, ironically enough, who hated pools. He swam in lakes and was always tan, and he was kind of a jerk. Alex had dated him for all of four months before she'd finally dumped him.

"Yeah," I said, mouth dry.

"Well," she said and inhaled deeply, "one day after one of his swim meets... Well, we were fighting outside the gym, and Kate was leaving the art studio late. She pretended to know me and got me out of there."

I swallowed, swirling a chip around the salsa and not making eye contact. "Did he, erm... Did he hurt you?"

Alex bit her lip, and she shook her head. "No," she said. "But it was one of those relationships where you just know that if you don't end it, it would get there. Does that make any sense?"

"Yeah," I said quietly. Guilt sank over me. *I* should have noticed.

She sighed and squeezed my hand across the table. "Emma," she said, "you couldn't have known. I didn't let anyone know."

"Okay," I said, shaking my head. I wanted to move on, to change the subject. "So, Katie?"

"Yeah, Katie," she said. "Well, after that, we started talking, and we sort of became friends. It was weird, because she was the mythical Katie. No one really was close to her. They just knew that Maverick had a kid sister." She frowned. "I mean, I know what you're going to ask. I don't understand how it happened. It wasn't really one thing. We just... We were just hanging out one day and she kissed me...or I kissed her. I don't even remember. We kinda just kissed each other."

I pondered her words as I took a sip of water. "Yeah," I said. "I mean, I can see how that could happen."

She sighed. "I should have told you, but I didn't want anything to change between us," she said. "There's such a stigma, ya know, and I'm not a lesbian, I guess… I mean, I still find guys attractive, but right now, I want to be with Kate."

The waiter approached with our order, and he spoke fast and in horrible Spanglish, but we were too preoccupied in our conversation to enjoy any of the spectacle. "Well," I said, picking at one of my tacos. "Why don't you stop 'hanging out' and tell her that?"

She tipped her iced tea skyward. "Maybe," she said, "if you set things straight with Maverick."

I looked up at her. "Okay," I said.

She lifted her glass and I raised mine. "Deal," we said in unison, toasting the promise.

Chapter Fifteen

I stared blindly at a blank spreadsheet and rubbed my temples. Traffic at the hospital was slow, and I wondered why they'd hired me, a second receptionist for this corner office. But I knew it was because of my mom.

Groaning, I pressed my face to my hands and the not-so-distant memories flooded back. Right there in the cubbyhole of the office, chill bumps rose on my arms. He'd slid his fingers along them I thought, but I couldn't decide what was fact and what was fiction... What was memory or how much was fantasy.

The nurse at my side nudged my shoulder and grinned just enough. I guess I must have had a glow or something. I flushed and looked over at her. "Your phone is about to burn a hole in the counter, Emma," she noted. "Why don't you take five?"

I frowned, sitting back, more focused now. My phone vibrated, jiggling against the countertop, and I blushed heavily. One word, one name, was enough to sell whatever 'glow' waited on my face. "Maverick," I mumbled.

"Take it," she said. "Go ahead."

I sighed, grabbing my phone. I walked into the hallway and swept across the screen to answer. "Hello," I said, leaning against the wall.

"Hi, there," he said, and a fresh flush sprang to my face.

That voice, I thought. *That face...* It would all be the death of me.

"Whatcha doing?"

I laughed. *So casual*, I thought. "I'm at work," I said.

"Oh," he replied, "sorry. You're at work? Where do you work?"

"I'm a receptionist at the hospital," I said. "Part-time, for the holiday, ya know?"

He paused. "When do you get off?"

My heart jumped in my chest, and I thought of the promise to Alex — to make things right. "I get off in an hour," I said.

"Cool," he said. "Ya wanna come over?" The words reverberated through my mind and I frowned.

"No... I mean, yes," I said, grimacing to myself. I wondered what he'd meant. *Come over for what?* I rubbed the bridge of my nose, glanced down at myself in my happy bunny scrubs and shook my head. "I'll be over about three-thirty?"

He laughed, and the sound shot right to my toes. "Cool," he replied.

"Yeah," I said. "Cool." The word tasted strange in my mouth.

"See ya later," he offered, and the line went dead.

I stared down at the grubby toes of my white Keds and wondered what kind of meeting this would be. I stepped back into the office, and Stephanie grinned knowingly.

"So…Maverick," she said. Stephanie was twenty-four. She'd barely crested the age of adulthood, and so far it didn't suit her. She beamed over, ready for the dish, and I hated that there wasn't much to tell her.

"Yes," I replied, "Maverick."

"Come on, Emma," she said, "I'm dying for some gossip."

My life wasn't exactly gossip-worthy. "He's a guy I have a project with," I told her, because that was the most truthful thing I could say. There were no labels, no intentions…just stolen kisses.

"*Just* a guy you have a project with?" She eyed me cautiously. "Then why are you blushing?"

I shrugged and regarded the computer in front of me. "I'm an easily embarrassed person," I said — and that wasn't a lie.

She shook her head, knowing there was more to the story but letting it go. "You win this round."

I was thankful and shot Alex a text.

Something with Maverick at 3:30. Wanna dress me?

She sent back a response.

Something?

I rolled my eyes, laughing.

Yeah, something. Do you want to dress me?

'Course I do! I'll be at your house at 3.

I smiled.

Thanks.

Stephanie smirked over at me. "Just a project," she repeated, shaking her head. "I wish I was eighteen again."

Chapter Sixteen

When I pulled up at my house, Alex was reclined against the side of her car in their driveway, grinning like she knew a secret.

"Hey," I said.

She waved and hustled over to open my door. "Come on," she said. "I've got work to do."

Well, I thought, *this might have been a mistake*.

I followed her into the house and she smiled, making a beeline to my room. "So," she said, "we don't know what you're doing, right? Could just be a work session, could be a date?"

I nodded as she thumbed through my clothes. "Right," I replied.

"Okay," she said, "let me think."

I plopped on the edge of my bed and imagined her movements cartoon-like. She worked with precision, an action figure in flight as she tried different outfits, ultimately deciding they were all wrong. She chuckled to herself then pulled out a final choice. "This," she said. She handed me what had grown to be called my 'fun jeans', because they hugged me in all the right places, and a silky-soft gray T-shirt. "Simple and cute," she announced, grabbing the locket from my stash of necklaces. "Add this and you'll be perfect."

"Thanks," I said.

"You'll be great."

"Ha," I mumbled. "Thanks."

She nudged my shoulder. "Text me if you need me," she said and headed out with a wave.

I stared at the clothes she'd picked out. "Well," I said aloud, talking to myself, "I guess Alex's word is law, right?" I quickly changed clothes and smiled at my reflection in the mirror. "Let's go, Emma." And so I did.

* * * *

A puff of dirt and gravel dissipated as I rolled to a stop in front of Maverick's. He stood beside the barn, just like he had before. His back was to me. He wore a pair of tight-fitting jeans and was brushing a horse.

Instantly, blood rushed to my cheeks and I came to the not-so-shocking realization that if this were to go any further, I would *always* be blushing. That boy left me quaking with something I couldn't quite identify and that fact left me trembling in my metaphorical boots.

I opened the car door and he twisted to wave at me. "Hi there," he called, gesturing for me to come over. "Don't be shy."

I walked slowly toward him. Well...them. Maverick was tossing a saddle over a giant quadruped, and I paused a few paces away, honestly nervous, because I'd never spent much time around horses—or really any animals outside of Stella. The horse was a deep chestnut with speckles and dark brown eyes. "What's her name?"

"*His* name is Rory," he told me, and I laughed out loud. He smiled. "Come here."

I frowned, unsure. "I think I'll stay here," I said.

He smirked. "I think it's gonna be hard for you to ride him if you won't touch him."

The blood drained from my face. "I'm *riding* him? Says who?"

"Me," he said, winking. It was heart-stopping. He extended a hand to me. "Don't be scared. This guy is a sweetheart, and he's a sucker for the ladies."

Despite myself, I giggled. "Okay," I said.

I extended a hand to Maverick, and he took it. Warmth spread through my chest, and he placed my hand on the horse's neck.

"Okay then," I managed.

He ducked down to kiss my cheek. "I take it you've never been on a horse before?"

"Unless you count Girl Scouts," I admitted, "no."

"This is going to be fun."

"You sure about this?" I wasn't.

"Breathe," he suggested, stepping behind me. "He can smell fear."

"Are you serious?" I asked with a frown.

"No," he said.

"So," I asked again, "are you sure about this? The horse?"

"Yep," he replied, sounding confident. "Hop up."

I frowned and just looked at him. "You're serious? What do you mean, '*hop up*'?"

"Okay," he said. "I'll help."

"Um" — I looked over my shoulder — "how?"

He smiled. "Hold on to me?"

"Sure," I said. "It's that simple."

He shook his head. "You're right. Sorry," he said. "Put your foot in the stirrup and toss the other leg over Rory here. He won't move. I promise."

With a resigned sigh, I stuck my foot in the stirrup clumsily. Maverick pressed his hands to my lower back, and my cheeks warmed. "Is this right?" I asked.

"You're making this too hard, Emma. Stop thinking," he said.

"Stop thinking? That seems like bad advice."

"You know what I mean," he chastised me.

I sighed, awkwardly tossing my leg over the horse's muscular back. Maverick helped, pushing my leg so it landed in the right place. "Whoa," I said.

"Stay there," he advised. "I'm going to go grab Pacman."

My eyes widened and I frowned. "Maverick, don't leave me alone on this horse."

He chuckled then reached out his hand, motioning for the horse to move. "I'm sorry," he said and nudged the horse forward.

He walked into the barn, holding Rory, and stopped to grab Pacman.

"So, Rory?" I asked, desperate for conversation.

He grinned over at me. "Yep," he said. "Rory."

I laughed. "And Pacman?"

"Yes," he said, nuzzling Pacman's muzzle with his hand. He stuck his hand in his pocket to retrieve a peppermint and fed it to him.

"Two very different names," I said.

"Yeah," he said. "Wanna guess who named which horse? Me or Katie?"

Katie, I thought, and a memory briefly called up a picture that was forever burned into my brain. I looked over at him, watching as he threw a leg over his horse, and I wondered if he knew about her—Katie, or Kate. I shook off the thought. *Not the time to dwell on that.* "Lemme guess," I said. "Katie named Rory. You named Pacman?"

He grinned. "How'd you know?"

I giggled and said, "I'm just a great guesser."

"Okay," he said. "I get it."

He nudged Pacman out of the barn and Rory followed. "Maverick," I said without thinking. He twisted, looking over at me with a grin. "Is this a date?"

"I haven't decided," he said. "What do you think?"

I flushed and looked down at the ground. "Yes," I said, "it's a date."

He leaned over to kiss me once, long and hard. "Good," he replied. "This is a date."

Chapter Seventeen

Church bells rang and I smoothed the black and white dress and brushed a hand through my hair. It was the Sunday before Christmas, and I stood in front of the massive Methodist church downtown.

Mama beamed, happily sated by the Christmas hymns. She squeezed my arm. "Wanna go to Uncle Ben's?" Uncle Ben's was the local bakery. Ironically, Uncle Ben sold very few baked goods, but he was known for the self-proclaimed 'Best Grilled Cheese in the Magnolia State'. I wasn't sure about that but had to admit that the sandwich was pretty good.

I smiled. "Yeah," I said, "sounds good."

We walked down the street toward the bakery and waved at our neighbors as we went. It was a nice thing. We're a small community. Mom and I rounded the corner to the large-windowed storefront that was Uncle Ben's.

Mom settled into a conversation with Stephanie from the hospital, and I stumbled to a stop in front of the store. There, two rows of tables into the little restaurant, were Maverick, Kate and Mrs. English. He wore a white shirt and a gray tie and sat beside his red-haired sister.

I frowned, glancing back toward my mom. She was gesturing with rapid-fire action as she and her co-worker spoke. Stephanie sang in the choir at our church and was arranging a caroling group.

I swiveled back to the window, watching Maverick draw a glass of tea to his lips. Blood flooded my cheeks as Mom's arm came around my shoulders. "Hey," she said, "what're you looking at?"

I blinked. I hadn't exactly mentioned Maverick to my mom. I mean, it hadn't come up or been the right time. But beyond that, I really wasn't sure what to say. Maverick and I hadn't defined the relationship. Were we dating? *Yes*, I thought, but I wasn't sure what that really meant, so I hadn't told my mother.

And there he was with his family, enjoying their grilled cheeses and soup, minding their own business.

"Um-m..." I said under my breath.

She shook her head. "Spill," she requested, rolling a scrunchie from her wrist and tying her hair into a loose bun at the base of her neck.

Biting back a blush, I nodded. "Um," I said, "I have to tell you something."

"Okay," she said, "shoot."

"Do you remember Maverick English?"

"Oh, that guy you had a crush on in middle school?"

Lovely, I thought. *What a time to bring that up.* "Yeah, him."

"Okay," she replied, "what about him?"

My gaze darted to Maverick through the window. He was beaming, handsome—and with tidy hair, for once. He glanced up at that moment, meeting my eyes, and he grinned. I swallowed. "We're sort of dating," I told her.

She laughed. "Oh," she said, "really? Why does that make you so nervous?"

"He's in there," I said.

"Okay," she answered, "so?"

It was my time to confess. "I hadn't told you."

"Well, now you have," she replied, shaking her head. "Let's go eat."

Sure, I thought, and we went inside, easy as pie.

Ariel, a perky twenty-something with artificially blonde hair, greeted us at the door. "Hi, there," she said. "Table or booth?"

My mom shrugged. "Either one is fine."

Ariel turned away, grabbing a couple of menus and chewing her gum. She led us to a table across the restaurant from the Englishes, and I let out a sigh of relief. I'm not sure what I thought was going to happen.

"Can I get y'all anything to drink?" she asked.

Mom ordered an unsweetened tea and I asked for water. Ariel assured us that our server would be over to us soon. I leaned back, quickly diverting the conversation from Maverick English and my middle-school crush. "So," I said, "are we going Christmas caroling with your Sunday school class again this year?"

"Maybe," she said, "though I think you might be going somewhere else."

I frowned, thanking Ariel as she deposited our drinks. "What do you mean?"

She opened her mouth to speak but closed it again.

"Can I interrupt?" Maverick's voice settled over my body. He wasn't looking at me. Instead, he'd extended a hand to my mom, thoughtful and smiling. "Ms. Cage, it's nice to formally meet you. I'm Maverick."

My mom played the part perfectly. "Well, hello," she said, shaking his hand. "Nice to meet you too, Maverick."

"My sister and I are having a little ugly Christmas sweater party tonight. I wondered if Emma would like to come," he said, looking at my mom for a fraction of a second longer, then he peered at me. "You can bring Alex. It'll be fun. There will be eggnog."

My mouth dry, I swallowed, grasping my water and taking a sip. My mom met my gaze. Cheeks warm, I nodded too. "Okay, yeah," I said. Idly, I wondered if the Alex comment had been innocent or intentional.

"Awesome," he said. "I'll see you tonight, then? Six-thirty?"

"See ya at six-thirty." I could barely get the words out, some combination of nerves and excitement, I guessed.

"Great," he said and lifted a hand to my mom, continuing to act perfectly. "Nice to see you, Ms. Cage."

"You too, Maverick."

My heart fluttered in my ribcage, and I snapped open my menu to hide behind it.

Maverick chuckled, ducked down and pecked my cheek behind the menu, and he sauntered back to his table.

* * * *

One infamous grilled cheese later, I sat on the edge of my bed, twiddling my phone between my fingers. I sighed, texting Alex.

Ugly sweater party tonight at the Englishes?

Seconds later, she replied.

I have the perfect sweater.

That was Alex, easy to please.
I swallowed hard, falling backward across the mattress before responding.

Hey, Alex?

Yeah?

Does he know about Katie?

She began typing, only to pause mid-stream. After a few staggered moments, she continued.

No…no one knows…other than you apparently.

I frowned, depositing my phone on my pillow. I was sure she'd been kidding, but her words still stung. It was just another reminder that she hadn't planned on sharing this with me.

I closed my eyes. There was something very intense about the change in our dynamic, and I wasn't ready for that to happen. Just yesterday we had been these little, starry-eyed freshmen, and now everything had become so complicated.

A shrill ding sounded from my pillow, and I groaned, rolling over and snatching it. Maverick's name had replaced Alex's, and I smiled. The text was a picture of Maverick. He wore one of those truly awful

Christmas sweaters with ivy wreaths, garland and Christmas lights, but Maverick was the main event. He wore a cheesy grin and flashed a thumbs-up, and I laughed because suddenly he appeared to be more of a goober than I could have guessed.

I texted back.

Nice sweater.

You're just jealous that my sweater is uglier than yours.

You wish.

Like how I charmed your mom?

Ha! Charmed her? She sees right through you.

I don't believe it.

We shall see.

A pause in the action, then,

I'm glad you're coming tonight.

My stomach tightened with the slight affection. Cheeks warm, I texted back.

Thanks, Maverick. I'm glad too.

I flipped the phone face down on the bed. There was no need to doddle, overthink or worry. *Nope.* For now, it was just fun. I hopped from the bed and walked over to my closet. I knelt down to grab the box from the back corner and pulled out my sweater.

I held it up and sighed. My phone was ringing.

I draped the sweater over the back of my chair and answered it. "Hey," I said. I'd caught a glimpse of Alex's photo and knew it was her. There wasn't much else to say, so I settled for deadpan.

She sighed dramatically, a shockingly lyrical sound, and I reclined in my desk chair. "Emma," she said, "I'm sorry."

I pulled the sweater from the back of the chair to peer down at the buggy-eyed reindeer on its front. The puffy, red nose of the reindeer made me grin, despite everything. "How long is it going to be a secret, Alex?"

Silence washed over us and I frowned, not wanting to upset her, but it was a relevant question. Finally, she responded, but her voice was small. "I don't know," she said.

I nibbled along my thumbnail. "I'm sorry," I said, and she giggled, shaking it off.

"No," she said, "don't be. We're going to have fun. You wanna drive or shall I?"

"Well," I said, "do you wanna drink?"

"Touché," she said. "I'll see you in a bit?"

The line went dead and I sat down on the edge of my bed. I pulled a book to my lap and started reading, because when in doubt, I read books.

* * * *

I gasped awake, frowning. The sky was dark, and it looked cold. I silently thanked winter for finally arriving in our little Southern town. A slow smile slid across my face and I rolled off the edge of the bed.

Tossing a glance to the clock, I sighed deeply. Despite my nap, it was only six, so I had plenty of time to get ready. I jerked my curtains closed, pulled the T-shirt from my shoulders and situated the sweater in place.

Twenty minutes later, I had curled my hair and tied it back with a white ribbon, and I pulled a pair of white stockings on my legs to counter the black skirt. *If I'm gonna do it, I might as well do it right, right?*

"Well, don't you look cute?" Mom called from the doorway.

I twisted from where I stood at the mirror. Mom was sporting her annual Christmas caroling look — a white top, red scarf and curled hair. "Thanks," I said. "Is Stanley going caroling?"

She winked. "Maybe," she replied and shook her head. "You kids have fun tonight — and be careful."

I smirked. "You too," I joked.

"I'll try my best," she said and waved.

I grabbed a jacket and texted Alex.

Ready to go?

She shot back not thirty seconds later.

Yep. I'll be right over.

With that, I tucked my keys into the pocket of my jacket with my phone and hurried outside.

A gust of wind pushed me back against the door and I laughed, staring at Alex's appearance. It showed a Christmas tree with pompoms attached to the front. "Nice sweater," I called.

"Right back at ya, sister," she said, winking and dropping into the passenger side of my car.

"How was your afternoon?" I got in and grinned, flipping on the Christmas carols.

"Uneventful," she said. "But it's about to get better."

"Yes," I replied. "Did you tell Katie you're coming?"

"Kate likes surprises," she told me.

I pulled out of the driveway. "Well, you'd be a good one, right?"

"I would sure hope so," she said.

"You know so," I replied, watching the road slip by.

"I wonder what kind of party this will be?" she mused, twisting a strand of hair around her fingertip.

"An 'ugly sweater party', remember?"

She cut her glance toward me then out of the window. "Yeah," she said, "I'm sure."

"What's that face about?" I asked.

"Nothing," she said and shook her head. "Sometimes it's just really cute how innocent you are."

I leaned over to shove her shoulder. "You're innocent."

She smirked. "You're a mess," she said and gestured to the road in front of me. "Yeah…that looks like an ugly sweater party."

I twisted, staring up the road. Party lights dotted the drive toward the barn that was teeming with people. "Lord," I whispered under my breath.

"Don't worry," she said. "I'm sure he won't drink so much."

I laughed awkwardly and pulled into the grass beside the other cars. "Really?"

"Really," she said and squeezed her hand. "Let's go."

Chapter Eighteen

Music mingled with the sweet smell of a Southern winter, and I looped my arm through Alex's. She waved as the partygoers ran past. They all wore sweaters and too much makeup. They carried drinks and were wide-eyed and bright.

"I wonder where *he* is," she mused, winking over at me, and I frowned.

"Don't start," I said.

She wrapped an arm around my shoulders. "Oh," she said, "I'm sorry. Did I offend you?"

I sighed, shaking my head and tugging myself away. "I wonder if there's anything non-alcoholic here?"

"Oh, yeah," she said. "I'm sure there's a Coke somewhere around here."

"Careful," I said. "Ask for Coke and get—"

"They're high school students, not addicts."

"Aren't they?"

"Come on," she said and tugged her through the crowd. "Let's find your man."

I frowned. "He isn't 'my man', Alex."

"I don't know," she said. "What do you think he is? Your make-out buddy? Cuz I don't think that's a thing — at least not for you."

I followed her. "I just don't know," I said. "We haven't really discussed it."

"There's not much to discuss," she offered.

I laughed and crossed the threshold of the house. We followed the flow of traffic into a large kitchen where Maverick reclined against the counter, reading a magazine. A few girls stood next to the fridge talking, but other than that, the room was empty. Alex winked at me, squeezed my hand and whispered, "My work here is done," in my ear before leaving me in the dust.

I crossed the room, triggering his interest. He dropped the magazine on the counter without another thought. "Nice sweater," he said.

"This isn't exactly the kind of party I expected," I said.

"I figured," he said, a sparkle in his eye. "Surprising you was more fun, though... Plus, I wouldn't expect your mom to be thrilled with this." He lifted an arm, gesturing to the girls by the fridge.

"What does that mean?"

"Just wait," he said, tipping his head toward them. They smiled Maverick's way and opened the fridge, grabbing a couple of beers. "That's why."

"Ah," I said. "Oh well."

"Want one?" he asked, nudging my shoulder.

"No, thanks," I said, but I leaned into his side.

He pushed off the counter and walked to the fridge. He grabbed a couple of bottles and outstretched one. "Here," he said.

I took it, inspected the label suspiciously and barked a laugh. "Orange soda?"

He grinned, twisting off the top. "Yep," he said and clinked his bottle against mine. "No drinking tonight."

"Really?"

He chuckled. "You sound so surprised."

"I am," I said, "a little."

He sighed, shaking his head and clasping a hand behind mine. Suddenly, he engulfed me, surrounding my senses with suppressed longing. When he spoke, his voice was even, if not measured.

"Look, Emma. I know something happened at the party," he said. "I just don't know what... I don't want that to happen again."

I nodded. "Okay."

He took a sip of his soda and shrugged. "Wanna head outside? It's about time for me to set up the bonfire," he said.

"A bonfire?"

"Yeah," he replied. "How do you feel about s'mores?"

"S'mores sound great," I answered.

"Awesome." He took my hand and led me out of the back door.

We walked and I watched the people. "Where's your mom?"

"She went to pick up our grandparents," he said. "She won't be back until the morning."

"Does she know about this?"

"Almost definitely," he said and kissed my cheek. He offered me his bottle. "Hold this?"

"Sure."

He began stacking the wood, and someone tapped on my shoulder. I twisted to see Kate. "Katie," Maverick greeted his sister, "having fun?"

"Yeah," she said. "I was going to ask Emma if her friend came."

Maverick heaved another piece of wood onto the stack. "Are you two friends or something?"

Kate met my gaze with a tight-lipped nod. "Yes," she said, "we're friends."

My skin prickled with the weight of the secret, but I played along anyway. "Yeah," I replied, "she's around here somewhere."

"Awesome," Kate said, obviously pleased. "Enjoy the s'mores."

Maverick smirked. "You aren't gonna stick around for one?"

Kate frowned. "Yeah, I will," she said. "I'll be back. I'm just gonna grab a drink."

A drink, sure, I thought and shook my head.

Maverick appeared none the wiser. "Cool," he said and turned back to the firewood.

Kate squeezed my shoulder. Something in the lilt of her gaze said she knew how strange our silence was. Maybe, just maybe, she wanted to end the secrecy too. "See ya in a bit," she said.

I leaned against the side of the house, watching Maverick work. He was all strong arms, messy hair and everything that made me weak in the knees.

"What's going on in there?" he asked, gesturing to his head then my own. "You're so serious."

I shrugged. "Nothing much." *If he only knew...*

He straightened and clapped his hands together. "You've got to loosen up," he said, crossing the yard.

He took his bottle from my hand and took a swig. "Stop worrying. This is a party. Let's have fun."

"I'll try," I said, nibbling my bottom lip.

He sighed and leaned down, pressing his lips to my ear. "You've gotta stop doing that."

I twisted to peer over at him, and his stubble grazed my cheek. I frowned, suddenly embarrassed. "What? Why?"

He smiled, rubbing my arms through the thin fabric of my jacket. "It's incredibly hot," he said.

"No," I said, "it's not."

He sighed and pressed a kiss to my forehead. "Babe," he said, his Southern accent peeking into his voice, "don't test me."

I opened my mouth, confused. "What are you talking about?"

A dark chuckle rattled through his chest, and he squeezed my shoulder. "Don't worry about it," he said. "Let's make s'mores."

Hesitant, I tucked a strand of hair behind my ear. "Let's," I agreed.

"Come on," he said and slid his fingertips along my arm to grasp my hand. He led me through the crowd and back into the kitchen where we stashed our bottles and he grabbed a grocery bag from under the counter. He held it up and winked. "Good, wholesome fun."

"Yeah," I said. "The masses didn't come for the booze."

"Nope. Definitely the s'mores."

* * * *

The party tapered down, and Maverick and I sat by the fire. He'd grabbed a couple of lawn chairs, and we'd laughed—like, really laughed. Suddenly, mid-conversation, his hand twitched in mine and he grinned. "Dance with me?"

"I'm a horrible dancer," I admitted.

"Come on," he prodded, standing and taking my other hand. "Dance with me."

"Oh," I mumbled.

He chuckled. "What?"

"Nothing," I said.

"Come on," he said. "What're you thinking?"

His eyes were warm, inviting...endless. I pressed my face to his shoulder. "Just that this is a much better party than the last one," I said.

"Good," he mumbled, brushing my hair with his lips. A shot darted down my spine, and I glanced up just in time for him to dip down and kiss me—like...*kiss* me. He framed my face and I slid my arms around his neck. I felt weightless, and he was strong against me. My mind darted to tomorrow, to school, to life after this, but one of his hands slid down to my waist, holding me fast, and I knew that I wanted this—no matter what *this* was.

A whistle forced us apart, and Alex emerged into my view. Her eyes were saucers, and she wore a shade darker lipstick than she had earlier, but there she was—Christmas tree sweater and all.

"Hey there," she said, half cat call, half serious, and I could tell she'd had a drink or two herself. She waved, her tan skin tinting red, and she plopped into one of the chairs by the fire. "Sorry to break up the party." She laughed. "Speaking of... Maverick, this is a great one."

He released my waist, settling for my hand instead. "Thanks," he said. "But, to be fair, I didn't do much."

"True," she agreed.

I shoved the sleeve of my sweater to my elbow and glanced at my watch. I sighed, leaning my head against his shoulder halfheartedly. "It's getting late."

Maverick groaned. "Yeah," he said, twisting to kiss my hair.

"We'd better get home," I told Alex.

She sighed. "Fine." She smiled at Maverick. "Thanks for inviting us. It has been great."

I gigged and tugged my hand from Maverick's. "Goodnight," I said, but his hands stilled me at my waist.

"Talk to you soon?" Then he grazed my cheek with his soft lips.

"Yeah," I said.

He tucked a strand of my hair behind my ear. "Goodnight."

"Night," I repeated, my cheeks warming heavily.

Alex giggled and linked arms with me as we walked toward the car. The last of the party-goers were staggering to their vehicles, and inwardly, I wondered why everyone liked to drink so much. Alex hadn't had that much, I guessed. She walked normally and sounded fine. Her eyes were only a little glazed and she seemed happier, but that might have more to do with the reason for her new lip color than the alcohol.

We got in the car and Alex flipped on the radio. Christmas carols flooded the car, and I laughed down at my reindeer sweater. "That was something," I said.

"Yes, it was," she said. "You two seemed cozy."

"Did you find Katie?"

In the glow of the dashboard, she giggled. "Yeah," she said. "Like I said, that night *was* something."

Chapter Nineteen

The fireworks were exploding in town a few nights before New Year's, unsanctioned by city lawmakers, but the cops didn't exactly care. As I lay in bed, staring at the ceiling and listening to the thunderous boom of poppers, I grabbed my notebook.

I'd been thinking about the project, and the more I thought about it, the more my fingers itched. We had come up with a concept — *the sulky teen and his relationship with his drug addict father?* It wasn't exactly romantic, but it was something.

I tapped my pencil against the page and scribbled, loving the angst of it and nearly jumping out of my skin at the next firecracker. *I get it*, I thought. *You're having fun.*

Hopping out of bed, I padded barefoot into the kitchen for a glass of water. I leaned against the counter, listening to the myriad explosions and glanced out of the window.

There Alex and Katie sat on top of a picnic table, talking softly. Katie's pale red hair was draped across her thin shoulders, and Alex wore polka-dotted pajamas. Their heads were bent together. *Innocent, unassuming*, I thought.

I frowned, placing my glass on the counter and trudging to the back door. I opened it, and they shifted, hearing the sound. "Emma?" Alex called.

"Yeah," I said. "Sorry, I just…couldn't sleep."

Alex nodded, waving me over. "It's all right. Kate just came over," she said.

I laughed. "It's late," I teased, and they both grinned.

Katie hopped off the table. "I only come out at night," she told me.

"You're hilarious," Alex said.

I watched them and rubbed the chill bumps from my arms. "It's finally cold out," I said.

"This *is* your kind of weather, isn't it?" Alex recalled.

"Yeah."

"I've got to go to the bathroom. I'll be back." She smiled and ambled into the house.

Silence bubbled between Katie and I, but she spoke after a moment.

"Is that why you're going to Rhode Island?" Katie's gaze fixated solely on me, probably for the first time.

I bit my bottom lip, and Maverick's voice rushed into my head, causing blood to spring to my cheeks. "No," I said.

She frowned. "It's just so far away."

I could tell she wasn't thinking about Rhode Island. No, her thoughts were in New York with Alex. "Look, Katie," I began, but she shook her head.

"No," she said, "it's fine."

I forced a smile. "I guess."

She nodded, rubbing her thighs to keep warm. "Oh," she said. "By the way, erm...you can call me Kate."

I gigged, awkwardly, but agreed, nonetheless. "Kate," I said. "I'll work on that."

Our conversation tapered to the ground between us, and she shrugged just as Alex heaved the sliding glass door open again.

"Think it'll snow?" Kate questioned, laughing halfheartedly, mostly joking.

Alex plopped down on the picnic table with a smirk. "Yeah," she said, "maybe in March."

Without thinking, I sat beside Alex at the picnic table. "I can't believe the break is almost over."

"I can't believe you're dating my brother," Kate noted.

I frowned, glancing over at her. "We aren't dating," I said.

"Sweetie," Alex said, "you're in denial."

"I think so too," Kate said.

I tucked a strand of hair behind my ear. "I just mean—" I started, but I retracted the statement before I could finish. "Never mind."

Alex shook her head. "No," she said, "talk."

"I just mean..." I trailed off. "We haven't exactly talked about things."

"Emma," Kate said, shaking her head, "Maverick doesn't really talk. He rides Pacman, and he runs track. Yeah, he drinks, but he's smart. He really likes you. My brother will figure it out. Give him time."

I leaned my head against Alex's shoulder like I had so many times before. "Yeah," I said.

Alex chucked under her breath. "Are you guys going to the New Year's Fest downtown?"

I shrugged. "I don't know," I said. "Maybe."

Chapter Twenty

In the right light, our little Southern town is perfect. I guess it's the nostalgia creeping into my existence, but as the New Year's Festival came into view, my heart clenched with affection.

Old Downtown gleamed with fairy lights and smelled of caramel apples and popcorn, and students and families swelled down the street. Businesses set up stands to sell food, and the city pumped in music and erected a Ferris wheel, a town favorite.

The Ferris wheel was parked at the edge of downtown. The spokes glittered with pink and gold lights, and it was the absolute perfect place to enjoy the fireworks at midnight.

I walked downtown in a pair of jeans and a T-shirt. The temperature was mild, and the wind had stilled. *It's a beautiful night*, I thought and tugged my hair into a loose ponytail.

"Hey," Alex called, waving as she came over from one of the food vendors. She wore a black dress and flats with her hair curled. "Have you found the funnel cakes?"

I shook my head. "What a greeting," I teased. "No, I haven't seen them."

"Gah, I've got to find one."

"Well, let's go find 'em," I said.

"Awesome," she said.

We passed Uncle Ben's table, and he waved. He was pedelling grilled cheese, hot dogs, corn dogs and grinned at all the passersby. "Emma! Alex! How are my favorite girls?"

I laughed. "We're good," I said. "Have you seen Miss Molly?"

"Ah," he said, "are you in the market for a funnel cake?"

"Yes," she said. "I like to have my dessert first."

He pointed down the street with a smile. "She's right down there," he said. "I'll see y'all a little later."

Alex waved and grabbed my arm, tugging me in the direction he'd pointed. "I saw Maverick earlier," she said. "He asked about you."

I flushed, looping her arm through mine. "Oh?"

"Yeah," she said. "I was walking along, minding my own business and making eyes at the cheese fry station, and there he was all *'Alex, have you seen Emma?'* Of course, I told him that you'd gone off with your boyfriend, Murphy—ya know the bassist in that band. What's it called again?" Her eyes sparkled, and I rolled mine.

"You're kidding, right?"

She grinned, pulling a ten-dollar bill from her purse. "Yeah," she said, "kidding."

I frowned at her tone, watching as she ordered a couple of funnel cakes from Molly. Molly wore a white dress with an eccentric red bow at the waist, and her booth was coated in colorful ribbons. It was a family operation, from her grandson hauling bags of powdered sugar to the tent to her daughter tearing tickets. New Year's Fest was her biggest event of the year.

Alex brought back the cakes, and I thanked her, worrying my bottom lip. She groaned. "Oh, Emma, I'm just messing with you. I told him you'd be here soon…and look! Here you are."

I nodded and tore off a piece of fried dough. Powdered sugar fell in slow motion, and I watched it go. "This really is the messiest festival food."

She plopped onto one of the benches along the square. "What would you prefer? A candied apple?"

I sat beside her, brushing off then straightening my shirt. "I'm not complaining," I said and peered up at the Ferris wheel. It was tall, with lights and the city crest—and my childhood memories. The thing was a landmark. "It's really beautiful, isn't it?"

Alex tossed her paper plate in the trash bin beside the bench. "Yeah," she said, "I guess."

"You *guess*?"

She stared skyward, as if surveying the thing. "I'm afraid of heights, remember?"

Awkwardly, I licked the powdered sugar from my fingertips. Molly didn't make it a practice to offer napkins. "It's not even about getting on it," I said, following her gaze. "I just think it's pretty. So full of history."

"I'm new to town," she said. "Less history for me."

I watched the children mingle and laugh. They ran through the streets, wielding lollipops for swords and wearing scarves as armor. "I know," I said.

"Ladies," a deep voice greeted, and we looked up to see Mr. Zelner standing hand in hand with his wife. "Having a good time?"

Alex beamed, popping up with affection. "Yes, sir," she said. "Mrs. Zelner! You look gorgeous."

Mrs. Zelner, obviously pregnant, placed a hand on her swelling belly. She wore a black and white dress that hugged her stomach and smiled broadly. "Alex," she said and hugged her. "You're sweet. It's good to see you."

I waved. "How's your break going?"

Mr. Zelner shrugged, holding his wife's waist. "It's going great," he said. "Did you get in touch with Mr. English?"

In typical Alex fashion, she answered for me. "Oh yes," she interjected. "She found him all right.

Mrs. Zelner nudged her husband. "I think you struck a chord, honey," she said. "Let's go get a funnel cake. Those look good."

"All right," he said and waved at us. "I'll see you both in class next week?"

"Of course," I said, watching them amble toward Molly's booth.

"Was that Mr. Zelner?" I knew that voice…Maverick.

I turned, a grin springing onto my lips. "Yes," I said.

"Hey," he said, waving and wrapping his arms around my waist. "What did he want?"

Alex ran a hand through her hair. "To enjoy the festival with his wife," she answered.

"Sounds good," he said, kissing my cheek. "Want to enjoy the festival?'

"Yes," I said, "let's enjoy the festival."

I'll leave you to it," Alex said, and she ambled away without another word.

* * * *

There is something about the possibilities of New Year's Eve, but I'd never experienced one like this. Actually, I'd never so much as dreamed of a New Year's Eve like this one. We ate, laughed and by eleven-fifty, we were in line for the Ferris wheel. The fireworks started, and Maverick nudged my shoulder. "Gorgeous," he mumbled, and I shivered through a gust of wind that had risen. "Are you cold?"

"A little," I said.

He pulled his jacket off his shoulders. "Here," he said. "You need to be warm."

"Thank you," I said and put it around me.

Seconds later, sixty-seven-year-old Edward waved from the front of the line, opening the gate to let us onto the Ferris wheel. "Have fun, you two."

Maverick led me to our seat with one hand on the small of my back. I slid into the bucket and he joined me, wrapping a strong arm around me. The Ferris wheel climbed skyward, and I rolled my head onto his shoulder. The stars peeked through the clouds, and he smiled. "Hey," he said.

I straightened to peer up at him. Warmth spread between us. "Hi," I replied.

He kissed my nose. "Happy New Year."

"A little early," I said.

He shook his head. "Yeah." His expression seemed measured, so I nudged his side.

"What?"

He shrugged, brushing his fingers along my hairline. "I want to kiss you."

"Okay," I said, "then kiss me."

It was slow motion.

He cupped my face with his hands, and the town echoed below us.

"Ten, nine, eight, seven, six, five, four, three, two, one," the people chanted in time with the fireworks, and he finally kissed me — the best kind of kiss…long, slow and beautiful.

In that moment, among the fireworks, the carnival food and the screaming kids, I realized just how real this was. I knotted my fingers into his hair and kissed him harder.

"Happy New Year," I whispered against his lips.

Chapter Twenty-One

Winter break disappeared, and suddenly I found myself sitting in the second row of history class, staring out of the window.

The teacher droned on and on and I doodled, remembering Maverick and my night on the Ferris wheel. Maverick had skimmed his hands along my shoulders and we'd crashed together without thought. Then, we'd walked along the crowded streets, snacking and laughing together. It had been perfect — or it had felt perfect.

The bell rang and I snapped my textbook closed. With my heart in my throat, I knew I would have to get the notes from Tammy-with-the-long-hair, but, for now, I stuffed my notebook into my backpack and trudged from history. The hallway teemed with busy students, distracted and excited.

It was lunchtime, and I would see Alex or Maverick for the first time today. Idly, I wondered what lunch would be like now. Alex seemed to flee whenever Maverick appeared — understandably, but still... In some ways, I missed the way things had been before that party. Between the secret, the truth and the undertones of romance, it was all eating me alive.

My skin crawled with the stupid burden of it all, and I rubbed my arms. The cool hallway and the distant faces reminded me that not everything had changed.

No, I thought. *Actually, very little has changed.*

I shoved open the cafeteria doors and merged into the line. From there, I could see Alex seated at our normal table. She was bent over her tray—texting, I thought—so I shuffled through the line alone. *She must have brought lunch today.* I smiled politely at the lunch lady, and she handed me a tray of lukewarm pizza. I thanked her anyway. It was just another day.

A few minutes later, I arrived at the table and slid across from my best friend. "Hey," I said, "who ya texting?"

She tucked her phone into the side pocket of her backpack. "Oh," she said, "ya know, just my Latin lover, José."

I shook my head, smirking. "Yeah," I replied, "José."

A thin blush crept onto her pale cheeks. "It was Kate."

I picked at the piece of pizza in front of me. *Just a little inedible*, I thought, laughing awkwardly. "How is Kate?"

"Good," she said and pulled a sandwich from her backpack. "She wanted me to come over tonight... Ya know, when Maverick's at your house working on that project."

"Oh," I said. "What about Mrs. English?"

A crease darkened her brow. "Well..." she said, twisting a strand of hair around her finger.

I looked up. "Alex," I said, "does Mrs. English know?"

"Know what?" A deeper voice joined the conversation and the color drained from my face. *Maverick...with bad timing*, I thought, but there was no way to retract the words. I looked up, obviously looking like a deer-in-headlights, and he frowned. "Is something wrong? What's going on?"

I sighed and shook my head. "Hi," I said. "Nothing's wrong." I flashed him a smile, faking it, but he frowned.

"Emma," he said, "you're a terrible liar."

"Maverick, it isn't Emma's fault," she said and stared over his head, avoiding eye contact at all costs. "You need to talk to Kate."

He frowned, and Alex grabbed her backpack and fled, leaving her sandwich behind. He looked at me. "What just happened?"

My cheeks burned, and my carefully honed illusion of safety waned. Our ease washed away with the crease in his brow. *The balance has returned to the universe*, I thought, dramatically, as he slid across from me with his tray. I opened my mouth to speak, but there he was, handsome and frowning with confusion.

"Emma, say something," he said.

I have no answers, I thought and shook my head. "There is nothing I can say," I said honestly. I reached across the table to touch his hand, but he pulled it away.

"What's going on?"

I sighed. "I can't," I said, because there was no realm in which I could say anything else. It wasn't my secret to tell. "Just...talk to Kate." I picked up my unfinished lunch and walked away. I slammed my tray onto the revolving belt and rushed from the lunchroom. Heat flooded my cheeks and I swallowed hard, pressing my back against the cool wall. The past weeks crashed down on my shoulders, and I was suffocating under the weight of it.

"I've gotta get out of here," I mumbled. Arms across my chest, I shoved the heavy, metal doors out of the way with my hip to step outside. Brisk air blustered against my bare arms, and I charged toward the playground.

Years ago, the high school had been renovated from an old elementary school, but the school distract had never removed the playground. Now, the artifact lived on the edge of our campus, slightly rusted, but it was a beacon. I knew Alex would be there.

I climbed the incline and saw her. Her back was to me and she was poised on a swing with her hands on the chains, uncertain and with her shoulders shaking.

I stood a foot behind her. "Hey," I said.

She twisted to peer at me. "Hi," she replied.

"Hey," I repeated then slid onto the swing that was next to hers. "Are you all right?"

She shrugged. "It all used to be so simple." There was a wistful tone in her voice.

This took a turn, I thought. "What?"

"Life," she answered and pushed off the ground an inch, kicking back just enough to move. "I remember this, ya know. The playground... Being a kid..." She kicked off, higher now. The sound of her voice was bitter and sad, but I let her talk. "I always thought I would fly. Ya know, eventually."

Air washed around us as she flew higher on the swing, a curtain of wind-blown hair and black clothes, and I frowned. "You still can," I said, a laugh quaking my body. "Well, metaphorically. Physically? Not so much."

She slowed to a stop, not really trying anymore, and glared at the trees in the distance. "This isn't the time for you to be cute," she said.

"What's wrong, Alex?"

She sighed, slumping in the seat. "I thought we should tell people," she said quietly and quirked her head up at the sky. "I mean, not scream it from the rooftops or anything, but I didn't want this huge secret." She lifted her gaze and her eyes shined. "I would have told you."

"It's okay," I said.

She nodded, but that didn't stop the tears from falling. "It's not," she replied. "She's embarrassed by me."

"Alex, that's crazy," I said. "Really, that's crazy."

She almost laughed, wiping tears away. "Yeah, that's me." A bitter smile ghosted her lips, and she shook her head with what I could only guess was underlying resentment. "Crazy Alex."

Affection blossomed in my chest, a blistering feeling unidentifiable to anyone but the one feeling it. Exhaling, I brushed a hand through her hair. "Alex, you know what I mean," I said. "These things are just complicated. It's probably about her."

She frowned. "That's easy for you to say."

"Yes," I said, "it is, because I know you. You're no one to be embarrassed by." I glanced at my watch and made a snap decision. "Let's get out of here."

"Get out of here?" She followed my gaze to the watch on my wrist. "It's twelve-twenty."

"I know," I said and stood, grabbing my backpack from the ground. "Let's get out of here."

Our eyes locked and she grinned, hopping down. "Okay," she said — and we left.

Chapter Twenty-Two

Dull blue-gray skies trailed alongside the car. I inhaled the sharp scent of seasons changing and drove with no inhibitions. With Alex by my side and my heart in my throat, we circled Nomansville until the sky turned pink, and my phone trilled to life in the cup holder.

I sighed, briefly contemplating ignoring it, but thought better of that plan. For all I knew, it could have been my mom. I jerked it from between us and flushed. *No,* I thought, *not Mom.*

I glanced over at Alex.

"Is that Maverick?" Her voice was thin. We hadn't been talking, not really, and she appeared bruised from the inside out, but when I held up the phone, she smiled. "Go ahead," she said. "Answer it."

Biting back a comment, I swiped the green button and maneuvered the car to the side of the road. "Hello?"

"Hey," he said, a simple word, but enough to make my heart rate accelerate in my ribcage. The voice on the other end sent chills down my spine. Brittle and disarmed, he sounded like something inside him had snapped.

"Hey," I said, my eyes trained on the road in front of me. "Are you okay?"

"I'm at your house." He avoided the question.

"Oh," I replied.

"You left," he stated flatly.

"Yeah."

"Why?"

"I needed to," I defended, and that got a chuckle.

"I always need to leave," he said, presumably as an easy joke, but a strangled noise emerged instead. There was a short pause, and he continued with measured speech. "I needed to see you."

My gaze twitched to Alex. Mesmerized by the black screen of her phone, she didn't appear to be listening, but God knew she had every right to. She had turned the device off the second we'd left the school, since it had become abundantly clear that the crumbling lie would snap.

I frowned. "What's wrong?"

"Emma," he said, "just come home."

I groaned. "I can't."

"Why?"

"You *know* why."

"Then, you *know* why I'm upset." His voice rose in pitch, and a chill ran down my spine.

"I can't."

A tense silence forged from our impasse, but Alex shattered it. "Emma"—her voice determined and strong and her arms crossed—"take me home."

A rush of air emanated from the other end of the phone, and Maverick began to speak, but I shook my head. "Gimme a minute, Maverick." I stowed my phone face down in my lap to muffle the sound, and I rounded to peer at Alex. "We don't have to go home."

She shrugged, rubbing the back of her neck, and finally met my gaze. "We can't drive forever, Emma."

"Yeah," I said. "I know, but—"

"But nothing," she replied. "I'm fine."

I sighed and jerked the phone to my ear once again. "We'll be there soon," I said then hung up.

* * * *

When we were three houses away, Maverick came into view. He was sitting on the steps, his eyes trained on the ground. His backpack waited on the sidewalk, like he was a child who'd forgotten his house key.

He looked skyward at the sound of our approach but lifted a hand in greeting. He had a begrudging smile on his face, strong and silent, but it looked marginalized, like it had been a rough couple of hours.

Beside me, Alex laughed, that same bitter noise I had grown to love. "He looks like a little kid," she noted.

"Yeah," I said.

She sighed, forcing a smile. "I'm really okay."

"You're not," I disagreed. "But just because you're not but that doesn't mean you won't be tomorrow."

She nodded, a weak action lacking conviction, and gripped my shoulders in a hug. "I love you," she said.

"Love you too," I replied. "Text me if you need me?"

"I will," she said, opening the door and practically running from Maverick.

He lifted his hand to wave but dropped it to his lap as she rushed away. *Gosh*, I thought, *he's trying.*

I shoved my door open and walked over. "Hey, I take it you talked to Kate."

"Katie," he said, quietly, rising to meet my gaze.

I frowned. "Katie?"

He pressed his face to my shoulder, inhaling deeply. "Katie," he repeated softly, and he sighed. "Can we go inside?"

"Yeah, of course." I pulled my backpack to my front so I could fish for my house keys. Matter-of-factly, he grasped the bag, holding it open for me. I jerked my lanyard from where it had settled at the bottom of my chaos and leaned up on my tiptoes to peck his cheek. "Thanks."

He forced a smile and looked at me intently. "Is Alex all right?"

"Yeah." I slid the key into the lock and pushed the door open. I extended a hand to grab my backpack from him, but he waved me off. "She'll be fine."

"I didn't mean to upset her," he said.

"I know." I sighed, leading him deeper into the house. "It... It wasn't really *you*."

He trudged after me, his eyes trained on the floor with a careful precision that made my heart melt. Suddenly, all his swagger was gone and he appeared years younger. My heart swelled. "I get it," he said.

"Well," I began, but I led him into the bedroom, and he deposited the bags on the floor beside the door. "How are *you*?"

"I'll be fine." He met me in the middle of the room, placed his hands on my waist — a careful movement — and drummed his fingers along my hip in a methodical dance. "I just can't believe this," he mumbled. "We don't... We don't keep secrets. Katie and I... I mean...we tell each other everything."

I sighed, rubbing his shoulders methodically. "I know," I said. "Alex and I were the same way."

He met my eyes, fingertips skimming over the skin of my forearm. "But you knew," he said.

Groaning, I slipped my arms around his waist and nudged his chin with my nose. "Not exactly," I admitted softly. "I mean, yes, I know now. But I've only known for a little while."

He frowned. "How long is a little while?"

I nibbled the inside of my cheek, slowly dragging my thumbs along his sides over his T-shirt. "Remember the night of the party at the lake house?"

He shook his head. "Actually," he said, shrugging a shoulder, "I don't remember much about that night."

I leaned over to kiss his shoulder awkwardly, trying to be comforting. "I kind of figured," I said. "That night was a little weird."

He frowned. "What kind of weird?"

"Well," I said, "I lost Alex and ran into you. Then things got—like I said—weird."

"You keep saying 'weird'."

Blood rushed to my face, and I knew I had to finally say it. "You keep asking me what I haven't told you about that night. Here is what it was. We kissed," I said, "sort of a lot."

He laughed. "Should I be shocked?"

I sighed and twisted away from him. "Well..." I was scrambling to put the words together to explain. "Anyway, we...sort of ended up against this door, and you opened it and we stumbled backward into the room. We looked up...and there they were."

He was silent for a minute. "So, I knew all along?"

"I mean, one or two drinks less and you might have remembered."

He sighed, side-stepping away from me and pressing his hands to his face. "Damn," he said, "I'm sorry."

"Why are you sorry exactly?"

"I could have prevented this," he said and dragged his hands through his hair. "We could've skipped all this middle stuff."

I frowned, tipping my gaze toward him. "Yeah, I guess."

He leaned down and kissed me once. "Okay."

"Okay, what?" I asked.

"Well," he said, dipping down to brush his lips to the corner of my mouth. "Just kiss me for a while? I don't want to think about it."

I leaned forward to press my lips to his. I sighed softly against the thin line of stubble along his chin. "I don't know how constructive this is."

"Yes," he assured me, skimming his hands along my sides, "it is *very* constructive."

He traveled his hands, firm enough to make my stomach turn, along my spine, and my heart flipped in my chest. Then there was a sharp *thump thump* on the wall, and I startled out of my skin.

"Hey there," Mom called from the door. It had been cracked. "Emma, is Maverick staying for dinner?"

Heat pulsed to my cheeks, and the knot in my stomach twisted. "Um-m," I said.

Maverick laughed. "I would love to stay for dinner. Thank you, ma'am."

Mom smiled. "Great," she replied and waved, deserting the hallway and leaving a blistering silence in her wake.

Seconds ticked in unabridged silence and he beamed. "Your mom likes me."

Groaning, I collapsed on the edge of my bed to catch my breath and steady my heartbeat. "Whatever…"

"Calm down," he said, placing one warm hand on my thigh. It burned through the fabric of my jeans, and he met my eyes. "So…"

I blinked, staring at him. "So?"

"Yeah," he said, a thoughtful smirk on his drawn lips. "This project?"

A shock of affection spread through me, and I shuddered a soft sigh. "Yeah, the project."

He grinned. "Okay, good."

Chapter Twenty-Three

Time lapsed in awkward silence and the routine set in—crawl out of bed, meet Alex for hot chocolate on the drive to school then meander through the halls as a zombified host until I saw Maverick. Yes, Maverick sparked something in me, and whenever I saw him, I couldn't help but be consumed by it. It was good.

That Friday, I reclined in my desk chair, writing, with Maverick at my side. Unfocused, he drummed his pencil against the edge of his notebook. "Hey," he said, leaning back and tossing a pencil in the air then catching it. "Hey, Emma."

I peeked up through the curtain of my hair. "Yeah?"

He grinned. "How about a double date?"

I crossed my arms in resistance. "Huh?" *Whatever has he have come up with now?*

"A double date," he repeated. After a pause, he amended the statement. "Ya know, with Katie... With Kate and Alex?"

I tucked my pencil behind my ear. "I'm not so sure about that."

"Come on," he probed, slinking his arms around my waist thoughtfully. He pressed his face to my shoulder, and I inhaled his scent. This whole thing had started about a month ago, I realized, and he was still here, tender and teasing. His voice rounded to a vulnerable lilt, and I couldn't help but grin. "To break the tension..."

I placed a hand on the back of his neck, massaging his heated skin. "I'm just not sure. That sounds really awkward."

He sighed and looked up at me. "Come on," he said, his eyes like those of a big child, and I sighed too.

"We can try," I offered.

"Thanks," he said. A tired smile slipped onto his lips, and I leaned forward to kiss his cheek. *He must be having trouble sleeping*, I wondered idly.

I shrugged. "Don't thank me. It'll be good."

"I don't know about that, but I want to try," he replied then kissed me. My skin burned against his. I breathed in salt and male, and he tugged me out of my chair and onto his lap. "I think John needs a girlfriend," he said, and I laughed. John was the main character in our story.

"Really," I said. "*John* does?"

"Yep," he said, teasing my lips with his.

"Joan?" I threw out.

"Equally unimpressive name," he said and stood, moving me carefully off his lap. Grabbing his phone, he texted his sister then turned to me. "Will tomorrow night work?"

"Sounds good," I said. I walked over to the calendar on the wall, studying it. We were more than halfway through January. The days were flying by and fear crept to my throat. The monster of time passing loomed.

He wrapped his arms around me from behind. *No,* I thought, *I won't let the ticking time bomb of our relationship consume me.* I turned in his embrace, and he brushed the hair from my face. "Are you all right?"

He slid his hands up my arms. "I'm good," I said.

He chuckled, and I knew he didn't believe me, but he didn't push. "So, John and Joan?"

"Yes," I confirmed, glad to have something to focus on that made me smile.

"Awesome."

* * * *

The double date consisted of dinner and a movie at the English house. Alex drove, wearing a pair of jeans and a sweater and looking impeccably uncomfortable. "You look like you've seen a ghost," I said, laughing awkwardly.

"I haven't yet," she said.

I groaned. "Alex," I cautioned and she sighed.

"I'm sorry," she said—and I could tell she was—"but this is weird."

Rolling my eyes, I flipped on the radio. "It's only weird if you make it that way," I said, and she let out a giggle.

"Ah-h," she replied, "I didn't know that was how it worked."

"Yep," I advised. "*You* control the awkwardness."

"Of course," she said. "My mistake."

I rolled down the window, embracing the tunnel of air against the side of the car. "It's good," I said, halfway attempting to convince myself. "Maverick is trying here. He wants things to be good... He is hurt, Alex—but not by you. Secrets hurt."

She frowned, rubbing the bridge of her nose. Suddenly, we were no longer talking about Maverick and Kate. "I know," she said, taking a wide turn down the English driveway and idling there. Her deep hazel gaze stayed magnetized to the steering wheel and she slid her hands along the cool surface, studying the rivets in the leather. "I'm sorry I lied to you."

The defeated lilt in her voice shattered something deep inside me, and I saw the door swing open at the end of the driveway. Sighing, I nudged her shoulder. There was no way for me to be mad at her, and I mean, had I ever really been? I understood—really, I did—and we were okay. I hoped we were, at least. The only remnant of strain in our relationship was the ache in my chest when I looked at her. It was a dull thing, a steady and unyielding reminder that she had kept something important from me and how much I hated secrets.

"Nothing has changed," I said. It was a lie. Everything was a little tainted and we both knew it.

Alex opened her mouth to speak but closed it. Releasing the brake, she put the car in gear and we rode up to the house, where she parked with a muted frown. She turned, mouth agape, but a shadow fell over the side of the car. It was Maverick. He waved, ducking to open my door with a wide-eyed grin. "Hey," he said, "you're late."

I rolled my eyes and shoved the car door open. "By five minutes," I said.

He rounded and opened Alex's door before she could. "Hi," he said, "you look nice."

"Don't be weird, Maverick," Kate called from the doorway, and my gaze snapped toward the sound. She leaned there, arms crossed, wearing a white sweater and leggings.

Maverick crossed back to me and tossed an arm around my shoulders. "Weird? Me? Nah," he said, making a beeline for the house and leading me along with him.

"Hey, Kate," I said.

She pecked Alex's cheek. "Hey," she said, "can we talk?"

Alex was quiet for a moment before continuing. "Yeah," she said, "I guess."

I looked at Alex, catching the arm of her sweater. "It's only weird if you make it that way," I repeated, and she shook me off, clearly unamused.

Maverick led me into the kitchen and frowned. "Was this a bad idea?"

I laughed like something was funny. "Yes, I'm almost positive it was."

"Don't play with me," he said.

Groaning, I pulled him into an off-kilter hug. "I'm sorry," I replied..

"I mean," he mumbled against my hair, kissing it, "I just found out that my baby sister is a lesbian."

"I don't think she's a baby anymore," I suggested. Then I looked up at him thoughtfully. "But really, Maverick, what has changed?"

I listened to his heartbeat, methodical and slow as he thought about it, then he sighed. "I mean" — he paused and closed his eyes — "nothing."

I pressed a kiss to the corner of his mouth. "Exactly," I said. "Now, what are we making for dinner?"

He shook his head and cast his gaze to the empty sink. "We're ordering pizza, I think. I forgot to thaw out the chicken."

Somehow I knew that everything would be all right.

Chapter Twenty-Four

The library smelled of mold and books — a dangerous combination for an avid reader like me. I stared down at my planner, pen in hand, and scribbled due dates and timings of senior activities, feeling the calendar as an albatross on my neck. These weeks with Maverick had taught me a priceless lesson. Time, finite and brittle, stopped for no man or woman and our time was limited.

I frowned and stared at the days, flipping past February, March and April to daunting May. The date of graduation mocked me — circles, dashes and confetti on paper from when I was glad it would be over.

A text lit up my phone screen and I snapped the planner closed, ending the relentless list of my deadlines. I sat up straighter, reading the text from Maverick.

Go to your locker.

I frowned and texted back.

Why?

Because, Emma.

Then, a second later.

Trust me.

Sighing, I tucked my books into my bag and trudged down the hallway. Heavy, I moved at the pace of a sloth until I spotted my locker. A single sunflower was stuck into the lock. My cheeks heated. "What the — ?"
My phone buzzed again.

Check inside.

Walking over, I pulled the sunflower lock from where it sat and quickly keyed in the combination. I opened the locker and a piece of paper tumbled to the ground. I grasped it, biting my bottom lip.

Turn around.

I spun, and Maverick was standing there, smiling at me. "You're silly," I said.
He sighed and kissed my cheek. "You're beautiful."
"Maverick, what's with the theatrics?"
He took my hand. "Isn't that what Valentine's Day is about?"
February fourteenth had never meant anything to me. My heart shuddered in my chest, a blossom of mid-winter warmth "Valentine's Day," I said. "I forgot."
"Whoa," he said. "That makes me feel great."

"Don't take it personally. I haven't had a valentine before, so I tend to ignore the day."

"But won't you kiss me?"

I flushed, glancing around the sparsely populated hallway. I blinked, raising on my tiptoes to kiss him once. "Okay," I said, "there."

"That was hardly a kiss," he said. "But whatever... So, I take it you don't have any plans for the evening."

"No," I said. "It just happens I'm an open book."

He stole another kiss right there in the hallway. "Good," he told me. "I'll pick you up at six."

"Awesome," I said. "Cool."

He squeezed my hand. "You're cute," he said.

I shook my head, and he laughed. "Don't do that."

He kissed my head. "I'm not laughing at you. I'm enchanted by your cuteness." He flashed me a grin. "I'll see you tonight."

I smirked and crossed my arms. "I'll see you in English," I countered.

"Right," he said, "in English."

* * * *

Hours later in class, I flipped through my English book, leaning over my desk. Maverick wasn't there, but that didn't surprise me. Alex nudged my shoulder, and I straightened. I'd been doodling while Zelner talked, so she whispered, "Hey, where's your head?

I laughed as she gestured. *I'm happy, I guess. Distracted.*

Zelner eyed us suspiciously and clapped his hands together. "Now," he said, "I hope you all aren't putting off your final projects. I'm excited to see what you've come up with. Does anyone have any questions?"

He was met with crickets. "That's what I thought," he said, shaking his head. "All right, seniors, let's call it a day."

Binders slammed closed, independent of thought or ideology, and Alex grinned toward me. "What's got you all smiley and bug-eyed?"

"Bug-eyed? Really?" I hadn't realized that Maverick and cupid's special day had affected me so much.

"It's an expression," she said.

I shook my head. "I'm pretty sure it isn't."

"Not the point," she argued.

"Oh," I said, ceding the question. There was no reason to make a big fuss. "I'm just happy."

"You have a date tonight," she guessed, a slow smirk crawling onto her lips.

"Yeah," I confirmed.

"Great," she said. "Want me to curl your hair?"

We had fallen back into normalcy, and I grinned in reply. "Sure," I said.

"Yay!" she exclaimed with genuine enthusiasm.

We shoved our books into our bags, and the sound echoed through the empty classroom. Zelner, behind his desk, waved us over. "Have you been able to get anything done with Mr. English?"

"Oh, she's gotten something done all right."

"Sh-h," I said. "Yes, Mr. Zelner, we're working together very well."

Zelner smiled toward the ground, like he'd known the secret all along. He probably had. I mean, teachers see a lot. I'm sure they hear a lot too. Nevertheless, I brushed off the comment.

"Great," he said. "Let me know if you need anything."

I shoved away from him, holding Alex's arm. "Alex..."

"Oh, Emma," she said, "calm down. It's okay. What does it matter if he knows?"

I replied, "It's just...weird."

"It doesn't have to be." She threw my words back at me, and I groaned. "It's only weird if you —"

"Stop!" I held up my hands in defense. "I know, I know."

"Come on," she said. "Let's go make you over."

"Really?"

She giggled. "I'm kidding. You're gorgeous. I just wanna fix you up a little."

"Your wish is my command," I agreed, shaking my head and hopping into the passenger seat beside her. "Let's go home."

* * * *

The radio in the living room blared the pop top forty, and Alex thumbed through my closet. She pulled out a pair of dark jeans and a lace top. "This is perfect," she said. "He'll love it. Simple. Understated. Adorable."

I laughed. "And my hair?"

She patted my desk chair. "Sit," she said and turned on the curling iron.

When it had heated sufficiently, Alex began working on my hair and I opened my notebook. "Do you have any plans with Kate tonight?"

"Yeah," she said, "but we're staying in."

"Dinner and a movie?"

"Sort of," she said.

"Oh," I said, nibbling the inside of my cheek. "*Oh*." Sometimes I really was an innocent.

"I'm kidding," she said. "We're watching a movie. What're you and Maverick doing?"

I shrugged, flipping through the project scenes I'd written with Maverick so far. "I have absolutely no idea."

She twisted strand after strand around the curling iron. "Oh, so it's a surprise? That's sweet — and romantic."

I watched her move and gave up reading, folding the corner of the notebook. "Yeah," I said, slightly surprised. Not a month ago, I would have never thought Maverick was romantic or sweet or any of that. Suddenly he seemed to be much more that way than any of us had ever imagined.

"You're thinking pretty loudly," she said, placing the iron on the desk and walking around to gather my bangs.

I laughed under my breath. "Yeah," I said.

"Care to elaborate?"

"Well" — I stared down at the words we'd created — "I just never thought Maverick would be like this."

She smirked, pinning my hair back. "Like what?"

"Like what you said — sweet…romantic."

She wrapped an arm around my shoulders to hug me. "I know. I know," she said. "I'm pretty surprised too."

"Good surprised, right?"

"Yeah," she said. "Of course, good surprised."

I beamed, straightening in the chair to peer at my reflection. "It's like a dream." I sighed deeply.

She released my shoulders. "I'm still not sure I trust him," she noted, halfheartedly.

"That's fine," I said, grabbing the skirt from where we'd deposited it on the bed. "I'm not sure either, but that's okay."

The doorbell rang and she smiled. "Well, I'll go distract him while you finish getting dressed."

"Awesome," I said. "Thanks."

She left, and I grabbed my clothes, listening to the hum of the radio and the lilt of my friend's voice in the entryway.

Chapter Twenty-Five

Eyeing my reflection in the mirror, I judged myself ready for the date to begin. *Maverick*, I thought, training my memory of the past month on him with a laser-like focus. So much had happened so fast, and it was infinitely possible — and probable — that it was happening *too* fast.

I grabbed my jacket and purse. It would be a good night, I knew, and being with him would make it even more perfect

Rounding the corner, I spotted them. Alex was sitting on the couch, holding a picture of the two of us from freshman year. Maverick was gesturing wildly. He wore a pair of jeans and a gray T-shirt, and his hair was messy. They laughed, Alex murmuring something, and I leaned against the wall to watch.

Then Maverick glanced up. Instantly, his eyes brightened and that set the radiator in my heart ablaze. "Hey," he said, "you look amazing."

I felt a warm glow at the compliment. "Thanks," I responded. "Are you ready to go? You two seemed to having a good time."

"Thanks for entertaining me," he told Alex, patting her shoulder. "Have a good night."

"Let's go," I said.

"All right," he replied, "let's go."

Alex smirked, following our movements. "Where are you two kids headed?"

Maverick glanced between Alex and me. "I'll text you," he told her.

"Really? You're keeping me in the dark?" I looked between them and frowned.

Maverick smiled, kissing my head. "I'm full of mysteries," he joked. "Come on. It's more fun this way."

I sighed, pulling my hand from his with a little laugh. "Let's go then." I fake-pouted, just for effect, but neither of them believed my act.

"Yes, ma'am," he said. He waved to Alex. "Night, Alex."

We crept into the cool winter evening, and in a display of chivalry, he opened the passenger side door of his truck. "So," I asked, "what are we doing?"

He leaned over to kiss me before I could get in. "Don't worry about it," he said. "Just kiss me again."

"You're teasing me and it isn't funny," I whined.

He smirked against my lips, and I leaned in to him. Chill bumps rose on my arms, persistent and threatening, and I shivered. He rubbed them for warmth. "I'm really not," he said.

I tugged him closer. "Where are we going?"

He dragged his lips along my jaw, resting them at the crest of my ear. "Ice skating," he said.

I frowned. "Okay," I said, laughing, "but there's one problem."

He chuckled. "What?"

"It's south Mississippi," I said. "It's fifty degrees."

He reached into the cab of his truck to pull out a coat and wrap it around my shoulders. "Not a problem," he said.

Shaking my head, I hopped into the cab. "You're crazy," I said, and he didn't disagree. He walked around the car and jumped into the driver's side.

"You're beautiful," he said.

I blushed and fiddled with the lace of my top. "Then where are we going?"

He sighed, pulling out of my driveway with a bobble of his head. "There's an indoor skating rink on the coast."

"Really?"

"Yeah," he replied. "It's tiny, but the owners are awesome."

"That sounds great," I said. "But I can't skate...very well."

"Don't worry," he assured me. "I'll catch you if you fall."

"Oh, I believe that." And I hoped he would.

* * * *

We took the back roads to the coast, listening to the twang of static and country radio in the background. He sang along, but I don't think he knew the words. He kissed my hand once as he drove, and I flushed, shaking my head.

"When did you get so corny?" I asked, half joking.

He placed a hand over his heart. "I'm hurt," he complained.

"Don't be a baby."

He grinned over the console. "You're a tough cookie to crack."

"The expression is 'tough nut to crack' but not really," I said.

"Be my valentine?" he asked, his voice steady against the bluster of the air conditioner and bad radio.

He...this...cemented reality before my eyes. I could feel his gaze on my uncertain smile. "Yeah," I said. "Of course."

He returning his eyes to the road with a shake of his head. "Damn," he said.

"What?" I asked, quietly wondering if he regretted it already.

He flipped on his turn signal and drove down a gravel road. "I just really wanna kiss you."

My cheeks burned, and I shoved the cup holder against the back seat to crawl closer to him. "Are we almost there?"

"Yeah," he said, "just another few miles." He paused, and I looped my arms around his shoulders. "You're gonna play like that?" His chest hummed against me, and he hit the accelerator.

I giggled against his throat. He smelled of salt and something sweet, and I knitted my fingers into his hair. "Maybe I wanted to kiss you too," I told him.

"Skating, right?" he mumbled, pulling up to the small building.

"Yeah, so you say." I unfolded myself from his side. Butterflies blossomed in my stomach, and he grabbed another coat from the back seat.

"Put this one on," he suggested. "It's freezing in there."

"Thanks," I said, handing him his coat that he'd given me earlier and donning the smaller one.

Outside the car, he wrapped his strong arms around my waist. "Almost two months," he mumbled against my hair.

"Yeah," I said. If there was too much silence, my mind would wander, and that was not for the best — not by a long shot. "Hey, let's go skate?"

He dragged his hand along my arm to slip his fingers around mine. "You're right," he said. "After all, Uncle Tucker opened especially for me."

I could hardly contain the joy of the special gesture that Maverick had arranged for us, but I hoped the warmth of my kiss on his cheek somehow let him know.

He led us along a dirt path. The building itself was brick and big enough to be a house, but there was a wooden two-by-four on the back wall that read *Ice Skating for Families — Open December and July.*

Maverick opened the front door, and we were met with a gust of icy air. "Oh, geez," I mumbled, stepping inside, "it *is* freezing in here."

He wrapped an arm around my shoulders. "Come on in," he said.

I followed him into the dimly lit entryway, and it hit me. We really were the only ones there. The room of exposed brick was lit with what must have been a thousand fairy lights. It smelled like ice and warm cocoa, and I twisted to see a table against the back wall with a pot of hot chocolate on top, next to a tray of cookies. "This is amazing," I said.

"Want some hot chocolate?" he asked, walking to the back of the room to grab a couple of cups.

"That'd be great," I replied.

He smiled and nodded to the metal bench in the corner. There were two pairs of ice skates waiting, so I shuffled over and plopped down by them. He brought over the cups, and we sat shoulder-to-shoulder.

"So, your uncle owns this place?"

He sipped his chocolate. "Yeah," he said. "He teaches junior high in town, but he runs the rink during Christmas and the summer. He says there isn't enough calling for it during the whole year."

"Ah," I said.

He chuckled. "You're sure are quiet."

"I'm a quiet girl, Maverick," I reminded him.

"Touché," he said and kissed my cheek. "Care for a cookie?"

I popped up and walked over to the table. "They smell delicious," I said. "Does your uncle bake too?"

He shook his head. "Nah," he said. "That would be his wife. She owns a bakery downtown."

"An industrious family," I noted.

He grinned. "Oh, you know it."

I picked up one of the cookies and sighed contently. They were actually warm snickerdoodles. "You undersold the cookies," I noted, spinning to look at him, but suddenly he was right behind me. I could feel my heart rate accelerating in my chest. "Hey."

He ducked down to kiss me. "Hey," he responded.

I pressed my face against the rough fabric of his shirt and he startled. "Are you all right?" I asked.

He spun me around in a fast-paced dance move, and a giggle escaped my lips. "I'm good," he said, popping a cookie into his mouth and releasing me.

He walked over to the bench and grabbed a pair of skates. I followed him and soon we were tumbling awkwardly onto the ice.

* * * *

"We're going to be sore in the morning." Maverick's arm never left my waist as we ambled to the truck. Exhausted, we leaned against each other.

"True enough," I agreed, happy to be with him. We'd both ended up splayed across the ice once or twice, but somehow we'd avoided serious injury. "But it'll be worth it."

He held the door for me and I got into the cab, moving to the center to be near him while he drove. He slipped into the driver's seat beside me, and I pressed a kiss to his shoulder. Warmth flooded the cab as he switched on the truck, and I shuddered.

He pulled out of the vacant parking lot, and we drove home in relative silence, seemingly in sync. I'd never thought this would be possible, and he'd proved me wrong. I lolled my head against his shoulder, and he looked down at me.

"What?" I said.

His response was simple. He kissed the top of my head. "You're my best friend."

Chapter Twenty-Six

My ankles rubbed against the smooth linoleum as I shifted, sitting against the wall. I was sitting outside Mr. Zelner's classroom with a book nuzzled in my lap. A shadow cast across the page. I groaned, blinking for sight. "Maverick," I whined without meeting his gaze, "I'm reading."

A laugh bubbled from above me, and I blushed. *No,* I thought, *that's not Maverick.* Instead, the sound was a distinctly feminine wind chime. "You've got the wrong English," the voice replied. *It's Kate,* I realized.

I tucked my finger into the book in my lap and peered up at her. Kate leered over me with her strawberry-blonde hair tied in a knot at the base of her neck. A single paint splatter tainted her cheek, but she slid down the wall to join me. "Hey," she greeted, fingering the book out of my hands. "What're you reading?"

"Just reading," I replied.

She flipped through the paperback then handed it back to me and began to roll a loose thread on her sweater between her forefinger and thumb. "So," she said. Our shoulders were pressed together and she smiled a little. "How're things with you and Maverick? Is he being a gentleman?"

I blushed, shaking my head toward the ground. "A gentleman? Maybe," I said, teasing him like he could hear. "It depends on what your definition of 'gentleman' is."

"Well, you haven't taken off running yet, so he must be on his best behavior." Her voice danced, low and sweet, and she sighed. "How's Alex?"

"Is something wrong between you two?" I worried my bottom lip. I didn't want to be in the middle of whatever was going on.

An awkward silence buzzed between us, and Kate shrugged. She scanned the ground, studying the dirty tile. "I, erm, well..." She sighed. "I mean, we knew things would change eventually."

"Oh," I said. Blinking, I peered over at her. "What do you mean?"

"The clock's ticking, ya know?"

"I'm sorry," I said. "What?"

She laughed, an echo of awkward bitterness. "You two... Well, you both are going to graduate and leave."

I tilted my head against the wall. "Oh," I said, "yeah."

"Don't get me wrong," she added. A beat of silence preceded her nearly whispered, "I love her." Her voice trembled. "I'm proud of her. It's just hard to be on the other side of graduation, to watch the person you care about walk the line and not be able to be beside them."

Her words rang in my ears. *'I love her. I'm proud of her. It's just hard to be on the other side of graduation.'* Grief washed over my senses, and I pictured them on that picnic table during Christmas break. Quiet, their heads bent together, they had seemed straight out of a storybook. Dread twisted in my stomach as the image morphed. Suddenly, it was Maverick — one hand on the wheel of his truck, the other in mine, and he grinned over at me as we flew down the highway. *It's all so damn beautiful*, I thought, and the sun crested against his cheek. *How can something so beautiful self-destruct so fully?*

A shadow interrupted the daydream, and I quirked my gaze upward. Alex wore a red skirt and a white top and her mop of hair cascaded over her shoulders. "Hey," she said, disturbing my inner monologue, "is everything okay?"

"Yeah," Kate said, scrambling to her feet. "How are you, Alex?"

"I'm all right," she said softly, and applied one of those fake smiles to quench the pain of both the obvious lie she'd just heard and the equally clear lie she'd told. "It's been a while."

Blinking, I thought about that and quickly realized I hadn't seen them together since... When? Valentine's Day? Frowning, I stood. I had been so wrapped up in the 'Maverick and Emma show' that I had forgotten to check up on my best friend.

Kate slipped one of her hands into Alex's to squeeze. "Text me."

Alex nodded, a small gesture, and her hand twitched in Kate's. "I will," she responded.

Kate told me goodbye then hustled down the hallway toward her class. The had-been-empty hallway flooded with students, and they swallowed Kate, leaving Alex and me in the dust.

My mouth dry, I spun to Alex. "I'm so sorry," I said.

She frowned. "Why are you sorry?"

"I was so wrapped up in Maverick, Alex," I said, my cheeks warm. "I had no idea there was anything wrong."

She didn't skip a beat. "It's okay."

"No," I said, "it's really *not*."

"Emma, calm yourself. It's fine."

I swallowed, looping my arm around her. "Seriously, Alex, we're supposed to pick each other up when shit gets rough, right? I'm sorry I wasn't there for you."

She sighed, collapsing into my hug. "I love you," she said, ignoring my apologies. "I'm all right."

As the corridor filled with our peers, I instantly scanned the crowd for Maverick, but I regained my composure and grinned at Alex. "We're having a sleepover," I announced. "No boys, no girls, no stress. It'll just be you and me and a smorgasbord of unhealthy treats and bad movies."

Her pinched smile grew genuine. "Like old times?"

I squeezed her shoulders. "Just like old times."

Mr. Zelner's door swung open, and he stifled a laugh. "You two are very enthusiastic about my class," he said.

"Yes, we are," Alex said. "It's the best class in this joint."

He shook his head and stepped out of the way. "Well then, by all means, come on in."

We shuffled past him to our desks, and he looked back at us. "I'll be back in five. I have to grab a cup of coffee."

As soon as Zelner was out of earshot, Alex turned to me. "So," Alex said, turning the conversation, "what were you and Kate talking about?"

I frowned, sliding into my desk and crossing my legs. "Wait, what?"

"Remember?" she asked. "You...my girlfriend...in the hallway...like five minutes ago?"

I giggled, jerking my notebook from my backpack. "Oh," I said, "*that*."

She flipped her textbook open. "Yes," she replied, "*that*."

Idly, I doodled a drooping panda in the notebook's margin. "She just asked about me and Maverick," I mumbled, shrugging a shoulder and tacking on the sobering truth as an afterthought, "and you."

She sighed and shoved her pencil behind her ear without meeting my gaze. "Oh," she said. "What did you say?"

"I didn't," I answered, simple enough.

"Oh?"

"Yeah," I said. "I just sort of changed the topic, ya know? I asked about the two of you instead... If there was something wrong there." I paused. "She didn't really answer." It wasn't a complete lie.

The classroom door opened, a falter, a skipped beat and our peers began to filter in two by two, like the ark. I watched, and the conversation halted for a moment.

Then Alex sighed again, straightening in her desk. "We're fine, I guess."

"You *guess*?"

"Things are just tense."

"That's what she said," I told her. I crossed my arms, a terse frown springing onto my face, and I nudged her shoulder.

Finally, she looked over at me. "What?"

I groaned. "Come on," I said. "Talk to me. Y'all seemed great during Christmas. What happened?"

She darted her gaze away from mine. "I don't know, Emma," she said, her voice frail and unyielding. She was silent for a minute then continued with a bitter sigh. "What was gonna happen? What *could* happen?"

"That wasn't my question, Alex... What *happened*?"

"Oh, fine," she said. She swiveled in her desk to look at me head on. "It was Valentine's Day."

I nodded. "Yeah?"

"Everything was good," she said. "We made dinner and we were sitting there eating and laughing. It was all good."

"It's always good until it's not," I mumbled.

"Yeah, well..." she said. "Then, I mentioned school. It was something offhand, ya know, like 'I wonder when they'll send out dorm assignments,' and she snapped."

"What does that mean?"

"Apparently," she hedged, shaking her head, "all I talk about is leaving."

"Oh," I said, recalling our conversations and the heavy burden of our impending graduation.

"Yeah," she said. "Well, that left a bitter taste in her mouth. She started asking all these questions about what my leaving means—and I don't know what it means. That just made it worse, I guess. It just became this big *thing*."

I just let her talk. She needed to let everything go.

"I didn't know what to say. I mean, come on. It's just one of those things. It's gonna be hard, but I can't change it by sheer will. It's gonna happen." She stopped talking and her face was red.

"It'll be okay," I said.

"I guess," she said. "It's gonna be fine."

I smiled halfheartedly and reached over to squeeze her hand. "Good."

She looked up over my head and laughed. "We have company," she said. I looked up and saw Maverick slide into the desk beside mine, smirking in his track sweats.

"Hey," I said, "how's your Friday?"

He jerked his notebook from the bag and scratched the date in the top. "It's fine," he said. "Yours?"

I shrugged. "It's all right."

Mr. Zelner slipped in at the sound of the bell, cradling his thermos, and he eyed Maverick and me with a small chuckle before spinning to scribble directions on the board.

Maverick poked my side to regain my attention. "You busy tonight?"

"Yep," I said instantly. "Tonight is Girl's Night."

He pouted. "Really?"

"No boys allowed," Alex said. "*No one* else allowed, in fact."

He stared back, incomprehension sprawling across his features, but seconds later, understanding dawned. "Okay," he said. "Maybe tomorrow, then?"

"Yeah," I said, "tomorrow."

Mr. Zelner clapped his hands at the front of the room, calling out, "Order, order," but his joke was only met with stony silence and uncomfortable giggles.

He laughed and shook his head. "That was funnier in my head," he said and sighed. "I'm sure all of you are ready for the weekend—and I am too—but first we have to talk about this final project. By now, you should have all gotten a good chunk of it done, right?"

There was a ripple of agreement through most of the class.

"Wonderful," he said. "Now, I want you to flip the script."

Panic spread through the room as we waited for an explanation, and my gaze darted to Maverick. Just the night before, we had printed our story. It was ready to be edited then could be filed into the one-less-thing-to-worry-about-before-graduation file on my computer.

"If you wrote a play, convert it to a screenplay. A song into a musical. A story into a play. Something. Make a change and expand your avenues. I'll be looking at both drafts to see that you took care with the project, but this is about creativity. English as a discipline is in its essence creative. Explore language, human emotion, but most of all, make me feel something."

I bore a hole in Maverick's head. I could already hear him saying, *'You've got to let loose and stop worrying. You'll explode.'*

Yeah, right now, I felt like I might just do that.

Chapter Twenty-Seven

We burned the third bag of popcorn. Alex and I collapsed on the ground in front of the couch in fits of laughter, and I grabbed the blanket from the back to heap over our laps. The movies were horrible, but the moments were real. It almost felt like nothing had changed.

The credits rolled on another movie, and the clock on the wall blared two-forty-five, but it only felt like about eleven. Alex's head lolled on my shoulder, but she hummed along to the early two-thousands pop number coming from the television.

"Can I ask you something?"

She straightened with a measured smile. "I think you're going to," she said, grabbing the remote from the cluttered coffee table to flip off the sound.

"Alex," I said. My voice was feeble, quiet, and her gaze burned into mine, but I stared at the patch in the corner.

An awkward beat of silence, and she poked my side. "Yeah?"

Here we go, I thought. "Do you love her?"

There was a few seconds of silence before, "Yeah." She'd said it quietly.

My heart swelled in my chest, and I wrapped an arm around her shoulders. "Have you told her how you feel?"

"Yes," she said, sighing in deflated release. "Well, yes and no."

"You've got to tell her."

She groaned and pressed her face to her hands. "I know," she said.

I grabbed the bowl of candy and plopped it into her lap. "You're going to be all right," I said. "We're both going to be all right."

"What's going on with you and Maverick? Is something wrong?"

"No," I assured her. "We're fine."

"What aren't you saying?"

I sighed. "I've just been thinking—you know—about what Kate said… About time."

She leaned her head against my shoulder again. "Oh," she said, "don't worry about it. We have time."

The screen went black in front of us. We leaned against each other.

'We have time.' Her words replayed like a melody in my head, but suddenly time compressed in front of my eyes. There wasn't enough for anything—not school, not Alex, not Maverick or Kate.

No, I thought. *There's not enough time.*

We fell asleep like that, tangled in our blanket and each other, and I woke up as the sky turned pink. My shoulder was pressed against Alex's and my skin burned. Groaning, I crawled away from our heap to peer out of the sliding door at the sunrise.

The morning, vivid and marked and cold, began to glow as the sun peeked over houses. Sometimes, in the early morning or late at night, I saw something more in this six-stop town—a glimmer of something like hope and nostalgia mixed into one technicolor moment. I loved the random beauty of it.

A shuffle interrupted my inner monologue, and I twisted to peer at Alex. She slumped against our pillow fort, her hair a mess and her cheeks flushed scarlet. The room itself was a disaster, but I could deal with that later.

I grabbed my phone from the coffee table and padded down the hall into my bedroom. I plopped on the edge of my bed and tapped the home screen. There, Maverick and I grinned back at the camera. We wore big scarves and puffy coats, and the relationship felt, well...*simple.*

Shaking my head, I unlocked my phone to blink at the notifications. A text from Maverick.

Hey. Hope girl's night was great. Wanna have lunch? Text me when you get up.

I smiled, noting the time. Seven-twenty in the morning. It was definitely too early for lunch, but I shot him a text anyway.

Hey there. Just woke up.

I flopped back on the bed, staring at the speckled popcorn ceiling. Then I turned toward my bedside table and noticed a book waiting under a half-empty bottle of water. I grasped it. The book wasn't mine, I realized. The spine was worn, and I flipped through the frail pages. At the bottom of the title page in small, scrawled script, Maverick had written, *'This was my favorite book as a child. You reminded me of it.'*

A deep flush coated my cheeks. It was a book of fairy tales. I fell back in the bed, cradling it to my body with a soft pinch in my chest. I held it up, opening the first page to a vivid tale—knights and princesses and beautiful drawings. *God*, I thought, *I wish they were real.*

"Why can't this be our story?" I groaned, and a hand came around to cradle the book from my hands. He kissed my shoulder and I gasped.

"It can be," he said, his whisper an electric shock to my spine. He grinned, his lips against my skin, and I leaned back against him.

"How?" I asked, hanging on every word.

He shrugged, nodding against the thin fabric of my pajamas. "Easy," he mumbled. His lips were against my neck and he was finding his way to the skin under my pajama top.

I nibbled my lip then asked, "How?"

He kissed me, hard, shaking his head. "What have I told you about the lip?"

I laughed. "Don't bite it," I said.

His eyes were molten lava as he cradled my face in his big hand. "Don't go," he said.

I gazed back at him. "Okay, I won't."

He beamed down at me, all kisses, a knight in a black T-shirt. "I love you," he said, a twisted knife in my back again. "I love you."

I groaned, arching into him. "I love you," I replied, my heart in my throat, and he brought me closer.

"Hey," he said. "Hey, Emma." I frowned, the change sudden. His voice wavered in pitch, his form slipping away.

Suddenly I held the book, alone on the bed, stretched out and cold.

Alex stood over me. "Are you all right?"

"Yeah," I said, "I'm fine."

"Your phone was ringing," she said and dropped it onto the bed. I straightened, and she waved me off. "I told him you'd meet him for lunch at noon. Will that work?"

"Yeah," I said, blinking and pressing a palm to my warm face. "What time is it?"

"It's ten." She appeared shiny and new in a fresh pair of clothes with her hair brushed back into a swept bun.

"You look nice," I noted.

"Thanks," she said. "You gonna be all right? I've gotta, ya know, go talk to Kate."

"Yeah," I said. "I'm good. You go. Good luck."

Her smile blossomed. "I don't need luck," she said with a twinkle in her eye. "I have a best friend."

I laughed, halfheartedly. "Go... Go. I'm good," I said.

"Oh, fine. I'll text you after?"

"Please do," I said.

She winked, and I watched her walk away. *What a dream*, I thought, my cheeks warm.

I dragged my fingers along the intricate spine of the storybook. Maverick would be the death of me. Of that, I was certain.

Seconds later, my phone buzzed from where Alex had discarded it somewhere on the bed, and I snatched it up, answering without bothering to look at the caller ID. "Hello?"

"Morning," he said, his voice warming my chest.

"Hey," I replied, "when did you put this book here?"

He chuckled, a deep rumble. "That took long enough," he noted.

I frowned. "Maverick…"

"What's wrong?"

I shrugged. "I wanna see you," I told him.

"Now?"

I walked to my closet to grab fresh clothes. "Thirty minutes?"

"Sure," he said. "Where?"

I thought for a moment. "I'll text you," I said, hanging up and walking into the shower. *Too many feelings, too little time*, I thought as I flipped on the hot water and stepped in for a cleanse — or so I hoped.

Chapter Twenty-Eight

Hair damp, I sat cross-legged on my bed. My heart raced and my skin crawled, waiting for Maverick to make the screaming of my soul cease. Fingers itching, I flipped open the calendar on my phone.

Today was March third. Spring break was next week, but they said it might snow. What could I say? Mississippi was weird. We'd had a cold snap before at the beginning of March, so, I guessed it would be a spring break of mittens and sweaters.

Systematically I flipped through the months. April showers... May showers, caps and gowns... June, July, then August and it would all be over. We would go up in smoke.

I plopped back onto the bed, and my phone clattered to the ground, buzzing on the way down. I groaned, flailing to catch the falling projectile, but it hit the shaggy black rug, nonetheless. I scrambled, grabbing it and reading the text.

I'm here.

I rolled, falling from the edge of the bed and landing in a misshapen heap on the floor. "Ow," I mumbled.

I appraised my reflection in the mirror, noting the ruffled hair. I'd put on a big, white sweater over black leggings, and I tucked my phone in the waistband to hustle to the door.

"Hey," I said, throwing my arms around his neck.

He snickered, probably surprised by my enthusiasm, and squeezed my waist, tugging me tighter. "Hey," he said, a gust of air blustering against my cheek. He smelled like aftershave and detergent. He pulled back to assess me. "What's wrong?"

I peered at him, all eyes and black T-shirt. There, in his arms, the fears in the pit of my stomach subsided and our time felt endless. Instead of speaking, broaching the questions, I closed the distance between us, a fiery clash of lips against lips as I leaned against him. He seared against me, and I singed right back.

He laughed, a sweet vibration, and framed my face. He steered me into the warmth of the house and shut the door behind us. "That was a nice distraction," he mumbled.

"I try," I said, softening, and he kissed my cheek.

He drummed his thumb along my jaw, smiling just enough. "What's wrong?"

"What's gonna happen?" My voice was thin, uninhibited.

He dipped down to graze my hairline with his lips. "What do you mean, Emma?"

"I don't know," I admitted, pressing my face to his shoulder blade, but I stepped away, unable to focus on anything but the smell of his skin when he was so close.

He groaned, trudging after me and wrapping his arms around my waist. "Don't hide," he mumbled against my head, and I flushed. We both knew what I meant. "Wanna go somewhere?"

I straightened. The future, four months away, festered in front of us, but I didn't want to revel in it. "Okay," I said.

He released me, skimming his fingers down my arm to take my hand. "Only if you want to," he said.

"Of course I do."

He glanced over my shoulder, toward the back of the house. "Is your mama home?"

"Yeah," I said, "but she's in bed."

He grinned, a slow action, and he gripped my waist. "Good." A rush of air, and we crashed to the couch, giggling against one another. There was nothing like it, being with him, so sudden and so pointed. Every moment was crystalline, and I relished it.

Our kisses slowed, and I could hear his heartbeat.

"How do you feel?" he asked.

"I'm all right," I said, sitting up and nudging his face with my hand. I tried not to think, instead forcing my insanity to silence. "I'm sorry I worried you."

He pressed a kiss to my temple. "It's all right," he said. "After all, it's my job."

I stood and tugged him after me toward the door. "What do you mean 'it's your job'?"

Sunlight illuminated his mischievous expression as we stepped outside, and he mussed my hair, a playful gesture. "Boyfriends worry about their girlfriends, right?"

So perfect, I thought and locked the door. An early afternoon breeze swept through his hair, and I teased my fingers through it. "Let's get out of here."

He led me to his truck. "Where are we going?"

I shrugged. "Anywhere," I said. "Somewhere."

"I can do 'anywhere'," he said.

He opened the door, and I climbed in. I slid to the center of the truck and he hopped into the driver's seat. The cab filled with warmth, and I sighed.

This — right here and right now — was perfect.

I nuzzled my face into the strength of his shoulder, kissing it. "Thank you."

He looked down and smiled, intertwining his fingers through mine. "Thank *you*," he replied, and we took off down the driveway.

Chapter Twenty-Nine

He drove, and I sang. The road in front of us spread out for miles, filled with flowers and fields and big houses in the middle of nowhere, and hope blustered in my chest. The early spring afternoon screamed of certain rebirth, and I smothered a kiss to his shoulder.

He squeezed my hand but released it. He smirked, drifting to the left lane.

I gasped, giggling, despite myself, and laid my hands on his, at ten and two, leading him back to the right-hand lane. "Maverick, stop," I insisted, my voice a pitch or two too high.

He hit the gas, riding the center line, and blood rushed to my face. "You're cute when you fear for your life." He kissed the top of my head and slid back into the correct lane once more.

I swatted his arm. "Maverick, really?"

He shook his head. "You've gotta let go," he said. He smirked. "I'm going to get you on the back of my motorcycle one of these days."

I barked a laugh. "Maybe," I told him.

"I think so," he said. "You hungry?"

"Yeah," I replied. "A little, yeah."

"Cool," he said. "I know a little place not far from here."

"We're in the middle of nowhere," I observed, looking around at the unfamiliar countryside.

"Yep," he said.

"More relatives here?"

He shook his head. "Actually, this is a friend."

"Oh," I said. "You and your connections."

He smiled, hitting the accelerator again and a road appeared on the left. "Yep, stick with me."

My blood boiled, and I traced a slow pattern on his thigh. "I intend to," I said, but an echo bounced through my mind, the itching reminder. *I intend to...until I can't.*

He turned down a skinny road off the highway. There was no marked path, but we passed a couple of houses and the road bottomed out at a gray cinderblock building that was surrounded by cars.

"Gary is busy today," he noted.

"Gary? Drug Bust Gary?"

His chest bounced, laughing, and he shook his head. "He doesn't like to be called that anymore."

I frowned. I remembered the senior who had been expelled when I was a freshman. "He has a restaurant now?" Back in high school, he'd worn baggy clothes and always had dirty hair and the kind of chuckle that made you uncomfortable.

"Yes," he said. "What'd you think he was doing?"

I didn't know but hazarded a guess. "Maybe prison?"

He shook his head. "You're a little judgy, aren't you?"

"Yeah," I admitted, "you could say that."

He pulled into a parking space in the back of the building. "You're a mess."

"What kind of food is it?" I was ready to change the subject after my apparently incorrect judgement of good ole 'not drug-bust' Gary.

"Good," he noted, hopping from the cab and rounding to open my door. "His specialty is pot brownies."

I stared back blankly. "That's a joke, right?"

He winked. "Sure," he assured me.

Frowning, I followed him into the building without another question, because I was beginning to not want to know. Sometimes, ignorance truly is bliss. Inside, the building had white walls and black booths. Patrons surrounded a bar in the center of the big room, and the place swarmed with full trays of food. "A buffet?"

"Yep," he said. "Good ole Southern cookin'."

I spotted Gary across the room. He deposited drinks on a table and spun around. "Is that Maverick English?" He crossed the room with open arms and bro-hugged Maverick. "Man, it's been a while. How've you been?"

Maverick shrugged. "I'm all right." He gestured to me. "This is Emma."

Gary extended a hand. "Emma, huh? You in Maverick's year? Ya look familiar."

Maverick wrapped his arm around my waist. "Paws to yourself, Gary." He grinned. "Yeah, Emma's a senior too."

Gary smirked. "You guys an item now, Maverick?"

"Yep," he agreed. "We've been together since just before Christmas."

"Good," he said. "I was beginning to wonder if you were into dudes."

"Can we get a table and *not* a hard time?"

"Maybe, but it'll be tough." He led us to the back of the building and sat us down. "Drinks?"

"Water."

"Iced tea."

Gary said, "It'll be right over. Go ahead and help yourself to the bar." He peered down at me. "The mac and cheese is the best in the county. Seriously... That's why I built way out here."

I laughed. *A joke, right?* "Thanks for the tip."

Maverick grabbed my elbow, leading me over to the buffet. "The real reason he had to get out of the county was that he was creeping out the natives."

"Don't be an ass," I muttered, and I grabbed a spoonful of macaroni.

"I would never." He shook his head.

As we walked through the line, he looked over at me and grinned. Finally, I frowned back. "Hey," I said, grabbing his elbow. "What's with that?"

"I can't smile at my girlfriend?"

I sighed and walked back to our table. "I don't know," I wondered aloud. "There is something behind it, isn't there?"

"Yeah."

"What?"

"I just wish you'd tell me what you were thinking this morning."

"I don't know, Maverick," I said, tiredly, and rubbed my temples. "I've just been thinking."

"Yeah?" he asked through a mouthful of potatoes.

"What's gonna happen?"

"And we're back to the same question," he said ruefully.

"After graduation," I finished.

"Oh," he said.

I went quiet, poking my rice with my fork. "Yeah."

"Well," he began, swallowing hard, "will graduation change how you feel about me?"

"Of course not," I said.

He reached across the table. "Then it won't change anything."

My heart swelled—but not with any sort of firm security. Instead, I frowned. "I'm leaving," I reminded him.

He sighed, nudging my cheek with his thumb. "You're not leaving until August. Let's go away this summer. Alex and Kate can come. It could be a month on the road—traveling, seeing places other than these dumpy Mississippi towns, just being together."

I just looked at him, my stomach in a knot. When he said it like that, it sounded so simple. "That sounds amazing."

He grinned. "Then let's do it. Let's go."

"Okay," I agreed.

"Good," he said and shoveled a spoonful of peas into his mouth.

"And hey," I interjected, pulling off a piece of my roll.

"What?"

"Mississippi isn't dumpy."

"I know," he said. "You know what I mean."

I blushed. I felt like I'd never been anywhere else. "I do," I answered.

"Go ahead and eat."

So, I did.

Chapter Thirty

The first day of spring break, the vacuum sweeper roared over the TV and I stood with a bandana tied around my head. I sang into a hairbrush and swayed along to a tune I couldn't hear. After all, there was no one around to judge.

It was the perfect kind of day—easy and quiet—but mid-verse a hand came down on my waist. I gasped out a yip. Then, Maverick kissed my neck.

"Oh," I said, shaking my head, "that's cruel."

"Hey," he greeted.

"Hi," I replied. "Please, don't do that...ever... again."

He smirked. "Why?"

"My heart nearly stopped," I told him.

"Semantics." He tugged my bandana, smirking. "You ready to go?"

I frowned. "Go where?"

"Oh," he said, "did I forget to tell you? We're going to the beach for spring break."

"Um," I said, "I can't just up and go to the beach."

He chuckled. "Why not?"

I crossed my arms. "Well, first of all, I have a mom who might notice that I've disappeared."

"I already okayed it with her. I told you she loves me."

I blushed. "Oh," I said, crossing my arms, "well..."

He nudged my shoulder. "Come on," he said. "Make it a trial road trip."

I thought of the course catalogs piling up on my bedside table. "Okay, okay," I said. "I'll need to pack a bag."

"Already in the truck. Your mom packed it."

"Whoa," I said. "How didn't I notice that?"

"Dunno," he answered, shrugging. "We expected you to ask questions, but this was far more fun."

I laughed. "Can I at least change?"

"I guess you can," he teased, smirking. "But I kinda like this look."

"Ha ha, funny. I'll be ready five minutes."

And I was. Before I'd really taken in what was happening, we were off.

I kicked my feet up on the dashboard as he drove, and he rolled down the windows. The cold front made the Mississippi weather...well, bearable, if not perfect. It was sunny but cool, and the farther south we drove, the air smelled more and more of salt. As we rode along, I relaxed slowly, becoming one with the bucket seat. Instinctively, I leaned up to kiss his cheek. "I'm glad you kidnapped me."

"I thought you might be," he said.

I worried my bottom lip and glanced over at him. "Where are we staying?"

"Well" — he chuckled under his breath — "we have a little house down on the coast. It's where Katie goes to paint."

"Oh," I said, "that'll be nice."

He paused, glancing down at me. "I sense there's something wrong?"

"No," I mumbled.

"Don't lie," he said. "What's wrong?"

I groaned, pressing my face to his shoulder. It was only now sinking in that we would be alone, like, really alone for the first time. "It's stupid."

"Oh," he said, turning down a skinny driveway into the woods. "Emma, that isn't what this trip is about."

My cheeks burned. "*That*?"

"Yes," he said, "that."

"It's not?"

"No," he promised, frowning. "I mean, yeah, I have thought about it, but no, that wasn't the point."

I was silent. His words reverberated in my ears, and I sat still, processing them. He flipped on his blinker, a steady tick-tock-tick-tock, then turned down a gravel driveway.

The electric air around us simmered, and I frowned toward the beachy white house. It was small, with a wraparound porch, and he pulled into a makeshift parking spot. The building was surrounded by big, gnarly live oaks and screamed our own little paradise for the weekend, but his expression was drawn.

"We can go home," he said. "I don't want you to feel like…" He sighed, banging his hand against the leather in resignation. "I wanted this to be fun."

I stared at the tense movement of his jaw as he shut off the engine, and my cheeks warmed instantly. "Hey, I'm sorry. I'm just nervous."

"I get it. It makes sense," he said. "*I'm* sorry."

"Don't be sorry," I whispered. "This sounds perfect."

"Are you sure?" His voice wavered "I don't want you to be uncomfortable."

"I'm not, Maverick," I assured him. "I just, well... I wasn't expecting it, ya know?"

He squeezed my shoulders. "Yeah," he said. "Surprises... They can go one of two ways, right?"

"Oh, will you just shut up and kiss me?"

"That I can do."

He crossed the space between us—the air simmering, our hearts shuddering—and kissed me. My arms found their way around his neck.

"Hey," he said, nudging his face from mine, "wanna go see the water?"

"Yeah, let's go."

"Head up to the porch," he said, idling at the car door.

I climbed the steps, leaning against one of the beams and blinking down at him. "What're you waiting for?"

"Sorry," he said, shrugging. "You're just beautiful."

"Come on," I urged.

He followed me up the stairs. He twisted our hands in a playful dance, and I giggled. Nothing I had experienced in eighteen years had compared to that feeling. Hand in hand, we were electric.

We ambled around the corner of the house, and he tossed an arm around my shoulders. Maverick was warm and handsome and perfect, and suddenly, I was staring out at the Gulf of Mexico.

The murky waves lapped against dirty white-blond sand, and I froze at the corner of the house. *Geez*, I thought. The water had always mystified me. It was beautiful, endless.

"It makes you feel so small," I mumbled.

He brushed my cheek with his hand. "You aren't small."

I didn't reply, merely released his hand and kicked off my flip-flops. "Thank you for this," I said. I slid my hand around to cradle his face and kissed him once, slowly.

He grinned. "You're very welcome."

I smiled, pressing a kiss to his cheek. "You're kind of romantic, aren't you?"

"Guilty as charged," he teased, skimming a hand through my hair. "I just love to make you happy."

I leaned up on my tiptoes and kissed him again, soft and slow. "You make me happy."

He cradled my face in his hands. "Good," he said.

I beamed up at him, smirking to myself, and I dashed down onto the sand. I shrieked, running into the frosty surf. "Catch me if you can!"

I spun, facing him, watching the bewildered and playful jolt in his movement as he shucked his shoes off. Mischief played on his face like shadows, and I giggled.

God, I thought, launching myself into his arms.

I couldn't think of anything more perfect.

Chapter Thirty-One

We frolicked, splashing and giggling in the surf, for what felt like hours then we stumbled up the sand toward the house. "Ready for the tour?"

"Yeah," I said, a giggle building in my chest, "but I'm pretty wet."

"Don't move," he said, jogging toward the house. "I'll get a towel from the truck."

"You're wet too," I called, but my words were lost in the surf. He was gone, rounding the corner. A minute later, he arrived with a giant beach towel and massaged the water from my hair.

"Better?."

"Yeah," I said. "I'm perfect now."

"Come on," he said, shaking the water from his head and wringing out the chest of his T-shirt. "There's no saving this thing."

"It looks good from where I'm standing," I half-joked, and he flashed me a smile as we walked the rest of the way back up the beach.

He rummaged in his pocket, fishing a key ring from its contents, and quickly unlocked the door. "It isn't much," he admitted, "but it's home."

I squeezed his hand and stepped into the house. The living room was sparsely furnished—just a couch, a coffee table and a boxy TV set across from the couch. "It's nice," I told him.

"Thanks," he said. "There are blankets and things in the closet."

I followed the corridor and poked my head into a small kitchen. It was standard. "Kitchen?"

"Yes," he answered. "It's very exciting, I know."

I turned and kissed his cheek. "Come on."

"Okay," he said, taking my hand and leading me to the back of the house. There were two doors, opposite each other, and he pointed at the one on the right. "That's Kate's room."

"Oh?"

He placed a hand on the small of my back and nudged me forward. "That's my room."

I grinned. "Can I see?"

"Sure, go ahead."

"This is so exciting." I bounced.

He laughed, plastering a kiss to the back of my neck. "It's really not that much."

"Oh, would you rather I not be excited?"

"No," he replied, "go ahead."

I opened the door and took a step inside. The room was small and smelled of socks and sand and adolescence. A queen-sized bed waited under a window, curtained in blue, and there were posters on the wall.

Warmth spread through my chest. "It's sweet."

"Sweet?" His breath ghosted my neck.

"You know what I mean," I offered.

"Come on," he said. "Ya wanna tidy up before we go to dinner?"

"Yeah," I agreed, casting a glance down at my sandy legs. "I probably should."

He grinned and led me back down the hall and into a small bathroom. "Here ya go. "There are towels in the cabinet if you wanna grab a shower. I'll go get your bag from the car."

I turned away from the door to step out of my shorts. I stood on the bathmat and stared at my T-shirt-clad form. Shoulders lax, I leaned against the back wall.

Listening to Maverick move through the house, I flipped on the water. I could hear him—closing doors, mumbling gruffly. *Oh, did he run into something?*

"Maverick, are you okay?"

"I'm alive," he called, his voice close. "You decent?"

"Always," I said.

"Well," he said, nudging the door open to hand me my bag, "here ya go. I'll give you a minute."

I smiled and jerked the T-shirt over my head, turned on the water and stepped into the shower without another word.

* * * *

Later that night, we walked into town for dinner. Apparently he knew a little place that served 'the best catfish'. I guess he was right. Dinner *was* good, but I was so happy that he could have served Vienna sausages without crackers and I wouldn't have complained.

At the restaurant, we sat outside, listening to the waves crash against the shoreline like clockwork, and he told bad jokes as the sun set.

"So," he said, swinging our hands in tandem as we headed back, "the house doesn't have cable, but we have a TV and about four hundred VHS tapes."

"Is that all?"

"There might be a couple of DVDs," he said. "I know we have Scrabble."

The distant house came into view, and I shuffled in the chilly surf. "Scrabble, huh? I don't know. That's a pretty hardcore game in my house."

"There might even be Yahtzee under the bed."

I shook my head. "Even worse."

Just like that, we watched a movie, curled together on the couch. I listened to the sound of his breathing, concentrating on the inhale and exhale, the back and forth. He encased me within his arms, and I rested my head on one of them.

I'm not sure when I fell asleep, but I woke up in a bed, alone. Frowning, I straightened, blinking. The room mirrored Maverick's, but instead of movie posters, there were painted canvases. In fact, the entire room looked like it had been the scene of a paintball tournament. The smell was unmistakable.

Here I am, I thought, *in his sister's bed.*

I climbed from the side and shuffled across the hall to find him, a Maverick-sized lump in the queen-sized bed. He lay haphazardly, with a lazy arm thrown over his face and half under the blanket, but he wore only a pair of black pajama pants.

Red flags went up, and I knew I should crawl back into Kate's bed. I mean, there had to be a reason he'd plopped me in his sister's bed — but I couldn't resist.

Careful not to wake him, I slid into place beside him, slipping underneath his blanket. It smelled just like him, and I maneuvered even closer to watch the hard lines of his face, mellow in repose.

It was true what they say. *People look younger when they're asleep.*

Without thinking, I leaned forward and kissed his cheek.

Then I closed my eyes, an infestation of butterflies in my ribcage, and nuzzled my face to his arm.

Yeah, I thought, *I can get used to this.*

Chapter Thirty-Two

A hand came down over my hip, and I shivered in my sleep. Blood flooded my cheeks. Slowly, like fallen rain, I remembered.

He nudged my cheek. "Morning, sleepy head," he grumbled.

I blinked the sleep from my eyes and peered up at him. Maverick wore a pair of gray jogging shorts and a black T-shirt, and I frowned. "Why are you not in bed?"

"I ran down the beach to grab coffee and donuts," he answered, chuckling under his breath. "I checked the fridge, and there's nothing in it but stale beer. I didn't think that would make the best breakfast."

"Coffee," I mumbled, heading for the kitchen. "Coffee is good."

He shook his head and followed me. "When did you come to my bed?"

"Dunno," I replied. "What was that about anyway? You bring me on this romantic spring break getaway and put me in your little sister's bed? Really?"

"I didn't want to assume," he said and smirked. "You *were* concerned about my intentions in the truck."

I grabbed a cup of coffee from the holder, cradling it to my chest. Warmth blossomed from it, and I sighed. "Well, assume that I want to be near you."

"All the time?"

"Yep."

"I don't think you mean that."

"Maybe I mean just that."

"Oh," he said, almost an involuntary sound, and he shook his head. "Don't tease."

Finally, I laughed, genuine and real. "Sorry," I offered, though I really wasn't. The dimple popped in his chin and his face flushed, a new color to his persona, and I loved it. "So, what are our big plans for today?"

"Who says there are big plans?"

I stepped away from him, leaning against the counter, and took a sip of coffee. *Mm-m,* I thought, *still warm.* "Most schemes are pretty well planned out, I think."

Shrugging a shoulder, he nodded. "True." Then he paused, likely for effect. "I thought that after breakfast we could go into town and buy groceries. Ya know, the essentials. Popcorn. Coffee."

"Okay," I said, setting the half-empty cup beside me on the counter. "Sounds good."

"Great, and tonight we can drive into town for a movie."

"What's the catch?"

"What catch?"

"Oh, I don't know. I just feel one coming."

He shook his head. "Don't worry so much." He plucked a donut from the box. "This is a fun surprise."

I crossed my arms, assuming my armor. "Maverick," I said, "you've already surprised me once this week."

"Yeah, with a trip to the beach." He looked proud of himself, but I could still tell there was another shoe ready to drop.

I groaned. "Maverick, come on. Tell me."

He sighed. "Oh, fine." He toyed with my hair, now sagging from its day-old ballerina bun. "Mom and Katie *might* be coming down Monday."

"'Might' or 'are'?"

"Definitely 'are'."

I frowned. "They're coming here? With *us*?"

"Don't freak. You already know Katie sorta well because of Alex, right? And Mom is pretty cool. She really wants to spend a little time with you."

I bit my lip and he drew a thumb along the curve of my jaw to trace the path. My gaze drifted to the box of donuts, at the gaping hole in the dozen, and I felt inadequate. I wasn't very hungry anymore. I opened my mouth to speak but the words caught in my throat.

"Come on," he said. "I promise, Emma... This is gonna be good."

"Okay." I lolled my head against his shoulder.

"Have a donut," Maverick offered.

I sat at the kitchen table and stared at the donuts in the box. "So—" I began.

He smiled fondly and sat beside me. "This will be fun."

I faked enthusiasm, grabbing a glazed donut from the box. "Okay," I said, unconvinced—but not willing to ruin his plans.

* * * *

We drove inland to a grocery store, and I reveled in the smell of salt in the sea breeze. I fiddled with the radio dial and settled on a local station that claimed to play oldies but goodies.

Maverick chuckled at the choice. "I knew you were an old soul," he said, and I giggled.

"I'm going to take that as a compliment," I told him.

He took my hand over the center console, which was down and housing a couple of drinks we'd gotten at a drive-through window. "It's definitely a compliment." He grinned. "That's why you're so smart."

I brought my straw to my lips, avoiding the statement.

He cut his gaze toward me. "Are you going to deny it? Really?"

"No," I replied, "I guess not. It's just not... I'm not smart. I'm not smarter than the average person."

He barked a laugh. "Oh, my mistake."

"I'm serious, Maverick."

"Okay, okay," he said, waving at a couple of tourists in shorts and island shirts as they crossed the road. "I'm just saying, Emma. Those fancy schools sure want you."

I shrugged it off. "Test scores," I explained. "It's easy to study and swing high if you don't have a social life."

"Damn," he said. "I guess so."

"It's like that meme. *'You can't have it all.'* School, social life, sleep... Something's got to give."

"That's pretty sad," he said. "You seem to be handling it pretty well now."

"Yeah," I admitted, smirking out of the windshield. "But you *are* homework, so..."

He shook his head and pulled into the parking lot of the grocery store. "God," he said, "I keep forgetting to thank Zelner."

"Yeah," I agreed wholeheartedly.

He cut the engine and rounded the side of the car to open my door. "Ya think he knows?"

I thought of the few not-in-class conversations I'd had with him and the sly looks he'd given us on occasion. "Yeah," I said. "I think teachers know a lot more than we give them credit for."

"You're probably right about that." He took my hand and we ambled inside. "They spend all day watching us. They're bound to pick up on things."

"A touch of the hand here, a peck there and boom, the whole faculty knows."

"I wonder if his wife has had the baby yet?"

"Probably," I said, "considering she was pretty far along at New Year's."

"Oh," he said, grabbing a cart, "right."

"So, popcorn and coffee?"

"Maybe some meals too."

"Whoa, that's a solid list you've got there, Maverick."

"I know. Isn't it great?"

"Okay, let's go shop."

He squeezed my hand. "Yes, ma'am."

Chapter Thirty-Three

"A large popcorn," Maverick ordered. "Extra butter."

He smiled politely at the teenager in the maroon vest behind the counter. She was our age, with black hair and a grimace. As she strode away to get the popcorn, Maverick squeezed my shoulders. "A movie isn't a movie without a bucket of popcorn."

The theater was a five-minute drive into town, but we'd left forty-five minutes early to snag snacks and the best seats. The mid-sized theater seemed as if it had stepped out of a time warp, with walls painted with an intricate mural of small-town charm in the fifties.

As we waited for the not-so-perky theater staff person to return with our popcorn, I listened to the chatter of the kids behind us. They were six or seven and clutched a twenty-dollar bill, buzzing about which snacks they would buy.

I twisted, grinning as I watched them. One of them wore a little pink dress, and her hair was tied back with a black ribbon. She bounced, excited, and giggled, along with her friend in purple. The innocence burned under my skin, and I blinked, noting the woman a few feet away. She watched them with her arms crossed, and she caught my gaze. Lifting her hand, she waved. Independence, I realized, but not too much.

Maverick nudged my shoulder. "Whatcha thinking about?"

I shrugged, releasing his hand to accept the popcorn from the girl behind the counter. "Thanks," I said.

"Can I get y'all anything else?"

"A cherry slushy for me," he said. "What about you?"

I scanned the list above the raven-haired girl's head. "Hm, a blueberry slushy would be great."

"Swell," she said. "One minute."

Maverick grabbed a fistful of popcorn and grinned. "So, how do you like it here?"

"I like the paintings."

"I thought you might," he said. "You are one for the story."

"I am." I found it a bit surprising that he really did know me so well.

The girl came back and took our money with indifference. Something in her persona made me laugh, and Maverick quirked an eyebrow at me. "What?"

"I always forget, ya know."

"Forget what, babe?"

"Oh," I said, maneuvering out of the line and toward the theater. "Sometimes I forget that people actually live here."

He grinned. "At this theater? Really? That's sad."

"You know what I mean," I said. "At the beach. People live and work at the beach. That's kind of crazy, isn't it?"

"Yeah," he said. "I guess that to them, it's just home."

I followed him to our theater. "I guess so."

The theater was dark, save the screen, running the last bit of the previous movie, and I frowned. The theater was nearly empty. "We'd better go outside and wait."

"It's all right," he said. "I promise. Where do you wanna sit?"

I gave his question quick consideration. "I don't care. Middle?"

He led me up the stairs with a chuckle. "You're really nervous, aren't you?"

"No." I worried my lip.

He kissed my cheek. "You're such a bad liar."

"It's just weird." I shrugged, sliding into a row in the back and peering over at him.

"Okay," he said. "I'll tell you this."

I plopped into a seat in the center of the row. "Yeah?"

He grinned, sitting beside me. "More anticipation, please. This is good."

"Go ahead," I said.

He placed an arm around my shoulders. "One day, we'll be the people living at the beach."

I smiled into the silence, kissed him and watched the end of the movie before we saw the beginning. For a moment, I forgot about August while I leaned against him, pretending there was a future in our perfect lie.

Chapter Thirty-Four

A cool breeze blustered through Maverick's open window, and I leaned against his chest. His skin smelled of early morning sunshine, and I listened to the roll and rush of waves against the shoreline outside.

It was Monday morning, sometime just on the other side of dawn.

There, in his arms, I felt safe. His featherlight heartbeat sang under my ear, and I drew finger hearts on his chest. *Is this what happy feels like?*

He tightened his arms around me, and I sighed happily. "Maverick," I whined, a halfhearted noise, "we need to get up."

"I don't think so," he said. "I like it here."

I rolled my eyes, shrugging out of his embrace. "I need a shower," I said. "What time are they coming?"

He groaned, tossing a muscular arm over his face. "I think they'll be here about noon."

"Okay," I said. I fished for my phone on the bedside table and instinctively cued up my school email address to check for any missives. A habit of habits, I guessed.

Maverick nudged my shoulder. "What're you doing?"

My gaze darted to him, and I forced a cough. "Nothing," I said.

"You're checking your email, aren't you?" He launched across me, reaching for my phone and knocking it from my hands.

I sighed. "Something important could have come in."

"It's spring break," he reminded me.

I shook my head, leaning over to kiss him once. "I'll be back."

He nodded, but his gaze burned a hole in my back. I stopped in the doorway and peeked over my shoulder to flash him a playful smile. The weekend had been wonderfully intense.

"What?" He smirked from his spot in bed.

I jerked the tie from my bun and shook out my hair. "Just looking at you," I said.

He chuckled. "Like what you see?"

"Nah," I said and shuffled toward the bathroom.

The door thudded behind me, and I stared at my reflection in the mirror. *Nothing special. Dull brown hair and pale shoulders dyed red from the sun. Gosh*, I thought, *sometimes I wish I could see what he saw.* I nudged the T-shirt from my shoulders and toed off my socks. *It doesn't matter*, I thought. *He sees it, and for now, that's enough.* I stepped into the shower, testing the water with my fingertips as steam filled the room. I pressed my palms against the wall and closed my eyes, relishing the waterfall on my shoulder blades and back. *Safe and warm*, I thought, and I began my mantra.

Today will be good.

The words rolled and shifted through my mind as I listened to the beat of water humming against tile. I massaged my scalp, inhaling the sharp and sweet scent of strawberries and vanilla, Kate's shampoo. Idly, I wondered if Alex liked the smell. It was strange, I thought — the situation.

A muffled noise startled me from my thoughts, and I craned to look at the door. Distantly, I heard Maverick's voice in the hallway, but I shrugged it off, rubbing my shoulders and massaging the skin to normalcy. I felt as two-dimensional as paper.

A sharp, salty scent penetrated the sweet smell of the shampoo. "Is that bacon?"

Damn, I thought. *Talking to myself, much?* I shook my head and flipped off the water. The faucet dripped once, twice and dried up, so I padded across the room to pull a towel from the rack. "Maverick," I called.

"Yes, dear?" he yelled back, a chuckle caught in his throat.

"Do I smell bacon?"

A pause. He was probably laughing, but I didn't mind. "Yeah! Put on some clothes and get in here."

I shook my head, my cheeks warm. "Okay," I said. I rubbed the water from my skin and pulled on fresh clothes.

I walked semi-blind from the bathroom, worrying the water from my hair with a big towel. I shuffled down the hallway toward the bedroom in a clean T-shirt and a pair of jeans and plopped on the edge of the bed to scoop my phone from where it had landed on the floor.

Tucking it into my pocket, I listened to the crawling drawl echoing from the kitchen and I headed that way.

"Morning," I said. I popped my head around the corner and grinned at Maverick. He wore an apron over his T-shirt, and a slow, Southern sound rippled from his chest.

He slapped a dish towel over his shoulder and flashed me a smile. There were plates on the table, along with eggs, bacon and toast. "Hey, I hope you're hungry."

"Yeah, I could eat."

He pulled my chair from under the table with a chuckle. "You didn't hear any of that, did you?"

I smirked. "Every single note."

He shook his head. "My cover is blown," he teased, shaking his head and sitting beside me.

"Mm-hm-m," I said. "Now I know your secret."

"Yep." He shoveled a pile of eggs into his mouth. "I'm secretly a star."

I buttered my toast. "Oh, yeah, didn't I see you on *American Idol* last year?"

He gestured with his fork. "Might've been the year before," he said. He took a long drag from his coffee cup.

"Meh," I said and nibbled the crust from my toast.

He leaned back in his chair, teetering on two legs. "You okay?"

I wasn't sure what to say. "Yeah, I'm fine."

He popped a piece of bacon into his mouth. "Wanna go swimming?"

"That sounds fun," I replied.

He nudged my shoulder. "I thought so."

"You know that means I have to change now," I said.

He grabbed my hand. "Change after breakfast."

"Yes, Dad," I joked, rolling my eyes.

"Pfft," he offered in mocking exasperation. We lapsed into a soft silence while we ate, and I smiled at his concern. Finally, when I finished, I stood.

"I'll be back in a minute," I promised, placing a single kiss on the stubble of his cheek.

"Okay, okay," he said. "Take your time."

I shuffled back into the bedroom to grab my swimsuit and hustle back to the bathroom. I yanked my phone from my pocket, dragging my thumb along the jagged crack straining from the bottom corner. It had been a tragedy in the moment, but now, I was more zen. *Well*, I thought, *it happens.*

I shook off worry about the blemished screen and turned the phone on, scrolling through unnecessary notifications — this person liked my picture, that person wants help on this game — to see a text from Alex.

So, guess where I am.

I leaned back.

Dunno.

Where are you?

I thought that an odd question.

Sitting on a toilet?

What?

What in the world did she mean? What was the point of all this, anyway?

Alex, what's up?

You didn't tell me!

I frowned, worrying a sliver of paint from the peeling wall beside me.

What didn't I tell you, exactly?

You're at the beach. With Maverick. Alone.

I guessed I hadn't told her. *Oops.*

Oh…yeah. Sorry, Alex. It all happened really quickly.

I mean, I guess it's fine. I just would have liked to know. That's kinda big.

Yeah…it is. Well, how did you find out?

Her thought bubble appeared but disappeared seconds later. I sighed, discarding the phone on the countertop to rummage through my bag. I stripped, listening to Maverick move in the other room. He mumbled, singing under his breath — or maybe talking. I smiled as I changed, and finally my phone dinged. I glanced at the text and sighed. *Well*, I thought, *this is going to be something.*

* * * *

"So, Alex is coming too?"

He twisted to look at me. "Yeah," he said, laughing under his breath. I watched the line of his jaw and wrapped my fingers around his wrist. We stood in the water, staring toward the vast nowhere that was the gulf.

"Why didn't you tell me?"

He kissed my cheek. "'Cause…"

"That isn't an answer, Maverick." I sighed.

He grinned and tugged me closer. "Don't be mad," he said, an inch from my lips.

I cut my gaze away from him, trying to stay angry, but every fiber of my being just wanted to kiss him. *God*, I thought, *this isn't fair*.

"You're pretty when you're mad." He dragged a thumb across my chin.

"You're crazy," I responded.

He just smothered me in a kiss. I looped my arms around his neck on instinct, and he grumbled a sound in his throat. The surf bit our legs, and he brought up his hands to hold my face. "You know what, Emma?"

I stared at him, the stubble on his chin, the intense tease of his gaze. "What?"

He dipped down to kiss me again, once, the slow and steady kind of kiss that I swear I could feel in my toes. Then he pulled back to look at me, all wide-eyed and mysterious. "I think I love you."

The bottom fell from my stomach, and I stared then opened my mouth to speak, but he shook his head. "Don't," he said. His voice was raw, almost quiet.

I frowned. "What? Why?"

He shrugged, dragging his hands down my arms to hold my hands instead. "Because I love you…and that's enough for now."

Chapter Thirty-Five

We stumbled away from the beach, laughing uncontrollably, but I stopped short, hearing voices. "It's not that bad, right?"

He kissed my head. "It's not *bad* at all. Come on."

"Okay," I said.

He wrapped his arms around my waist in a single, swift hug, then swung the back door open. "Mom, hi!"

Mrs. English was reclined on the couch in the living room. Her capri-clad legs were kicked up on the coffee table, and she was reading a magazine. She glanced up with a smile.

"Hey," she greeted, "come on in."

Maverick released my hand to hug her. "We didn't hear the car. Y'all been here long?"

"No," his mom said. She shook her head, plopping the magazine on the coffee table. "The girls are just getting settled in."

Feeling distinctly like a puppy dog, I followed after him to lean against the wall across from them, feeling awkward. "Mrs. English! How was the drive?"

"It was great." She nudged Maverick's side and scooted farther to the center of the couch. She patted the empty cushion. "You know that Alex of yours can really sing."

"Yeah," I replied, giggling at the wording. *My Alex.* Then, I walked around the coffee table to sit beside her.

"Emma, don't worry," she said. "I don't bite."

"I promise. Eighteen years I've lived with her and not one bite," Maverick offered.

"Yeah, sorry. Y'all been having fun?" his mom inquired.

"It's been great. This is such a nice place," I told her, and I meant it sincerely.

She grinned. "Thanks. We love it." She glanced over at Maverick. "Did you tell her about the house?"

Maverick's gaze darted to the floorboards and he shook his head. "No," he said and backed to the door. "I'm gonna go say hi to Kate."

He scuttled to the back of the house and I frowned. "Is he okay?"

His mom watched him go. "Yeah, he'll be fine."

I swallowed and forced a smile. "So, what is it about this house?"

"It belonged to my husband," she told me.

Oh, I thought. Suddenly, Maverick's reaction made a lot of sense. We had been in the seventh grade when Maverick's dad had gotten sick. A year later, he'd passed away, and Maverick had missed a week and a half of school. "Maverick's dad?"

"Yeah," she said. "See…David, Maverick's dad, was raised in a tiny town in the Delta. When he graduated college, though, he packed his bags and came down here, looking for his muse. He had an art degree and a German Shepherd." She sighed. "Then, he met me."

"That's sweet," I said.

"Yeah," she said quietly.

"How did y'all get the farm then?" I asked her.

"Well, about a year after David and I got married, we found out we were going to have Maverick. David decided he needed a real job." She tucked a strand of hair behind her ear. "We moved and opened the farm, but we never sold this place" — she swallowed — "not even when David died."

A sad silence stretched between us but it wasn't uncomfortable. She shook her head. "I'm sorry," she said and slapped her knees to stand. "I'm a little tired... I'll see you kids later."

My shoulders slumped against the couch, and I watched as she slunk into the master bedroom. *Wow*, I thought and rubbed my temples. Suddenly, the depth of my ever-sullen mystery man increased tenfold.

"Hey," Maverick interjected.

"Hi," I answered in kind, standing. He leaned against the doorway, eyes cast down, and I crossed the room to nudge his jaw. The stubble tickled my palm as he shifted, meeting my gaze. "Are you okay?"

He nodded, soberly. "I'm fine."

"You miss him," I noted.

He pressed his forehead to mine. "Yes," he said.

I dragged my fingers along the rough stubble of his jaw. "It's okay."

He exhaled. "Emma?"

"Yeah?"

"Just kiss me," he said.

"That I can do," I said and kissed him. It was long, sad and slow, and set something in my chest ablaze.

Suddenly, I knew it was true.

I loved him too.

Chapter Thirty-Six

I meandered through the house, listening to the sound of the waves lapping against the shore outside and my best friend's giggle emanating through the walls. I stopped to lean against Kate's doorframe to spy on Thing 1 and Thing 2.

Kate sat cross-legged on the floor in front of a canvas. She wore a white T-shirt and gray shorts and her hair was already braided. Alex leaned over the bed, rummaging through her bag. She wore a white sundress with her hair tied back.

I coughed, announcing my presence, and Kate waved at me. "Emma," she said, "Hi!"

At that, Alex hopped up, spun and thrust her arms around my neck. "Did you hear us?"

"Actually, I did," I teased. "Y'all are loud

She pulled back, appraising my appearance. "How are you?"

"I'm good," I said. "Wanna take a walk?"

Kate lunged over, knocking the red Solo cup of paint brushes onto the ground. She groaned, giggling and collapsing to collect them. "You two go on," she said. "Talk. I wanna get a little painting done."

"Okay," Alex said, scooping a paint palette from the desk and handing it to Kate.

Kate giggled. "That could have been a massacre," she said, opening it.

"See you in a bit," Alex said, a dreamy smile poised on her lips as she shuffled back into her flip-flops. "Let's go."

In the white-walled hallway, I told her, "Did you know that Kate gets her love of painting from her dad?"

"Oh?"

"Yeah," I shared. "He had an art degree."

"Huh," Alex mused. "I never knew that. Kate doesn't talk about him much."

We lapsed into a muted silence, and I heard Maverick moving around in the kitchen. He shuffled and the coffee maker bubbled. I blinked, stepping through the living room and onto the patio. We shucked our shoes and stepped into the hot sand.

"So," she said, "how's the secret vacation going?"

"I didn't mean to not tell you," I explained.

"I know," she replied. She walked a pace ahead of me, a pinched smile on her rosy cheeks. "I just like to hear about the small things, ya know? Like, for example, impromptu sleepovers by way of romantic getaways."

Instantly, an incoherent fire filled my veins, and I stilled on the sand. I stared at my toes, the little half-chipped daisy I had painted on my toenail a few nights before, and I grappled with myself and the monster growing in my chest. I wanted to scream at her. She had completely hidden her relationship from me for well over a year. Who was she to even tease me about secret-keeping?

I swallowed the venom, though, because we were past it — and even if we hadn't been, it wasn't the same. Finally, I huffed a breath and leveled my gaze with hers. "I know," I admitted.

Alex barked a laugh. She stood in the center of the sand, and her skirt danced in slow motion like an old black and white movie. "I know, I know," she said. "But you've got to give me something."

"It's just been so..." I trailed off, unable to qualify the emotions or compartmentalize the moments enough to share them. The past few days had been so much, such an overwhelming cannon of feelings. Recounting them appeared to be fundamentally impossible. I mean, there was no way to bottle the butterflies rampant in my stomach and show them to my best friend.

An exasperated sound lurched from Alex's throat, interrupting the spiraling narrative in my head, and I met her gaze seriously. "Emma," she groaned out, "come on. You aren't saying anything. Did something happen? Do I need to kill him?"

Suddenly shocked by the turn in the conversation, I turned to her once again. Incomprehension toiled in my gaze for a moment, and seconds later, the moment shattered. "Oh, gosh, no, Alex. No. No."

"Okay," she said. "Now, please. Say *something*."

"Don't get me wrong," I said, hedging a hand through my hair. Suddenly, the relationship felt like just that. We weren't playing around, not anymore, and the future loomed, an iceberg on the horizon. "It's been so good."

"Okay," she said. "I need for you to give me more."

I sighed, exasperated. "I don't know what's wrong with me."

"I do," she stated flatly.

I frowned. "What?"

She crossed the sand to wrap her arms around my shoulders. "Graduation," she said simply, and I released a breath I hadn't known I'd been holding.

Yep, I thought, *that's it.*

I tugged from her grasp and crept to the surf. I stared, inhaling, as the cool, sharp bite of water lapped at my toes. "Do you ever think about just leaving?"

Alex sifted through the sand to reach my side. "Huh?"

I twisted my gaze from our toes in the water to the endless horizon of the Gulf of Mexico. "Right now," I said. "We could hop on a boat and just sail away from all of it."

A fond, tired smile slipped onto Alex's face, and she linked our hands. "That wouldn't make graduation go away," she said softly. Her voice sounded like the waves, and I grappled to remember a time she wasn't my saving grace, but I couldn't. No, she was always there, holding me up, and I was always there holding her up—for another six months, anyway. Big tears of frustration peaked in my gaze, and she shoved them away yet again with a joke.

"I mean," she hedged, "even if we skipped for the rest of the semester, we would probably still get our diplomas in the mail."

I closed my eyes, listening to the croak of birds overhead mixing with distant laughter from the house. That was Maverick, I knew. I would recognize that sound anywhere. I rubbed the back of my neck and finally looked at her. "He told me he loves me."

Alex's hazel eyes turned saucer-like, and she caught my arm. "What did *you* say?"

"I didn't say anything," I replied.

She frowned. "Emma," she began, but I held up my hand in defense.

"Don't start," I said. "He told me I wasn't ready."

"Are you?"

I shrugged, leaning my head against her shoulder. "No."

"Then it's okay," she said. "He understands."

A bite of silence echoed around us, and I stared at the rolling waves. A boat crested ing my line of vision, and I blinked, thinking of home and what would happen when I left.

Chapter Thirty-Seven

The house smelled of coffee and cookies, and I inhaled the captivating scent like heroin. Alex, at my side, dashed toward the kitchen, a white blur.

"Slow down," I teased, but she was already gone.

Instead, a strong set of arms engulfed me. "Good talk?" The words were a breath against my hair and heat rose to my cheeks.

"Yeah," I said. "Really good."

"So," he mused, kissing the back of my neck once, "this was a good surprise?"

"Yeah," I replied. "It's good having her here."

"I thought so," he said.

I twisted and took his hand. "Who's making cookies?"

He chuckled. "That would be Mom."

I smirked. "What's funny?"

"It's not so funny." He rubbed my shoulders.

"Well," I said, "what is it?"

"She bakes to take her mind off Dad." He sighed and kissed my forehead.

"I'm sorry," I said.

"Don't be," he told me. "Come on. It smells like snickerdoodles."

I skimmed my fingers down his arm to take his hand. "Yeah, it sure does." I followed him down the hall and into the kitchen. As I rounded the corner, I called, "Something smells good."

Mrs. English was leaning over the kitchen counter, stacking cookies on a platter. She wore a red apron over her jeans and glanced up with a nervous smile. "Hey," she said. "Chocolate chips and snickerdoodles."

Maverick grinned. "They smell great, Mom." He snatched one from the cooling rack and dropped it immediately.

"They're hot," she warned.

He blew on his fingers, chuckling to himself. "Yes," he said, "I see that."

Mrs. English spun, placing the platter of cookies on the kitchen table. "So..." she said as she turned to appraise us, "what have y'all been up to this weekend?"

"Swimming, mostly," I interjected . I knew exactly what she was implying, and my cheeks burned.

Maverick shook his head, slinking an arm around my waist. "Well, the first night we watched an old VHS tape and ate down the beach. You know, at the — "

"Crab Shack. Yes, go on," his mom finished.

"Of course, the Crab Shack." He shook his head. "Then we went shopping for actual groceries."

She faked surprise. "Are you, Maverick Andrew English, cooking?"

"It isn't that uncommon," he said to me.

She smirked. "Pretty uncommon," she said. "I'm just proud that poor Emma doesn't have food poisoning."

"I'm beginning to think this was a bad idea," he said, obviously joking.

* * * *

"Oh, gosh, Maverick, please stop with the accent," I begged, giggling over a counter full of taco bar fixings. The kitchen smelled of spices and warmth, and Maverick was browning the meat and butchering a Spanish accent.

He grabbed a plate, shaking his head and scooping a heap of cheese into his taco shell. "But why?"

I shrugged, unscrewing the cap on my water bottle to take a sip. "It's just...really terrible."

He groaned. "That hurts," he said.

Alex barked a laugh and shook her head. "Maverick. *Habla español*?" Spanish rolled off her tongue, easy and smart, and Maverick looked over at her, puzzled.

"What?" he asked through a bite of his taco.

"*Qué?*" Alex asked.

"*Lo siento*, Alex. Maverick *no habla español*." I stated the obvious.

Maverick looked between us. "What is happening?"

Kate shook her head. "Maverick, did you even go to Mr. Montez's class?"

Maverick looked from his mom to Kate and back. "Of course, I did," he said.

His mom shook his head. "Maverick, really," she said, "you've got to go to class. You're smart. Act like it." She gestured to the three of us. "These three could plot your death in Spanish and you would have no idea."

He nodded. "You have a point."

"The tacos are good, though," I told him.

"I know," he said. "Tacos, I can do. Spanish, not so much."

Kate faked disgust. "Y'all are painful to watch."

Maverick beamed, shoving an arm around my shoulders. "We try."

Alex swished her water around her mouth, shaking her head. "Okay, okay," she said. "I took a look in the front closet."

Maverick gasped. "Oh no."

"What?"

"Nothing," he said. "I was gonna make a joke."

"You're really outnumbered, aren't you, Maverick?"

His gaze pierced my focus, and he kissed my nose. "Yes," he said, "I really am."

Shaking her head, his mom swiveled to look at Alex. "What were you saying before my son decided he was going to try to be funny?"

Alex giggled. "Anyone in for a game night?"

Chapter Thirty-Eight

Hours of Boggle and Uno later, I leaned against Maverick's headboard. Just down the hallway, water pounded against tile as Maverick took his shower. Mrs. English had turned in after the third round of Uno, and I had waited with Alex and Kate, but Kate had taken to painting Alex, so I'd decided to give them a little privacy.

I shifted in bed, snuggling into Maverick's covers and listening to the pitter-patter of the water from the bathroom. I scanned the room, noting the traces of Maverick.

The room smelled of aftershave and salt, and his sheets were navy-blue reminders. Idly, I wondered how many other girls had occupied this room, but I shoved the thought away. There was no need to open that particular can of worms.

Instead, I kicked my legs off the side of the bed and crossed the room to study the pictures on his dresser. Maverick stared back at me—younger, more innocent, and smiling at the camera. He stood in the surf with his mom and sister and…his dad, who wore a striped button-down and shorts. He had pensive dark eyes and tan skin. He beamed, framing his little family like an arch.

I flushed, picked the photo up from the dresser and walked back to the bed. I slumped onto the edge and stared at the little family. They had been so happy, I realized, and carefully placed the frame on his nightstand.

I ached for him and his mom and sister.

Settling back into bed, I swallowed a breath and nudged an old yearbook from his nightstand. The book was thin, from middle school — seventh grade, I thought — and I swallowed awkwardly. I wondered why it was here.

I opened the book, smiling at the black and white inserts. I skimmed my fingers along signatures — long, detailed scribbles in messy thirteen-year-old scrawl.

A pinch of sadness crept through my chest as I remembered those signing days. I'd hid on the sidelines and, instead of asking my peers for signatures, my teachers had offered to sign. Now, this year, finally I would venture for actual signatures. I had made friends, and I felt something for someone, but it would shudder to a crashing halt in an increasingly few number of days crossed off the calendar.

I flipped past the signatures to skim the glossy pages. The pictures made my head spin. Faces slipped by in real time, and I stumbled upon a picture I had forgotten existed — Maverick and me at the middle school Homecoming Dance.

I wore a lacey red dress and my hair was bushy. He wore a tie and mismatched socks. In the picture, I was blushing. We hadn't even gone together, I remembered. One of the teachers had caught us at the punch bowl and shoved our heads together. *Diverse pictures and all that*, I thought.

Dragging my fingers along the photograph, big, warm tears welled in the corners of my eyes. A black Sharpie-stenciled heart throbbed around the picture, looping around our heads, and making mine spin.

"Whatcha looking at?" Cheeks hot, I looked up to see Maverick standing in the doorway. He stood under the door frame—his hair dripping and with a towel tucked around his waist—and my mouth went dry.

"Just this yearbook," I said, lifting the book to show him the cover. Without thinking, I pointed to the page in front of me. "I forgot this picture had been taken."

He crossed the room to peer over my shoulder. "Oh, yeah," he said. "That's a good one."

A slow, creeping smile snuck onto my face. "There's a heart around it," I noted.

He laughed under his breath. "Katie did that," he said, nudging my face with his forefinger. "I think the little smartass already knew I had a thing for you."

"Well," I said, "okay…"

He leaned down and kissed me once. "What?" he mumbled. "Did you not know?"

I shook my head. "No, I didn't."

"Well," he confessed, "it's true."

"Oh," I said. Speechless… That's what I was.

He walked over to the dresser to grab a pair of pajama pants. "Sorry. I forgot these."

I swallowed, averting my eyes and flipping through the book instead. "No problem."

Seconds later, the bed shifted and he nudged me to the side and slipped an arm around my shoulders. "Are you okay?"

I snapped the book closed and plopped it on the bed beside me. "It's a little weird, isn't it?"

He chuckled. "What is?"

"I don't know," I said. "Your mom is here."

He pressed a kiss to my cheek. "And we're gonna sleep," he said. "Goodnight, Emma."

"Night, Maverick."

Chapter Thirty-Nine

Mrs. English snapped her wristlet closed and sighed, clapping her hands together. "All right," she said. On our last night on the coast, Mrs. English decided she would venture into town to visit her brother, the notorious owner of the ice-skating rink, so we were left to our own devices. "You kids be good tonight."

I beamed, a rosy shade of not-so-pale. It was just Kate and I seeing her off, since Maverick was in the shower and Alex was still getting dressed. "Of course we will be, Mrs. English."

Maverick's mom tugged a light jacket onto her shoulders. "Emma, dear," she said, releasing her ponytail so that her black tresses fell flawlessly into place, "just call me Abby."

I blinked because, honestly, the idea itself was incomprehensible. "Okay," I said with a choked nod, "Abby."

Kate giggled. "Whoa," she said, "that sounds weird."

I shook my head. "Yeah, Mrs. English, I don't know if I can do it."

Mrs. English smiled. "You're too polite for your own good," she joked. "I'll see y'all later. Have fun."

Kate grinned. "We will. You be good too."

Mrs. English laughed. "You're funny."

"Sorry, Mom," she said, plopping onto the couch. "Have a good time with Uncle Tucker."

Mrs. English waved and headed outside. The door thumped closed behind her, and I slid into the armchair across from Kate, happily uncertain of our evening plans.

"Mom likes you," Kate noted in a matter-of-fact tone that made my stomach clench with the recognition of it. She fiddled with a loose thread on the threadbare blanket.

I giggled awkwardly. "That's, erm…good."

A slow grin crept to her lips. "You're good for him."

"Oh," I said, swallowing. "I'm just…me."

"Well, turns out that 'just you' is pretty good for him."

We lapsed into a guarded silence, and I kicked my legs over the arm of the chair. My stomach knotted artfully into a web of butterflies, and I hugged the pillow like it was my lifeline. Since we'd arrived on the coast, my emotions had been in hyper drive, constantly overwhelming me and sending me into fits of unadulterated something…those three words I'd not said constantly hanging in the balance.

"Silence," Maverick interjected, hustling into the room wearing jeans and a flannel shirt. "What's up?"

Kate tightened the blanket that was around her shoulders. "Nothing much," she said. "That's an interesting outfit for spring break."

He methodically dragging his hands along my shoulders. "It's supposed to be cool tonight," he said.

I twisted to kiss him once, unable to keep the silent smile from my lips. "Where are we going, anyway?"

"One of my buddies is having a bonfire," he said. "I thought it would be a nice finale."

A spark dashed up my spine. *Yeah*, I thought, *sounds perfect.* "Awesome."

"Yeah," Kate said, "what time does it start?"

Maverick shoved up the sleeve on his flannel to glance at his watch. "In about an hour, why?"

"No reason," she announced almost immediately, but I was realizing she was kind of like me. Kate, well…she wasn't that great a liar. Her voice pinched, her cheeks flushed and her eyes trained on something well away from Maverick's prying gaze, she continued, "Alex and I," she noted, tossing her legs over the side of the couch for a quick escape, "just have to get ready." With that, she rushed from the room.

"Howdy," he said with a fake drawl that sent a chill down my spine. He ducked to kiss me, and the butterflies' assault overpowered me once again. "How do you feel?"

"I feel good," I said. "How do you feel?"

"I'm good." He glanced toward where his sister had disappeared and chuckled awkwardly. "Wanna take a last walk on the beach?"

I jerked off my flip-flops. "Yeah," I said, "let's go."

"Okay," he agreed, taking one of my hands and shucking his own shoes, "let's go."

Seconds later, we tumbled into the sand. My bare feet sank in and I shuddered as a laugh burst through my chest.

"It's a little chilly out here," he said, walking a few paces ahead of me.

The cool breeze danced in my hair, and I flushed against its bite. "Yeah, it's nice."

"True," he said, kissing my hand and releasing it to walk down the beach. "I'm going to grab a jacket for you before we leave. It'll get colder when it gets dark."

"All right," I said. "I'll just raid your closet."

He wrapped his arms around my waist. "I know. I have the greatest sense of fashion."

I pressed my face to his shoulder, inhaling the delicious scent of his body wash. "Maybe it isn't your fashion sense I like."

He kissed my head. "Hm-m," he said. "Maybe I like you too." His words from the other day echoed in my ears, and my cheeks burned.

"Maverick," I whined, looping my arms around his neck.

He kissed me once. "Oops," he said. "That wasn't nice."

"I'm sorry."

He shook his head and kissed the hollow of my cheek. "There's no need to be."

I leaned against him, listening to the hum of the water in my ears. *It's so perfect*, I thought. Mouth dry, I leaned up on my tiptoes and kissed him. My skin tingled, and I sighed against his lips. "Maverick..." I breathed.

He sighed. "What's wrong?"

I leaned my head against his shoulder. "Nothing. I love this."

"That's a start," he said, hugging me tighter to his chest.

I sighed. "I guess."

He released me, skimming a hand down my arm to take mine, and we walked, hands swinging between us. He spun me around like the rejected ballerina I was, and he kissed my cheek. "You're beautiful."

"I'm just me," I said quietly, uncomprehending. I would never understand why someone like him had chosen someone like me.

He caught my wrist again, swinging to wrap me in a tight hug. "Well," he said, "I love *just* you." Mid-dance, he dipped me. My blood boiled in my veins, and I pressed my hands to his face with the kind of kiss that lights fireworks and ignites —

"Hey!" Kate shattered the illusion, and I lost my balance, crashing to the sand in a fit of uncomfortable laughter. "Whoa, lovebirds. It's time to go."

Maverick groaned, scooping me from the ground. "Time to go, then," he said. "You okay?"

"A tad mortified that Kate witnessed that, but…"

"Well," he said, tossing an arm around my shoulders. "that was some kiss."

"Don't flatter yourself."

He smirked. "The fall was pretty graceful, too."

"Will there be food at this bonfire?"

"Last time I went, there were hot dogs and s'mores," he noted. "That was probably six years ago."

"Then this information is outdated and useless to me," I teased.

"I'm sure there will still be food," he said. "Come on." He shuffled past his sister.

"I thought we needed to go," Kate noted.

"Yes," he said, "but Emma needs a jacket."

Kate looked between us but she didn't argue as we maneuvered our way through the back of the house. Instead, she whispered with Alex as Maverick's door slid closed behind me.

"Hey," he said, "what'd ya do that for?"

I shrugged, slinking my arms around his neck once again. "I don't know. Care to finish that kiss?"

"Oh?"

Insecurities blossomed in my chest. "I mean," I hedged, but he cut me off with a kiss.

"Don't second guess yourself," he told me.

So I didn't.

Chapter Forty

The party, scarcely occupied but welcoming, peaked at the edge of a farm. The fire, built into a huge fire pit, roasted the chilled mid-March cold snap, and pallets had been disguised as furniture. Fairy lights, so popular nowadays, draped across every surface, and the local teenagers buzzed around the fire.

Maverick and I sat on a picnic table, him on the seat, and me on the tabletop with my legs flanking his sides. It was warmer that way, I convinced myself, but really, I just liked being close to him. His hair smelled like musk, like him, and I loved every bit of it.

Love, love, love. I chanted the word. My heart flipped in my chest, and I kissed his hair.

He frowned. "Are you okay?"

I hugged him tighter. No answer seemed quite right.

"That isn't an answer," he said.

I nodded, squeezing his neck. "I'm all right."

"You're thinking pretty hard," he mumbled.

I shrugged. "I'm good."

"I'm good too," he said, chuckling.

"Really good?"

"God, you're a nerd."

I swatted his shoulder playfully and sighed. "This week has been perfect."

"It's sad that it has to end," he said.

"That's true," I mumbled, closing my eyes.

The fire warmed my already-flushed skin, and I unfolded myself from him to pull off the flannel shirt. I tied it around my waist and climbed from my perch. Grabbing a marshmallow from the wicker basket at the end of the table, I grinned at him. "Hey," I said, "wanna get out of here?"

He gestured to Alex and Kate across the fire. "What about those two?"

"I doubt they'll go far."

Shaking his head, he gripped my hand in his. "Okay."

We walked a few paces away from the fire, just beyond the tree line, and I stopped, leaning against one. I watched him walk, the simple gesture of his feet on the mucky dirt. "Why do you think they come out here? Can't you do a fire on the beach?"

"Probably," he said, dragging his hand along the bark of a tree. "Maybe they get sick of it, ya know? Living here and all."

"Somehow, I doubt that." *How could anyone tire of this?*

"Ya wanna do something fun?"

It was dim. Distant voices laughed, and I placed my other hand on his waist. "What's that?"

He rummaged in his pocket and I held my breath, not sure what was going to happen. Seconds later, he pulled out his keys. "Let's carve our initials into this tree."

I fingered the bark thoughtfully, trying desperately not to giggle. "Like kids?"

"Just like kids."

I fumbled, dragging my hand from his hair to his face and kissing him. Cool air blustered against my cheeks, but nevertheless, I was toasty. "Okay," I said, my heart heavy. *God*, I thought, *how in the hell am I going to leave him in August?*

He knelt, key in hand, and carved our initials into the bark at the base of the tree. Then, he stood and took my face into his hands. I was on fire, I was sure, despite the cold. He kissed me, and I knew he felt it. His hands were strong and rough, and I leaned into him without remorse.

Damn, I thought.

I love him.

Chapter Forty-One

Trees soared by the window, and Maverick drove five miles per hour over the speed limit but still held my hand. The roar of his engine sated something deep in my chest, and I sipped a chocolate-chip milkshake as I watched his steady hand on the wheel. "I'm not ready to go home," I said.

"And you didn't want to come."

"I never said that."

"You weren't thrilled," he reminded me.

"I don't like surprises." I rolled down my window, leaning forward so that my hair flew back in the wind.

"It was a good surprise, though." He put both of his hands on the wheel, flexing his arms.

I leaned my head against the headrest. Eyes on the faded green, I twisted my mossy brown locks into a messy braid. "We have to present the play next Friday," I said.

"Of course," he said, shaking his head. "I guess we should rehearse."

I grabbed my phone from the unoccupied cup holder. I opened the document, glad I had saved it there. "You'll be John?"

He barked a laugh. "You have it on your phone?"

I giggled. "Are you surprised?"

"Okay," he said, "I'll be John if you'll be Jane."

I shook my head. "Damn."

He smirked. "That was kinda hot."

"Oh," I replied. "Really?"

He shook his head. "Anyway," he said. "Go on."

I shrugged. "I was just gonna say that we could have thought of better names."

"I dunno about that," he said. "They're thoughtfully bland."

"Well," I said, "I don't know how I feel about it."

He glanced over. "Wanna change them?"

"I didn't mean about the names," I said. "I meant about me being Jane. I'm not a performer."

He returned his gaze to the road. "Oh," he said. "You wanna be behind that pen all your life?"

I frowned. "Maybe."

He smirked. "I don't believe that."

I took a drag from my milkshake and studied his expression while he drove. His hard gaze made my cheeks flare. I sighed, leaning against his shoulder. "Maybe I don't believe that either."

* * * *

"Hey," Alex said. We sat at home, poised over our homework, pretending to be productive. Really, it had been a lot of ogling and giggling over our beach trip. Now she had her calendar open on her lap. The book was nearly empty. Alex wasn't exactly a planner. "What are you doing May nineteenth?"

I grabbed my calendar from my desk, flipping to the page. "Nothing on paper."

"Good," she said. "Then you're free."

"Pretty much." I paused. "Why do you ask?"

"We're having a graduation party." She scribbled it down then started to hand me her pen. "Mark it."

I shook my head. "Sure, but not with that. I have the one I need."

"Oh, sorry," she said. "I forgot about the color system."

I plucked a blue pen from my desk drawer. "What time is this party?"

"Seven," she said.

I jotted down her words. "Okay, it's down."

"Now, text Maverick. Invite him." She handed me my phone.

"Yes, ma'am," I said, shooting him a text. "Now what?"

She looked a little vacant, like she had no clue. "We'll figure that out when we come to it."

"We will?"

"Yes." She smiled softly. "Can you believe it, Emma?"

I frowned. "What?"

"We're about to finish high school," she said. "Doesn't it seem like just yesterday?"

I bit my thumbnail. "Yeah."

She sighed. "I can't believe we're going to graduate." She stared at the calendar, at the big red circle on graduation day. She paused, faltering for a moment before she continued. "I can't believe we're going to separate schools."

Yeah, the decision had been made. I was going to Rhode Island and she to New York. I knocked her shoulder. "It's just a two-hour drive."

She reached over to hug me. "It's still far."

I sighed. "Not as far as home."

She pulled back to look at me. "You love him, don't you?"

I closed my eyes, rubbing them with the back of my hand. "Do you love her?"

"You didn't answer my question," she reminded me.

"Yes," I said. I exhaled then tucked the pen behind my ear. "I love him."

"You should tell him."

"I know," I said. "I just don't know how."

"Open mouth. Say words," she answered.

I groaned, shaking my head. "You know what I mean, Alex."

"I know. I know." She snapped her calendar closed. "Emma, it's only been a week since he told you. Don't be a drama queen."

I plopped facedown onto the bed. "Saying it..." I trailed off, shaking my head into my comforter. "It's hard."

Alex groaned, and the shuffle of her footsteps were hushed across the carpet. The bed shifted under me, and she shoved my shoulder gently. "Don't let it be hard."

I sighed. "It *is* hard," I said.

Alex paused for a moment. "Wanna know what Kate told me?"

I twisted to meet her eyes. Her expression was measured, so I nodded awkwardly. "Yeah."

"Okay," she began, leaning against my headboard. She tapped the Home button on her phone, checking the time or the notifications or both, and she sighed. "This isn't official."

I laughed. "Well, yes."

She twisted the hem of her T-shirt, seemingly turning the words over before she spoke. "Kate told me that Maverick... Well, Maverick hasn't never been serious with a girl."

"Define 'serious'?"

"I dunno, Emma. It sounded like... Well, she said he'd told a lot of girls he loved them before, but he never meant it, ya know? She said that he seems so different when he talks about you."

I frowned toward the ground, not knowing anything about anything. "God, I'm horrible."

She sighed. "Emma, what does that even mean? That's not true."

"I'm leaving." I groaned into the pillow.

"Emma," she said, "look at me."

I did. "What?"

"You are not a bad person for falling in love," she said, her eyes suddenly serious. "Actually, it's quite the opposite. Love is a beautiful thing."

I shook my head. "I wish it was that simple," I said.

She exhaled. "Emma, it *is* that simple. You have this thing, and yes, it may have a deadline, but it's great."

"Why couldn't this have happened when we were thirty or after college or something?"

She sighed then said, "Life isn't that easy, Emma."

I pressed my face to the mattress. "I am going to miss you so much."

"Me too," she echoed softly.

I rolled off the bed and walked over to the mirror. "I have to tell him."

"Yeah," she agreed, watching me.

I swiveled to look at her seriously. "How do I do that?"

She shrugged, tossing her legs over the side of the bed and staring at me. "I don't know, Emma," she said. "Don't overthink it. Just tell him how you feel."

I slid into my desk chair and placed my face in my hands. "I love you."

She laughed. "I love you too."

"I mean," I said, "I do love *you* – but I was practicing."

"You can't practice that."

"I just did." I giggled. Something blossomed in my chest and I groaned, frustrated at myself. "Open mouth. Say words. Right?"

"Yeah, yeah," she said, kneeling to grab her backpack from the floor. "Now, all you have to do is open mouth, say words to *him*."

"Yeah," I agreed, and she flashed me a smile.

"I've gotta go," she said. "Thanks for 'studying' with me."

"Any time, NYU."

"Sure, Brown."

We rolled our eyes, and she hustled out of the door.

Alone, I yanked my phone from the desktop to see a text from Maverick.

Party? I'm in.

I blushed and shot him a text.

Can I come over?

He shot back, seconds later.

Sure. Just working on the motorcycle.

I stared at the text and courage welled in my veins.

236

Maybe I could take you up on that ride?

There was a pause. Then…

I'll grab an extra helmet.

Here goes everything, I thought. I adjusted his flannel shirt on my shoulders, two buttons undone. No…one. It smelled like him.

"I love you," I told my reflection, and it stared back.

Go get him, my reflection told me.

So, I did.

Chapter Forty-Two

Windows down, hair in my face, short jeans — I was a whirlwind of young love and heartbreak and every stereotype in the book. I stared at the road in front of me, tumbling toward the English family farm with high stakes — mostly because I didn't know what I was doing. *I should just go back home*, I thought, but I shook it away. Turning back wasn't an option. Not now.

The house came into view and I hit the brakes, slowing down. The sun hung overhead, and I worried my bottom lip. Maverick's truck was parked beside the barn, as always, so I slid in beside it.

"I love you," I repeated, turning the words over in my mind. They sounded brittle and small and wrong, but they were *the words* — the spectacular words that changed everything. Dragging my hands along my steering wheel, I closed my eyes to regulate my breathing. *No stress*, I thought.

There was a knock on the glass and I gasped, swiveling to see Kate on the other side. "Hey," she said when I unrolled the window. "You okay?"

I swallowed. "I'm fine, yeah."

"You look nervous."

"I'm not, okay?"

"Okay," she said, holding two paint-stained hands up in defense. "Have a good date, then."

I opened my door, and she walked over to the truck. I gestured to her. "Where are you going?"

"Going to a movie with Alex."

"Things are good there, then?"

She stared down at Maverick's keys, searching for the right one and unlocking the door. "Things are good enough." She pushed a longer bit of her shaggy bangs behind her ear. "New York is far away."

I studied the uneven dirt path that led to the barn. *Too far*, I thought. Heart in my throat, I said, "So is Rhode Island."

She offered an off-handed grin. "We're really living for the moment, aren't we?"

"That's the positive way to think of it."

She hopped in the driver's seat of Maverick's truck with a shrug. "How else is there to look at it?"

She didn't leave room for a reply. Instead, she closed the door, and I watched dust rise from under the tires, a toxic cloud rising into the crystal-blue spring sky. I shoved away from my car and trudged into the barn. Pacman stuck his head out of the stall, and I rubbed his ears thoughtfully. "Hiya, Pacman."

There was a tinkle of metal against metal, and I diverted my eyes from the horse in front of me to see Maverick. He was toying with one of the bikes, wearing a white T-shirt and jeans that hung low on his hips.

Heat rushed to my face. "Hey," I said.

He twisted to flash me a million-dollar smile, and I returned it, despite myself, launching my arms around his neck. Suddenly, the monster of fear washed away. I held him, a chokehold and hug.

"Good morning," he said, surprised. "How ya doing?"

"I'm good," I said. "How are you?"

"I'm great," he said, kissing my cheek. "I like you in my shirt."

I peered down at the bike. "We aren't riding this one, are we?"

"Of course," he said, shaking his head. Then, "Nah, this thing doesn't move yet. My bike is around the corner."

"Okay," I said, "let's go."

He followed me. "What's with the sudden interest in taking out the bike?"

I watched him scoop a helmet from the ground. "No reason."

He laughed, outstretching the helmet. "I doubt that."

I shoved the helmet over my head. "You only live once."

He tossed a leg over the bike with a smirk. "Did you just YOLO me?"

"No," I said. *In omnia paratus.*"

He grinned and put his helmet on. "Should I know what that means?"

"Probably not," I said. I hopped on the bike with a wink. "It's Latin."

"For?" He revved the engine.

"Ready for anything."

* * * *

Maverick slammed on the brakes behind the barn, chuckling, and I tightened my grip around his waist. I buried my face in the crook of his neck, inhaling the sharp scent of awakened earth as he shut off the engine.

I hopped off the back of the motorcycle and shucked the helmet with a blush. "That was amazing."

"Exactly," he said.

I leaned up on my tiptoes to kiss him. He had to be almost a head taller than me, but it was perfect. He hugged my waist, leaning down to meet me, and I sighed against his lips. It was the kind of sigh that questioned nothing — *pure, unadulterated contentment*, I thought, despite avoidance.

I said, "I could eat."

"Wanna go out or order a pizza?"

I laughed. "Definitely pizza."

"Cool," he replied. He pulled off his helmet and linked his hand with mine.

Confidence blossomed in my chest, and I flashed him a smile as we walked up the steps to his house. With the blossom of spring in Mississippi, the English farm was lit up like the phantom of Christmas — lilac and pastel renderings of possibility.

I twisted in his arms to stand on the porch and survey the fields. "It's beautiful."

"It's home," he said. "*You're* beautiful."

Blood flooded to my cheeks, and I leaned back against him. "I never saw you coming," I mumbled, half under my breath, and he kissed the hollow of my neck.

"Well," he said, "here I am."

"Yeah," I said. I twisted in his arms to press a playful kiss to his lips. "Here you are."

He cupped my chin with one hand. "Here I am."

I twisted in his arms and pressed my lips to the stubble of his cheek. "You'll be the death of me," I mumbled, and he smothered a kiss into my hair.

"No," he said, rubbing my forearms, "just love me."

"Yes," I said. "What do you like on your pizza?"

He shrugged. "Pepperoni and bacon typically."

"Sounds good. Light on the sauce?"

He fished his phone from his pocket. "I'll make the order."

"Thanks."

He unlocked the front door and held it for me before disappearing into the kitchen to make the call. As I stepped into the living room, it struck me that I had only ever been there during the party.

I walked over to the entertainment center and picked up a framed picture of Maverick and Kate. They might have been around seven and four. Maverick wore a Superman cape, and Kate had a tiara.

Unable to stop myself, I laughed as Maverick shuffled into the room. I grasped the picture and extended it to him. "Halloween?"

He barked a chuckle. "God," he said, "I wish."

I giggled and replaced the photo on its shelf. "Are you serious?"

"Yep," he explained. "I wore that cape about a month that summer."

"That must have been cute."

"Oh yeah." He wrapped his arms around my shoulders once again. "Cute's the word."

"It *is* cute," I argued

He dipped to kiss me once. "You haven't had the formal tour, have you?"

I shook my head. "Nope."

"Good." He gestured to the room around us dramatically. "*This* is the living room. Ya know, your basic couch, chair, embarrassing child photographs, TV, the works."

"Very nice," I told him — and I meant it.

He laced his fingers with mine and led me down a small hallway. We hadn't ventured this far into the house at the party. My cheeks heated. He slowed, gesturing to an open door on the right. "That's Kate's room," he said. "Go ahead and peek."

I stuck my head around the corner. Kate's room was cluttered. The desk and floor were piled with books, magazines and CDs. I smiled, imagining Kate there.

Awkwardly, I shifted a step inside. An easel rested in the corner, and on the thick canvas was a single image. It was the watercolor of Alex. She wore a yellow sundress, and she was beaming with her hair pinned back on each side, but the detail astounded me. Kate had everything perfect, down to the dimple on Alex's right cheek but not the left.

"Maverick," I said, "Kate's really good."

"Yeah," he said, "she's amazing."

I squeezed his hand. "They're really happy, aren't they?"

"I think so," he said and sighed. "Come on."

He nudged me from the room, and we idled in the hallway. Across from Kate's room, another door waited, slightly ajar. "Is this your room?"

"Yeah," he said.

I released his hand, crossing the hallway with a curious smirk. "Can I?"

He forced a smile. "Okay."

I twisted the doorknob to cross the threshold. The room was simple. His bed was an unmade mess of black sheets. A red pillow lay half on the floor. A stack of books waited on the bedside table with a half-empty bottle of water.

I skimmed my fingers along the knickknacks on his desk. My cheeks burned. *Is it hot or is it just me?* I spun from the desk to sit on the edge of his bed and normalized my breathing.

He leaned against the doorframe, watching with an even gaze, but after a sober second, he crossed to tower over me. "Hi," he said, taking my face in his hands.

Heart in my throat, I replied, "Hey."

He leaned down and kissed me. "It isn't much," he noted.

"Maverick," I said.

"Is something wrong?"

"No, no, no," I assured him. I scrambled to stand, skimming my hands along his arms to his shoulders and into his hair. I stared, and the words flew from my mouth, a flustered rush flooding from my lips. "Maverick, I love you."

"What?"

Naturally, I laughed. "Maverick, I love you."

He grinned, eyes wide. "I love you," he said. "I love you, too."

Beaming, I tugged his hair once. "Kiss me, then."

"God…" He circled his thumbs along my cheeks and kissed me, a hard reminder. "I love you."

"I. Like. That," I said, punctuating each word with another kiss.

He gripped my waist, and I groaned softly. "I like that too," he said. "Say it again?"

I struggled closer to him. "I love you," I repeated. He rubbed my back, and I hitched a leg around his waist.

"Emma," he said, his voice rough as coals. Red flags flew, and caution racked my heated body—the point of no return vastly approaching. *Gosh*, I thought, *what am I doing*?

"Sorry," I said, desperately attempting to untangle myself from his limbs.

"Emma," he said. Sighing, he grasped my hand to inhibit my escape, "come back."

I avoided his gaze. My skin burned against his, and I fumbled an awkward kiss to his neck. "I'm sorry."

He dragged his hands up my back and cupped my face. "Emma, stop saying you're sorry," he said. He paused, strumming his fingers along my sides. "Do you even know what you're apologizing for?"

I laughed, awkwardly, and shook my head. "No," I admitted.

He placed a hand on my hair. "For being so damn sexy."

I kissed him, listening to the empty house — the hum of the refrigerator, a bird singing outside. We crashed backward with not another thought and were on the road to no return — our hearts beating in tandem, arms intertwined, kissing and giggling and loving one another.

Then the doorbell rang, and the moment shattered.

"Saved by the bell," he mumbled, shaking his head and stilling our movement.

I blushed and untangled myself from him. "I almost forgot I was hungry."

He rolled to the edge of the bed. "I didn't," he said, but I knew exactly what he meant.

Chapter Forty-Three

Mr. Zelner had arranged for our presentations to be in the auditorium. Maverick and I sat side by side in the front row, and Alex sat on my other side. She shot daggers at her partner, a raven-haired cheerleader with about as much ambition as the size of her waist. She wore her uniform and a perky smile, scrolling through her phone instead of paying attention to the star-crossed lovers on the stage.

Maverick nudged his hand into mine. The lovers began an interpretive dance, and Alex physically cringed. She leaned over to whisper in my ear.

"This is terrible," she said.

I slapped her shoulder. "Alex!"

"Come on. There's no excuse for it. I even got Sparkles over here to play ball in a hauntingly tragic poetry reading."

I laughed, shaking my head. The pair onstage ran away from each other, darting around standard set pieces and off stage. Silence. Crickets.

Zelner stood, slow clapping. "All right! Thanks for starting us off, Roger." He coughed. "Bella."

They peeked around the corner, mock-surprised by the applause and taking their swooping bows. Bella's sway skirt threatened to expose her to the entire theater, and Roger fumbled to grab her hand, quickly steering her down the steps without that particular misstep.

I fidgeted in my seat, watching Zelner scrutinize the crowd before him. *Countdown to the next victims*, I thought, and he pointed at a couple of girls in the middle of the auditorium. They groaned, trudging toward the stage. One of them had red hair and the other was a bleached blonde, but they both appeared equally bored.

"This is our short play," the redhead said. "I will be playing the typical soulless redhead, and Zoe here will be my victim." She wore all black, red hair ablaze with stereotype.

Zelner stared at them, wide-eyed and suspicious. "Okay," he said finally. "Let's have it then."

Zoe, the blonde wearing all white, lay on the floor of the stage. "I can't believe it! I knew you were trouble."

The unnamed redhead laughed, mythically, and leaned over the blonde. "Trouble? That's my middle name, little Zoe." She knelt beside the other girl, grinning and stroking her cheek. "What do you think I should do with you?"

Zoe whined pitifully, shaking her head. "Make it stop."

"Make *what* stop?"

"Everything," she said.

I swallowed, feeling Maverick's warm hand in my own. The air in the room sizzled with awkwardness, but no one dared to move. Instead, we all watched in shock. Idly, I glanced at Zelner. He looked like I felt…concerned.

"You've got to say more than that." She pulled a pillowcase from her purse and put it over the blonde's head.

"Kill me," the blonde said, squirming.

"Gladly," the redhead replied. She tightened the pillowcase, and the blonde squirmed before going still.

The auditorium was silent.

The redhead yanked the pillowcase from the blonde's head, and they both popped up.

Silence.

"Okay… I'll see you ladies after class," Mr. Zelner announced. Their shoulders slumped, and they returned to their seats in silence, somehow seemingly surprised by his reaction.

Mr. Zelner was quiet for a moment, rubbing the bridge of his nose in muted frustration. "How about Emma and Maverick?"

Pins and needles tingled my skin, and we nodded, synchronized. We had abbreviated our scene. There was no need to be on stage any longer than necessary. We climbed onto the stage, and Maverick dropped my hand.

I sat on the edge of the stage. My ballet flats dangled, and the blood drained from my face. The lights were hot, and my skin burned in the gray T-shirt dress over jeans. I heard Maverick pace the stage, voice crisp like autumn leaves in spring. "I'm sorry, Jane. I know I shouldn't have done it, but it happened. That doesn't change anything. That doesn't change the way I feel when I'm with you. It makes me want to be better."

I stared at my shoes. Black, simple…just like me. Not built for the stage.

He groaned, and I imagined him running his hands through his hair, just like we'd practiced. "God, Jane," he pleaded, frustration bending his voice like metal, "say something. Anything."

I sighed, climbing from the side of the stage to look at him. We centered ourselves, and I met his gaze. His facial expression translated to thoughts and rushed to my ears. *They aren't here. Look at me.* I swallowed, averting my eyes, back in character.

"I don't know what to say," I proclaimed, turning to stride away from him toward the curtain, but seconds later, I reared around to stare him down once again. "I look at you, I see everything that has happened and I think that maybe we aren't supposed to have that happy ending."

He tilted his head, his eyes fire and molten lava.

I felt sick. It suddenly seemed so real, standing there.

"What does that mean, Jane?"

I sighed, casting my gaze to the ground. "I don't know, John."

There were a few snickers from the crowd reacting to our name choices, but Maverick forged ahead without skipping a beat. He crossed, taking my face in his hands. His eyes were on mine, and my mouth was dry. "You won't get off that easy. You can't just say that, not when I love you more than anything that has happened."

I twisted away from him, but he held my hand steadfast—a single pressure against my palm. "I think the nature of the human condition is despair," I said, hushed enough that the blonde and the redhead three rows up might not have heard.

Maverick groaned, offhandedly. "Jane, stop talking in riddles," he almost yelled. Frustration showing on his oh-too-handsome face, and he caught himself. He took two long, measured breaths then he continued, his voice softer now. "Jane, you've got to give me something."

I shook my head, real tears bubbling in my eyes. I knew how the words felt, but now I knew joy just as much. "I watch others," I opened, shaking my head and looking at him, pleading. "I feel it myself, sometimes. Underneath all this high-pitched laughter and these tight grins, I see one common denominator." I pressed my face to his shoulder.

"What?"

"There is so much pain," I answered.

He frowned, framing my face with his hands. "But?"

I turned my gaze to him, biting my lip like I knew drove him crazy, and I continued. "Every once in a while, there's a glimmer of something else — something whole and beautiful and bright, like we're driving down the road to nowhere with the windows down, singing like no one in the world will ever hear."

He smiled fondly and pressed a kiss to my forehead. "Don't give up on me," he said.

I sighed, letting him enfold me in a hug. "I love you," I whispered into his chest, not entirely sure if I was in character or not. It was unscripted but loud enough for our baffled classmates to hear.

Real tears wet the front of Maverick's shirt, and I flushed heavily, not wanting anyone to see. I shook my head against him, and they began to clap. Cheeks damp and, I was certain, blood red, I kissed his shoulder and spun to rush backstage. I had been in middle school band — a quiet, unassuming clarinet player of two and a half years — so I knew every way on and off the stage. I veered down the back stairwell and opened a cobweb-covered door, piling into a vacant hallway. For most of the school, I was reminded, it was a normal class period.

I brushed the thought away and hurried into the bathroom to calm down. I sat on a toilet seat, balling tissues to blot mascara from my face. *God*, I thought, *I have too many emotions.*

Unsurprisingly and all too quickly I heard the bathroom door swing open. "Emma," Maverick said, his voice gruff and out of place but concerned, nonetheless.

I sighed, unlatching the stall door and stepping into the yellow-green bathroom light. "Hey, welcome to the girl's bathroom," I said—but I was glad he was there.

He enveloped me in seconds, wiping a stray tear from my cheek. "You really sold that performance. Sure you don't wanna ditch Brown and hit up New York with me?"

"Sorry." I laughed and leaned against him.

"You've gotta stop saying that."

"I love you," I said.

"You deviated from the script," he teased.

I shrugged. "Now that I've said it, it's hard to stop."

He massaged my shoulder. "Damn."

I smirked. "What?"

"Oh, nothing," he said, chuckling under his breath. He kissed my hair, a somber action, and he released my shoulders to take my hand. The bathroom door slammed behind us, and he led me toward the conventional entrance of the auditorium.

"Come on," I said. "What were you going to say?"

He chuckled. "We're just such a cliché."

Without protest, I giggled. "I don't know about that."

Outside the auditorium door, Maverick stilled, jerking me into another hug. "You gonna be okay?" His voice was a breath against my hair.

If I could just hold it together, maybe he wouldn't worry, but no. I had to be a mess.

I stretched to kiss him once. "I'm fine," I said. "I'm good."

He exhaled, propping the auditorium door open. "Let's get back to it, then," he said. "I think Alex and Sparkles were on deck."

I shuffled past him. The auditorium swelled with background noise and readjustments as Alex took the stage with her peppy partner. A hushed silence greeted our presence.

I blushed, forcing a small grin to Mr. Zelner, and slid into place in the middle of the front row. In the dim light, Maverick pressed a kiss to my temple. "It's okay," he said, and I knew it was true.

I would be okay.

Alex pulled a stool to the center of the stage, and Maverick squeezed my shoulders. Suddenly, my smile melted to genuine.

"I love you," I whispered back in the near silence.

On stage, Alex clapped her hands together, flashing me a thumbs up, and she plopped on the stool beside Sparkles.

"Saying 'I love you,'" Alex announced, her voice sharp and provocative in the style of pointed slam poetry, "is never easy."

Maverick's hand slipped into mine.

A couple of people laughed.

I did too.

We would be okay.

That, I realized, I knew for sure.

Chapter Forty-Four

Days flew off the calendar in a whirl of laughter and sharp-edged kisses. The last week of April was Senior Week—a title, more than anything. 'Celebrating Our Seniors' didn't seem very accurate. Actually, the big activity was simply to pick up our caps and gowns at the end of the week. *I guess that's exciting.*

Seniors buzzed through the hallway, running like scattered ants, and Maverick and I waited in the center of the chaos. The line of nearly a hundred people and counting had formed somewhere between the front office and the counselor's suite, and my gaze darted in every direction.

Purple and white robes swung from the counselors to the students, and I stood on my tiptoes, searching the crowd. I shoved my hand into my pocket to text Alex. We had been together at lunch, but somewhere between the surprise orange soda floats and robe distribution, I had lost her.

Maverick nudged my side. "Who're you texting?"

I frowned. "Alex," I said, automatically shooting the text message. "I lost her after lunch."

"Yeah," he said, ruffling his hands through his dark hair. One of his buddies from the track team strutted by in his uniform, and Maverick waved. "Hey, man," he greeted.

"Maverick," he said, "is this your girl?"

"That's my Emma," he said.

The track guy shook my hand. "Good to meet the girl distracting our boy Lightning." He shook his head, glanced at his watch and groaned. "Look at that," he said. "I'm late for practice…again."

Maverick smirked. "Better run then," he said.

The guy walked away, and I quirked an eyebrow at Maverick. "Lightning?"

"Ugh," Maverick said, shaking his head and changing the subject. "Want me to text Kate? Maybe she knows where Alex is."

"Kate should be in class," I told him.

He cut his gaze toward me. "Alex *should be* in line."

I laughed, uncomprehending for half a second. "Oh," I said.

He pulled out his phone and sending his sister a text. "If they're together, though, I doubt they're paying attention to their phones."

"Ew," I said, giggling under my breath.

He smirked. "Oh, hey, don't 'ew' about my sister."

"I'm 'ewing' about my friend, not your sister."

He shook his head. "Oh."

There was a rustle of feet on linoleum and Alex shot into my arms. "Emma, Emma," she chanted and I blushed.

"Yes?" I asked, settling with a giggle.

Alex's face was rosy, smiling, and she bounced on the balls of her feet. "I'm valedictorian."

My eyes widened. "Alex, you beat out Marshall?"

Marshall and Alex had been neck and neck in academics since Alex had spiraled into Nomansville. It was worth noting that Marshall was probably be in love with her — not that she realized that. To the rest of us, it was painfully obvious. He taunted her relentlessly, and hours after Alex had declared herself a New York University Bobcat, he'd snatched the title for himself too. Still, somehow, this valedictorian didn't see what was right in front of her face.

"Yeah," she said, beaming with pride, "I did."

"Great timing, Alex," Maverick said. He shifted and kissed my cheek before sidestepping out of the line. "I've gotta get to practice."

I frowned, grasping his hand in mine. "What about your cap and gown?"

"Don't worry. I'll get everything later." He flashed a grin at Alex. "Congrats, Alex."

"Thanks," she said, still beaming.

I leaned up, kissing him once, there in the hallway. Suddenly, with graduation looming and our deadline a flashing sign in the distance, public displays of affection didn't seem so bad. "I'll see you later?"

He released my hand, jogging away toward the gym.

Alex opened her mouth to speak but closed it again. I frowned. "Alex?"

She sighed. "Emma, is Maverick graduating?"

"What?" The line crawled forward at a slug's pace. "Of course, he is."

She laughed, obviously unbelieving. "I love you, Emma."

"I love you too," I said. I crossed my arms. We were next in line now, and Mr. Zelner waved at us.

He held a clipboard at the end of the table and smirked. "Names," he joked, checking us off his list.

I bit my thumbnail, and Alex dropped her arm from my shoulder. "Your favorite students, Mr. Zelner."

"Maybe," he said, reaching behind himself to rummage through a box of cords.

Mrs. Pannell, the guidance counselor, with gray hair and half-moon glasses, thumbed through the robes and handed one to each of us. Both robes were deep gold. The top ten wore gold. The rest of the school wore either purple or white. That had been easy, simple, and I tucked the robe over my arm. "Thanks," I said.

Mr. Zelner placed a bag of cords in front of each of us. "Congratulations, ladies. You'll be well decorated."

I blushed, taking the bag and signing the form Mrs. Pannell slid in front of me.

"Graduation rehearsal is tomorrow at eleven," she said. "Wear your cap and gown. We're taking a class picture."

"Then yearbook social, right?"

Mrs. Pannell, who had been all business, finally smiled. "Yes, Alex," she said, "then yearbook social."

"Awesome. Thanks, Mrs. Pannell."

We shuffled away from the chaos, arm in arm, carrying our loot to the parking lot. Alex popped her trunk, and we tucked our robes in the back so that we could appraise our bag of cords – a white stole for top ten, a black cord for highest honors and a purple one for honors. We both had a single silver cord for National Honor Society, but Alex had a pink one for theater and I had a yellow for newspaper staff.

Warmth spread through my chest as I stared down at the rainbow of our high school careers. "Well," I said, "there it is."

"What?" Alex asked.

I shrugged, gesturing to the rainbow of memories strewn about the trunk of her car. "High school."

She leaned her head against my shoulder. "We made it."

"Yeah," I said, quietly, "I guess we did."

* * * *

Corralled into the auditorium, Alex and I sat side by side. Mrs. Pannell argued with Mr. Zelner on stage, and Alex frowned over at me. "Where's Maverick?"

I bit the raw inside of my cheek and sighed. He hadn't called the previous night. He hadn't so much as texted. "I don't know," I admitted.

The two on stage finally came to a decision and Mrs. Pannell started reading off the top ten. "Start a line at the back of the auditorium, one to ten. Highest honors stand up. We've got to alphabetize you quickly."

The room buzzed, and Alex and I hurried to the back of the room. Marshall stood between us, number two, and we talked over him, quietly. He leaned against the wall with a defeated sigh. "Alex, wanna swap spots so you can talk to Emma?'

Alex grinned, fiercely. "I think I'll stay here, but feel free to take Emma's place if you're such a gentleman."

He slumped against the wall, and the door to the auditorium opened. I inhaled sharply. It was Maverick in his cap and gown.

"Maverick!" I wrapped my arms around his neck. "I was getting worried."

He pecked my cheek. "Sorry," he said. "I'm always running late."

I kissed him once and he ambled away toward the crowd to join the mass of classmates. The next group joined the line, and Mr. Zelner joined us at the front. "Ladies, ready to walk?"

Marshall coughed. "Mr. Zelner?"

"Oh," he said. "Sorry, Mr. Stevenson."

Alex giggled, holding her shoulders high. *Yes, after four years, she's ready.* Mr. Zelner led the brigade, and we walked in synchronized steps — Alex then Marshall, and I followed after them, casting my gaze over my shoulder toward Maverick as he waited to be sorted. He smiled, waving, but seconds later he was out of sight. Our future was clear, and my heart clenched in my chest.

One foot in front of the other…but not together.

The sun burned my scalp through the cap, but I turned my gaze toward it.

There were blue skies but I had a storm in my heart.

I closed my eyes.

We still have time, I thought.

A whole summer.

God, I thought.

A summer isn't enough.

Nevertheless, I kept walking, my heart in my throat.

Sun, sound, breath — and I inhaled.

It would have to be enough.

Chapter Forty-Five

I slid into place on the cold, stone bench outside the auditorium and flipped open Maverick's yearbook. The glossy pages mocked me. The white pages were flooded with at least a hundred signatures, and I stared at them. *Gosh*, I thought, *so many people love him and he has chosen to love* me.

I flipped to the back of his yearbook, and blood flooded my cheeks. I could say so much to him on these pages.

A hand slid around my chin, and Maverick pecked my cheek. "I'll give you a minute," he said, snagging my yearbook from beside me and disappearing into the crowd.

Alex slid onto the bench beside me, knocking my knees, and smirked. "Whatcha gonna write?"

I truly didn't know, so I answered the best that I could. "There's a lot I could say."

She bopped my knee, a gentle tap. "Don't overthink it."

"Yeah," I said, staring at the blank canvas, "right."

"Okay, Rhode Island. Write a novel in his yearbook." She pulled a pen from behind her ear and poising it on the corner of the page in front of her. "I guarantee he won't forget you, either way."

I exhaled. *Maybe*, I thought, *that's what I'm afraid of...his* not *forgetting me.* I dragged my hand along the white insert and clicked the pen.

"*Maverick*," I wrote big at the left margin, finally putting pen to paper. "*You've made my past four months perfect, and I love you for it. I can't wait to spend the next two making memories with you. I love you so much.*"

"That's shorter than I expected," Alex teased as I signed my name.

I sniggered. "You think so little of me."

"No," she said, "I just know you. You are long-winded."

I shut the book, and she closed the yearbook she'd been signing on the table. "Whose is that?"

She shrugged. "Not really sure," she said.

I smiled. "So, the standard, '*Have a great summer! Love, Alex*'?"

"Exactly."

"So," I said, "what now?"

"Free ice cream," Maverick said, plopping across from me. He was balancing three cups in his arms, along with my yearbook, and extended two of them to us. "Happy Senior Day."

"Thanks," I said as he passed them out. "Is this caramel syrup?"

"Yep," he said. "That okay?"

"Perfect."

Alex dipped her spoon into her ice cream. "You're a good friend."

He chuckled. "I know."

"Good friends bring friends ice cream," I added, and we clinked cups.

He shoveled a spoonful into his mouth. "It's a little late to friend-zone me, Emma," he joked.

"You're hilarious," I shot back.

"I know," he replied. "And I brought the ice cream. So, don't I get a couple of bad jokes?"

"Yes, I guess you do."

Mr. Zelner walked over, a camera dangling from a strap around his neck, and he snapped a picture of us.

Alex groaned. "Mr. Zelner! No candids."

"Okay," he agreed. "How about looking like you like each other." Maverick and I leaned into Alex, holding our ice cream and beaming. With pure, unadulterated joy, I hummed, and Mr. Zelner ate it up.

"That's great." He checked the photo and glanced toward the stairs of the auditorium. "I better take that group shot before half of my seniors run off."

He cupped his mouth with his hands to announce the photo op. "Okay! Can I get all my graduates on the steps?"

There was synchronized laugher, and we hopped off the bench, tumbling toward the stairs. Our class of just shy of three hundred people stacked onto the steps side by side, and Mr. Zelner climbed a ladder. He pointed the camera at us and flashed a winning grin.

"All right, class of 2019," he called. "Say 'Bulldogs'."

There was an outburst of giggling and shaking heads. Inside, I guessed, we were all screaming the same thing. *It's over.*

Mr. Zelner snapped the picture. "All right, disperse. I need the top ten now."

Maverick squeezed my shoulders. "I'll be in the grass with the other peons," he joked, pecking my cheek.

I blushed at the rapid fire of Mr. Zelner's camera. "Okay," I told Maverick.

"See ya in a minute," he said, his voice gruff against my hair.

The crowd dwindled to ten, and Marshall gestured to the vague formation we had assembled. "How do you want us?"

Mr. Zelner shrugged. "I don't know," he said. "Two rows? And come on...smile." There was a twinkle in his dark eyes. "You've made it."

A giggle escaped our collective, and we shuffled into two lines. Alex and I stood front row center, arms thrust around each other's necks like the best friends we were, and I could feel Marshall's stoic gaze behind us. I ignored it—and him.

"Start together, finish together," I said, and we linked hands.

A single squeeze, and we met each other's eyes.

"One," she mouthed.

Mr. Zelner poised to take the picture.

"Two," I mouthed.

I gathered myself.

"Three," we finished together, and we soared. Just as Mr. Zelner snapped the picture, we jumped skyward.

"Ladies," he said, "you blocked Marshall."

Alex grinned. "That was part of the point."

Marshall groaned, placing one hand on each of our shoulders. "Take the picture now, Mr. Zelner, before they get loose."

He snapped another. "I'll send these out after graduation."

"Thanks," I said, dropping Alex's hand.

"All right, y'all have a good weekend." He collapsed the ladder, waved and hustled away with his camera on his shoulder.

The crowd dissipated. "So," Alex said, "any big plans with Maverick this weekend?"

"Maybe," I said. I scanned the crowd, spotting him. He was reclined against the auditorium wall, chuckling as he talked to a lanky guy with red hair.

Alex waved a hand in front of my face. "Earth to Emma," she said.

Heat flooded my cheeks. "Sorry," I said. "What?"

"Any plans? With Maverick?"

"Oh," I said. "I think we're going to have a movie marathon tomorrow night."

Alex smiled slowly. "Where will you do that?"

"I'm not sure," I replied. "Maybe his house, maybe mine."

"That's hard and fast planning."

"I know," I admitted.

"Look at that," she teased. "My little Emma...without details."

I shrugged a shoulder. "I love him."

She smirked. "You don't love me?"

I giggled. "You know what I mean."

"He's changing you," she noted. "And you're changing him."

I blushed. "Is that a good thing?"

"I think so," she answered, rolling on her heels to stare at the puffy white clouds with a thoughtful grin. "You bring something good out of each other."

I looked over heads to watch Maverick. He jogged in place, laughing at something his buddy said and shaking his hands. Hyped, I guessed.

"Hey," I interjected, "have you ever been to a track meet?"

"No," she said, snickering unconsciously, "I can't say I have."

"It's the last one of the year this afternoon," I told her. "Wouldn't it be girlfriendy to go to his last track meet?"

She smirked. "Do you even know what happens at a track meet?"

I thought for a moment. "I don't know," I said. "Running?"

She grinned. "Precisely," she said.

"Right," I replied. "So, ya wanna go?"

"Sure," she said, shaking her head. "But if we're going to a sporting event, we need to go home and change."

I frowned, blinking down at the black T-shirt I had thrown on under my robe. "Why?"

"School spirit, Emma," she said.

"Oh," I said. "Okay, let's go."

"You don't wanna say bye?"

I shrugged. "I'll see him in an hour."

"Okay," she said, "let's go."

* * * *

I thrust my cap and gown over my shoulder as I got out of the car and headed into the house, rushing the clock with a giggle. In the past four years, I had probably been to a grand total of six sporting events, all of which I had been covering for the school paper. Now

I had another reason entirely, and that sent my heart on a whirlwind or spiral, I wasn't sure which.

I stuck my robe in the coat closet and dashed back to my room, almost stumbling past my mom. She laughed, carefully working her earring into her earlobe. "Where's the fire?"

I prepared to be the victim of slight mockery. "Maverick's track meet," I said.

"A *sporting* event?" Mom was incredulous.

"Don't mock," I said. "It's the high school experience."

She smiled skeptically. "It's your boyfriend."

An offhanded blush overtook my cheeks, and I nodded. "Yeah, well..."

"All right, then," she said. "Carry on."

I hustled into my bedroom and jerked my favorite purple and white spirit shirt from the contents of my closet. It sported a proud bulldog and a frilly font, and I knew Alex had the matching shirt in white, so I quickly swapped out the black T-shirt for it.

"So," I called, displacing one fabric for another in one fluid motion, "where are *you* headed?"

Mom rounded the corner to lean against my doorframe. "Nowhere," she joked, playfully shaking her hair.

I giggled. "Off to see Stanley, then?"

Mom winked. "Maybe."

I smirked. "Well, you kids be good."

"I could say the same," she said, straightening her skirt. "Going to a sporting event..."

"Oh," I said, slipping on a pair of white tennis shoes and tying my hair into a loose ponytail, "it isn't *that* weird."

She crossed her arms and leveled her gaze with mine. "For you?"

Unable to keep a straight face, I stared at my shoes. "Yeah," I said, "you're right. It's weird."

* * * *

Track, it turns out, is a low-key sport—no raging crowds, marching bands or cheerleaders. A middle-aged man in black and white held a stopwatch while the teams warmed up, stretching and chuckling among themselves.

Alex and I slid into place on the first row of bleachers, listening to the crickets and the swell of music echoing from the band's graduation rehearsal half a mile away. "Well," I said, "this is track."

Alex grabbed her phone from the pocket of her a-little-too-tight jeans. "Maybe I can harass Kate into leaving the studio."

"Maybe," I said. "Guilt her. I mean, it's her big brother's last game as a high school student."

"It's not a *game*," she reminded me.

"Not the point." I giggled.

"It kind of is," a gruff voice interjected, and Maverick jogged into view. He wore purple shorts and a white T-shirt, and he looked surprised to see us...well, me. "Hey... What're you doing here?"

I launched myself into his arms, feigning interest in the best of ways, and pressed a kiss to his cheek. "I thought you could use a cheerleader," I said.

"I'll take one," he said, winking. "Y'all look cute."

Alex beamed. "Thanks," she said. "I had to convince your girlfriend to have school spirit, but it was worth it."

He grazed his lips along my jaw in a single, pointed movement. "Really?"

"I don't...cheer," I said.

He nudged my shoulder. "Well, I'm glad you're here. If you want, you can come with us to get pizza later."

"Maybe Kate too?" Alex asked.

He faked a cringe. "I dunno," he said. "Little sister might crash my style."

I shoved his side. "She can't... Kate is much cooler than you."

He groaned, throwing a hand over his face in dismay. "That hurts."

"English! Look alive," Stopwatch Man called from the field. He wore a whistle and a disgruntled frown, and I giggled.

"You'd better go," I said.

"See ya after," he promised, pecking my cheek again before jogging off toward the coach.

Alex kicked her feet up on the bleachers and chortled. "You two really are disgustingly cute."

I rubbed my hands together, shrugging slowly. "Thanks?"

"You're welcome," she said, shoving my shoulder. "You're my favorite weirdo."

I peered at the field thoughtfully. "Sports," I said.

She barked a giggle. "I just don't get it."

The boys on the field started running, flying really, and I blinked. *It seems like a pretty strange sport*, I thought, but Maverick's hair flew backward and his grin was relentless. Something in my heart accelerated with each pump of his feet on the ground.

Maverick, I mused, was the only person I would plop on these bleachers for. Yeah, love twisted the pragmatic sensibility of my heart and made it this unstable thing.

Great, I thought.

He flashed me a smile, and I warmed to the idea. Maybe, just maybe, it *was* great.

Chapter Forty-Six

One track meet later, we piled into the local pizzeria, a group of nine and counting. I trailed after Maverick, laughing at the inane jokes coming from his track buddies. It was weird. I realized that this was the first time I had spent any time with his friends.

The redhead, Nick, slung an arm over his girlfriend's shoulders and flashed Maverick and me a grin. "So," he said, sliding into a chair at the head of the table. "Emma, right? I haven't seen you around much."

Maverick chuckled. "Emma's pretty focused."

The girlfriend leaned across the table, pointing thoughtfully. "Oh," she said,"you're in my history class, right?"

"I was." I nodded, suddenly realizing exactly where I had seen her before. She sat in the back corner of our AP US history class, often twiddling her hair and staring idly out of the window.

She sipped her sweet tea then said, "You *were*?"

Internally, I groaned. Her distance and questions flooded back into my memory, and I swallowed the giggle. "Yeah. It's pretty much over now, isn't it?"

"Wow," she said, "you're right."

"Crazy, isn't it?"

"What is?" Alex asked.

Kate sighed, giggling under her breath and pressing her face against the curtain of Alex's hair. "School's over," she answered.

"Oh," the girlfriend's voice tapered off and silence quelled the outright excitement. But moments later the symphony of conversation tumbled to life once again and laughter returned to center stage.

Maverick's hand burned on my knee, and he squeezed once—a gentle reminder, or an apology or both. I didn't care. I was just happy to be with him in that moment...to see him smile.

We ate our pizza, and soon he walked Alex and me to her car. He braced his arms around me and offered me one of those grins that set my heart ablaze. "I had fun tonight," he breathed into my ear.

I flushed and tugged him closer. "Thanks," I said. "I had fun too."

He grazed my cheek with one of his hands. "No, you didn't."

"Hey," I said. "I did have fun."

He kissed me—right there in the middle of the parking lot with his friends cat-calling all the while. "I love you," he said under his breath...a cool, quiet sound that made my toes curl.

"I love you," I echoed.

Kate and Alex made fake gagging noises and Maverick groaned. "Goodnight," he said. "Thanks for coming."

"It was fun," I said. "You're fast."

"I try."

"Big brother," Kate interjected, "it's time to go."

Maverick twisted to flash his sister a smile. "Yes, dear," he said, pecked my cheek once more and opened the car door. "Talk to you later."

I hopped into the front seat. "Goodnight."

"Night," he said, waving and jogging back over to the truck.

The car jolted as Alex closed the door and giggled. "You two," she said. "I can't."

"Just drive," I told her.

She revved the engine. "Okay, okay," she said. "You've gotta admit. Y'all are pretty cute."

I shrugged a shoulder, leaning my forehead against the window to watch Maverick's truck in the rearview mirror. "I guess," I admitted.

She drove, slowly, unfazed by the hour or the glare of headlights. "Are you gazing?"

Blood flooded my cheeks, as common an occurrence for me as breathing. "Maybe," I said.

"You're just the cutest," she said, veering right down our street and leaving Maverick and his truck on the main drag.

We lapsed into a familiar silence, and too soon she cut the engine. I padded into my house. Mom wasn't home. *Probably at work by now*, I thought, and ambled into my bedroom to change clothes.

I caught a glimpse of myself in the mirror as I straightened my soft, gray 'happy cloud' pajama pants, and I giggled. A goofy smile stretched across my flushed cheeks, unconscious and unyielding.

My phone buzzed across the room, and I tumbled to bed and scanned the notification.

What're you wearing?

Listlessly, I shook my head.

Don't text and drive.

Seconds later, he texted back.

I'm not driving.

I snuggled into my blankets.

How are you already home?

A pause, then...

I drive fast.

You're going to get yourself killed.

I love you.

Stop distracting me. I'm trying to be mad at you.

You're not.

I grinned.

You're right.

Still want to have movie night tomorrow?

Duh. My place. Seven?

Sounds perfect. I'll bring the snacks.

I placed my phone facedown on my bedside table. *Yeah*, I thought. *Sounds perfect.*

* * * *

At a quarter to seven, I plopped down on my bed, wearing a pair of faded purple sweats with a worn white tank top. I twisted my hair into a messy bun and grabbed my phone from my nightstand to text my wonderful distraction.

Hurry. I miss you.

Three minutes later my phone vibrated.

I'm outside.

I rolled my eyes.

Then come inside. It's unlocked. Come find me.

I listened to the creak of the door opening and studied a speck of peeling paint on the wall. He moved through the empty house, a shuffle against hard wood, and blood rushed to my bare shoulders. I heard him at the door.

"Come here." I beckoned him over.

He smirked down at me, lingering at the edge of the bed. "You're gorgeous," he said, sliding a hand across my shoulder.

I snorted. "In sweatpants and a tank top?"

"Always," he said.

I shook my head. "Maverick," I whined, "come here."

He chuckled at my insistence and crawled over me. "Hey," he said, dragging his fingers along my jaw. His stubble against my cheek sent my heartbeat reeling, and I wrapped my arms around his neck. "This is movie night?" His probing voice singed my eardrums, and the apples of my cheeks burned.

"It's previews," I said quietly. I wove my fingers into his hair, tugging the dark strands. "Alex says you're good for me."

He laughed at the offhand comment and slid his hands along my bare shoulders. "Kate says you're good for me too," he replied.

I grazed my lips along his neck slowly. "I love you," I said.

"I love you." He peppered kisses along my shoulder, and I gasped against his skin.

Exhaling, I rolled over to cuddle against his chest. "Hold me?"

His heartbeat hammered through his chest. The sound was music to my ears. *Perfection*, I thought, realizing I hadn't felt this safe in a long time.

"Any time," he mumbled, pressing a kiss to my forehead. I shuddered, overcome with emotion, and he dragged his fingers along my shoulders to tug me closer. "What's wrong?"

"I love you." *Do not cry.*

"I know," he said. "I love you too."

I kissed his lips for the first time that night.

"God, Emma."

I frowned, pressing my face to his chest. "Sorry."

He shook his head. "You've got to stop that, baby."

"What?"

"Being so sorry," he said. "You didn't do anything wrong. Kiss me again."

"Okay." Blood rushed to my cheeks, and I rolled on top of him. I kissed him and he grinned.

"Hey," he said, and I pulled back.

"What?"

He shrugged a shoulder, rubbing my sides through the thin fabric of my tank top. "I have a proposition for you."

I smirked, staring down at him. "What kind of proposition?"

He kissed the corner of my mouth. "No more thinking," he said.

"No more thinking? That seems dangerous."

"Oh, let me finish, will you?" He slid his hands carefully underneath my tank top to slowly massage my skin. "No more thinking about August."

I frowned. *God*, I thought, *I wish I could do that.* "Maverick," I began to protest, but he shook his head.

"Come on, Emma," he said. "I want to enjoy this summer with you. I want to travel. I want to love you. I want to not think about the fact that in three months I won't be able to hold you like this."

I frowned and kissed him. "Okay," I said, "we won't think about it."

He smiled tiredly, dragging a hand along my neck to cradle my face. "We'll love each other."

I nuzzled my face against his neck. "Yes," I said, closing my eyes and letting him hold me. "That sounds perfect."

He nodded. "The perfect summer."

Chapter Forty-Seven

Two movies later, we snuggled on the couch. I hummed against his chest and groaned. "I'm hungry," I whined.

"I want pancakes," he countered.

"That can be arranged."

We untangled from one another and stumbled into the kitchen, and I frowned at the clock on the stove. "Damn," I said, under my breath.

He rubbed my sides, a habit, always trying to calm me down, I realized. "What?"

I shrugged, leaning against him. "It's just getting late."

He kissed my shoulder. "Want me to go?"

I shook my head. "No," I said, "I never want that."

He opened the pantry to pull out a pancake mix. "Good."

I grinned. "Wanna make things interesting?" I reached around him to grab a bag of chocolate chips, holding them behind my back.

"Always," he said.

I beamed, tossing him the bag of chocolate chips. "Let's go."

He tugged me closer, and I sighed against his chest. We were magnets, and I leaned back against him. "I love you," he said, his voice ashes against satin.

"I love you," I repeated, pressing a kiss to the apple of his cheek, then to the tiny dimple.

He smiled, rubbing my shoulders. "I probably *should* get home," he said, casting a glance over to the clock. "Rain check on the pancakes?"

I sighed, pressing my face to his shoulder. "Yeah," I said, "I guess."

He hugged me tightly, lifting me an inch from the ground. "Don't make that face."

I kissed him again. "I know. You're right."

Lips against my temple, he hummed. "I'll see you Monday."

"Text me tomorrow?"

"Yep," he said and pulled away. "Come lock the door."

I giggled and trailed after him. *That stupid grin*, I thought as it hung on my face. "Drive safe," I said, and he dipped to kiss me once.

"I'll do my best," he replied with a tempting wink.

"Goodnight."

He backed down the driveway with a grin. "Goodnight, Emma."

My gaze trailed after him until his headlights had disappeared around the corner, and I collapsed against the door facing. "Gosh," I mumbled, "I love you."

I shuffled from the doorway back into the kitchen. I flipped the radio on and replaced the pancake materials in the pantry, humming along with the music. Idly, I grabbed an apple and made a beeline for my room.

Well, I thought. *I'm wide awake. Might as well study.*

I grabbed my laptop and tabbed open my history notes.

Finals were this week, graduation this weekend.

I stared at the Word document and nodded sharply.

Let's go.

* * * *

The remainder of our semester strained in the foreground of my sanity, and I drummed my fingers against the wooden tabletop. The library assistants mumbled behind the counter, suspiciously eyeing the copious few of us who had huddled in the stacks for much needed study sessions.

Much needed, maybe, but my focus darted everywhere but history, the topic of today's torture. The names and dates spewed from my fingertips as I scribbled yet more notes in the margins of my notes — the wars, the leaders, those that fought, blah blah blah. All of it blurred and nothing stuck. Or maybe it had, I thought idly and groaned. *No more.*

I rubbed the back of my neck and grabbed my phone to text Maverick.

Hey.

I placed the phone face down and bit the eraser on my pencil. The phone vibrated on the tabletop.

I shuddered, seeing a single word in reply.

Hiya.

I leaned back against the chair.

You studying?

Seconds later, he sent back a response. I barked a laugh, and the librarian shot me a glare.

Emma, who are you talking to?

Rolling my eyes, I responded with a measured smirk.

Are you busy, then?

Well, I was about to take a run around the gym. Wanna come with me?

Ha.

It's calming!

How about this? I'll come and watch you run.

There was a pause, and I saw his thought bubble blossom.

That sounds good too.

I smiled, slamming my textbooks closed without bothering to yank my notes from the pages.

See ya soon.

I shuffled into the hallway, clutching my history book to my chest, and stopped at my locker to discard it. My heartbeat in my ears, I shoved the gym door open and stepped inside. My footsteps echoed against the floor. From behind, I spied Maverick on the bleachers. He was leaning over, his leg outstretched to lace his tennis shoes.

"Hey," I called.

He grinned, waving me to him.

"How did your trig final go?" I climbed the steps to join him on the bleachers, listening to the croak of the old metal under my feet.

He shrugged. "Pretty well," he said. "As well as trig can go."

"Good?"

He chuckled. "Yep. How are you?"

"I'm all right," I said. "Just been studying for history but I couldn't look at it anymore."

"Lucky me," he said and pecked my lips. "You sure you don't wanna do a lap with me?"

I shook my head. "I'm good, thanks."

He held up his hands in defeat. "All right, all right," he said. He jogged backward, watching me stare at him, but a few seconds later he doubled around to face the track. From the sidelines, I watched the arch of his back and listened to the steady pump of his feet against the linoleum. *He's really mine*, I thought through a thin haze of adrenaline.

Halfway around the building, he slowed to a crawl. "Do you remember our homecoming dance freshman year?"

I blushed. "Yes?"

"Well, I do," he said. He swiveled to run back over to me. He skidded to a stop in front of me and nudged my chin with his fist.

I giggled, skimming my hands along his shoulder. "Oh?"

"Yeah," he said. "Well, I remember I was dancing with Heidi in the center of the mob, making a real ass out of myself, trying to impress her."

I fisted my fingers into his hair and tugged. "Oh, right," I said. "Heidi... That blonde girl you dated, right?"

He grinned, playfully, making fun of himself. "Yeah, that's specific."

True enough, I thought. The parade of scantily clothed girls who had sashayed in front of Maverick had been particularly blonde. Internally, I scanned through the faces, the names. "Heidi was older, right?"

"She was a sophomore," he said.

I crossed my arms. "Older."

"That's not the point," he said, dragging his finger along my hairline.

I shivered at the gentle touch. "Sorry. Your point?"

"The point *is*" — he paused for dramatic effect — "that I remember glancing up just as you walked in, and God, Emma. You had your hair all curled and wore this insane white dress, and suddenly you had legs." He leaned back, rubbing my shoulders. "I remember thinking *'What the hell am I doing?'* and I stopped dancing to watch you toddle in on those little red heels. Damn, that made Heidi mad, but I didn't care. You mesmerized me."

"I remember that, actually," I said. "Heidi *was* so mad."

"Yeah," he said, "she stormed off, and I went to get you a cup of punch, but when I got back, you were gone."

My cheeks warmed and I leaned forward to kiss him. "I didn't know you were looking at me," I said.

"Who would I have been looking at?"

I shrugged. "I don't know," I said. "Anyone else."

He placed a bruising kiss to my lips, shaking his head. "You were so beautiful," he said.

"I had braces and zits, and I didn't even want to be there," I said. "Alex made me go."

"Yeah," he said, strumming my cheek cautiously, "bless Alex for that."

I kissed his shoulder lightly. "I thought you said you had a crush on me in middle school."

"I did," he said, slumping on the bleacher beside me to take my hand in his. "But ya know middle school crushes. They're kinda innocent. I always thought you were cute and smart and whatnot, but when I saw you in that white dress? Damn." He kissed me once, harder than before, and my blood boiled. "You weren't a cute little girl anymore."

My cheeks burned, and I kissed him back. I jerked him closer, and he grinned against my lips. We didn't speak. We lost ourselves in each other, hands on hips and smiling.

Then the bell rang, and it was time for my final.

I pulled back. "I've gotta go."

"Knock 'em dead," he said, his eyes on mine.

I laughed, a sharp, strangled sound in the back of my throat. "Maverick, they're already dead."

He grinned, pulling me in to kiss him again. "God," he said, "I love you so much."

"I'll see you later," I replied, grabbing my bag and hurrying off to my final without another care.

Chapter Forty-Eight

Wheels spun as we flew down the highway, soaring on hope and excitement. With the windows down and the wind in my hair, I leaned out, screaming into the current. Alex danced in the driver's seat, her right foot on the peddle and her right hand in Kate's. Maverick had his arms wrapped around me, and he plastered a kiss to my neck.

Finals are over, I screamed the thought.

"I love you," Maverick whispered in my ear, squeezing my waist.

I twisted to kiss him. The wind whipped in my face through the open window, and I whispered a chant to his lips, "I love you, I love you. I love you."

Shocked by the sudden contact or the assured lilt to my voice, he fell against the seat, and I cemented my face to his chest, laughing uncontrollably. The four of us were giddy, driving fast to nowhere, and for a moment, everything was absolutely perfect. Our summer was stretched out before us, and I kissed the taut skin of his neck. "I love you."

"I love you both, but please…not in my car." Alex made a gagging sound and Kate joined in.

We all giggled, and the sound rang in my ears. It was beautiful, so beautiful, and suddenly I forgot our ticking time bomb. I straightened and Maverick followed. Still, we scooted together, magnetized. His arm around my shoulders, he smiled toward the front seat. "Sorry," he said. "Where are we going anyway?"

Alex peered at us in the rearview window and her eyes sparkled. "Anywhere," she said.

Alex was right. *Time*, I thought, *is our enemy*, but we had taken control of it. I snuggled to Maverick's side, and he rubbed my shoulder.

"Then let's go," I said, and she hit the accelerator, mischief in her bright eyes.

* * * *

I walked solemnly across the stage and stared down at the rest of our class. I saw the tip of Maverick's hat and his sloping shoulders. Caps flew into the air, and Alex reared around Marshall to hug me. "We did it," she said.

"We did it," I agreed wholeheartedly.

The occupants of the bleachers flooded to the field, and we rushed down the stairs of the stage. Seconds later, I flung my arms around Maverick's neck, and he was kissing me.

Mr. Zelner snapped a picture, and Maverick groaned. "Were you a photographer in a former life, Mr. Zelner?"

"We all have hobbies," he said. "I'll send that with the class photo."

Someone tapped my shoulder, and I turned to see Mom.

"I'm so proud of you," she said. "You looked beautiful on that stage." She looked at Maverick. "Can I take your picture? Where did Alex run off to?"

"Of course," he said, coupling for another picture. "I'm sure Alex will turn up. The crowd must have eaten her."

Mom giggled. If I were being honest, Maverick really had charmed her. "True," she said, snapping the picture.

"Look who I found," Alex interjected, gesturing to Kate.

"Alex," she said, "we're taking pictures."

We smiled for the camera, linking arms, high on life and everything else, and Mom suggested we take off the robes. Maverick caught the look. "What was that?"

I shrugged. "Oh, nothing," I said, unzipping my robe. "You'll see."

He followed suit. Under the robe, he wore a white button-up shirt and black slacks. "Okay," he said, "let's have it then."

I shoved the robe from my shoulders, and Mom caught it. His jaw dropped, and I giggled. "I still have it," I said. It was the white dress from freshman homecoming. It was a little shorter now, because I was a little taller. Now, it even fit better in the chest.

Maverick smirked and pulled me to his waist. "We'll talk about this later," he said. He dipped his lips to my cheek, and Mom snapped a picture.

"All right, everyone, smile," she sang. I stood in the middle of Maverick and Alex, and Alex popped a hand on my shoulder. "Kate, wanna hop in this one?"

Kate held up her hands, shaking her head, but Mom insisted. We took several shots like that — silly, serious and every emotion in between. Other students rushed past us, and I leaned against Maverick with ease. My emotions were swirling high.

"Mama, we've got to turn in our robes," I told her. "We'll be right back."

"All right," she said. "Then we're going out to eat. I'll go find your parents, Maverick."

Maverick grasped my hand and we all rushed toward the gym. My heart in my throat, I stepped into the tunnel. Maverick then took his revenge, pinning me to the wall. "You're such a tease," he mumbled, kissing the hollow of my cheek.

Alex and Kate waved, backing down the hallway. "We'll, erm, give you two a minute."

I knitted my fingers in his hair. "I take it you still like this dress?"

"You look gorgeous," he said. He dug his fingers into my waist, his breath hot on my shoulder.

I flushed. "I grew into it," I said, quietly.

"You were beautiful then," he said, chuckling. He massaged my sides, dragging his hands upward slowly. They burned through the silky fabric, and my heart flopped in my chest. "But yes, you're right."

"Maverick," I said, shaking my head, "we have to stop. We have to turn in our robes."

He groaned and released my waist. "I know." He sighed. "Sorry."

"Kissing me isn't something to be sorry for."

He pressed another kiss to my forehead. "Robes," he said. "Cold showers."

I frowned. "What?"

"Nothing," he said. He took my hand, leading me down the tunnel and into the gym. "We've got to turn in our robes, remember?"

"Yes," I said, biting my thumbnail. "I remember. I wasn't sure if you did."

He chuckled. "How could I forget?"

"Maybe when I kiss you?"

"Good thought," he said, pressing a kiss to my temple as we walked into the gym. The room was divided by last name. Seven teachers were stationed at seven tables, and I sighed. *Time to split up*, I thought. "I'll see you in a minute," Maverick said as he turned to leave. He squeezed my hand. "See you."

* * * *

We huddled around a huge table at the pizza place. Most of Nomansville was already closed post-graduation, but the underclassmen had strewn fairy lights around the restaurant and wore taut, tired half-smiles as they served. Their expressions read like a book. *'Well, it's our turn now.'*

Maverick sat beside me in the arch, and Alex grinned on my other side. My mom poked at a salad, peering at Kate. "Kate," she said, "what grade are you in again?"

Kate nibbled the end of her breadstick uneasily. Her hands, I noticed, were permanently stained blue and green. "I guess you would say I'm a sophomore now. Right, Mom?"

Mrs. English sipped her water. "Yes," she said. "These kids are growing up."

"Not a freshman anymore, eh?" Mr. Fisher picked up a slice of pizza. "Alex, how did you and Kate meet again?"

A hush fell over the four of us. I frowned. As forward thinking as Alex had 'wanted' to be, I doubted she'd told her parents. They were front row Southern Baptists and not exactly tolerant.

"Oh," she said. "Remember, Dad? I was at school late, working on a paper, and she was in the art studio. We ran into each other on the way out. I offered her a ride."

The safe story, I noted. It wasn't so far from the truth to be a complete lie but still not the whole truth — an anxiety-laden grapple for honesty in their messed-up scenario.

"Yeah, Dave," Alex's mom said. She studied her nails, painted a frosty pink. "You really should listen more."

I looked between them and cast my gaze back to Maverick. "Well, new friends are always nice," I said.

"Yes, they are," she said, manicuring the fragile silence. "I think we should toast." She held up the plastic cup with a forced smile. "To graduation and new friends."

We clinked our glasses together, and Maverick squeezed my hand under the table. "To summer," he said, countering with a wide-eyed grin.

I leaned over to kiss him.

They all laughed, and silence bubbled under the conversation.

"Kate, are you going to this party the girls are planning?"

"I wouldn't miss it."

"Won't that be great?"

The voices merged, losing shape before they made it to my ears.

All I could see was the sun and Maverick. I could hear Alex and Kate tittering, somewhere. I was laughing, I was in love — and somehow that was enough.

* * * *

Heat blistered across my shoulders and the slope of my back, and I listened to the slosh of water against the poolside.

"I love this weather," Alex exclaimed from beside me, and I rolled my gaze to peer at her.

"I miss the winter," I noted.

"The winter, really?" She didn't believe me.

"Yeah," I said. "This isn't bad, though."

She grinned. "Exactly," she said, dragging her sunglasses off her face and into the mop of her hair.

"The sun can be good," I mumbled, tossing my forearm over my eyes.

"And yet you constantly hide from it," she teased.

"A little sun goes a long way." I explained.

"It's good."

I peeked around my arm. "This is nice."

"It is," she agreed, without opening her eyes.

"Seriously," I said, watching little kids toddle around the pool in their inflatable water wings and goggles, "we haven't spent much time together lately — ya know, just the two of us."

"Right." She turned her face to mine and smiled weakly. "Yeah, it's been…different."

"Good different," I said.

"Yeah," she agreed. "Change can be good, right?"

I swallowed, staring at the cool aquamarine of the pool water. "That victory dinner was really something."

She ran a hand through her hair, listlessly tugging at the roots. "Yeah," she said, "it really was."

I swallowed down my questions—no point in opening the wound now—and tossed my legs over the side of the lounge chair. "We might as well actually get into the water, right?"

"Definitely," she said. "Water plus sunlight equals a fast tan."

I giggled. "True."

"So," Alex said as we climbed into the pool, "I know you're excited for this party." The cool water lapped around our shoulders.

"Yeah," I said. "You know me."

"I do know you," she said, dipping her head under the water in one fluid motion and popping back up with all the elegance of a seasoned swimmer.

"So, what exactly do you have planned for this soiree?"

She kicked off the wall, darting to the other end of the pool. "Nothing," she called over her shoulder.

"Nothing?" I questioned, treading water to trail behind her. "That seems very un-Alex-like."

She winked. "Don't worry your pretty little head about it. Just put on a dress and heels, and we'll party the night away."

"Okay," I said. "I'll try to do that."

"Try hard, Emma," she said. "This is our time."

My heart warmed with the comment, and I closed my eyes. "You're right," I said. "I love you."

She mussed my hair. "I love you, too," she said. "Now, let's swim before we burn."

Weird logic, I thought, but I smiled, diving after her.

Chapter Forty-Nine

It rained the night of the party. The *pitter-patter* of droplets hit the roof, and I jerked the black lace fit-and-flare into place. Instinctively, I appraised myself in the mirror. My shoulders, a little too wide, were straight and semi-tan from our trip to the pool the previous day. I had curled my hair into long, beachy waves, and Mom had done my makeup.

Now, she sat on my bed, smiling. "That really is a pretty dress," she said.

"Yeah," I said. I twisted playfully in front of the mirror to watch the skirt swing. "And I just found it in my closet."

She beamed. "Well, sometimes that happens." She shrugged a shoulder. "What are the big plans for tonight?"

I worried my bottom lip. "I haven't heard any," I said. "Alex just told me to put on a dress and show up."

"Classic Alex," she said. She picked up a picture from my bedside table of Alex and me freshman year and she sighed. "Can I ask you something?"

I slid into my desk chair and crossed my legs. "Yeah," I said, "what's up?"

"Alex," she opened, still studying the picture. "Is she dating Maverick's sister?"

Mouth dry, I nodded. "Yeah," I said, "she is."

Mom replaced the picture on my bedside table. "I thought so," she said. "They wouldn't look at each other at dinner." She laughed awkwardly. "I mean, *zero* eye contact. I just wondered. Of course, I won't tell anyone."

"Thanks," I said.

"Do you think she'll tell her parents?"

"I'm sure," I said, staring down at the toes of my peep-toe heels. "If it gets...serious...or sticks, ya know?"

"Ah," she said. "The relationship or the liking women?"

I thought for a moment before I answered her. "Maybe both."

"Okay," she said, "I just wondered." She stood up, smoothing her skirt. "Have a good time tonight. Call me if you need me."

I kissed her cheek. "I will. See you in the morning," I said.

My phone vibrated, a text from Alex.

Get your cute butt outside. Oh, and ditch the heels for rain boots and a rain jacket.

I frowned.

Where are we going?

The party.

And you don't see my confusion?

Cute. Butt. In. Car.

I chucked my heels for the red rain booties. "Okay," I said. "Whatever happens happens."

I shuffled, confused, out of the door, and saw Alex's head pop out of her car. "In the back seat. We've gotta go pick up the Englishes."

I trudged toward the car, hopping in the assigned seat. "Where are we going? I thought we were having a party?"

She wore a pink swing dress with a plunging neckline and wiggled her eyebrow suggestively. "Don't ask questions," she said. "I have a plan."

"You're insane," I told her.

"I know," she agreed. "That's why you love me."

I didn't argue, watching our town slip by through crystalline raindrops on the windshield. "It's a beautiful night."

She smiled at me in the rearview mirror. "It's raining."

"I like the rain," I said, nibbling my lip. "I told my mom."

She frowned over at me. "What do you mean?"

I sighed, leaning my forehead against the cool glass of the window. "I told her about you and Kate. Well, you know," I said, shaking my head, "she asked. I didn't wanna lie."

She responded with an even voice. "I wouldn't want you to lie to your mom, Emma. That wouldn't be fair of me to ask."

"She asked me something else," I said, my voice small.

She pulled up to the English house and twisted to look at me. "Yeah?"

I frowned. "Are you ever gonna tell your parents?"

She sighed. Her gaze tipped toward the house instead of me, she studied her black fingernails. "I want to," she said, "but I can't. Emma, they won't understand."

Of course, I knew what she meant and how she felt. "I love you," I said.

The front door swung open and a thunderclap sang above our heads. In the doorway, Maverick and Kate emerged. Kate wore a navy rain jacket, artfully splattered with paint somewhere along the way, over a white sundress, and Maverick grinned through the downpour. He sprinted, all black slacks and a button-down, and slid into the seat beside me, shaking the water from his ink-black hair.

"Hey," he said, "have they told you where we're going?"

I giggled. "Nope," I said. I wove my fingers into his wet hair and jerked his lips to mine. "I have no idea what's going on."

"We're having a party," Alex said, linking hands with Kate over the console.

Maverick nodded, chuckling to himself. "So, where are we going?"

"Well," she said, "out to the lake."

"Why?"

Alex shrugged, a playful smile on her face. "Because we have all we need for the best party ever right here."

Something in my heart blossomed, and I pressed my face to the damp skin of Maverick's neck. He smelled of rain and cologne and him, and I kissed just under the collar of his shirt. "She's right," I whispered, my heart electric in my chest.

He wrapped a heavy arm around my shoulders and dipped to peck my cheek. "I love you," he said. "Let's go."

* * * *

The Fisher family's lake house wasn't far from the lake house that had started it all. The stone structure shone from the road, and memories flashed behind my eyelids. The day they'd bought the house, Alex and I had spent the night huddled around the fireplace, giggling over circumstance and bad TV. That summer, we had sprawled on the lawn more afternoons than not, soaking up the Mississippi rays and inhaling the sweet scent of freshly mown grass and summer. It seemed only fitting for the house to usher us out of our high school careers too.

The rain had subsided for a moment, so we tumbled from Alex's car — hand in hand and heart in heart — and hustled to the front door. Alex fished her house keys from the pocket of her rain jacket, quickly unlocked the door, and we filed inside.

I stepped over the threshold and smiled instantly. Alex had strewn fairy lights around the perimeter of the house, and its homey warmth spread through my chest. Maverick wrapped his arms around my waist, and Alex giggled from the doorway. "I'm going to call the pizza guy," she said. "Kate, can you pop the popcorn?"

A cool blush coated my shoulders as her words rushed over me. They were subtle, thoughtful but pointed. *Let's give them a minute,* they said.

Alex and Kate shuffled out of the entryway, giggling about pizza toppings, but suddenly, I didn't care. Maverick's thumbs drummed a steady beat along my sides, and his breath sizzled against the back of my neck.

"Hey," he mumbled against my skin. He skimmed his hands along my hips to the curve of my stomach, and an icy chill shot up my spine.

"Hi," I whispered, breathless as his fingers gently pried my rain jacket from my shoulders. My stomach knotted as a burst of air conditioning hit me, and Maverick's lips replaced the chill.

"I love your dress," he whispered, a gruff murmur against my neck, and I gasped a giggle.

"You haven't seen it yet," I said.

He chuckled, and the tension broke. "Oh," he said, "sorry."

I giggled, shrugging a shoulder. "Don't be," I said, catching my breath, only to have it knocked from my chest again almost instantly.

He dipped and spun me, a fluid dance of limbs, and he appraised my appearance, smirking. "Yep," he mumbled, "I was right. I love your dress."

"Thanks," I said, closing my lips around his in another kind of dance entirely.

He gripped my shoulders tighter. "Mm-hm-m," he said under his breath, "any time."

I retreated, cementing my face to the nape of his neck and inhaling the sharp scent of him. Idly, I massaged an uneasy pattern along his back. "You look pretty handsome yourself," I mumbled, an afterthought.

"Emma, I'm soaked," he noted against my hair.

He was right, of course. His dark hair was plastered to his head, and his black clothes were a second skin. *Perfect*, I thought, and I kissed his neck. "Yeah," I said, smirking and diverting his attention, "but I love you."

"Gosh," he said, hands carving around my face. He kissed me — long, slow and absolutely perfect. "I love you, too."

Our private utopia shattered with the scrape of feet against the hardwood floor as the other two rejoined us. They had both discarded their rain jackets and padded in stocking feet to where we had landed, mid living room. Kate held two big bowls of popcorn, and Alex slapped a map down on the coffee table.

"What's this?"

Alex grinned, gesturing to the map. "Where are we going?"

Realization dawned on me — our trip, our swan song of a summer — and I beamed at them. "Everywhere."

Maverick kissed my temple, his shoulders shaking with quiet laughter. "That might take a while, babe," he said.

"Right," I said, giggling. We had two months, maybe a month to travel and probably not even that. I burrowed my face into his shoulder. "New York?"

"Via?"

"Everywhere," I repeated.

He shook his head but surrendered. "Okay."

Chapter Fifty

My back ached. I rolled over, grasping reality in slow waves. The four of us had collapsed doggy-pile style on a makeshift pallet of blankets in front of the fire. I blinked, counting the bodies and listening to the patter of rain outside the house.

Maverick's arm lay across the hardwood, probably having fallen to the floor when I'd moved. A blanket was over his waist, likely a victim of the war of bodies, and Kate's head was on Maverick's ankle.

I scanned the room for Alex but came up dry, so I scrambled to my feet and hustled out of the living room. Long shadows cascaded across the hallway, and I hummed under my breath. "Alex?"

Lightning shocked across the dim hallway, and I nearly jumped out of my skin. "Gosh," I mumbled, inhaling sharply, "Alex?"

"I'm in here," she called softly, and I shuffled through the near-silent house after her voice.

"Marco." My voice echoed, bouncing off every surface like a boomerang.

The soundboard of her giggle targeted me. "Polo," she said, just as I rounded the corner. She was sitting on the closed porch, gripping a cup of warm coffee, the ghost of which I had caught a whiff of as I'd passed the kitchen. The word was something so simple, I thought, but she'd sounded so sad... Her voice had diminished to the level of near silence.

"Hey," I said. "are you okay?"

She shrugged, rubbing her upper arm and taking a sip of coffee. "I'm all right," she said and straightened her shoulders. "I just... They're selling the house."

I frowned. "Your parents?"

"Yeah," she said. She took a long drag from her coffee. "Dad got a new job. They're moving at the end of the summer."

I sighed, plopping beside her on the bench. "That's..."

"Yeah," she said, leaning her head against my shoulder.

Silence drooped between us, and I let it. *Sometimes*, I thought, *that's all you can do.*

* * * *

Music blared from Alex's speaker, and I sprawled across her bed. I hummed, studying the ceiling. Stars spotted the white, peeling paint, and I imagined a child must have lived here before Alex.

Now, the room felt incredibly small. Clothes and books were piled the ground, an abstract representation. *Alex's life*, I thought. *Ladies and gentlemen, gather 'round.*

I flopped onto my stomach, bending my knees to the air, and watched her jerk the wreckage of high school from the bottom of her closet.

A giggle rippled through her chest. "Oh, God," she said, lifting a wrinkled T-shirt from the mess. "Remember this night?"

I blushed, studying the garment with calculated curiosity as she unfolded the cascading fabric. "Is that? Oh, God," I breathed, giggling to myself as that particular night tumbled back to my consciousness.

The night Alex had earned her driver's license, we'd flown. Brazen and reckless, she'd driven and I'd navigated with nothing but a wrinkled map and a faded flyer from the school bulletin board. We'd ditched last period to visit the Department of Motor Vehicles and grab one driver's license and a bag of mini donuts.

Then we'd veered southward. Alex's dirty-blonde hair had rushed behind her. We'd been like fireworks, spiraling down the highway to see some quirky band with a name we couldn't even pronounce. They were playing at a casino on the coast.

Then, sixteen and stupid, we'd lacked the maturity to know that casinos require the twenty-one and over crowd with ankle tattoos and a license to drink. Luckily, Alex had flashed a toothy smile and the bouncer had slid a neon warning sign onto our arms. *Do not sell these kids alcohol*, it screamed.

We'd stumbled, drunk on life, into the blaring lights and bumping music. Bodies, I remembered, and the sharp, dirty scent of burned cigarettes. Ashes and darkness flooded my senses, and Alex shucked the T-shirt at me.

"Earth to Emma," she said. "Do you remember that night?"

"How could I forget the night my best friend ditched me to make out with a sleazy drummer," I teased, raking my fingers through my hair.

"That isn't fair! He bought me a drink," she said, giggling.

I ran my fingers along the thin fabric of the shirt. It was soft, with electric lettering and funky colors, and the night flooded back to the forefront of my mind. Bodies, drunk and not, had ground to a pop-funk mixture that I hadn't been able to quite identify — folksy mandolins, banjos of country and the harsh drumline of rock.

The crowd of twenty-somethings had swayed and danced, bouncing on heels and in slinky dresses. I remembered the rush of excitement, the flickering lights and the belief that anything was possible. I'd felt so grown up... Free, even.

"And look at us now," I said, followed by a deep sigh.

"You're right," she agreed. "Look at us now — brilliantly smart, epic love stories in the process, reasonably attractive." She winked over the piles. "I think we've hit the jackpot."

"Yeah," I said. I shoved my face into one of her pillows, inhaling the sweet smell of her perfume. *Crazy*, I thought. She smelled like home. My thoughts dashed to her with that drummer, that guy, and I nibbled my lip. "I guess you're right."

"Oh, come on, Emma," she said. She climbed over the piles of clothes and plopped down beside me. "You okay?"

How do you say it's still weird? The lies? The swift change? Maybe everything? I groaned, an inward sound, and bit my nail.

She growled. "Stop chewing your nails, Emma."

God, I thought. She knew me like no one else. Well, Mom, but other than that—no one else. I opened my eyes. "There's nothing wrong," I said. "I just love you. Ya know that?"

She offered a sidelong smile. "You're my best friend. Ya know *that*?"

I knocked her shoulder with mine playfully. "Yeah," I said, "I do."

"This trip is kind of crazy," she noted, giving up and changing the subject.

I giggled. "Yeah," I said, "it is."

"But great... Don't get me wrong."

"I understand," I said, flipping over onto my back. I idly counted the glow-in-the-dark stars on the ceiling. "I want to see more. I've only ever been here."

She twisted to look at me. "Define 'here'," she said.

"You know what I mean," I said. "I've never been out of the South—Mississippi and Alabama really." I paused, laughing halfheartedly. "Well, we went to Orlando once for the parks."

"Oh," she said. "We should go to Chattanooga. The aquarium is great, and the skyline is so *tall*." She giggled. "You'll love it."

"I'll go anywhere." As I heard myself, I wondered where this confident Emma had come from, but I guessed it was from senior year—and Maverick.

"That's true." She shrugged. "I wanna go to Washington DC," she said.

I smirked. "That's a little out of the way, isn't it?"

"Monuments and political figures and whatnot."

"Ah," I said, rubbing the chill bumps on my arms. "We could go to the Library of Congress."

"You're such a nerd." She shook her head, smirking.

A knock broke our focus, and Mrs. Fisher waved through the crack in the door. A letter was tucked into the pocket of her apron, she waved and straightened at the waist. Her hair stuck up on the side. "Oh, hi, Emma," she said.

I blushed, rolling off the side of the bed to appear presentable. "Hey, Mrs. Fisher. How are you?"

"I'm good," she said, gesturing to the explosion of clothes on the floor. "Alex, this is a mess."

"Yep," she said. "I'm cleaning out my closet."

Mrs. Fisher flashed her daughter a thumbs-up and backed away. "Awesome," she said. "Keep doing what you're doing."

Alex unfolded herself from the bed. She stared down at the piles with a measured sigh. "It's more afraid of me than I am of it, right?"

"Of course," I said. I glanced at my watch. *Ten till Maverick*, I thought.

"No," Alex said, groaning, "don't say it."

"Maverick's picking me up in ten. We're going swimming, I think."

"Of course you are." She pouted, jerking her prom dress from its hanger and hugging it to her chest. The magenta strapless number had sent every eye in the room reeling and wondering why this gorgeous girl had chosen to go stag to the prom. Only a choice few of us knew the truth of the matter. The entire night Alex had leered at Kate. They had even danced once, a fast shuffle that turned into a slow dance, but I knew it wasn't enough.

"Oh, don't be like that," I said.

She groaned. "Don't be like what? Honest?"

"You know what I mean." I scratched my hairline, frowning to myself. "You'll only be four hours away."

She sighed. "I know. I know." She spun back to the closet. "I'll see you later."

"See ya," I said and headed back home to change.

Chapter Fifty-One

I pulled the red and white polka-dotted tankini into place and peered at my reflection in the mirror— awkward smile, not-so-thin shoulders. I groaned, shoving a hand through my hair and knotting it into a low bun. *There*, I thought.

The front door creaked open, and I straightened. One thing about Maverick... That guy was punctual...if he wanted to show up.

"Maverick," I whined, shaking my head. I swung to check the time on the clock on the wall. I still had three minutes. "You're early."

"You sound mad," he called. \

I listened to the hum of his laughter. *Gosh*, I thought. That six-foot two-inches of trouble shot a silent shiver up my spine. He emerged in the doorway, holding a hand in front of his eyes *just in case*. He wore black swim trunks and a white T-shirt, and his hair stood on end. "I thought early was good."

I giggled. "It is," I mumbled. "Put your hand down."

"Yes, ma'am," he said and swiftly approached. He leaned against me and whispered soft and silent lullabies to my skin. They landed like feathers on my shoulders and shattered any illusion of control I'd gained on the situation. My heart skipped an off-kilter beat.

"Yeah," I said. "I was running late. I just got back."

His lips grazed my bare shoulder. "Where have you been?"

I quirked a playful eyebrow at him, saucy with uncensored flirtation. "Alex's," I said, spinning in his arms to wink at him. "Ya know, pillow fights and all."

He groaned, a grunting sound in the back of his throat, and flopped on the edge of my bed. "Don't tease me," he said.

"I'm not," I said. "You should have been there."

He grasped Rori the bear in his big hands. He turned the tattered bear over once, twice, three times and he chuckled. "What were y'all up to, Em?"

I ruffled his hair. "Cleaning out Alex's closet," I said. "Ya know that her family is moving at the end of the summer?"

"Yeah," he said and kissed my hand. "Kate's upset."

I sighed. "It's sad."

He frowned. "I don't get it," he said. "Alex is going to school anyway. What's the big deal?"

I massaged his scalp slowly. "Look at it from Kate's perspective," I mumbled. "What will be Alex's motivation to come back here? Or even if she wants to...it'll be harder since her parents aren't here. If her parents were here, that could be a cover, an easy in, but since they'll be in Washington... How can she justify Christmas in Mississippi when her family is in Washington?"

"Oh," he said, drumming his fingers along my spine, "I guess I get it."

I worried my lip. "Yeah," I said.

"Okay," he said. "So, y'all were cleaning out her closet?"

"Yeah," I said, kissing his neck slowly and biting back a giggle. "Well, *she* was cleaning out her closet. I was watching her clean and offering comedic commentary."

He chuckled under his breath and tugged me into his lap, tickling my sides. "Does Alex have any beloved stuffed animals with gender-inappropriate names?" He pressed kisses along my forearm, his lips burning against my bare skin.

I rolled my eyes. "Rori can be a girl's name," I whined, holding myself together as best I could.

He shook his head, dragging his lips to my neck. "Not buying it, love," he said.

I groaned softly. His lips were warm against my pulse point, and I swallowed hard. "Don't make me look it up," I said, as if I actually could. Right now, I couldn't see straight, much less type.

He gave me a sharp kiss, a targeted motion. I boiled under his touch, under his kiss, and I wove my arms around his neck. "Go ahead," he said, teasing, daring me to try it. "Look it up."

I crashed against him like the waves against our feet the first time he'd told me he loved me. "Keep it up, and we won't go swimming," I said in a rush of breath against his collarbone.

"I love you."

I flushed, and he cupped my face. The kiss softened, and I sighed against his touch. "I love you too."

He pulled me into a hug, lingering and slow. "Then let's go swimming."

Heart aflutter, I nodded, knowing I could have stayed there with him forever.

* * * *

We dove under the water, and I gasped a sharp breath. The chlorine burned my eyes and nose. Maverick's hands found purchase on my back. I pivoted, grasping his forearms for support.

An uninhibited giggle bubbled through my throat. "Geez," I breathed. "This water is so cold. It's great."

"Nah," he said through a shiver, tightening his grip around my waist, "*you're* great."

I kissed him. "Oh, God." I giggled.

"What?"

I shrugged. "Nothing… We're just…*that* couple."

"*That* couple?"

"The couple that makes everyone sick," I said. "The romantic comedy waiting to happen."

"Shit… I had no idea."

"It isn't a terrible thing," I explained. "It's good for us."

"Good point," he said, cradling my face in his warm hands. "I love you."

I swelled with emotion in the pool water, tangling my legs with his in a fluid motion. "I love you."

Always teasing, he said, "Oh?"

I blinked the drops from my eyes. "Yeah."

He bobbed in the water, chuckling under his breath and ducking out of my embrace. "Let's at least pretend to swim."

I smirked, watching his muscular back, beaded with water and retreating. "What does that mean?" A thrill up my spine, I called after him, and he doubled back to jerk me into his warm embrace.

"You're so innocent, and it's so sexy," he breathed. His dark hair dripped, soaked from his halfway swim, and his gaze pulsed against mine — one of those fearless stares that could last an eternity, even if we couldn't.

"Ah," I said, scraping my fingers along his back, "I don't know what to say."

He chuckled. "Don't say anything."

"But—"

His hand struck the water, splashing me in a wicked act of war. "Catch me if you can," he antagonized, darting out of my grip. He catapulted toward the other end of the pool.

Again, for a moment I froze, dumbfounded. Temptation rolled down his back, a silent call, and I splashed with frantic urgency as I launched after him.

I tackled him in the middle of the pool, linking my legs around his waist and covering his eyes with my hands. "I can," I heaved into his ear, giggling.

"Damn," he said, half winded. "You swim fast."

I climbed around him, spider-monkey-style, and kissed him. "Quickly."

He groaned, pressing his face to my shoulder in an open-mouthed kiss. "Girl," he said, "you're a smartie, aren't you?"

"Yeah," I said, "I guess."

He pulled me tight to his waist. "How could you doubt it? Third in the class. Ivy League college. Sexy as hell," he said, kissing my shoulder.

I peered up at him then skimmed my fingers down his arms, slow...like staggered satin. "Hey," I said.

The playful sparkle in his blue-green eyes darkened, and he dragged his hands down the slippery back of my swimsuit. "Hey," he breathed.

I inhaled the scent of chlorine and sunshine and cast a glance over my shoulder. The lifeguard propped one tan leg on a longue chair and shoved his hand through his sandy hair. He wore red swim trunks and dark sunglasses, but I could tell from the sly smirk on his face that he was watching us. "Wanna get out of here?"

Maverick shrugged a shoulder, teasing my hairline with a single finger. "I'm not sure," he said. "It's such a nice day."

I kissed him hard, looping my arms around his neck. I grazed my lips down to his neck, pressing knife-edged words against his ear. "Let's get out of here," I said.

He wrapped his arms around my waist. "Okay," he replied and laughed, but it was humorless. "Damn, it's good that this water is cold."

"Um," I said, "should I get that comment?"

A manly sound rippled from his chest. "No."

Suddenly, anxious flutters rushed up my spine. "Okay."

He dipped to kiss my head. "Let's go."

"Okay," I agreed, and we hustled out of the pool.

Chapter Fifty-Two

I jerked a beach towel around my shoulders, shaking off the droplets and giggling under my breath. My hair was slick with chlorine and pool water, so I massaged the strands with another towel right there in the parking lot.

"Come on," he said. "You're dry enough."

"I'm trying to save your truck," I called back as I tossed my bag into the bed. "Where are we going anyway?"

"Dunno," he said. He kicked the back-passenger tire, peering at me with a watchful stare. He'd pulled on his T-shirt over his swim trunks, and the thin fabric clung to his stomach, sending a shot up my spine.

"Well," I said, forcing an even tone and crossing my arms. "I'm all wet. You're all wet. Home might be the best option."

He groaned, leaning against the cool metal of the cab. "I'm not sure I'm ready to go home."

"Oh?" I crossed to stand in front of him with a playful wink. "What do you propose then?"

"I don't know."

"Oh," I countered. "What a predicament."

"We could go back to my place and watch a movie," he offered.

"I dunno about that," I said, gesturing to myself. "I'm all slimy." It was only half a joke. I had always hated the feeling after a swim—all chlorine and unmentionable germs.

He smirked. "Okay, fine," he said. "We'll take a shower *then* watch a movie?"

My joke had backfired. The color drained from my face and I stuttered a response. "I...uh," I managed, but laughter caught in his throat like acid wind chimes.

"You should see your face," he said.

Mortified, I shook my head. "Maverick..."

"What?"

"Not funny," I replied, probably fifty shades of red.

"Oh, but it was funny."

I groaned, pressing my towel to my face in defeat. "You're mean."

"Yeah," he said, "a little."

I peeked around the scratchy towel. "Well?"

He exhaled, shaking his head with a measured stare. "How about this? We go home, take separate showers, order Chinese and watch a movie?"

"Maybe kiss a little?"

"I'm not gonna argue with that."

He opened the door for me and I hopped into the front seat of the truck, tucked in my towel. I stared through the windshield as he loped around the front of his truck. *Yeah*, I thought, *this will be the perfect summer.*

Maverick and me and Alex and Kate.

* * * *

My reflection in the mirror was timeless, focused —
damp hair, drawn gaze, one of Maverick's soft blue T-
shirts. I yanked a pair of shorts up my hips and closed
my eyes. The house was warm and quiet. My swimsuit
hung from the rack in the tub, drips falling as soft as
tiny pebbles. Mrs. English was at work. Kate was with
Alex. Maverick moved, somewhere in the house, not so
quiet.

"Hey," he called from outside the door, "want
anything to drink?"

I toyed with my hair. "Water?"

"Got it," he said, shuffling away.

I plopped on the edge of their bathtub, idly counting
shampoo bottles and discarded body wash containers,
and I jerked a pair of socks onto my feet then
meandered down the hall.

The TV was already on in the living room and I slid
into place on the couch, tugging a pillow onto my lap.
"What're we watching?"

"*Girls Gone Wild*," he teased from the kitchen.

"Oh, really?" I scanned the living room with muted
interest. In the dim light, it all seemed homier. An
upright piano was nuzzled against the wall.
"Maverick," I called, "who plays the piano?"

A shuffle, then, "What?"

I unfolded from the couch and walked over to slide
onto the bench. "The piano," I said, sliding open the
cover and poising my fingers over the keys.

"Oh," he said, suddenly from behind me. "Mom
does."

I dragged my fingers along the keys in a slow,
fumbled scale. "Is this new?"

"Yeah," he said. "She got it earlier this week to practice."

I formed a chord, all white notes, but it rang, nonetheless. "Practice for what?"

He plopped beside me on the bench, looping an arm around my shoulders. "She's playing for the church." He sighed against my neck. "I didn't know you could play the piano."

"I'm not all that great," I admitted.

He smirked. "Really?"

"Yeah," I said. "I took lessons as a kid, but that was years ago."

He kissed my cheek soberly. "Play me something?"

I blushed, shifting on the bench. It was a little unstable under both our weights. "Like what?"

He nudged my shoulder. "Whatever you want," he said and paused. "Whatever you know."

"Um-m," I said. I flexed my fingers over the keys. "Okay."

"Have at it, then," he said.

I shoved his shoulder. "Well, I'll need the bench."

"Oh, okay," he said. He got up to lean against the wall, watching me with a soft gaze. "Let's hear it, Maestro."

Heat flooded my cheeks, and I groaned, rubbing my eyes with the backs of my hands. "I can't," I said. "I haven't played in years, Maverick."

He leaned down and pressed a kiss to my head. "Please," he said, half-jokingly. "Play for me. I think you can."

I sighed. "Okay," I said, wringing out my hands.

Just breathe, I thought. Then, I ran my fingers across the ivory keys. They were worn and old. I pressed out chords I hadn't touched in ages. It was a simple

315

rhythm, a dance of hand against instrument. This used to be a part of me—the keyboard a mere extension of my fingers.

Now, I fumbled. I shuddered against the keys, unfamiliar and laughing. Playing the piano, I guessed, wasn't so much like riding a bike. It was a practice, a discipline that I had long since fallen out of.

"You aren't bad," he said.

A strangled noise escaped my body, and I slammed the cover over the keys. "You're funny," I said. "I used to be good."

"Hey," he whined, "I liked that song."

"That wasn't even a song."

"It was," he argued.

"You're right," I admitted. "Four chords can make a song, right?"

"A pop song."

I slid off the piano bench and hugged him. "True," I said. I kissed him—lazy kisses like summer rain.

He mumbled, a quiet jokester with a crooked grin and a bad boy attitude that I loved more than anything else. I inhaled against his chest. He was so warm. His skin radiated strength and possibilities, and I pressed my face into him.

"Hey," he said, "what?"

I shrugged. "I'm excited."

"For the trip?"

"Yeah," I answered.

"I'm glad." He led me to the couch, hand on my back, and smiled. "Maybe we can camp somewhere along the way."

"You're kidding?"

"No," he said, curving his arms around my shoulders. "We could get a couple of tents and sleeping bags and sleep under the stars..."

I giggled. "Yeah... Maybe."

"What?" His breath brushed my hair. "Not a big camper?"

I couldn't tell if he was serious or not. "Yeah," I said, "I'm really not."

"It could be fun."

"I doubt it. Bugs... Humidity..."

"Moonlight... Snuggling..."

"Snuggling?"

He nodded. "Definitely."

I kissed him, holding his face in my hands, and he tugged me closer. Something boiled between us, and I ran my fingers into his hair. We moved in tandem, hearts and limbs, laughing softly.

"Okay, lovebirds." Kate's voice interrupted our bliss. Her voice tapered off, quivering, and I jerked away from him.

Swallowing hard, I quirked my head toward her. She held my phone, gesturing. Her eyes were red. "Kate, what's wrong?"

She shook her head. "Nothing," she said. It was a lie.

"What's going on?"

She exhaled. "I think you need to call Alex."

My heart shuddered, dropping to my stomach. Something was very wrong. I could see it in her all-too-pale face. I scrambled from Maverick's arms and gathered my things. "Um," I said, "Maverick, I've gotta go."

He frowned, surprised by the sudden mood change. "Yeah," he said, "it's fine. I'll drive you home."

I grabbed my phone from Kate's hands. "Thanks," I said.

She shook her head, rushing into the back of the house.

I frowned to myself. Fragile possibilities blossomed in my imagination, and I followed Maverick to the truck. I was stone-cold silent the entire ride home.

Chapter Fifty-Three

A tense seven-minute drive later, Maverick rolled to a stop along the curb in front of Alex's house. He nudged my chin, as a gentle reminder. "Hey," he said, "call me later?"

"Yeah, okay." I swallowed hard. My mind darted about, preoccupied and endlessly concerned. The ghost of Kate's expression clouded my judgment, and I'd hardly heard him.

He probed my shoulder, forcing my gaze to his. "Emma," he said, "whatever it is, it'll be fine."

My stomach twisted, caught in a knot he couldn't untangle. "I know," I said. "I, erm... I've gotta go. I love you."

He skimmed his fingers along my shoulder. "I love you, too," he said. "Talk to you later?"

I nodded but didn't reply beyond that. I climbed from the truck and stared up at the house. My heartbeat pounded in my ears, and the floodgates flew open. I had walked up the worn path a thousand times since the Fishers had joined the neighborhood.

Now, with a lump in my throat, I shuffled to the front door to examine the perfectly striped white paint. Every summer, like clockwork, Mr. Fisher repainted it. It calmed him, I think.

I inhaled deeply and knocked on the door, a hollow echo in my chest, and it occurred to me that I should have changed. There I was in Maverick's pale blue T-shirt and shorts.

The door swung open, and Mrs. Fisher beamed from the doorway. She had ditched the apron and she wore black slacks and a white top. Her grin confused me, mismatched from the somber expression mirrored on Kate's pale face. "Have you heard the news?"

I blinked. "News?"

"Yes," she said. "Alex got a letter earlier...from NYU."

I swallowed. "A letter from NYU?"

"There's a special orientation," she explained

My heart clenched in my chest. "A special orientation?"

She stared back at me, the colorful excitement draining from her face. "Come on," she said, leading me by the elbow through the house. The house, I realized, was in boxes — or at least beginning to be. The photos and paintings had been stashed away, so the walls were bare and the house smelled of new paint.

We rounded the corner into Alex's room, and Mrs. Fisher smiled. "Alex," she said. Alex was reclined on her bed, piles surrounding her, her legs limp and off the side, and she was staring blankly at the letter. Her eyes were red, and a shot of anxiety dashed up my spine. "Look who's back."

The letter fell from Alex's hands, fluttering to the carpet, and she tumbled off the edge of the bed and launched into my arms. "I called you a million times."

Mrs. Fisher rubbed her forearms, a pinched frown on her tidy face. "I'll give you two a minute."

I hugged Alex tight, giggling despite the persuasive fog between us. "I think it was six, but go on," I said. "What's up? Are you okay?"

"I'm fine," she said and shook her head. "No. That's a lie. I'm *not* okay."

I held her at arm's length. "Alex, what's going on?"

She slumped on the edge of the bed again. "We got a letter today," she said, jerking the band from her hair, "from the university."

I knelt down beside the bed to grab the thin piece of paper in my hand. *Amazing,* I thought, *that something so insignificant could cause so much damage.* "And?"

She groaned, shaking her head. "I have to leave."

There it is, I thought. Her four words had fallen in shards, and I gripped the paper. I shuddered, scanning along the thin type on the official letterhead — early orientation, pre-courses and student activities.

My mouth now dry, I met her eyes once again. "When?"

She stared skyward and opened her mouth, only to close it a second later. The silence stretched. "The middle of June," she finally said softly. "In three weeks."

Our summer slipped away as I slid down the wall opposite her. "Okay," I said, nibbling my thumbnail, my voice as calm as I could muster.

"Okay?" She sounded incredulous.

I sighed, rubbing the bridge of my nose. "What should I say?"

Her shoulders shaking, she shrugged. "I don't know."

"I'm sorry," I offered.

She straightened. "It's not your fault. I'm just..." She shook her head. Her eyes were drawn and red, sad. "We had plans."

I scrambled from the floor to the bed and wrapped my arms around her shoulders. One of us, I realized, had to keep it together, and right now, that had to be me. "I know, I know," I chanted, rubbing her back methodically.

A broken sound ripped from her chest—a sob or something worse. "I just can't believe this," she said. "We had *plans*."

"I know. I'm just in shock," I explained. "Did y'all even know this was on the table?"

"Nope," she said. "I had no idea about this two-month-long detour."

I sighed. "Still," I said, "this has to be a pretty big deal, doesn't it?"

She groaned. "I guess. It's for valedictorians or early admissions or scholars or something. I don't really know."

I smiled. "That's great, Alex."

"Not really. It's basically summer school, but the classes are only available for this select set of students that they have deemed ready because of test scores or GPAs and blah blah blah."

"It's going to be wonderful, Alex," I said, hedging the fringes of dangerous territory. "It's just the beginning."

She buried her face in her hands. "The beginning of the end," she mumbled.

A strangled noise gripped my throat, and I scrambled for words that would comfort her. "No, Alex, the beginning of the next chapter of your life, and it's going to be amazing. You should be proud."

"Ordinarily I would be," she said, mussing her hair, clearly frustrated. She jumped up from the bed to pace the cluttered floor. "I would be, but—"

I repositioned a leg under my body and turned to keep her pinned in my line of vision. "Kate," I said in a whisper. "I know."

She sighed. "Yeah."

"I know," I repeated. The words were dry in my mouth. I bit the inside of my cheek. "But come on, Alex. Even Kate, when she calms down, is going to be so proud of you. We all are so *proud* of you." I forced a smile, my heart a lump in my throat. So far, I thought I was holding up well.

She stilled, rocking to a standing stop, and leaned against the wall. She twisted away from me, and I knew she didn't want me to see her cry. *Ever as strong as she's smart, that Alex*, I thought.

"It's gonna be okay," I said from the bed, unsure of how else to comfort her.

I stared at the carpet, and my stomach turned. Our planned summer together flashed behind my eyelids, a flood of unforeseen and unfulfilled memories—Alex and me in flashy outfits, giggling over plates of bad Italian food in The Village.

Alex shook and grappled with the doorknob to capture a moment of privacy. She collapsed against the wood as if it was all that could hold her up, and she closed her eyes, brushing the fitful tears from her eyes. "Mom's so excited," she said.

"I know," I mumbled. Her voice was so small, and she slid to the wooden floor.

On the ground, she yanked her knees to her chin. "I mean," she said, "she's already packing. Half of the house is in boxes. She just doesn't get it."

The strangled monster welled in my stomach — of secrets and lies shattering illusions and promises. I straightened. "Well," I reminded her, "she can't get it, Alex."

Alex laughed bitterly, almost like she hadn't heard me. "She just keeps saying that I'll be there soon, like a chant…over and over again. Then, it's *'Emma will be only four hours away in no time, Alex. Don't be a baby about this. It's a big deal.'*"

Alex shook her head, purely venting now. "Does she think I don't know that? I know, Emma," she huffed, borrowing my catch phrase of the afternoon. "I know."

I swallowed the monster again and crossed the room to kneel beside her. She needed me, so I linked my arms around her in a genuine hug. "I'm sorry, Alex."

She shrugged. "I know you are," she said, quaking under me. "I'm sorry. I hate this."

"Don't," I said. "I'm proud of you."

She sighed, resting her head on my shoulder in silent contempt. "I'm not ready to leave yet."

"Yeah," I said, "I'm not ready either."

Chapter Fifty-Four

Limbs heavy, I crawled into bed. I closed my eyes, but sleep lurked just below the surface. I lamented, an internal battle, and curled into the fantasy of our summer together.

God, I thought, *such a perfect lie.*

"Hey," Mom's voice interjected, and I straightened.

"Morning," I said, lukewarm with exhaustion.

A rustle and she sat on the edge of the bed. "Honey, are you okay?"

I shrugged, a lump under the covers. At Alex's, I had held it together. Now, alone, I'd crumbled. "I'm fine."

Mom frowned, unamused. "You don't seem fine."

I groaned, peering through the gap between my blanket and the curtain of my hair. "I'm fine," I said. "Really. I'm just sad."

"What happened?"

"Alex has to be in New York in mid-June," I told her.

Mom's expression faltered. "They really can't live without her at NYU, can they?"

I closed my eyes. "No," I said and frowned. "I'm not sure if I can either."

"Hey," she said, "don't say that. You two are strong together, but you'll be just as strong apart—and you'll be together again before you know it."

"I know," I mumbled quietly.

She offered a weak smile. "Come on," she said, patting my side and walking toward the door. "Let's have some dinner."

I climbed from the bed, tucking my blanket around my shoulders. "Mom," I said, under my breath.

She turned. "Yeah?"

"I'm not ready for things to change," I admitted, and she sighed.

"I know, sweetie," she said and enveloped me in a hug. She held me there, sudden and slow, and my heart shuddered against her. "It's going to be okay."

Tears pooled in my eyes. "I know," I said. "I love you."

She squeezed me tighter. "I love you too, Emma."

A violent grumble echoed in my stomach. "Come on," I said. "I'm starving."

She grinned. "Let's go. There's potato soup."

"My favorite," I said.

"Yeah, I know."

And we ate.

And giggled.

And for a moment, I felt okay.

* * * *

I slept soundly that night. In fact, I slept past my internal alarm. I awoke to my phone vibrating violently against my bedside table. My heart, sound and focused, stuttered a beat in my chest. *God*, I thought, *who could that be?*

I swatted the table and blinked, grabbing my phone to scan the text quickly. *Maverick*, I thought. *Of course.*

Hey.

Okay, Romeo, I thought, shaking my head with a halfhearted laugh.

I didn't think to answer. I lay on my side on top of my comforter. It was half past noon. *A good night's sleep doesn't change everything*, I thought.

The screen lit up again.

Emma, are you okay?

A second later, another text shot through the atmosphere.

Emma, come unlock the door.

There are pros and cons to the boyfriend package, I thought. This was both. I rolled off the bed and sulked to the front door. "Maverick," I whined his name.

He held up a paper bag covered with Chinese characters. "Have you eaten yet?"

"I'm not hungry," I lied.

He shook his head. "You need to eat. Can I come in?"

"Yeah," I said, stepping out of the door frame, "come on in."

He wrapped an arm around my shoulders and led me through the house to the kitchen. He smiled weakly and grabbed a couple of forks from the silverware drawer where I pointed.

He placed the paper bag on the kitchen table and kissed my cheek. "Plates or out of the carton?"

I didn't respond. "Kate told you, didn't she?"

He nodded, opening one of the cartons and sticking a fork in the fried rice. "I'm sorry, Emma," he said, his voice gruff.

I shrugged. "It isn't your fault."

He shoveled a forkful of rice into his mouth then wiped with a napkin. "It isn't anyone's fault, though, is it? Somebody has to say they're sorry."

I popped a piece of sweet-and-sour chicken into my mouth and swallowed hard. "I think her mom knows."

He frowned. "About Kate?"

I nuzzled my face against the hallow of his neck. "I don't know why," I said. "I think she might have applied for these classes for her because she knew."

He exhaled. "Did you say anything to Alex about it?"

I stared at my hands. "No." If my suspicions were correct, I wasn't going to be the one to open that Pandora's box with Alex.

He kissed my head. "That's probably for the best."

"Thanks for this," I said.

He chuckled. "For what?"

I giggled. "The food," I said, taking another bite. "I was starving."

"You were asleep," he noted, smirking.

"Still starving."

He nuzzled my shoulder. "How're you holding up?"

"I'm fine," I said. "I guess… I just can't believe all this is happening."

"Yeah."

"I mean, we were going to do so much," I said.

"What if we could still go?" He scooped a big forkful into his mouth.

"How?" I pinched a piece of rice between my fingers.

"I'm not sure," he said. "I haven't figured that much out yet."

I took a tentative bite. "Oh."

He closed his eyes, thinking, then he kissed my shoulder. "We're going to go," he promised and stood up, leaving his carton on the counter. "I'll work it out."

With that, he left the room, and I stared after him, confused.

* * * *

That night I lay in bed, inhaling the scent of Chinese food and decaying possibilities. A white light flickered on my laptop, and my alarm clock glared red neon. I sat up, slumping against my headboard.

I flipped on my bedside lamp to grab my book. I flipped it open and studied the words. It was poetry — sonnets and limericks by some obscure writer. Mom had gotten it for me as a joke years before, but now I kind of loved it. I stared at the words, unable to read them, my heart just not in the pages.

Listless, I sighed and snapped the book closed. I shoved it back onto the bedside table and loosened the bun I'd worn to bed. *I have no focus*, I thought, idly, and snuggled back into my pillow.

My phone vibrated, and I grabbed it. A text from Alex.

Hey, I'm sorry I freaked out yesterday.

I sighed into the darkness.

Don't be. I understand.

Well, I just hate this ending.

I glanced across the room - to the suitcase I had started packing before everything had gone up in smoke.

Yeah. Me too, Alex.

Another text popped up—this one from Maverick, and I switched screens.

Okay. One week?

He wanted us to take our trip anyway? For one week?

I don't know.

He replied.

Ask, then.

Yeah, I thought, *okay*. I switched over to Alex's thread.

You have three weeks, right?

There was a pause before she responded.

Yeah, why?

Spend one of them with us.

Then, I continued, a little stronger.

I mean, we've already cleared it with the parents. We could still do New York. Maybe a couple of other stops along the way. It could still be great.

My mouth dry, I scrolled to text Maverick again.

I asked Alex.

And?

She's deliberating.

I love you.

I love you too.

Then, finally, two words from Alex set the plan in motion.

I'm in.

Chapter Fifty-Five

The door creaked open with the first rays of sunshine, and I awoke from a fitful sleep. I rolled from the edge of the bed and padded barefoot into the living room. Mom was just dropping her purse onto the couch.

"Hey," she said softly. She glanced at her watch and smirked. "You okay? It's seven a.m."

"Yeah," I said. "I'm fine, I guess."

She frowned. "What's wrong?"

"I don't know," I said. "It's been such a roller coaster."

"I get that," she said. "Want some coffee?"

"Yeah, thanks." I picked up a picture from the coffee table. It was a new one, the four of us, arm in arm at the beach during spring break. We stood in shorts and swimsuits, ankle deep in the water, waves lapping at our feet, just grinning…absolutely happy.

She nudged my shoulder. "That's a great picture."

"It was a fun trip," I replied.

I followed her into the kitchen and slid onto a bar stool. "We can still go," I said.

"On y'all's trip?" She flipped on the coffee maker and pulled a couple of mugs from the cabinet. "Oh, really?"

"Well," I said, "we can make the trip in two days, skip all the stops and still have enough time to explore for a few days."

Mom frowned and slid me a mug. "Oh," she said, mentally doing the math.

I cupped the warmth between my hands. "It won't be the same, but it'll be something."

"It will be," she said.

"Yeah," I agreed.

She sipped her coffee. "When are you leaving?"

I nibbled my bottom lip. "Today," I said, quietly, "if that's okay."

"Yeah," she said. "You were going anyway. This is just a little sooner than we expected, right?"

"Exactly," I agreed.

She sighed. "You'll be careful?"

"Yes," I said. "We'll take turns driving and stop when we're tired."

She wrapped an arm around my shoulders. "You'll call me?"

"Yeah," I said, "I will."

She smiled. "Well, why don't you get a little more rest? It's still early."

"That's probably smart."

I took another fleeting sip from my coffee cup then hopped from the stool and rushed back to my bedroom. I folded a leg under my body and grabbed my phone from the bedside table to text Maverick.

Morning. Hey. Whatever greeting is appropriate. I'm all packed and ready. Just call me when it's time to head out.

I flipped on the sound, curled into my pillow and closed my eyes.

* * * *

My phone rang, an angry wail into the morning sunshine, and I grappled to answer it. "Morning," I said, my voice rough with sleep. There was no answer, and I frowned to myself. "Hello?"

"Hey." It was Alex. Her voice was small, thin, quivering. "Can I come over?"

I straightened in the bed. "Yeah," I said.

I rubbed my eyes and tossed my legs over the side then headed to the front door. "I'll come unlock the door. Is everything all right?"

She sniffled on the line, but I could hear her on the porch. She was already here, I realized and jerked the door open. Her face was red, her eyes welled with emotion and she held her suitcase by the handle. "No," she said, "not really."

I took her arm and pulling her inside. "What happened?"

"Mom knows."

My stomach heaved. So my guess had been right. I'd never wished so much that I'd be wrong.

"And I take it she didn't react great."

She walked to the back of the house and collapsed on the corner of my bed. "I can't believe her."

I sighed, sitting beside her. "What happened?"

"I don't know... I woke up, and I was happy. Ya know, genuinely happy, excited for one last hurrah before they shipped me off. Then she stomped on it. She started saying these things — leading statements, ya know — and I just couldn't believe it."

I took one of her hands, dragging my thumb along her palm. "I'm sorry."

"Finally, she said it." She shook her head, shoving a hand through her greasy hair.

I could tell it had already been a day, and my heart clenched. She hadn't taken the time to shower. That much was obvious.

I waited for her to continue but was met with an uneasy silence. "What, Alex? What did she say?"

Alex laughed bitterly. "She said *'You aren't going anywhere with her. You're not going anywhere with that girl.'*"

I closed my eyes and stared down at our hands. "Oh," I said. "I'm guessing she didn't mean me?"

Alex leaned against my shoulder, and I could feel her shaking. "Nope, she didn't."

"How did she find out?" The question flew out of my mouth before I could retract it.

"I don't know," she said. "I didn't exactly ask."

I frowned, rubbing her back. "What did *you* say?"

She twitched her hand away from mine, so she could pace away. "I told her that I'm eighteen and I could go wherever I wanted with whomever I wanted," she said.

"Oh, Alex..."

She shook her head, a swift action. "I said that I'm eighteen, that I'm going to the school she wanted me to go to, that I'm leaving when she wants me to but that I am going to take this trip with my friends, because after June nineteenth, God knows when I'll see them again."

I nodded. "And?"

"And nothing," she said. "She stalked out of the room, and I grabbed my bag and came here. I've got to go, Emma. I've got to get the hell out of here."

I shrank back. Alex's words were a slap, but not against me, so I straightened, grasping her arm. "Hey," I said, "it's gonna be okay, but you can't just leave like this."

She groaned, pressing her face to my shoulder. "I figured," she said.

"Want me to come with you?"

She shook her head. "No," she said. "I'll be back."

"Okay," I assured her. "I'll be here."

She crossed her arms and peered down at her suitcase. "Can I leave that here?"

"Sure."

She straightened herself and frowned toward the ground. "Emma?"

"Yeah?"

"What happens if she doesn't understand?"

I sighed. "I don't know," I said, even though I didn't understand completely myself.

"Yeah," she said, "okay… See you."

She walked away, and I watched her go. I collapsed on my bed. Moments later, my phone buzzed beside my head and I snatched it up. "Good morning."

"How do you feel?" It was Maverick.

"I'm okay," I said quietly.

"Ya sure?"

"It's just been a rough morning."

Maverick paused. "What happened?"

I shrugged like he could see me. "I don't know. Alex's mom knows. Apparently, it got volatile."

"You mean…Alex's mom knows about her and Kate? She didn't know already?"

I rubbed the bridge of my nose. "No."

"Well, that sucks."

I pressed my face to my pillow. "It really does."

A pause. "I'm outside."

I stumbled to the door, opened it, and Maverick peered down at me. "Hiya," he said.

"Hey." I walked back to my room, and he followed. "Where's Kate?"

He surveyed the two suitcases already packed and in my room. "She's still packing."

I sat down at my desk, pulling my calendar into my lap and flipping it open. I scanned over the months. They had passed like trees fly by the window when we drive, so fast that they blur and merge together. The ink under my fingertips lost its form, and I finally looked up at him. He was leaning against the doorframe, arms crossed.

"Does Kate know about Alex and her mom?" I wondered.

He shook his head. "I don't think so," he said. He walked over and scooped the calendar from my hands. "You're thinking."

I sighed. "How can I not?"

"Today is a good day," he said. "They'll work it out."

"Yeah," I said. "It's that simple."

"I know," he said. "I don't exactly know them."

"They aren't exactly open-minded," I said.

He kissed my cheek. "Don't worry so much," he said, looping his arms around me so that I would stand. "It will smooth itself out."

I sighed. "How do you know that?"

"Wanna know a secret?"

"Yeah," I said.

He pressed his lips to my forehead, methodically shaking his head. "I don't know that."

I groaned and hid my face in his chest. He was warm, and I clung to that for fear of losing it. "That sounds like faith," I said.

He nodded, hands on my back. "Just a little, yeah."

"In what?"

He was quiet, and I could hear a bird sing outside. "I dunno," he said after a moment. "Something bigger than us. The universe, maybe."

I stared up at him, imagining the words forming in his head, and my stomach formed a hard knot. *Yeah*, I thought.

Have a little faith in *something*.

I closed my eyes against his chest and just let him hold me until the doorbell rang.

Chapter Fifty-Six

My stomach ached. I knew my best friend, and my best friend never rang the doorbell. If she did, well, that meant something. Our brief paradise clouded.

I broke away from Maverick's embrace and trudged through the house to the front door, with him following. *Inhale, exhale*, I thought, preparing for the all-time worst, though I wasn't sure what that would be. The moment, extended by the fabric of anticipation and chance, dragged on.

I jerked the door open and released a gasp of relief. Kate had propped her painted tennis shoes on her suitcase and was looking down at her phone. *Blissfully unaware*, I thought, and I opened my mouth to speak, a jarred sound. "Oh," I managed. "Kate, hi."

Her bright gaze darted between us and the timid excitement drained from her face. "Hey," she hedged, shoving her phone into the pocket of her jeans. "What's with you two? You look like you've seen a ghost."

Huh, I thought. *Maybe. It depends on your definition. Perhaps the ghost of happiness past?*

Maverick swooped in, patting me on the back. "Oh, nothing," he said. "I just forgot to grab the suitcases."

"Yeah," I said, "that's all."

"Y'all are acting weird."

I bit my lip, probably harder than I should have, and shook my head. "Yeah…no," I said, probably sounding as mixed up as I was.

"Hey." Alex's half-breathless voice suddenly interjected. She rushed to Kate's side and forced a smile. She had showered and smelled of lavender and mint, and she wore an overall dress over a white T-shirt. "Sorry I'm late."

I scanned her face for signs of the conversation, but it was fresh with makeup. "Is everything okay?"

"Yeah," Alex said, "everything is taken care of."

"Really?" I asked.

"Hey," Maverick said, nudging my shoulder. "Why don't y'all go grab your suitcases? We'll meet you at the car. Katie and I will go ahead and put ours in." He snagged his car keys from the bowl inside the door where he'd dropped them and pecked my cheek. "See ya in a minute?"

I watched them shuffle to the car. Cradled in uncomfortable silence, I bit my nail. "Alex," I said, "what happened?"

She forged past me into the hall. "More fighting," she said.

"Well," I said, cutting her off before she could grab her suitcase, "was there a resolution?"

She frowned. "Not exactly."

"And you're just going to leave?"

Alex nodded. "I have to."

"And I guess you're not going to tell Kate?"

"Nope," she said, simply.

I waited a beat, ready for a reply I likely wouldn't get. "Why not?"

She knelt to grab her suitcase, her shoulders slumping. She plowed ahead, with words heavy as her gaze, and she paced the rug. "Do you really have to ask?"

I gripped the handle of my suitcase till my fingers were white-knuckled. "Alex, please."

She scoffed. "Is it fair that my mother won't even look at me?" She stared over my head. "All I've done is fall in love."

"I know," I said. *God*, I thought, *when did our lives become this complicated?* I rubbed the bridge of my nose, thinking of the night after the party... The shock of the entire Alex–Kate thing had been severe, and I'd felt neglected. Alex had lied to me. My heart had been heavy. Suddenly, I understood Mrs. Fisher.

"Earth to Emma," Alex said. "Is that all you have to say about it?"

I groaned. "Maybe just give it some time, Alex. It's an adjustment for her."

"That's why I have to go," she said. "I need time. Mom needs time."

Air rushed from my body in a stunned murmur, and I knotted my hair into a low bun. My limbs were heavy and my heart uncertain. "But why keep it from Kate?"

Alex snapped up the handle of her suitcase. "Why ruin the trip for her too?"

Yeah, I thought, *I know, I know, but I also know my best friend. If she keeps this secret, it will weigh on her like an albatross.* "But—"

"But nothing," she said. "This is my decision, you know, and I say 'no'."

The tone in her voice was final. 'No' definitely meant 'no'.

* * * *

Kate drove the first leg in Alex's car. Maverick and I sat in the backseat with the windows down, exchanging glances, and Kate turned up the radio. She felt it, I'm sure—the dark cloud over the car—so she squeezed Alex's hand on the console.

"It's okay," she said, simple words to cover the way we all felt, though she couldn't know the full extent of why. It was a mixed bag of emotions, I guess, and my chest contracted.

I was running, feet on pavement, and it started raining. Showers pelted the asphalt, and I sprinted faster and faster, but I knew there was no use. There was no use running. I stopped. I stood in the center of a hurricane and cried, listening to the beat of water against trees and wondering what it would be like to exist in such solitude — the quiet of the highway disrupted by nothing but the occasional teenage driver with the radio blaring.

I stumbled, my legs burning, my heart achingly heavy, and collapsed in the middle of the road. The rain stopped, and I inhaled. The earth rose and fell with my heartbeat, and I swear I could feel its orbit.

No, I realized. I could hear the persistent hum of a car barreling toward me, and I screamed. The noise gutted me, and I shook from head to toe.

Then, Maverick's arms were around me. My eyes fluttered open. *When did I fall asleep?* I frowned, shifting my head against his shoulder. "Sorry," I said. "Bad dream."

"It's okay," he said. His gaze darted to the front of the car. "We were thinking about stopping for a bite to eat. Are you hungry?"

I straightened, scooting away from him and toward the window. "Yeah," I said, "a bit. What time is it?"

He glanced at the time on the dashboard. "Four-thirty-five. We've been driving about six hours." He chuckled. "I could use a hamburger — and a bathroom."

My heart still beat erratically in my chest. *Time*, I thought. *Always our enemy.*

"There's an exit in a few miles," Kate interjected. I met her eyes in the rearview mirror. She wore a tight-lipped smile. "We'll stop there for a while."

Maverick grabbed my hand. He brought my palm to his lips, kissing the center with a frown. "Are you okay?"

I shrugged. "Yeah," I said, "I'm fine."

It was one of those horrible half-truths. My heart throbbed, but there was nothing I could do about it. The tension bottled between Alex and me was unfounded, but I couldn't shatter the silence and neither could she. I wondered, thinking of the lie she had woven between us for an entire year. She had done the same to her mom and dad. In a cryptic way, I understood. Even now, I understood the horrible situation that lying had put us all in.

I turned toward the trees, wondering if we would ever be the same.

Maybe, I thought, and I threaded a hand through my fallen bun.

Maybe.
But maybe not.

Chapter Fifty-Seven

Kate took a right-hand exit into a small town in northern Alabama. During my dream, the radio had turned to static, and she pulled into a shopping complex. All faded paint and exposed brick, it was still a welcoming area just off the highway.

Kate parked in front of a diner. "Emma, I'm going to run into the store and grab a couple of CDs. Wanna come with me?"

Cheeks warm, I nodded. "Yeah, let's go."

Maverick caught my hand. "You want chicken?"

"Sounds good," I said and kissed his cheek. "We'll be right back."

Kate and I hustled down the sidewalk, shoulder to shoulder, and I held the door for her at the drug store on the corner. "I think we need candy," I said.

"I think you're right," she agreed.

I strolled through the aisles, avoiding questions like the plague and looping around a corner. "Hey, here are the CDs."

Kate rounded behind me, thumbing through the stack. "What a selection," she noted, shaking her head. "How do you feel about reggae?"

I giggled. "Seriously?"

She grinned. "Well, it's that...or country's greatest hits," she noted.

"Oh, nice," I said. "Well, we are in the Deep South." I nudged her shoulder and joined the search, chuckling. "Ooooh, here's a gospel medley."

A giggle rippled from her chest. "Nice," she said. "Maybe we'll just stick with the candy?"

"We'll pick up a radio station soon enough."

She swallowed and ambled down the aisle. A tense silence settled between us and she sighed. "Hey, Emma?"

I grabbed a basket and surveyed the candy counter. "Yeah?"

She followed, her eyes trained on my face thoughtfully. "Is everything all right?"

I shrugged, grabbing a couple of bags of M&Ms. "Yeah," I said, though I didn't sound convincing, even to myself.

"Oh," she said quietly, clearly not believing me, and she grasped a bag of Twizzlers. "Alex's favorite."

"You're right."

She exhaled and closed her eyes. "Let's get out of here. I'm hungry."

"Yeah," I said and rounded to the checkout. There was a line—an elderly man with a bouquet of flowers and a twenty-something girl with a magazine wrapped around a packet of cigarettes. "Kate?"

She glanced up, strumming through the magazine rack. "Yeah?"

"She loves you," I said, and the girl's ears perked up, suddenly interested. Sometimes the human condition was so universal and painfully obvious. "I just... Don't forget that."

Her composure faltered, but she didn't argue. "Yeah," she said, "I know."

I sighed as the old man thanked the checkout girl in the blue vest. "Thank you, young lady," he said. "It's my Cathleen's and my forty-sixth anniversary."

The checkout girl tucked a strand of dyed blue-gray hair behind her ear. "I'm sure she'll love them, Mr. Grayson."

The man smiled fondly. "Yes, Kendall," he said, "I'm sure she will." He shuffled away, nodding at each of us in turn, and the line moved forward, but it wasn't until the door swung open that the checkout girl, Kendall, swiped the girl in the bomber jacket's pack of cigarettes.

"You all right?" Bomber Jacket asked. Suddenly, I got the feeling this was the kind of town where an outsider stuck out—everyone a thread of the same fabric.

Kendall swiped the barcode on the magazine. "Yeah," she said. "Mrs. Grayson died a couple of years ago. He takes her fresh flowers every month. He wears her favorite sweater and takes the same bouquet. It's just sad."

My heart swelled in my chest. *Love*, I thought. *Universal.* Checkout Girl called it sad. I kind of thought it was beautiful.

"Oh," Bomber Jacket said, "okay."

Kendall handed Bomber Jacket her receipt. "Well, have a nice day."

Bomber Jacket shuffled out of the store, and soft country music filtered between us as we plopped an assortment of snacks onto the counter. "Y'all must be passing through," she noted, a friendly enough expression on her pale face.

"Yeah."

"Sorry about that," she mumbled, carefully piling the snacks into a brown paper bag and reading off our total.

Kate shook her head. "No worries," she said. "He was sweet."

Kendall accepted the twenty from me and counting our change. "Yeah," she replied, offering a handful of wrinkled bills. "He is. Y'all have a safe trip."

We waved, ducking out of the store and heading back down the street. The sun overhead slanted across the horizon, painting the first rays of sunset. I inhaled the sweet scent and peering through the window of the diner just down the road.

Alex and Maverick sat across from each other. Maverick looked like he was attempting conversation, only to be dashed by Alex, who was swirling her straw in her soda. Her hair fell in awkward tendrils over her shoulder, and she jerked a napkin from the holder in front of her and tore off the corner, a nervous habit she'd picked up from me.

"Well," I said, "those two look like they're having a great time."

Kate laughed. "Should we put them out of their misery?"

"Yep," I said, holding the door open for her.

Alex whipped around. "That took you long enough."

"Don't be like that," I said, plopping into the chair beside Maverick. "There was a line, an old man and a beautifully sad story."

He slid me a glass of lemonade. "Should I know what that means?"

Kate shook her head. "Nah. The bad news is that the music selection was country or gospel. The good news is we've got candy."

Maverick fist-bumped his sister. "Good call."

A vibration rattled the table and Alex jumped. Her phone, I realized, as she scanned the screen, all slumped shoulders and worry. After half a second, she melted, less anxious, and tucked the phone in her purse.

Kate frowned. "What am I missing here?"

Before any of us could answer, the server appeared. He was friendly and grinning as he passed out down home favorites like chicken and waffles and hamburgers and fries. We ate.

It wasn't an earth-shattering meal or anything, just enough to keep our stomachs out of our throats as we drove the last few miles to the Tennessee border. Kate's question lingered in the air, but we didn't breach it as we scarfed down the wonderfully greasy diner favorites. Instead, we made chit-chat about the weather and our plans, avoiding the topic like the plague.

"All right," he said, "who wants a milkshake?"

Alex swallowed. "Strawberry?"

"Gotcha," Maverick said. "Katie?"

Through a veiled frown, she nodded. "Vanilla."

Maverick flashed her a smile. "No, you're not, Katie," he attempted to joke, but Kate just looked at him, so he chuckled. "Man, tough crowd. Emma, wanna help me carry?"

"Yeah, sure," I said.

Around the corner, Maverick wrapped an arm around my shoulders. "It's going pretty well," he said.

I shrugged. "Did she say anything while we were gone?"

He shook his head. "Nope."

"Radio silence?"

He walked to the counter to order. The teenager behind the counter wore the same getup as the waitress, sporting a red and blue button-down shirt and a welcoming grin.

Maverick ordered, leaning across the counter. A few seconds later, he whipped around, holding a receipt. He squeezed my hands. "Emma, dear," he said, "stop worrying. It's okay. Stop thinking."

"Ugh," I said, dropping my head to his shoulder. "I'll try."

He winked, rubbing my back gently. "Seriously," he said, "let's just try to have fun."

"Sir…" the kid behind the counter said.

Maverick cringed. "Sir," he mocked. "That graduating really ages you."

I nudged past him to grab the tray of milkshakes. "Thanks."

We sat down at the table, and Maverick smiled. "Milkshakes for my ladies."

"Thanks," Kate said, ripping the wrapper from her straw and sticking it into her shake.

"Sure," he said, "although apparently I'm an old man."

"The guy was just being polite." I giggled.

For a moment, the tension broke. "I'm sorry, what?" Kate asked.

"Oh nothing," he told her. "The kid at the counter just called me 'sir'."

Kate groaned. "You're a drama queen."

"Of course... That's me."

I took a long drag from my milkshake. "But he's *my* drama queen."

He pressed his lips to the apple of my cheek. "And you're my worrywort. Who woulda thought?"

Laughing, Alex shook her head, a fresh light in her eyes. "Not me."

"I wondered if this would ever happen," Kate said, smirking. "He always had this huge crush on you."

I quirked an eyebrow at Maverick. "Oh?"

"Yep," he said. "Ya know...between the *others*."

Alex shook her head. "We don't talk about 'the others', right?"

Kate sipped her shake. "Exactly."

Maverick slipped an arm around my shoulders. "So," he said, plucking the car keys from the table. "We'd better get back on the road. I'll drive."

I stood, throwing the strap of my purse on my shoulder, and we walked outside. It was almost six, and the sun hung low in the sky. I stopped at the trunk and pulled out a puffy blanket.

He frowned. "You cold?"

"Nah," I said, shrugging. "I just like this blanket."

"Come on," he said, steering me to the front seat.

Kate and Alex settled into the back, and Maverick grinned down at me. In a blink of a second, he pinned me to the car door and kissed me once. "Are you having fun?"

"Yeah," I said, not exactly lying.

He squeezed my waist. "Emma, you're a horrible liar."

"I love you," I said. "Thanks for this."
He rubbed my shoulders. "You're welcome."
"Let's go," I said. "We're burning daylight."
He opened my door. "Yes, ma'am."

Chapter Fifty-Eight

The clock on the dashboard displayed a quarter to ten, and Maverick rubbed his eyes with the back of his hand. A road sign announced the next town, a dark exit a few miles down the road. "Y'all ready to stop for the night?"

A beat of silence, and I glanced over my shoulder at the backseat. Alex's head lolled on Kate's shoulder. Both of their eyes were closed. Exhaustion had melted their anxiety, and now, they were relying on one another.

I swiveled to nod at Maverick. "Yeah," I said, "let's stop."

He pulled into one of those not-so-nice but not-so-terrible roadside motels. He cut the engine, unhooked his seatbelt and twisted to the backseat. "Hey, you there," he called, "wake up."

Kate moved a little, fighting for consciousness, jolted then shifted, intertwined with Alex. "Ugh," she mumbled, not particularly coherent.

352

"'Ugh' is not an answer," he said. "Hop out. We're going to get a room for the night."

Alex jerked from her position and straightened, threading a hand through her hair and looking confused. "Where are we?"

I pushed the car door open. "On the side of the highway," I said, "stranded."

"Um-m," Kate hedged, concern peeling across her tan cheeks.

"We're fine," he said, slamming the door behind him and rounding the back of the car to unpack our bags from the trunk. "Just making camp for tonight."

Kate and Alex climbed from the backseat, and we hustled into the slightly dodgy motel lobby. Filled with yellow light and mismatched furniture, the place smelled of cleaning spray and coffee. Behind a low counter in the corner, a man in a stained gray button-down eyed us. "Checking in?"

Maverick fished in his pocket for his wallet. "Yes, sir."

The man smirked over the desk. "Is your mother in the car?"

Maverick thumbed through his wallet, extending his driver's license. "I'm nineteen."

The man surveyed the card for a moment, suspicious. He might have been in his early thirties. He had dark hair and ghostly pale skin, like he lived in his parents' basement or worse. "You kids in trouble or something?"

Alex caught the look and shook her head. "Just on our senior trip."

The man smirked. "Stopping here?"

Kate chuckled, an awkward sound to break the tension. "Where else?"

"All right," he said and pointed at Maverick. "Nineteen, you'll sign for it. It looks better on the books."

Maverick agreed and stepped up to the counter to make the transaction. Alex excused herself to go to the restroom. Kate and I dragged our luggage and collapsed on the couch in the lobby.

Curious, I peered at her. "Nineteen?"

"You caught that, huh?" She laughed. "Yeah, Maverick didn't start school until he was six."

"Isn't that illegal?"

Kate shrugged. "Mom's a rebel, I guess."

I looked over at Maverick, at his strong jaw and the straight slope of his back. I swallowed as he turned, his backpack swinging from one of his shoulders. "We ready?"

He extended a hand to me. "Where did Alex go?"

"In the restroom," I said.

He smirked, handing me a key. "Oh," he said. "I thought you girls went to the bathroom in groups."

Kate hopped up, rolling her eyes. "Maverick, we've talked about this," she said.m"About feminine bathroom habits?"

"No," she said. "Don't oversimplify women. It's demeaning."

"Oh," he said. "Sorry."

"Also, this is a motel. Single stalls."

He smiled. "Ah, right."

Kate popped her suitcase onto its wheels. "I'll wait for her. You two go on."

"Room one-fourteen," Maverick told her.

She flashed him a thumbs-up and dissolved into her phone. Maverick grabbed my elbow and led me out of the front door and toward a door adjacent to the car.

Chuckling, he nudged my shoulder. "Nice place, yeah?"

"Charming," I replied, a bit tongue in cheek.

He kissed my head, sticking the key in the doorknob. "You feeling any better?"

I nodded. "Yeah."

He ducked and kissed my head. "Good," he said and kicked the door with a groan. "Ole Stan wasn't kidding. The door does stick."

I giggled, despite myself. "High-class."

"I know, I know," he said, holding the door for me. "But it's cheap and on the highway."

"Cheers," I said, shuffling past him into the room.

The motel room was small, with two beds and a box-like TV on top of the dresser. Not-so-white sheets were topped with gray-golden pillows, and the plastic curtains were drawn.

I wheeled my suitcase to the corner and peeked out of the window. The empty pool was backlit by a streetlamp, but the sign blared 'Closed' in red. I inhaled sharply and Maverick slid his arms around my waist.

"Hey," he breathed in my ear, and I shuddered against him. "Question..."

I twisted in his arms. "Yeah?"

He grinned against my hair. "Am I snuggling with my sister or you?"

A blush flared in my cheeks and I teased his lips with my own. *So tall*, I thought, weaving my fingers through the thick hair at the nape of his neck. "Don't you dare sleep with your sister."

"Good." He squeezed my waist. Yep, you can bunk with Alex."

"So funny," he said.

"I know, I know. Just kiss me, will you?"

"I don't know about that," he said. "We wouldn't want the others to walk in."

"Give me a break." I raised on my tiptoes, kissing him once, long and slow.

"Definitely." He pressed his lips to mine once again, only to be interrupted by the knock at the door. He groaned, skimming his lips along my cheek. "Why?"

I giggled. "It's your sister," I said. "Be nice."

He crossed the room, opened the door and forced a smile. "Hi, ladies."

Kate groaned, grabbing her suitcase and hustling past him. "What did we interrupt?"

I blushed, shaking my head. "Oh, nothing."

"Nothing," he said, turning toward the bathroom. "I'll be back."

Kate slumped onto the bed by the window and flicked the TV on. "What to watch?"

Alex groaned, face-planting on the opposite bed. "Sleep," she said.

"I second that," I said. The few hours I'd had the night before hadn't really done it for me.

The bathroom door swung open, and Maverick crossed his arms. "There's a girl in my bed — and it's not my girlfriend."

"Hey," I said, "straighten up, buddy."

"Damn," he said, feigning hurt. "Demoted already."

"I'm going to call Mom." I pivoted to the door. Outside, the stiff, warm air blustered against my cheeks. I paced to the edge of the parking lot and speed-dialed my mom, kicking gravel with the toe of my tennis shoe. Seconds later, her phone went straight to voicemail.

Oh, I remembered, *work.*

"Mama, sorry. I forgot about work," I said to the robot. "We're good. We stopped for the night. Erm, I hope work is good."

The rumble of cars on the highway was hypnotic, and I groaned internally. "Well," I said, "g'night."

The night air was sticky, and I peered skyward, counting stars and possibilities. Then I returned to knock on the hotel room door and rejoin the party. Seconds later, the door cracked an inch, and Alex peeked around the corner. "Hi, I'm naked."

"Okay. Where's Maverick in all this nudity?" I thought that a very valid question.

"I'm in the bathroom," he yelled. "Also not wearing pants."

I bit back a giggle and stepped through the barely widened crack in the door. I smirked down at her. "You're not naked," I said, raking my hand through my suitcase to find my PJs.

Kate sat cross-legged on the bed, French-braiding her hair. "We're messing with him."

"Y'all are so mean," I teased, quickly stepping into my pajamas.

Kate shrugged. "I'm his sister. It's what I do."

Alex nodded. "And I'm her accomplice."

"You two are weirdos," I said. "I've gotta use the bathroom now. Wanna let him off the hook?"

"Okay," she said. "Maverick, come on in."

I tucked my dirty clothes into my bag and leaned against the wall across from the bathroom. Maverick came strutting out, wearing a patented playboy grin, a pair of black shorts and a white T-shirt. "How was your mom?"

I frowned. "At work," I said. "I forgot."

He kissed my forehead. "Ah, right. That's okay. You'll talk to her tomorrow."

"Yeah," I said, "I will."

I smiled and stepped into the restroom. It was small, almost claustrophobic, but it was white-tiled and clean. I leaned over the counter, my palms on the cool surface. My cheeks were pale, makeup long worn off, but I splashed water on my face anyway.

The dull murmur of the conversation in the other room warmed the rotting pit of conflicting emotions in my stomach, so I opened the door and trudged back into the room. "Lights out, kiddos," I teased.

Maverick was stretched on our bed, an arm tossed over his face. "Okay, Mom."

I blushed heavily and slid into bed beside him. "Sorry." I twisted in his arms so that I could see him, half in the dark.

"Goodnight," I said softly.

"Goodnight." He kissed me, and I draped my arm over his chest, holding him.

Kate groaned from the other bed. "Please, feel free to stop anytime you want."

Maverick pressed his lips to my forehead. "Don't word it like that or we won't."

Alex laughed. "Night."

I pressed my face to his T-shirt and closed my eyes. "Night."

Then, I let go of it all and he kissed my cheek. I was safe in his quiet embrace and I fell asleep, cradled in his warmth.

Chapter Fifty-Nine

A shudder rocked my body and I jerked out of bed with a start. *A bad dream, maybe,* I thought, but then I heard a near-silent murmur from the bathroom. Frowning, I tossed my legs over the side of the bed and surveyed the room. Maverick lay half under the covers beside me, a pinched, childlike grin on his handsome face, and Kate was curled on the other bed, a small ball in the center of the mattress.

Exhaling, I padded across the brittle carpet in stocking feet to knock on the door. "Alex?"

The muffled sound caught in her throat and went silent for a beat. "Em," Alex mumbled from the other side of the door. "Did I wake you?"

"No," I said, not really lying. "Are you okay?"

"Yeah," she replied, "just great."

I tried the door, but it was locked, and I groaned. "Lemme in," I said.

Her uncertainty was tangible, but the lock clicked, nonetheless. Through a sigh, I scooted into the bathroom. The small security light flashed a dull green but, otherwise, the room was dark. Her red eyes were set deep in her pale face, and I wondered how long she had been in there. "Hey," she breathed, her voice a thin line.

I sat on the edge of the tub and tucked a strand of her hair behind her ear. "Alex," I said, "what's wrong?"

She was plopped on the toilet lid. "I can't do this," she said.

"Do what?"

"Be here," she said, a reply and a sob all in one.

I released a breath I hadn't been sure I was holding. "What do you want to do?"

She shook her head, not making eye contact. "I don't know," she said. "I hate fighting, knowing they're angry with me."

"Alex," I said, nibbling my bottom lip, "look at me."

A sigh caught in her chest, but she leveled her gaze with mine. "Yeah?"

I forced a smile. "Let's go home."

"What about the trip?"

I shrugged. "We'll go some other time."

She gave a deep sigh. "It feels like we have no time at all."

"Don't be dramatic. I'm pretty sure we still have a lifetime," I said. "Besides, New York isn't going anywhere."

She blinked fresh tears from her eyes. "What about them?"

The million-dollar question, I thought. "I don't know about them," I said. "But for now, we'll be all right."

"Okay," she said. "We'll go home."

I twisted my hand to illuminate the blue-green light on my watch. "Maybe in the morning."

"What time is it?"

"Two-forty-five."

She stood up. "Yeah, in the morning."

I stood and caught her hand. "What are you going to do?"

"About Mom?"

I nodded.

"I don't know," she said.

"I love you," I told her. "You're going to be okay, no matter what."

A sad smile shone on her face. "I know," she said. "Thanks."

Seconds later, I climbed back into bed, and Maverick snaked his arm around me. "Everything okay?" His lips were pressed to my ear.

"Yeah." I pressed my face to his shoulder. "We have to go home."

He was silent for a minute then he agreed. "Yeah," he said, "okay."

I sighed and snuggled against his chest. "Thanks."

He chuckled. "For what?"

"For being so great about everything," I told him.

He kissed my hair. "Don't thank me."

Lost in the moment, I ran a hand through his dark hair. "You're pretty."

He snorted. "Thanks. But you're prettier."

"Oh," I said, my cheeks warming against his chest, "thanks."

He tightened his arm around my waist.

"G'night," I said.

Sleep washed over me again and I swam.

We were in the pool at midnight, giggling, and I heard someone talking. A man, on his cell phone, walked past. He had a long beard and tattoo sleeves – dragons and fire…crazy things.

Alex grinned. "Ever think about getting a tattoo?"

"Nah," she said. "I don't think so."

I shoved a hand through my damp hair. "You haven't thought about it or you don't want one?"

"Both?" Alex shrugged, swimming a long stroke across the pool.

Maverick sat on the edge with his feet in the water, surveying us with a haughty grin. He eyed his sister. "You want one, I'm guessing?"

"I don't know," Kate said. "Maybe a small one. A butterfly or something."

Alex barked a laugh. "Not a butterfly, please."

Kate rolled her eyes. "Hey, by the time I'm old enough to get one, you probably won't have to look at it."

The color drained from Alex's face and we frowned, an intense silence surrounding us. Suddenly Maverick was beside me and dragged his hands along my back. "It's over."

"What?" My voice caught in my throat and I shuddered.

He snickered. "Don't make it harder than it has to be."

Alex nodded, standing straight. "Okay," she said. "Kate, no."

Kate appeared disinterested. "I'm only being honest."

"It's over," they said, a chant.

The water lapped against my waist, and Alex and I struggled under the current. Was it the pool or the ocean? Suddenly, I couldn't tell.

The scent of iron wafted toward me, and I cast my gaze down. Scarlet seeped into the aqua-blue water, and I gasped for breath. Maverick released me and disappeared.

Alex and I were swimming in shark-infested waters, and she stroked once, twice. Her gaze drifted, eyes wandering, and she darted away from me. Suddenly, I was alone.

I gasped a breath, caught in the dream, but rays of sunshine blistered against my face. It was morning in the hotel room. Blissful morning.

The TV was on a local news station but muted. Kate seemed to be the only one up. She twirled a bottle of nail polish in her hands. "Emma, are you okay?"

I ran my fingers through my hair. "Yeah," I said. "I just had a bad dream."

She unscrewed the bottle of polish and yanked off her socks. "Dreams like that suck."

"Yeah." I leaned against the headboard of the bed and stared down at Maverick's sleeping form. His head was nuzzled under his pillow, and he was snoring.

Kate carefully painted her toenails and smirked toward her brother. "Sorry about that."

I pushed his hair out of his face. "It's kind of cute."

She sniggered. "You must really love him."

"I do."

"Good morning," he mumbled, rubbing his eyes with the backs of his hands.

I smiled, leaning down to kiss him once. "Morning."

Kate grinned. "You two are adorable." She shook her head. "It's kinda gross."

"We'll try to tone down the love." He stretched and hopped out of bed. "I've gotta shower."

"Gah," Alex groaned, tossing an arm over her face. "Talking... Sunlight..."

"It's morning, Alex. You've got to get up. It's time to get going."

Maverick rummaged in his suitcase. "About that," he said.

Kate frowned. "Yeah?"

Alex groaned. "We've got to go back home," she said.

"Why?" Kate asked.

Maverick straightened. "I've gotta get back," he said. "I forgot that I have a thing."

"Um-m," she said, "what?"

Alex groaned, standing up. "No," she said, "he's just saying that."

Maverick sighed and walked to the bathroom. "I'll be in the shower."

Well, I thought, *I guess I'm here.*

Alex sat up a little straighter. "My mom found out about us." Her voice was quiet.

Kate blinked, her braid sagging against her tilted head. "What? How?"

"I don't really know," Alex said. "All I know is that she knows, and I left kind of in the middle of a fight."

Kate rubbed the bridge of her nose. "A *fight*?"

"Yeah," she said. "I'm sorry I didn't tell you."

I closed my eyes and listened to the buzz of the air conditioner. "Guys, should I go?"

"No," Kate said, and I opened my eyes. Then, "I don't know."

"I'm gonna go see if there's breakfast," I lied, shuffling out of the door.

Well, that went well.

Chapter Sixty

Alex drove the last lap. A weight lay over the car, silent and pressured but somehow less painful. One hand on the wheel and the other hand in Kate's, she smiled. It was a soft expression, timid and nervous. That night, Alex would talk to her parents.

Thirty minutes from town, the silence broke. "It's a nice day," Maverick noted. "Why aren't the windows down?"

"Honestly," I said, unwinding the window.

Kate twisted the volume knob. Soft rock pulsed through the radio, the kind you can gyrate to all night. "God," she said, "I love the wind."

Alex glanced at her girlfriend. "I love you."

Heat flooded my cheeks. I had never heard Alex say the words, but they sounded sweet coming from her mouth. How could something so beautiful be wrong?

* * * *

I went to sleep early, exhausted in the best way. The next morning, I awoke early. My head pounded and my heart raced. I pressed my face to my pillow. My life — our lives — blared in surround sound, a pounding in my ears punctuated by the noise of the front door slamming.

I hopped out of bed and followed the sound of my mom's footsteps to the kitchen. "Hey."

She was at the coffee maker, her back to me, and she jumped. "Oh, Emma."

I snorted. "I live here."

"Well," she said, "I thought you were going to be gone for a week."

I shrugged. "That was the plan."

She surveyed me thoughtfully. "Did something happen?"

"No," I began, then, "yes, sorta."

"Want some tea? Coffee?"

"Coffee," I replied. "Coffee would be good."

"Perfect." She filled then slid me a mug. "So, what happened?"

"Alex needed to be home."

"Oh," she said but didn't press. "Things gonna be okay there?"

"I don't know," I told her.

She smiled weakly. "Eventually it'll all smooth out."

"Yeah," I said, "I hope so."

She nodded. "I know so."

Comfortable silence bubbled between us, and I crossed to the kitchen window. Huge, dark clouds hung in the summer sky, and I sighed. "It's going to rain, isn't it?"

"Yeah," she confirmed.

"Great," I said, sliding onto a stool. "So nature reflects our lives."

"Okay, Writer Brain," she said, kissing my head. "It's gonna be all right. Take it easy today."

I propped my feet on the bar stool. "I will. Go to bed, Mama," I said. "I'm all right."

"Goodnight," she said. "Wake me up if you need me."

"I'm good. Night."

She shuffled off to bed, and I made myself some toast. Feeling hollow, I leaned away from the window and listened to the bottom fall out of the sky and the rain on the ceiling.

"Well," I mumbled, "welcome to summer in the South." 'Rainy and humid' or 'unbelievably hot' were the only real options.

A knock on the back door stunned me out of my stupor, and I hustled over to the door. Maverick was leaning just under the awning, but he was soaked to the bone. "Hey," he said, gesturing wildly, "come out here."

I opened the door just enough. "It's pouring rain, Maverick. Why don't you come inside?"

"Come out."

He took my hand and jerked me into the backyard. Rain soaked my pajamas. "Maverick!" I gasped.

He spun me around. Alex and Kate stood in the center of the yard, and we all laughed. "It's okay," he said.

Alex hugged me. "It's okay."

The laughing morphed into dancing and, as the rain pelted our bodies, we collided. Limbs and giggles were synonymous in friendship and love, and I leaned closer and closer into Maverick's embrace. His body was warm and inviting, and I let him cradle me in something I couldn't explain. We slowed to a crawl, holding each other, because what else could we do?

"I love you," I whispered.

He chuckled. "Let's go inside."

We piled into the house, wet, and I thundered to Alex's side. "What happened last night?"

Alex shook her head. "I talked to Mom."

"And?"

"It's okay." She paused, sidestepping into the bathroom to grab a couple of towels. She came back in and smiled weakly. "Or at least it will be."

Maverick snagged a towel and rubbed the water from his hair. He nudged his sister's shoulder. "We'd better go."

I frowned. "You just got here."

He leaned down and kissing my forehead. "I'll see you later. Kate's gotta help me with something."

I walked over and leaned my shoulder against Alex's. *Best friends*, I thought, recalling those first months together. It had been a whirlwind. We didn't fit in, no, but we fit together. "See ya later?"

Kate took Alex's hand, squeezed once, and the siblings left us to silence.

Crickets.

Then, I turned to Alex. "So…"

She ran her fingers through her dirty-blonde hair. "Yeah?"

"Ever think about getting a tattoo?" I asked.

"Um-m, not actively, no."

"Well?" I prodded.

"Well?"

The repeated word rang in my ears. "I had a dream about it while we were gone. Well, a nightmare really."

Alex spread her towel on the couch and plopped on it. "Yeah? Then why dwell on it now?"

"I dunno," I said. "That wasn't the nightmare really...the tattoo."

"Well, then what *was* the nightmare?"

"I didn't just lose Maverick. I lost you too," I admitted.

Her expression softened. "You're not going to lose me," she promised, wrapping her arm around my shoulder. "You're my best friend—forever, no matter what."

I smiled, hugging her back with a wicked twinkle in my eye. "Permanently?"

"Yes," she confirmed. "Why're you acting weird?"

"I don't know," I said. "I've just been thinking about it."

"About what?"

"Tattoos," I said.

"Oh." She giggled. "Really?"

"A little one."

She grinned. "Interesting..."

"What?"

She nudged my shoulder. "Emma Cage," she said, "you're a secret rebel."

"I'm not. It would be *basic*, ya know. Nothing *rebellious*."

She sobered and crossed her arms. "Oh, then what would it be?"

"I don't know."

She smirked. "Liar."

"A heart," I decided, holding my thumb and my index finger to indicate size, "a really small one."

"Okay," Alex said, standing and brushing off her soaked jeans. "Let's do it."

"No," I said. "That'd be... No."

"Come on, Emma," she said. "Live a little."

"I don't know how," I said, shaking my head. I studied my hands, red and blotchy, and I sighed. "You know that."

"You're my best friend. Ya know *that*?"

"Yeah, I do." I studied her, frowning. "You're my best friend too."

She squeezed my hand. "My job as your best friend is to make you do the things you wanna do that you're too scared of."

I worked a hand through my hair. "Okay," I said.

She beamed. "Really?"

"No."

"You're sending mixed signals, Emma."

"I don't know," I admitted.

"I don't know either." She laughed. "You've always been indecisive."

A slow smile slid across my face. "Yeah," I said, "I have been."

"Well..." She stopped in front of the mirror and peered at herself, straightening. Her blonde hair hung like a curtain around her face, and she toyed with it in her reflection.

I pulled my leg under my body. "Do you want one?"

"I dunno," she said. "I would probably. A heart would be nice."

"Wanna get matching tattoos?"

"Let's do it."

"Okay," I agreed.

"For real?"

"Yeah," I said. A thrill buzzed in my chest. I felt like a rebel. A rebel without a cause, as it were. Well, I guess my cause was a heart tattooed in playful black ink across my shoulder or hip.

"All right," she said, "let's go."

Chapter Sixty-One

"I can't believe you went through with it," Alex said, releasing a high-pitched giggle.

I twisted in front of the mirror, and heat flooded my chest. A tiny black heart now resided on my shoulder. Honestly, I hadn't been sure I would go through with it either, but I'd played the game. "Oh, really?"

"Do you like it?" Alex asked.

"I think so."

She laughed at me. "You're so indecisive."

I nodded. "And you love me anyway."

Alex grinned. "Of course. What would I do without my little straight and narrow?"

"I dunno," I said. I paused and the air sizzled between us. "I guess we'll find out."

She sighed. "I don't want to talk about that."

"Okay," I said, turning to thumb through my closet. "When are they supposed to get here?"

Alex glanced at her watch and joined me at the closet. "Fifteen minutes," she said. "So, do you wanna show off your new little friend?"

"Maybe." Blushing, I pulled out a peach off-the-shoulder number.

"Awesome," she said, already halfway out of the door. "I'm going to run home and change. See you in a few."

I eyed the tattoo in the mirror. It was small enough to be a freckle, I guessed, but not really. I jerked my T-shirt over my head and shucked my shorts. Cool air blustered against the skin of my calves and back, and a thin layer of heat rushed across my shoulders.

A smile sprang to my lips, and I shrugged the slinky smooth fabric over my shoulders. The cool texture brushed across the bodice and I grazed the fresh ink with tentative fingers. Idly, I wondered if Maverick would like it.

I straightened my posture. "Doesn't matter," I mumbled. "I didn't do it for him. I did it for me." I twirled, watching the peach skirt fan around my legs.

"But not today," I mumbled. I quickly swapped the off-the-shoulder number and replaced it with a simple black T-shirt dress. *Chicken*, I thought, fisting the cotton in my hands.

I blinked at my reflection and tied back my hair. The plans had been sketchy, quiet — a shrug and a giggle. In fact, instead of explaining, Maverick had just grinned, kissed my head and told me not to worry about it. So, here I was, staring at the slope of my shoulders in the dark dress.

"You changed your mind." Alex's voice echoed from the hallway.

I scanned her appearance. "Your red dress," I said. "I approve."

"Don't change the subject," she said. "What happened to that cute little peach number?"

"I don't know," I said, kneeling to strap on my sandals.

She waltzed to the mirror to tease her fingers through her hair. "You concerned that boy-toy won't like it?"

"Of course not," I said. "I did this for me, not him."

"It's fine," she said. "I get it. I'm a little nervous too."

"Ha!" I smirked. "Kate'll love it."

"Oh, really?"

"Of course," I said.

She slid into my desk chair, and we lapsed into silence. The air sizzled with the realization that tomorrow was our deadline.

I straightened the hem of my dress. "I'll miss you."

"Well…" she said softly. She thumbed my yearbook from the bookshelf and flipped it open idly. "You'll be in Rhode Island in no time."

I straightened, my stomach turning at the very thought. "Yeah," I said. "Only four hours away."

She smiled and nudged my shoulder. "Come on," she said. "Don't be so sad. We have tonight, right?"

I forced a laugh. "I wish it was enough."

She sighed. "Life is hard."

"Life *is* hard."

The doorbell rang and the moment shattered.

I jerked upright, smoothing my skirt. "Well, here we go."

Alex followed suit. "To have fun."

We hustled to the front of the house, and I opened the door. Maverick wore a pair of jeans and a white button-down shirt, and a shot of anticipation spiraled through my spine. "Hey," he said, dipping to kiss my cheek. "You look nice."

I beamed. "Thanks," I said. "So, what're we doing?"

"Nothing too exciting," he said. "Just dinner."

"Where's Kate?" Alex asked.

He gestured to the driveway. "She's keeping the car running."

Alex hurried out, leaving Maverick and me in the doorway. Without thinking, I leaned up on my tiptoes to kiss him. The night air was lukewarm, and I pressed my lips to his in a slow dance.

"I love you," he said against my lips. He pulled his hand from his pocket and held it out, letting a necklace dangle from his fingers.

"Maverick," I said, "it's beautiful." It was simple — a gold heart on a gold chain — and my shoulder throbbed irrationally.

He ducked to kiss me again. "Kate helped me pick it out," he explained. He fumbled with the charm and carefully unlatched it. "It's a locket."

I peered at him with a soft smile. "Maverick," I said, taking the locket to look at the picture. It was the first selfie we'd taken together. "It's perfect."

"You're beautiful," he said.

"Will you help me put it on?"

He looped his arms around my waist and squeezed once. I tugged my hair out of the way, and he fastened the necklace, pressing a kiss to the hollow behind my ear. "How does it feel?"

I beamed, casting my glance at the necklace. It was heavy against my chest, and I twisted it between my fingers. "It feels great," I said. "Thank you."

He pressed his hands to my face. "You're welcome."

"Hey!" Alex called from the car. She sat in the passenger side with her head out of the window and waved.

Kate crawled across her to smirk. "Yeah, yeah, you're in love. We get it."

Alex nodded. "But *we're* hungry."

I kissed Maverick's cheek. "I'm hungry too."
"Come on then," he said, chuckling.

Chapter Sixty-Two

That nighttime melted. The scene was timeless. Maverick's watch, a sloth, slaved for our memories, nuzzled against my ear and ticking lazily. Maverick, Alex, Kate and I lay on our backs on a blanket, staring up at the stars and laughing like wind chimes in the breezy summer night. We lolled under a thin sheen of sweat that was veiled in tears.

Maverick snuck his arms around my waist, and the soft groan of his breathing echoed in my chest. *In, out,* I thought and dragged my fingers in an intricate pattern along his forearm. Squinting, I counted the stars, one by one.

I sighed, and the words tumbled unhindered from my lips. "It's really over now, isn't it?"

"No," Alex said, lolling her head from the cradle of Kate's arms. Moisture sprang to her eyes, but she shook her head. "No, it's not over." Her voice was a whisper in the wind, something I had internally recorded over years of slumber-party softness and class mumblings.

My eyes flickered closed. "Promise?"

Kate shuddered. "Promise?" she begged, an echo.

Alex's voice quivered. "Promise," she said, but it was a lie and we all knew it.

"I love you," he mumbled, bringing his lips down to my hair.

A harsh breath shuddered across my collarbone, a bitter tidal wave of anger. *Like it isn't too late*, I thought. *Like we aren't out of time.* "I love you," I whispered against the rough fabric of his shirt, and the earthy scent of understatement and Maverick rose to meet me.

A terse beat of silence pulsed through our quartet, but Kate shattered the ice with an uneven voice. "I love you too, big bro," she said.

He chuckled and cicadas sang in the bushes. My skin crawled, and I pressed my cheek to Maverick's neck. We burned against one another, and a softer hand, Alex's, found mine.

We inhaled together, a chain of intertwined fingers, and our heartbeats slowed to an even tempo. Just like that, we fell asleep under nature's blanket.

The four of us were walking a tightrope, and it was ready to snap.

* * * *

A wave of ice water startled me awake, and I groaned, swatting it away. *God*, I thought, shooting straight up. Bodies flailed and I gasped.

Rain? I questioned, darting my gaze around.

No, I realized. A summer rain shower in Mississippi steamed. It was the sprinklers.

Unable to control myself, a laugh escaped my throat. The memory of the day the Fishers had installed the sprinkler system flooded my body, and I giggled uncontrollably. They had been fish out of water in our town and thought sprinklers were normal in Nomansville.

I scrambled from the ground and grappled for Maverick's hands. My dress wet, the locket cold against my skin, I grabbed his hand and we sprinted. Alex shrieked. Kate gasped. We rocketed from the blanket under the stars, darting through the landmine of sprinklers and onto the patio. Giggles sounded around me and, for a moment, my spirit warmed.

Maverick shot between us, wagging his unruly black hair like a dog. "Who has sprinklers in Mississippi?" He heaved a chuckle in the muggy air.

Alex giggled. She doubled over, catching her breath through waterlogged lungs. "We're transplants," she said, awkwardly.

Despite everything, a muted smile grounded across my face. "Welcome any time."

Kate giggled. "Minus the sprinklers."

A pause of silence deflated our sunny dispositions, and Alex cast a glance at her watch. She swallowed, her gaze tipping toward the ground. "My flight is in three hours."

Maverick sighed. "Do you need help packing the car?"

Alex shook her head. "No," she said, "it's already packed. There isn't much.. Ya know, the plane and all."

The air fizzled between us, and Alex hugged me. "You're my best friend, you know that?"

I offered a deep sigh that said it all and clung to her with all my might. Nobody liked change. I knew that and laughed at myself because only six months ago — just six months ago — this hadn't been a problem. I had been beyond ready to flee this nowhere town.

Now? I clung to Nomansville, and tears welled in the corners of my eyes. "I'll see you soon," I said.

Emotion swelled in her gaze, and she nodded sharply against the nape of my neck. "Yes," she breathed. It was one of those infinite hugs, one that made an impact. "I'll see you soon."

I released her and she turned to Kate. Their eyes met and I took Maverick's hand. "We'll give you two some privacy."

"Bye, Alex," he said. "Good luck in New York."

He trailed his fingers down to loop with mine and squeezed once. We crossed the yard between the two houses. "You gonna be okay?"

"Yeah," I said. "I have to be, don't I?"

He chuckled. "I guess."

I tilted my head to meet his gaze. "I love you."

He grazed my cheek with his hand, making me feel safe and warm. "I love you too."

Chapter Sixty-Three

June disappeared in a cloud of smoke, and I listened to the constant, hollow hymn of summer's joyful expression. I gripped the memories for dear life, leaning into them in a desperate attempt to hold on.

Maverick grazed my shoulder with his fingertips and I giggled uncontrollably. "That tickles, Maverick."

"Sorry," he said, soberly weaving his arms around my waist. "I just love you."

"I know that."

"Damn, that's harsh," he said.

Heat flooded from my cheeks to my chest. "I love you," I told him.

He framed my face. "I know."

"Good," I said, giving him a playful smile.

He drummed his fingers along my palm and gripped my hands. "Come here."

A giggle rippled through my chest. "What?"

He grinned, extending a hand. "Dance with me."

"There isn't any music," I said, half a lie. The TV was on. A commercial rolled a numbing song, and it switched to a fast-paced jive and back.

"There is music. Dance with me."

I blushed and clasped his hand. "Um-m, okay."

He jerked me closer to press his forehead to mine. "You're beautiful," he whispered.

My skin prickled, and I strummed a loose chord on his shoulders. "You're handsome," I replied, "and I love you."

He winded his arms around my waist. "You just told me that," he noted halfheartedly.

I shrugged, swaying my hips in time with the commercial track and pressing my face to the crook of his neck. "Yes," I breathed. His scent intoxicated me, and a thrill rushed up my spine. "I just don't know how many times I'll be able to tell you that I love you."

He inhaled sharply and his hands on my back stilled. He paused, and a breath caught in his throat. "Emma," he said, tightening his grasp on my body, "don't talk like that. Don't say that."

I blinked, fresh tears in my eyes. "Then what?"

"Kiss me," he mumbled, but he did it for me. I begged God to freeze this moment, but I knew it was fleeting. We both knew it, but we crashed in time with the rhythm onscreen.

The commercial cut off, shattering the illusion. "Want to get out of here?"

He chuckled, a warped sound in the back of his throat. "Yeah," he said. "To wherever you want."

"I could use a cup of coffee," I admitted.

"Coffee sounds great. Ben's?"

"Ben's? You, sir," I said, smirking, "know nothing about coffee."

"Okay," he said, smoothing his shirt. "Where are we going, then?"

"Jitters," I said.

"Jitters?"

I smiled, rising on my tiptoes to kiss him once. "You're such a jock."

"Ha," he said. "What does that mean?"

"Nothing," I teased, grinning. "Put on your shoes, lover boy. Let's go."

* * * *

Years ago, Jitters had been nothing more than an independent bookstore. Now under new management, my favorite bookstore had become a local hotspot for free Wi-Fi and crumpets with cream cheese. The perimeter of the square brick building was a coffee bar, but there were ten rows of bookshelves and an artsy sitting area.

Maverick and I slumped onto the loveseat in the lounge, listening to the hiss of the cappuccino machine. He flipped through a book of poetry with his head in my lap, and I sipped my latte like it was my lifeline.

The book drooped to his stomach, and he mussed my hair. "Ya got a little something..." he said.

I had been people watching, lost in a sea of uncaptured emotion. "Huh?"

He brushed a bit of whipped cream from the tip of my nose and popping the remnant into his mouth. "Yum," he said.

"You're one to talk."

He chuckled. "What? Do I have muffin on my face?"

I shook my head, bending down and kissing him once. "No," I said. "I just love you."

He swiveled his legs, which had been balanced over the arm of the couch, to the ground, and popped up to wrap his arms around my waist. "I might love you a little too."

"Maverick," I said. His name caught in my throat like sweet poison.

"Sorry," he said, standing and pacing to the window. It was papered with flyers, mostly old and faded, but he jerked one from the mosaic.

"What?"

He held up the flyer. "We have a date," he said.

I straightened, interested. "Do we?"

I skimmed the flyer with a blush. *End of Summer Dance* it screamed in newsprint lettering, and all I could think was *no. Maybe when Alex was here, but now?*

"I don't know, Maverick."

"Come on," he urged, nudging my shoulder. "It'll be fun."

"I don't know," I repeated, putting my coffee aside and standing with an anxious frown.

"One last blowout," he said. "Just you and me."

I smirked. "You and me and the whole town."

"You and me and the whole town and a gorgeous dress," he continued with a sneaky smile.

I leaned up on my tiptoes, teasing his lips with mine. "You really wanna go?"

He shrugged. "I think it'll be fun."

"Okay," I conceded, "maybe it will be."

He grinned, squeezing my waist. "Yeah, it will."

I laughed, awkwardly. "I guess I'll have to get a new dress."

"You should take Kate. She's been, erm…moping."

"That can definitely be arranged."

He spun me around like a ballerina. "Sounds good."

"Very good." Then I kissed him.

Chapter Sixty-Four

I drummed my fingers along the tabletop at the ice cream shop and stared out at the downtown with a lump in my throat. Kate and I sat on the outside patio, drinking root beer floats and watching cars go by. Kate's strawberry-blonde hair was knotted into a limp bun, and she wore all black. She curled her fingers around the float cup but didn't make eye contact. Instead, she peered idly at the streetlight, watching its slow crawl from green to yellow to red and back again.

I rubbed the back of my neck and poked at my float with a straw. "You sure you wanna do this, Kate?"

Her voice had been heavy, as if dress shopping sounded like a life sentence, and Kate looked bad. It seemed cruel, but her eyes had sunk into her skull, and dark circles had taken residence under her steely blue gaze.

Thoughts of Alex danced over my consciousness, an albatross in their own right, and my heart clenched. I missed her too. A month ago, she'd flown out of

Nomansville and into the rest of her life, but she still called every night.

Her voice, a mellow tune in my ear, had rung a pinch lower than normal. The classes... Well, the classes were *'solid, interesting'*. Apparently, New York was only a little cooler than Mississippi, but her roommate was a pothead — or maybe an alcoholic. As if on cue, there had been a clang somewhere in Alex's room and her voice had softened.

'Sorry,' she had said. *'Who am I to judge? She's probably just away from home for the first time.'*

I had sighed from my perch on the edge of my bed. *'I miss you.'*

She had paused, allowing silence to stretch across the thousand plus miles between us. When she spoke, her voice shook. *'I miss you too,'* she'd said, swallowing hard. *'How is Kate?'*

Kate fingered a complimentary cherry from the bowl on the table. "Alex could tie them with her tongue," she noted.

Damn, I thought, *she didn't even hear me*. "Kate," I said, "are you sure you wanna do this?"

She flicked the cherry to the floor, and it rolled across the porch. "Brother-mandated, remember?"

"Well," I said, "yeah."

She nodded. "Brother knows best, right?"

I sighed. "He just hates to see you hurting."

"I know. I just need to perk up."

I plopped my half-empty cup on the table. "Not right now."

"Thanks." She smiled weakly.

I glanced down at my phone, which was facedown on the table. "Does she call you much?"

Kate glanced down at her watch. "Probably too much."

I laughed. "It's never too much."

She took a final swig of her root beer float and chucked it into the trash can in the corner by the door. "We'd better go. Gotta get you a dress, right?"

"Yeah, right," I said.

Seconds later, we walked down Main Street, peering in storefronts. She pointed to a small boutique a block down, and I bobbed my head with an awkward giggle. "I don't know," I said. "Alex always dressed me."

"This should be fun, then," she said, opening the door.

I trailed after her, watching her graze her hands along the shelves. "Sometimes it's fun being useless."

"Why?"

I had slept in a bun, so now my hair fell in loose mermaid waves just past my shoulders. "I get my own personal shoppers."

She groaned. Her phone was ringing in her pocket. "Ugh," she said. "it's probably Maverick checking up on us."

I shook my head. "Let it go to voicemail."

"Nah," Kate said, jerking her phone out. "He'll just keep calling."

I followed her gaze to the caller ID, to the picture of Alex in a vibrant yellow dress. She smiled — grinned really — and her eyes twinkled. "Is that a new picture?"

"From orientation," she noted.

Joy bubbled in my chest. "Who looks that good at orientation?"

Kate giggled. "That's what I said." She slid the bar, answering the call, and pressed the button for speaker phone. "Emma's personal shopper, how can I help you?"

Alex's voice was muffled for a second, through laughter maybe. "I'm sorry. What?"

I took the phone, allowing Kate to continue her work at the shelves. "Kate is helping me shop."

Alex's words flooded out in a rush. "Great," she said. "I was worried about your wardrobe."

"But you weren't worried about me?"

"You'll be fine. Your clothes, on the other hand, I was scared for," she said. "What are we shopping for exactly?"

Kate tossed a colorful blanket of dresses over her left arm and took the phone from me. "Apparently the 2019 class council can't let go."

Alex paused, waiting for the end of her sentence. Then, she continued. "Wait," she said. I imagined her in her dorm, cross legged, her eyebrows scrunched together while she bent over a magazine. "What?"

I grasped the phone once again. "They're throwing an end-of-summer dance."

"Oh," Alex said.

"The whole town is invited," I added. "They're trying to make it a kind of a town shindig instead of a school one, ya know?"

"Shindig? Did you really just say 'shindig'?" Alex sounded incredulous.

"I miss you."

Kate shifted, grabbing another dress from the rack. "How's the roommate?"

"She's here," Alex said, "and a little *too* happy."

I placed the phone on a display case and thumbed through another rack. "How can anyone be 'too happy'?"

"I don't know," Alex said. "She just is."

Kate held up a dress for me to look at. The flowy dress was a mustard-yellow with bold burgundy, white and black flowers, long, billowy sleeves and a plunging neckline. "How do you feel about this?"

I frowned. "I don't know."

"Come on," she said. "You're trying it on."

"Yes! Do it," Alex cheered. I could hear the grin in her voice. "Wait! What are we looking at?"

Kate answered, "Mustard and burgundy."

"Oh! Emma, go try it on," Alex said.

Kate extended the dress toward me and I peered between her, the phone and the dress. "I'm feeling ganged up on."

Kate shook her head. "Don't worry so much," she said. "What will trying it on hurt?"

"Okay," I said. I thrust the dress over my arm and rushed into the dressing room. There was, I decided, no real reason to argue.

I quickly stripped and slid the colorful dress into place, leering at my reflection in the mirror. My otherwise pale skin glazed pink as the skirt swung midway up my thighs. A sizable valley of cleavage peaked from the low-cut top, and I frowned, pivoting to the side.

Awkwardly, I managed to convince myself that the dress looked nice. It really did, but my chest was warm and I felt exposed.

"Emma," Kate called from the other side of the door, "how does it look?"

"Okay," I hedged.

Alex's laughter reverberated through the speaker. "You don't sound very convinced."

"It's very...booby," I complained.

"Oh, geez," Kate said. "Here ya go. Try this one." A dress appeared over the door. It was long and white with a red-flowered print. "It's off the shoulder," she warned.

"What else?" Alex's voice questioned, thoughtfully.

Kate explained as I changed. "Well, it's long and white, but it has these artsy red flowers — like, sparsely flowered, ya know, not obnoxiously so."

"What? Ya know what? This is ridiculous. You should FaceTime me," Alex said.

I straightened in the dress, and it felt close. The skirt of it fell nearly to my ankles, and I smiled. Only my shoulders were cold.

"How does it look, Emma? You're being quiet," Alex interjected into my inner monologue, and I flushed.

I gave myself one more look. "I like it."

"Can we see?" Kate knocked on the door.

I nudged it open, and she held out the phone. Suddenly, Alex sprang onto the screen. She wore a magenta top with a bow at the shoulder, and her hair was tied back. She grinned. "I love that," she said, throwing a thumbs-up.

"Yeah," Kate said, "it's very pretty."

"I thought so," I said, surveying my reflection thoughtfully.

Alex coughed, watching me sway the skirt and shaking her head. "Kate, can we see anything shorter? Our girl here has good legs."

The skin of my chest, already enflamed, burned even warmer. *Okay*, I thought, *take the compliment.*

"We can do that. What do you think, Alex? I have a blush, off-the-shoulder number with a ruffle top and a very-belted slight fit-and-flare."

Alex twisted her nose, thinking. "Hm, what color is the fit-and-flare?"

"White lace top and a sort of muted golden taffeta skirt," Kate replied, eying the dress thoughtfully.

"Try the fit-and-flare," Alex said, and Kate moved to swap the dresses.

"Thanks," I said. For a moment, it felt like it had before Alex had left.

"What?"

I shrugged. "I'm just happy."

Kate nodded. "Me too," she said.

Alex beamed between us. "Ditto."

The door closed between us, and I listened to their soft chatter, slow and uninhibited. *Long distance,* I thought to myself, shaking my head. Maverick and I hadn't talked about what would happen *after*. We'd pushed the conversation away.

I maneuvered the dress down my thighs, shaking my head. It danced to just above my knee, and I thought of the fingertips test from elementary school and how crazy the concept was. My gaze drifted upward, heartwarming with my skin.

"You can come in," I told Kate.

The door snuck open, and our smiles were in sync.

"Yeah," Kate said, but Alex finished her thought.

"That's it."

Chapter Sixty-Five

"Emma, are you sure you don't mind me coming to this dance?" Mom lingered over me and fidgeted with my hair. She wore a navy maxi dress with a high neck and a white belt tied at the hip. Her hair was twisted into a playful bun at the base of her neck.

"Yeah, of course."

"Good," she said. "It sounds like fun."

"I hope so." I eyed her skeptically. "Do I finally get to meet Stanley tonight?"

She grabbed her mascara from the counter. "I guess so. Are you okay with that?"

"I'm excited, yeah. I've heard so much about him."

"He's pretty great," she said. She straightened, studying her reflection in the mirror. "I'll admit. I didn't expect to meet anyone at the hospital."

I patted on my lip gloss and giggled under my breath. "The scrubs really seal the deal, don't they?"

She shook her head, leaning against my door. "More likely the suits at church."

"Oh," I said, "right."

The doorbell rang, and Mom smirked. "I wonder if that's yours or mine?"

"Dunno," I said. "Let's go see."

We crossed into the living room, and Mom opened the door. On the other side stood Maverick and the man I assumed was Stanley. Their shoulders brushed, and they were joking and laughing.

Maverick wore a black button-down and slacks, and his hair was carefully messy. "Hey," he said.

Stanley's gaze zeroed in on my mom. With a sly smile, he swooped down to kiss her cheek. He wore a white button-down and a gray tie, and his sandy-blond hair was styled to a tee. "You look beautiful." I liked the look he gave her. It warmed me to know she had someone who cared about her like that, especially since I was leaving soon.

Stanley turned to me, extending a muscled hand. "You must be Emma," he said.

I shook his hand. "Yes. It's nice to finally meet you, Stanley."

"Nice to meet you too," he said. "Your boyfriend here is pretty charming."

"Thanks," I said. "I like him."

Mom squeezed my shoulder. "We'll see you guys a little later."

"We're going to get some dinner before we crash the party," she said.

"Okay," I giggled. "You kids be good."

Mom locked the door. "You too," she said. "We'll see you soon. Happy dancing." They hopped into Stanley's Ford Focus, and Maverick laid his hand on my hip. "God," he said in my ear, "you look beautiful."

My skin burned, and I leaned up to kiss his cheek. "Thanks," I said. "Ready to go?"

Maverick nodded. "Yeah."

His hand against the small of my back while we walked sent a thrill up my spine. "Stanley seems like a nice guy," he noted.

"Yeah," I said. "He goes to our church."

Maverick opened the truck door for me, and I climbed into the cab.

He cupped my face, kissing me hard. It was a single kiss, a focused one, an intense kiss that seeped to my toes, but seconds later, he pressed his forehead to mine. "I love you," he said under his breath.

I squeezed his hand. "I love you too," I said.

He closed the door behind me. I watched the slope of his shoulders as he rounded the truck to jump into the front seat.

He chuckled. "What're you looking at?"

"Nothing," I said, dusting my fingers along his hairline. "You."

He placed a solid peck against my lips, and it seared my heart. "Why?"

I ran my fingers into his hair and kissed him back. The scent of fresh linen and citrus flooded my senses, and I gasped into it. "You're pretty to look at," I said.

He brushed his hand along the hollow of my cheek. "Thanks," he said. "You're pretty pretty to look at yourself."

I shoved his shoulder, happily embarrassed. "Just drive, okay?"

He revved the engine and drove toward the high school for our one last hurrah. I gazed at the lines of his jaw as he drove, my heart stuck somewhere south of my throat.

He looked over. "Emma, that's creepy. Stop staring at me."

"You really know how to charm a girl," I said.

He twisted to kiss my palm as he drove. "Oh, shush," he said. "Ya know I love you."

I flushed, leaning my head against the window. "Is Kate coming tonight?"

He ran a hand through his hair. "No," he said. "She's got a fun night of sulking and FaceTiming her girlfriend... Your best friend."

I worried my lip. "Ah," I said. "How's she doing?"

"Better since you two hung out." He swallowed. "She's been happier."

"Good." I smiled.

"Thanks for that."

"Anytime," I said and kissed him.

He sighed. "Until next week."

"Come on, Maverick. I just want to dance with you."

"That I can do," he said and kissed my hand. "Come on."

* * * *

I lolled my head against his chest, listening to the slow hum of the band on stage. I felt warm, bubbly, and I exhaled. "Maverick..." I breathed against the fabric of his shirt. He smelled like summer. "I don't want this to be over."

He sighed, rubbing my back. "We still have a week."

He was right. It was the last day of July. In a week, I had to get on a plane and fly to Rhode Island.

"A week isn't enough," I said.

He pulled me tighter by the waist. "It's been so good."

I stared up at him. The lights were low, but I could see the rough line of stubble along his jaw. I traced it, frowning. "It has been."

He rubbed his fingers along the small of my back. "Want some chicken?"

I laughed. "Chicken?"

"It smells good, doesn't it? I think there are wings."

Shaking my head, I dropped my hands from his neck. "Yeah, I could use some *chicken*."

He led me to the food table in the back of the room. "Punch or water?"

I trailed behind him. "Punch sounds good."

He poured a couple of glasses and handed them over. "Here ya go," he said. "Wanna go grab a table? I'll fix a couple of plates.""

I nodded. "I will."

I maneuvered away from the dance floor and plopped down at a table in the corner. I sniffed the punch and a wry smile slid onto my face. It smelled like childhood and summer and everything ending.

I sipped and nearly spit it out. "Whoa," I said, "that's strong."

As if on cue, Maverick slid into the chair across from me. "What?"

I held up the clear plastic cup. "This is really strong."

He deposited the plates on the tabletop and sipped the contents of his cup. He groaned and shoved the cup to the side. "Yeah," he said, "that's spiked."

"Really? That's really a thing people do?"

He kissed my head. "You're so innocent."

"I am *not*."

"You are," he said. He teased my hairline, cupping my face with thoughtful correctness. I didn't reply. Instead, I nibbled a cookie from my plate.

He popped a potato chip into his mouth, surveying the crowd. "It was probably the new seniors — ready to claim their status and all that."

"What?"

"The punch, Em."

"Oh," I said. I blushed, laughing under my breath. "Mischievous."

He leaned over and kissed my cheek. "You hungry? Have a wing." He shoved the plate of chicken wings toward me and I picked one up.

"Okay," I said, only half listening.

I scanned the room and spotted Mom and Stanley across the room. She danced like a happy teenager, and it warmed my heart.

Maverick nudged my face with his hand. "You okay?"

"Yeah, I'm good."

He squeezed my hand and continued eating. I watched him with my heart on my sleeve, and I worried my bottom lip. So much excitement bubbled in the room — seniors, new and old, prepared to be thrust into the next phase of their lives and parents ready to burst themselves with the pride and excitement of it all.

A few minutes later, he slipped a hand into my hair. "You're thinking pretty loudly."

"Let's dance," I requested.

He chuckled but stood up, leading me to the dance floor. The song slowed, last call, and I wrapped my arms around his neck. He linked his arms around my waist, jerking me closer.

A flash startled us from our moment, and I peeked over his shoulder. Mr. Zelner stood a foot away with his camera. His wife, holding their little bundle of joy, was at his side, and my cheeks heated. "Mr. Zelner, hi."

He waved. "Hey." He let the camera fall to his chest. "You two look happy."

Maverick rubbed my shoulders. "Yeah," he said, "we are."

Mrs. Zelner smiled, shifting the baby onto her hip. "It's good to see."

I leaned back to beam at their new daughter. She wore a pink and white dress and had a small bow in her wispy hair. "She's so pretty," I said. "Can I hold her?"

"Sure," Mrs. Zelner said. She handed me the baby carefully, and I cradled her head.

Maverick watched us and rubbed my back slowly. "Mr. Zelner, what's her name?"

Mr. Zelner cringed. "I think you can call me Chad now, Maverick."

"Okay," Maverick said. "What's her name, Chad?"

"Scarlet Whitney Zelner," Mrs. Zelner answered, gingerly mussing the baby's hair.

Maverick smirked. "Very Southern."

I bounced her slowly. The baby giggled. "It's a pretty name for a pretty girl."

"You're right." Maverick kissed my head, and I sighed, relinquishing the baby.

"Thanks," I said.

She nodded, and Mr. Zelner held up his camera.

"One last picture?"

I leaned into Maverick, placing a hand on my hip, and he wrapped his arm around me. We smiled, and a horde of butterflies fluttered in my chest.

The camera flashed, the song ended and we said our goodbye to the Zelners.

Sighing, I pressed my face to Maverick's chest, and we swayed.

The night wasn't over. Not yet.

So, we just kept dancing until the decorations were packed and the students had vacated. Then, we drove home slower than the speed limit.

Chapter Sixty-Six

My life in boxes, I sat on the bed. My stomach was in a knot and I peered down at the floor. My suitcase and backpack waited, packed and ready, but I felt ill. Tomorrow was daunting, and I thought my heart would burst.

"Goodbye," I muttered, testing the taste of the word in my mouth. Heavy, I fell backward on the bed to stare at the ceiling.

"Damn" — Maverick's voice interjected into my self-loathing — "I guess I'll go." He was leaning on the doorframe.

I twisted to meet his gaze. "Hey," I said quietly.

He walked over to me. He sat, knocking his shoulder against mine. His eyes were sad, but he was smiling, nonetheless. "Are you all right?"

I twisted to kiss him, shaking my head. "I love you."

He sighed, slipping his arms around my waist. "Yeah," he said, holding me. "I love you too."

I pressed my face to the crook of his neck. "Will you stay with me?"

He rubbed my shoulders. "Yeah," he said. "Need any help packing?"

I cast a look toward my closet and my desk, and I shook my head. "No, I'm done."

He kissed my hair. "Okay," he said. "Wanna watch a movie?"

"No," I mumbled.

"Wanna get something to eat?"

"No."

"Wanna play a game?"

"No."

"What do you wanna do?"

I leaned against him. "I don't know," I said. "Not go?"

Sighing, he shook his head. "You've got to go."

I groaned. "Why?"

"To be smart," he said.

"Smart is overrated."

He laughed. "You're going to love college."

"I don't know."

He smirked. "You know you are. You're going to meet new people and have new adventures."

"But you won't be there."

He groaned, tugging me closer. "No," he said, "I won't." He kissed my shoulder. "You're going to find somebody."

"Oh." The color drained from my face and my heart skipped a beat.

He frowned. "What's wrong?"

I shrugged, exhaling under my breath. "I don't know," I said quietly.

He sighed. "I'm sorry." His voice was soft, but I shook my head against his shoulder.

"Don't be."

"Hey," he said, "look at me."

"Okay, what?" I twisted my head toward him.

He slid his hand toward my face. "I love you," he said. "You know that?"

I leaned forward, kissing him slowly. "I know that."

He smiled, mussing a hand in my hair. "I know you love me."

I squeezed his hand. "Good," I said. "Because I do...love you, I mean."

His hand slipped from my hair to my face. "I know you do," he said. "But that doesn't change anything."

I leaned my forehead against his. "Two thousand miles is pretty far, isn't it?"

"You rounded up," he noted.

"I know," I said, shaking my head. "What is it? A thousand four hundred?"

"Yeah," he said. "Something like that."

I pressed my face to his shoulder. "It's too far," I said. "I don't wanna go."

He dragged his fingers along my shoulder blade. "You've *got* to go," he repeated. "I love you, but you've *got* to go."

I leaned forward, kissing him softly. "I know I do." I wove my fingers into his hair. "Just stay with me?"

"That I can do," he said. "Wanna change? You look uncomfortable. You can have my T-shirt."

"Okay." I pulled back, watching him jerk his T-shirt over his head. My cheeks burned, and I threw my arms around his neck.

He grinned against my lips. "That good, huh?" His voice was quiet and understated, masking the heaviness of the air.

I swatted his chest, flushing even more as I grazed his skin then climbed off the bed. I walked across the room, carefully undoing my top. I faced away from him, my skin burning, watching him in the mirror. The fabric pooled at my feet, and his eyes zeroed in on the one thing he didn't know existed.

"Why, Miss Emma," he said. His voice deepened, and he crossed the room in one long-legged stride. Suddenly, his warmth enveloped me, and my stomach lurched. "You have a tattoo."

I blushed, and he pressed a kiss to my collarbone. "Yeah," I said.

He chuckled, his hands on my waist, and I shrugged a shoulder. He dipped down again, kissing my neck, and I stared at the ceiling.

"When'd that happen?"

"Before Alex left," I said. "She got one too."

His breath was hot on my shoulder. "You got matching tattoos? How cute."

I pulled the T-shirt over my head, inhaling sharply. When I turned, he was sitting on the edge of the bed again, staring at the floor, and I joined him, linking our hands together. "Do you like it?"

"It's kinda perfect," he said.

I smiled, shaking my head and crawling to the foot of the bed. "Yeah," I said, "I like it."

He slid to my side. "Why didn't you show me sooner?"

"I don't know," I said. "I didn't know if you would like it."

He groaned, tugging me to his chest firmly. "Don't worry," he said. His chest vibrated against my skin he spoke. "I do."

I laid my face against his shoulder. His skin was warm, and I lightly pecked his chest. He tasted like salt. "This is nice," I said.

"You should get some sleep," he said, kissing my hair. "You have a big day tomorrow."

I exhaled. "No," I said, closing my eyes. "I don't want to sleep."

He grinned against my hair. "You should really get some rest."

"No," I groaned, "no sleep."

"Emma," he said. His voice even, he dragged his hands along my forearms, raising bumps in his wake.

I tilted my head, meeting his gaze. "What?"

"I love you," he said.

I smiled, weakly, but I didn't reply. Instead, I wrapped my arms around him and pressed my lips to his. He smelled of warmth and possibilities, and a breath caught in my throat. "Maverick?"

He clasped my face in his hands. "Yeah?"

I inhaled deeply and pressed a hand to his chest. "I don't wanna sleep," I repeated.

"Emma," he breathed, a heartbeat against my skin.

"Maverick," I muttered.

He massaged my sides, traveling his hands up to cup my face. "Okay," he said, softly, and his love crashed over me like a wave to the sand.

* * * *

Morning shuddered into existence, and I groaned, suddenly cold. I rolled over, grabbing the blankets, but

Maverick's warmth was nowhere to be found. I was alone, flushed and cold. My skin was exposed as I rolled onto my side.

Blinking, I frowned. "Maverick," I whined, tossing an arm over my face.

I heard him shifting and the wrinkling of paper. I forced my eyes open to find him leaning over my desk. His jeans hung low on his hips, and his taut skin bore memories untold.

"What're you doing?"

He released a sigh and shrugged his shoulders without turning. "Nothing," he said.

"You aren't that great a liar, either."

After a measured beat of silence, he twisted to appraise me. "Sorry I woke you," he said, crossing the room to graze my cheek.

I kissed his hand and tugged him back onto the mattress. Wrapping my arms around his waist, I swallowed the lump in my throat. "It's fine," I said. "What time is it?"

He kissed my head, shaking his. "About six," he said. "You missed your flight."

I rolled my eyes, laughing under my breath. "That must be why I feel so well rested."

He leaned down to kiss me again. He slipped his arms around my waist, and I groaned under my breath. "Don't go," he mumbled.

"I have to," I replied, pressing a featherlight kiss to his shoulder.

'I know," he said, tugging me closer. I closed my eyes again. His voice, a lullaby, lulled me back to sleep again. "I know you do."

Chapter Sixty-Seven

I slid into the airplane seat and gazed out of the window. The runway stretched out in front of me, and I listened to the drone of the flight attendant's speech. Her words, a routine, went in one ear and out of the other. My heart in my throat, I latched my seatbelt. We were moving, and I was breathing. Wasn't I?

My hand darted to the chest of my pale pink sweater dress, and I clutched Maverick's locket. I felt alien in my own body. I hadn't known how to dress that morning. I hadn't known what to wear. *What is the weather in Rhode Island in August? God*, I thought. *I didn't think this through.*

I sighed, pulling my backpack onto my lap, and I unzipped it, searching for something, though I didn't know what. There, at the back, out of place, was my yearbook. I bit my bottom lip and flipped to the front page. I hadn't opened it since the day we'd gotten them and had our signing party. It had been on my desk, under a stack of papers. I hadn't thought I'd packed it. *How did it get into my backpack?*

I slid my fingers along the glossy memories. *A lot of the same*, I thought. Luckily, Alex's scrolling scrawl waited at the bottom of the page, a promise of something, but I didn't know what.

Emma, you are my best friend. No matter what, you have been there for me, and I love you so much. Thank you for standing beside me, even when I lied, even when I made it hard for you to love me. You've been kind and understanding, and I am proud to have been a part of Project Emma. You're all grown up now. You're smart and driven, but you've loved and known love – and I couldn't be more thrilled. Now, you're going to Brown, and you are ready for this adventure. I know it. I love you so much, Emma. I'm glad you'll only be four hours away. Love always, your Alex.

My eyes welled with big tears, and I rubbed my eyes with the backs of my hand. "Miss? Are you all right?" It was one of the flight attendants. He was pudgy, and his face was red, but he looked kind.

"I'm fine, thanks," I said. It wasn't really a lie, I guessed.

He offered a weak smile. "Let me know if you need anything."

Inhaling deeply, I peered down at the book again. I knew Maverick's message would be on the back page, but I wasn't sure if I could take reading it. Nevertheless, I gave in. I wanted to see his handwriting, to feel close to him, even now.

On the back page, I frowned. There, beneath Maverick's simple *I love you, Maverick English* was now a whole page of text. It was written in messy scrawl and with a red pen. I frowned.

Hey, Emma. I know you're the writer in our relationship, but I've got a couple of things to say. Sorry if it's a mess. I've got to write this before you wake up.

A fresh blush sprang to my cheeks. He had written this...*after*. He'd written it this morning. And he'd put my yearbook in my backpack for me to find.

First off, I don't know when you're reading this, but I'm Maverick. We dated senior year of high school. Well, part of it – the best part of it. You probably don't remember me.

A breath hitched in my throat, and I shook my head. "Of course I remember you, you idiot," I said to the book and imagined his wry grin as I read.

Second, I wanted to remind you of a few things. You have a beautiful smile. I love the way you laugh at me with that half smirk and the way you pretend to not sing along in the car. I love the way you say you're sorry at inappropriate times, and I love that reindeer sweater you wore to my party. Seriously, you should wear that more often. I love the way you love me, I love the sound of the words against your lips and I hope you never stop saying it. Tell people you love them, because it is a beautiful thing, Emma.

Finally, I want you to promise me something. That's kinda crazy, I know because I'm not there and I can't enforce the promise, but bear with me, will you? I want you to promise me to have adventures. Let someone make that beautiful smile. Make friends like family, eat good food, study hard, sing like nobody is listening and love unashamedly.

I bit my quivering lip hard.

I love you, he'd written in a messy scrawl. I imagined him bent over my desk, pen in hand, glancing over to see if I was awake yet.

Tears burned in my eyes, and I shoved them away. An old lady in a sweater handed me a tissue with a tired, knowing expression.

"It's all right, honey," she said. "It does get better."

I smiled at her weakly, just to be polite — but then it struck me. In just a few months, Maverick English had taught me how to love and be loved. He'd taught me to let go and laugh at myself — and no matter what my future would hold, because of Maverick English, my first true love, that woman was right.

Want to see more from this author? Here's a taster for you to enjoy!

The Artist and Me
Hannah Kay

Excerpt

"Lucas!" A firm hand rapped against my door and I growled, rolling over in bed to peer at the alarm clock poised atop my ever-growing stack of books 'to read'.

It was seven-forty-five on Tuesday morning. Tuesday, May twenty-third, to be exact. Today I would begin my internship with Alexander Swift, proprietor and, for all intents and purposes, editor of the *Carltonville Gazette*. It wasn't the *New York Times, The Boston Globe* or anything of the sort, but it was a real news office and it would most certainly be a step up from the *Eagle Newsletter* at school, where Sally Rainwater was editor only because she'd been the most popular person in the room on a random Thursday during assembly.

About twenty minutes later I arrived in the kitchen, freshly showered and wearing black slacks and a blue button-down shirt. Mom was setting loaded plates out on the table—four bright yellow plates to match the sunshine streaming through the open windows. My mom, wearing a pair of jeans and a simple black T-shirt covered with a tattered apron, loved sunshine. She was a kindergarten teacher during the school year, the perfect career for her demeanor.

My father was bent over the newspaper, but don't be fooled. He wasn't scanning its contents for new writing techniques or anything remotely creative. He was checking for stocks—reported straight from the Big Apple. The collar of his white starched shirt stuck up in the back. Classic Dad, the ever distracted businessman.

Clara, my younger sister by a year, was reclining in her chair and wearing a thin green T-shirt over her—surely—skimpy bikini to prevent Dad's annual freak-out over her choice of swimwear. Did I mention that for most of Carltonville High's student body, today was just the first day of summer vacation?

Clara rejected the plate Mom placed in front of her, instead plucking an apple from the bowl in the center of the table. "Alyssa is picking me up in five." She took a bite.

Dad's ears perked up. "Going out to the beach?" He didn't wait for a response. "Who's going?"

The inquiry went on as I ate my eggs, toast and bacon, the same inquisition that occurred every first day of summer. Dad dug around for information and Clara skirted around the truth. It was the same result. Dad, charmed by his baby girl, believed Clara and her two best friends were going to the beach sans boys to soak up some sun on the first day of summer when in actuality it would be Clara, her two best friends, plus practically the entire student body of Carltonville High—boys included—as it had been since Clara was thirteen.

She stood at the beep of Alyssa's horn and pecked Dad's cheek for good measure, grabbing her bag from where it'd been tucked under her chair and bouncing out of the front door without another word.

My mom, completely aware of Clara's real plans, bit her toast carefully, checking her watch. "You'd better head out too, Lucas. Don't want to be late on your first day."

With that, Mom bought me time to run by and grab some coffee, something she and I had in common. I was about as far from a teacher as you could get, but I could put away a cup of coffee in under three minutes on our 'commute' to school — the high and elementary schools of Carltonville were basically the same entity. In fact, the idea of a 'middle school' had been eradicated from our schools long ago. Needless to say, my dad detested coffee so much that he banned it from his house. He was definitely the stricter of our parents, the iron fist to mom's soft lilac.

I climbed in the front seat of Hendleson, my beat-up black Ford, and slammed the door behind me — not out of anger. It jams easily. My grandfather bought Hendleson on March twenty-seventh, 1972 — also known as the day my dad was born. Granddad drove that truck until my dad went off to college and he passed it on. My dad was never very fond of Hendleson, though, so the second he raised enough money to buy a car, Hendleson took up a dusty corner of the garage until I got the keys on my sixteenth birthday. Unlike Dad, I loved that piece of scrap metal.

Sign up for our newsletter and find out about all our romance book releases, eBook sales and promotions, sneak peeks and FREE romance books!

About the Author

Hannah Kay is a cowbell ringing, true maroon wearing writer of young adult fiction and a graduate of English from Mississippi State University. Hannah teaches high school English as a relatable language and hopes to instil a love of reading and writing into her students.

A self-proclaimed wallflower, Hannah published her first short novel, The Artist and Me, with Finch Books in April of 2016, and followed with The Separation in March of 2017. When Hannah isn't glued to her keyboard, she can be found curled up on the couch watching reruns on TV or singing show tunes at the top of her lungs. Feel free to connect with Hannah on social media for updates!

Hannah loves to hear from readers. You can find her contact information, website details and author profile page at https://www.finch-books.com

www.ingramcontent.com/pod-product-compliance
Lightning Source LLC
Chambersburg PA
CBHW020636020726
47494CB00001B/212